Where Bees Swarm

Don Windle

Clocktower Books

San Diego, CA USA
www.clocktowerbooks.com

THE OPEN PRESS
21628 Oak Dr., Box 4
Cassel CA 96016

Email: openpres@citlink.net
Website: www.citlink.net/openpres

Where Bees Swarm
by Don Windle

Clocktower Books

San Diego, CA USA
www.clocktowerbooks.com

Copyright © 2000 by Don Windle

CLOCKTOWER and design are trademarks of C&C Publishers.

Cover art and design by Brian Callahan

ISBN 0-7433-0020-3

Chapter 1

The Continental DC-8 was on final approach to the Da Nang airfield, coming in low over the South China Sea. The pilot and copilot were going through their landing check-off list when the Da Nang air controller yelled over the radio: "Abort approach! Abort approach! We have incoming mortar rounds. All traffic go on visual till I contact you from underground bunker."

The pilot gave the large plane full throttle, pulled it into a steep climb, banking hard to the right. The first indication Navy Lieutenant Bill Dawson had of the problem was his body pushing hard into the seat, then the increased roar of the engines. From his window seat on the starboard side, his view suddenly was filled with houses and streets instead of sky. The tree tops looked too close, zooming by fast. As they banked and climbed, he recognized the small puffs of smoke and dust made by mortar shells exploding near the runway. Remembering the high arc of mortars fired for long range, Dawson felt the sudden rush of fear in his stomach.

Unwittingly cracking his knuckles, Lieutenant Dawson said to the enlisted man on his left: "Looks like our new home is under attack. The pilot better get some altitude quick. If we take one of those mortar rounds, we've had it." Prompted by his own fear demanding action, his words burst out involuntarily. When he saw the panic erupt in the young man's eyes, Dawson quickly added, "Don't worry, they're aiming at the airfield. It's not likely they'll hit us."

The pilot announced, "The air base is being shelled. We are climbing to a safe altitude and will hold there until it's safe to land. So relax. We're in no danger."

At 10,000 feet, the plane leveled off and flew in lazy circles over the South China Sea east of Vietnam. Mortars exploding around the airport like white balls, seemed to grow out of the ground and then quickly disappear. Now, with the plane out of immediate danger, Dawson relaxed and watched the action through alert eyes almost the same color as the gray at his temples. A gas storage tank near the runway erupted into a huge orange ball. After a few seconds the orange ball contracted into yellow tongues of flame that quickly enveloped the area around the fuel storage berm.

Lieutenant Dawson leaned his long, wiry body back in the seat as he admired the checkerboard of dark-green foliage and brown squares of freshly plowed fields, surrounding the sprawling city of Da Nang. He knew such peaceful illusions can mask the death and destruction inherent with war. From a distance blood running in the foxhole and mortar trench is obscured by the beauty of the land. Dawson closed his eyes thinking: To some it's only a police action; to others a little, worrisome war. To me it has been a remote war. Now it's an immediate, personal war. His thoughts went back two weeks to the telephone call that started him on his journey to Vietnam.

The beautiful fall day was cool enough for a long-sleeve shirt to feel comfortable. From his office at the Patuxent River Naval Air Test Center in Maryland, Dawson watched multicolored leaves drift lazily to the ground as he answered the telephone. "Lieutenant Dawson speaking."

"Hello Bill, this is Rocky Rhodes."

Dawson raised his eyebrows in surprise. "Captain Rhodes?"

"That's right."

"But I heard you were in Vietnam," Dawson said, wondering why his old mentor was calling.

"You heard right. I'm calling from my sand-carpeted office on Red Beach, north of Da Nang. How would you like to pay me a visit?"

Dawson hesitated. "Well, sir, before I commit myself, I'd like to know what you have in mind. A visit? What for?"

"I'll give you a quick sketch. As you may know I have the Regiment out here, headquartered in Da Nang. Things here are building up fast. I've got..., well, I can't give the number on the phone. Anyway, I've got several battalions of Seabees here in-country providing support for the armed forces. A major problem is inadequate communications. You wouldn't believe the mess we have here with telephone communications. Each camp or unit has its own field switchboard and is linked with from two to six other commands. Visualize one-hundred units connected like that, trying to contact each other.

"Hell! Sometimes I have to go through five switchboards to reach a command only five miles from here. At times I've found it faster to drive over there. I want you to set up a central system, or whatever you call it. As I recall, you specialized in the communications field when you were a Seabee electrician. As for how long you would be here; I guarantee not over a year."

"A year!" Lieutenant Dawson exclaimed. "That's a full tour of duty, Captain- or I guess I should address you as Commodore now that you have the regiment. I have a while to go on this assignment. I like it here. It's a good job."

"I know it's a lot to ask, Bill. But I don't know anyone else in the Navy who can do the job as well as you." There was a pause. "I need you."

"You must want me pretty bad, Commodore, to blow a lot of smoke like that. It sounds like you're asking me to volunteer. But I'm sure with your pull you can get a set of orders cut for me with one call to Washington. Is that what happens if I don't volunteer?"

"No, Bill, unless you agree, you won't have to come out here now. And I'm not blowing smoke. We do need you. This job requires someone with a good technical background, who can coordinate between four services, sometimes at high-command level, and most of the time under emergency conditions. I know from the work you've done for me before, that you're the right man for the job. Bill, this is the most important undertaking the Seabees and the Civil Engineer Corps have been assigned since World War II.

"One promise I can make is, when your tour is completed here, I'll do my best to see that you go where you want for your next tour of duty. One further thought; it's almost certain you will be sent here when your present tour is finished-then you may not get such an interesting job."

"Well, I'm involved in some hot projects here. I don't know how long it would take to get a relief in and brief him on my job. How soon would I have to be there?"

"Give you a week to get things squared away-don't worry, they'll be able to cover things there. Then you'll have one week at Port Hueneme, California for combat training and indoctrination. So I'll see you here in about two weeks."

Now, circling above Vietnam, Dawson still wasn't sure why he let himself get talked into it. He had been in the Navy long enough to know better than to volunteer for anything. Part of the reason, he thought, was a response like an old fire horse running in the pasture at the sound of the fire bell. But his primary motivation was a feeling of patriotism, of duty; and the desire to keep more people from falling under the Communist yoke. The challenge of the job added motivation. It had been a long time since he had been involved in a telephone project. He looked forward to working, on large scale, with communications-the technical field he preferred.

Working with Commodore Rhodes, his mentor of years past, was a definite bonus.

Dawson thought back to the first time he had served with, then, Lieutenant Commander Rhodes on Adak Alaska. At the time Dawson was a third class construction electrician, and Rhodes saved him from being placed on report by a shavetail ensign who thought all rules must be obeyed. They served together again while Dawson was still enlisted, and then shortly after he received his commission. In his mind, Rhodes was the epitome of what a Naval officer should be.

The pilot's voice on the intercom broke into Dawson's thoughts: "It's all clear below now. We'll be landing in a few minutes."

As they were landing, Dawson saw two mortar craters in the edge of the concrete runway flash by, and eight more craters near the runway. When they turned onto the taxiway, they passed near the gas storage area that had been hit. The fire was still burning, but appeared to be contained to the one tank.

At the bottom of the metal stairs, a sergeant in Air Force fatigues directed the disembarking passengers to one of the low, tin-roofed buildings near the taxiway. Dawson entered the building with louvered walls, and looked for a Seabee whom he expected to meet him. Not finding one, he asked the airman behind the counter, "Is this the Da Nang main air terminal?"

"Yes sir. This is it," the boyish-looking airman replied.

Dawson decided to wait until he had his baggage before calling the regiment. *Maybe someone will be here to meet me by then. He was probably delayed by the mortar attack.* The heat combined with high humidity made Dawson uncomfortable in his Navy blue uniform. *Seems sort of dumb having to report in Blues in a place like this,* Dawson thought, as rivulets of sweat ran down his face. He could feel one slowly trickling down his spine.

The men swarmed over the string of baggage gondolas, each man rummaging for his own. For five minutes they resembled a mass of writhing worms. Dawson waited on the outer edge of the mob until he saw his bags. Then he elbowed his way in to the gondola and dragged two bags out through the crowd and into the terminal.

A half-hour later, after all other arriving military men had departed in buses or cargo trucks, Dawson decided he had waited long enough. "How do I contact the Thirtieth Naval Construction Regiment by telephone?" he asked the Air Force airman behind the counter.

The airman hesitated, looking at three telephones on the long counter. One was a conventional black telephone without dial, the others, field phones with cranks. The man conferred briefly with another airman in the small room behind the counter. Then he told Dawson: "The easiest way to get them is to use the field phone at the end of the counter. You'll have to go through three switchboards. Our operator is Moment, ask him for Parchment, when you get him ask for Pitch Blend, and then ask for Zion-that's the switchboard at the Seabee regiment. And, Lieutenant... Good luck!"

Lieutenant Dawson gave the hand crank a quick twist and picked up the receiver.

A crisp, efficient voice responded, "Operator."

"Connect me with Parchment, please."

After considerable delay, a more distant voice answered, "Parchment."

"Connect me with Pitch Blend, operator."

"Yes sir."

Dawson waited several minutes with no answer. Trying to curb his impatience, he turned the crank again.

"Operator."

"Which operator are you?"

"This is Parchment operator."

"Ring Pitch Blend again, they didn't answer." The Parchment operator gave a long ring this time.

"Pitch Blend," came over the line.

"Operator, please connect me with Zion."

"Sorry, that trunk is busy."

"Do you only have one, Operator?"

"That's right. Sometimes we don't have that. Do you want to wait?"

"Yes, I'll wait." That he did for five minutes. He resisted several impulses to ring the operator, knowing it would ring all three switchboards he was connected through. Finally he gave the crank another twist, as he wiped sweat from his face.

"Operator."

"Operator, I've been waiting for five minutes, can you ring Zion now?"

"Sorry, but Zion isn't on my board."

"What? You... Five minutes ago you told me... Just a minute. Which operator am I talking with?"

"This is Parchment. Who do you want?"

"Ring Pitch Blend again," Dawson said in a barely tolerant voice, as he looked at the airman, who shrugged.

"Sorry, that line's busy."

"Busy? How in blazes can it be busy? You should still have me plugged in there."

"I pulled the plug to Pitch Blend when you rang me back.. Wait, there's an open line now. I'll ring."

"Another voice came through the receiver, "Have you finished?"

The color mounted in Dawson's face, "Finished? Hell no. I haven't even got started. Which operator are you?"

"This is Moment operator."

"Leave the line, Moment. I'm waiting for Pitch Blend to answer."

"This is Pitch Blend. What number do you want?"

"Operator, I am trying to get through to Zion. You left me waiting for over five minutes before. What's wrong over there?"

"You were number two waiting for that line. And then I got a disconnect before the other party was through. I can ring them for you now."

"Zion. What number please?"

"Zion, do you have a transportation section there?"

"No. This is the Regiment. You'll have to go through the Battalion for transportation."

"Operator, connect me with your Officer of The Day."

Lieutenant Dawson heard a loud click about half way through the operator's, "Yes..."

"I had to pull the plug on you. Sorry, but there was an operation-immediate call."

"I can't believe it! Which operator do I have now?"

"This is Pitch Blend. Do you want to hold till I have an open line again?"

"Yes, Pitch Blend, I'll hold. I doubt I could stand the stress of working my way back to you again. Please ring Zion as soon as you can."

Dawson looked at his watch. He had been on the telephone for more than ten minutes. I understand why Commodore Rhodes is frustrated with this system, he thought, taking another swipe at sweat running down his right cheek.

After a few minutes a voice came over the phone. "Zion, what number do you want?"

"I want to speak with your Officer of The Day."

"Command Duty Officer, Lieutenant Case speaking."

"This is Lieutenant Dawson. I'm supposed to report to your command. I'm at the Da Nang airport. Can you send someone to pick me up?"

"Sure thing. A driver will be there in half an hour."

Dawson was hot and tired and irritated after the telephone ordeal. Looking out across the large shed for a comfortable place to wait, he saw only rows of hard, unpainted wood benches without backs. He dragged his bags over to one placed against a wall and sat down resting his back and head against the rough board louvers. He removed his hat and ran his fingers through his crew-cut; then closed his eyes, letting his thoughts roam undirected. Well you've had an introduction to the problem you're supposed to correct-Hmm, and it does need correcting-should have let some one else do it though-should have thought of that before. You're here now, and you got another big problem-keeping yourself alive.

His senses closed out more of the world, letting him slide into the fuzzy state between musing and dozing. He faintly heard sounds of men coming and going from the building, the sound of small engine-driven planes, and the roar of fighter-bomber jets taking off or landing regularly.

His mind dwelt on the communications mess for a few minutes. I wonder how long it'll take to get an efficient system installed. Well, there's nothing I can do about it now; I'm sure I'll have plenty of time to worry about that in the days ahead.

"Lieutenant Dawson?"

He came to with a start. "Yeah, you from the Regiment?"

"Yes sir. I'm Carney. Jeep's right outside the door. I'll take one of those bags for you."

From what he had seen from the air, Dawson figured they were skirting the business section of Da Nang. "How far to the Regiment, Carney?"

"About twelve clicks, Lieutenant."

"Twelve clicks?"

"You know, clicks-kilometers."

Dawson laughed, embarrassed at having forgotten American military slang for kilometer. His mind did some quick calculations: Let's see, a kilometer is five-eighths of a mile, so must be about eight miles-guess I'll have to get in tune with the metric system again. The hot air blowing through the open jeep dried the sweat and almost felt cool.

Carney wove skillfully through the maze of bicycles and pedestrians clogging the street at numerous points. The scene reminded Dawson of other parts of Asia where, as a career Navy man, he had been stationed in years past. The streets were narrow and without sidewalks. At sometime in the distant past they had been paved with a thin layer of asphalt, but weren't designed for the heavy military vehicles now using them. In places the pot holes seemed to occupy as much area as the smooth surface.

Other than military, there were few motorized vehicles. The people either walked or rode bicycles. A few motor scooters dodged around vehicles, and occasionally they passed a bus overflowing with people. The buses were mostly old, low-slung, converted trucks with a rear entrance and a large baggage rack on top. Some of the smaller ones reminded Dawson of jitneys in the Philippines.

On the surface, little evidence of a war in progress presented itself. They passed no bombed-out areas. But as they got out of the densely populated area an occasional crater in or near the edge of the road gave evidence of an exploded mine.

Children played in the streets with little concern for traffic except when it stopped. Then they swarmed around American vehicles, hands out, begging for gum, candy or cigarettes. An occasional young couple walked along hand-in-hand. Seeing many more young women than young men along the streets, provided a subtle reminder of war.

When they stopped and Dawson could study faces, the haggard, beaten look of the older people told of war. There was another look Bill Dawson couldn't identify. It wasn't the same expression he had seen on the faces of people in other war-torn countries. The expression was more disturbing, more perplexing than the look of defeat worn by people whose country had been conquered.

The suburbs of Da Nang were interlaced with flooded rice paddies, mounded graves and areas of natural vegetation. As they approached the beach area, Dawson watched the sand dunes grow. He breathed deeper, enjoying the fresh salt air. Just before they arrived at Red Beach, as they were leaving a small village, countless shacks sprawled across the sand on both sides of the road. They were made of cardboard and wood, of tar paper and tin, or other metal salvaged from every imaginable source. The shacks were strewn across the sand like a patchwork quilt. They were like unwelcome appendages to the village. It reminded Dawson of the depression-era hobo jungles he had seen around Omaha as a young boy.

"What's this area called?" Dawson asked.

"We call it Refugee Village. Most of the people living here are from North Vietnam. Some have been here a long time, but most of them escaped recently. Sad lookin' ain't it?"

"Sure is. Most of the people look hungry. What do they eat? Can they find work?"

The driver, gave a slight shrug. "They collect garbage from military bases. They scrounge through our dump for material to make those shacks. We hire some of them to work at the Regiment, but we got to be careful because some V.C. are mixed in with them, and can cause big trouble. They have to be screened first."

Old men and women, and children straggled along both sides of the road to Red Beach. Some dragged pieces of cardboard, tin, or bundles of small boards. Some struggled with cloth bags filled with junkyard minutiae. The old people didn't look up as the jeep passed. The shame and degradation of having to beg and scrounge for their existence was easier to bear with averted eyes. Only the young children showed spirit. They waved and called out as the jeep passed. They ran and pushed each other in play as they carried or dragged their booty home.

Dawson noted in detail the lay of the land as they approached Red Beach. They left Highway One, the main artery running the length of Vietnam, and turned right onto a gravel road leading toward the beach. After three hundred yards they came to the main gate and guard post. Heavy razor-wire entanglement protected the front of the search lights and sandbagged bunkers.

Carney took Dawson to the only two-story building and directed him to the CDO's office on the second deck. He was surprised to find a Pasco metal building in a forward war zone. The large building housed all regimental offices. Reaching the second deck, Dawson stopped and looked around. Desks and file cabinets clustered around a large open area in the center. The rhythmic tat, tat, tat of typewriters and chatter of a half dozen voices filled the air. Around the perimeter were rooms divided by partitions with space at the bottom and the top-no doors, just 2 x 4 entryways.

A lieutenant greeted Dawson, "I'm Roger Case. Glad to meet you finally, Bill. I'll get you checked in and squared away. The Commodore said he wanted to see you as soon as you've stowed your gear. Give me your orders and records, and I'll have a yeoman process them while we get your gear over to your room."

Case carried one of Dawson's bags across loose sand flanking the packed gravel road, to a long narrow building on stilts two-feet off the ground, sided with wood louvered strips. "I haven't had anything to eat since breakfast. I'd like a snack before seeing the Commodore," Dawson said.

"Sure," Lieutenant Case said. "Chow is over but I'll get a steward to fix you a sandwich."

Dawson followed Case into one end of the building, entering a corridor running the length of it. On either side were cubicles formed by plywood sheets, with a foot opening at the floor and open above the plywood to the corrugated metal roof. There were doorless entries to each of the small rooms. Case stopped at the second opening on the right. "You can have any room that's empty. I suppose there are half a dozen. This one's directly across the hall from my room."

"This is fine with me," Dawson said, dropping his bag on the plywood deck.

Case placed the bag he carried beside the other one and said, "OK, let's get you a snack."

They entered the kitchen end of the officers' mess, across the gravel road from the officers' barracks. Going through the kitchen and into the dining room, Case located one of the stewards and told him to fix Dawson a sandwich. He turned to Dawson. "As soon as you finish, come back to the headquarters building and I'll take you in to see the Commodore. Sorry I can't stay, but I've got a pile of work waiting for me. That's one thing you'll find no shortage of here-work."

Dawson had eaten half of his sandwich when in the distance he heard, whump, whump. Ten seconds later a siren sounded right outside the mess. He jumped to his feet. For a second, panic welled up inside-he didn't know where to go. When he saw the stewards heading for the back door, Dawson followed. He jumped into the mortar trench two seconds behind them-just as another pair of whumps sounded near by.

"Do all new arrivals get such a warm welcome?" Dawson quipped.

"No sweat, Lieutenant. Charley's shooting at the Marines across the road. But we gotta go on the alert just in case he misses." one of the men said with a knowing smile.

As Dawson squatted in the two-foot wide trench he thought, with a twinge of irony: When the Commodore told me what a good job I would have, he didn't mention the down side. Well, that's why they're giving me combat pay.

Chapter 2

When Lieutenant Dawson entered the Commodore's office, a tired looking Captain Rhodes greeted him. The lines in his face were etched by strain and worry; but his blue eyes sparkled and his voice was filled with the enthusiasm Dawson remembered, even though five years had passed since they last served together.

"Bill, you can't know how glad I am you're here," the Commodore said, returning Dawson's grip with his large, rough hand. "Sorry I couldn't give you time to get settled, but that will have to wait until tonight. This communications problem has been weighing me down. When you have that resolved, it'll be one big monkey off my back. We don't have much time right now; I have another meeting, but I want you to start getting a firsthand view of the problem."

"Yes sir, I understand. I got a good feel for the problem when I tried to place my first call from the airfield to the Regiment. It took..."

"Fine," the Commodore interrupted. "There's a fresh-caught ensign standing by who will be your guide for the next week. He'll show you the location of all the commands and introduce you to people you need to know to get your job done." The Commodore yelled out to his yeoman, "Sampson, get Ensign Clark for me," and turned to Dawson again. "You'll Like him. He's a sharp young man who's been with me since we first opened up shop here. Bill, one week from today I want you to report to me with your plan of action. Tom Ramore, the Operations Officer, will be your boss, but I want you to know you have an open door here anytime."

He smiled and gave a quick chuckle, at his unintended pun. Pointing to his doorless entrance, he said, "As you can see, that applies actually as well as figuratively."

Commodore Rhodes swiveled his chair at the knock on the bare, two-by-four framework of his office entrance. "Come in, Ken. Meet Lieutenant Bill Dawson. Bill, meet your personal tour guide, Ken Clark. Now gentlemen, I have to get across town," the Commodore said, rising and strapping on his .45, as Dawson and Clark shook hands. As they left his office, the Commodore called after them, "Bill, use my name all you want to get what you need to do the job."

Ensign Clark led Dawson into a long, semi-enclosed room on the east side of the building. He pointed to one of six desks. "That's your desk, Lieutenant. Mine is the one right behind it. The other desks in here belong to Project Liaison Officers. That's my job most of the time. Here's our ace Liaison Officer, Lieutenant Case. Meet Lieutenant Dawson."

Case replied in mock seriousness, "I'll ace you my young friend if you're not careful. And I've already met the new arrival. Bill, don't believe all this young stud tells you. Although he's new in the Navy, he has learned to shoot the bull like an old salt."

Dawson watched the friendly exchange between the two men, and knew he would get along well with them. Case, the larger of the two, was square and sturdy. Tough, dependable, Dawson thought. He knew Case by reputation through mutual friends in the small group of ex-enlisted men who comprise the Civil Engineer Corps, Limited Duty Officers, (LDOs). Within the Navy family they were called Mustangs, and earned the title for the innovative and unorthodox way they got the job done.

Case was known as a hard-charger, a workhorse, and was one of the most knowledgeable officers in the construction business. Even more important, Roger Case had the reputation of being an outstanding leader. He knew how to develop the right attitude in a crew of men to get more out of them than they thought they could produce. And they could still end the day with a laugh, no matter how unpleasant the job. Case knew how to set the right tone with Seabees.

At first sight, Dawson liked Ensign Clark. From his many years in the Navy, changing location and jobs at least every two years, and having new working associates, as well as social contacts, Dawson had learned to make accurate snap judgments of men. Although the Seabee greens worn by officers and enlisted men were hardly the spit-and-polish uniform of the Navy, Clark wore his with obvious pride. It was clean and pressed; and Clark had the build to make any uniform look military. He was 5'10" with a stocky build, not pudgy, rather, hard and compact. His direct, concise speech matched his decisive, sure movements. Yes, I can see why the Commodore likes him, Dawson thought. Definite career potential.

Clark pointed at battle gear covering the desk top. "This is your gear, Lieutenant. The Commodore said he didn't want your time wasted, so I checked this out from the armory. Please sign these custody cards. I can take them down later and get myself off the hook."

Dawson quickly checked off the gear on the cards, and signed them. He tightened the helmet liner to fit his head, adjusted the wide webbed belt to his waist, cleared the .45, and loaded the two clips, inserting one in the .45 and the other into the pouch on the webbed belt. He then holstered the .45 saying, "I'm ready. By the way, what is Command policy about wearing all of this gear?" he asked, hefting the heavy flack jacket.

"Everyone's supposed to have his weapon with him at all times. The rest of the gear? Well, the Command recommends wearing it, but leaves it up to the individual's discretion. I like to keep it handy. It depends on where I am whether or not I wear it."

"Well, Ken, what I want to know is, what are the odds of us getting shot at this afternoon?"

"Every place we'll be going today is considered under friendly control. There's not much chance of us being shot, other than by random sniper fire. The only battle gear I'm wearing is my weapon.

"Now, if you're ready, I'm supposed to get you in to meet the Operations Officer before we start on our tour of military bases. His office is in the next room. Do you know Commander Ramore?"

"Not well. I met him once in Washington at a cocktail party, but we've never worked together."

Leaving the Commander's office, Dawson and Clark piled into Clark's jeep and toured the immediate camp area. The regiment's camp was small; only large enough to provide office space, along with messing, and berthing facilities for a small staff. All of the offices were in the one large metal building, and a small one of wood. The other buildings-an officer's mess, and two hooches, a shower, one two-hole outhouse, a chief's mess and barracks, six large hooches for enlisted barracks, two shower hooches, and eight two-hole outhouses were of tropical wood construction.

Not exactly like home, Dawson thought. But I should complain? I'm sure thousands of troops in fox holes and mortar trenches would consider this plush.

The 30th NCR was flanked on either side by two of its construction battalions, which, besides protecting their own camps, also provided security for the regiment. The South China Sea, with gently sloping beach, ran along the east side of all three units. Barbed wire entanglements, and bunkers manned only at night, guarded the beach. To the west, flat, open, sandy terrain stretched for a hundred yards; then a ridge of rolling sand dunes rose up between the three Seabee units and Highway One. The gate Dawson came through earlier was the only entrance to the three commands. No physical barriers existed between Mobile Construction Battalion 9 to the north of the 30th NCR or MCB-3 to the south.

"You refer to the barracks and other buildings as 'hooches' is that a legitimate name or slang?" Dawson asked.

"It's the only one I know. That's what we call all of the tropical buildings we build here."

They left the Seabee camp driving south for one kilometer, on Highway One toward Da Nang, and then turned west into the Marine 7th Engineers' camp. They drove through it with Clark giving an overview of its function and pointing out the location of the communications center. Exiting the west end of the camp, they were in more hilly terrain. Then, in less than a half-kilometer, they entered the First Marine Tank Command camp.

"The roads we've been on so far," Clark said, "are considered safe for travel in the day time, but not at night. Travel between commands at night is done only when absolutely necessary."

"I don't intend to take any more chances than I have to," Dawson said. "So I'll limit my travel to day time."

The Marine guard waved them through as they exited the west end of the Tank Command and started down a narrow, gravel road that wound its way through rugged, uninhabited hills. Clark explained this road was considered safe to use on some days and closed on others, depending on intelligence reports of Viet Cong activity in the area.

"Looks like bad country to me on any day," Dawson said, as he nervously scanned both sides of the road. They could hide a company of V.C. in these hills, he thought. "How far is it to the next military camp?"

"I still have trouble with the kilometer-miles business. The map shows it at twelve clicks-Let's see, that's about seven miles. When it isn't safe to use, the Marine sentries on either end of the road give us the word. The mine detail sweeps this road each morning before it's opened to travel."

"This is one road I'll not use if I can avoid it," Dawson said.

"I've never had any trouble. But I follow the Marine's recommendations, using it only when they say it's safe."

Dawson caught himself cracking his knuckles, one after another. He didn't know why; maybe to relieve tension. As a boy he had done it a lot. He developed three ways to crack his large knuckles-pull, twist, and bend. It was a habit his mother scolded him for regularly. "Don't do that, Billy. It will make your knuckles big."

After driving in silence for a while, Clark said: "Things aren't done here like we were taught in OCS. We address Commanders and above by their rank. But most officers within our command, from Lieutenant Commander down, call each other by first names, which was difficult for me to get used to after the rigorous discipline at OCS. I still don't feel free to call my seniors by first names unless I know that's what they prefer."

Bill smiled, appreciating his diplomacy. "First name's fine with me, Ken. Spit and polish has its place in the military, but out here I believe informality within a small group of officers can build camarad...."

Dawson's reply was interrupted by the windshield between the two men shattering, and the sound of a shot arriving almost instantaneously. Clark tromped the accelerator to the floor, disregarding the winding road and possibility of meeting another vehicle.

Seeing the hood of the jeep covered with glass shards, Dawson knew the shot had come from behind them. He pulled his .45, chambered a round, and looked back. There was only bare,, rocky hills in view. He continued looking behind as Clark performed controlled four-wheel drifts in the curves on the gravel road. After two kilometers, Clark slowed down.

"Probably a lone sniper," He said. "Too many hills between us for him to get us in his sights again. You see anything?"

Dawson was glad his level of fear had diminished to the point it didn't show in his voice. "Nothing moved. We're lucky he was a poor shot. I think I'll modify my opinion about the safety of this road."

"Me too! I've driven this road a dozen times, with no trouble. Going back we'll take the long way."

When they got to the guard post at the Marine ammunitions storage area, Clark stopped and reported the shot to the guard.

"I thought I heard a shot from that direction," the Private said. "I'll call and get the Tank Command to send out a patrol. Those buggers are getting brave coming out in the daylight when they don't have good jungle cover."

As they continued down the road it passed to the east of ammo storage berms and bunkers. Immediately beyond the ammo storage area a small village with a few huts bordered the road. Flooded rice paddies came up to the back of the thatched huts, and dense growth closed in on the other side of the road. Dawson thought, I'll bet the Vietnamese didn't vote for putting an ammo dump in their backyard.

After winding along the narrow road for a few miles, with the jungle overhanging both sides of it, they arrived at another check-point Clark said was the entrance to the First Marine Division Headquarters complex. From the main road, he pointed out the headquarters building perched high on a hill, and, as he drove slowly along the well traveled road, explained where the smaller Marine commands fit in the overall command structure.

When Dawson could push aside the constant threat of danger, he admired the beauty of the countryside with its many shades of green; the dark green of the jungle, the pale, delicate green of tender rice shoots, and the sea flashing its emerald radiance. Countless rivers and streams rushed from the mountains in torrents of cool, clear water; and then turned brown and sluggish as they wandered through flat lands making up much of the Da Nang area. Some of their names sounded melodious to Dawson, although he had difficulty pronouncing them. The Song Han split Da Nang and Da Nang-East, and three miles north of Red Beach the

Song Cau De brought life to fishermen as it flowed into the South China Sea. A smaller stream called Khe Thanh Khe, ran between Red Beach and Da Nang, where the laughter of children bathing mingled with the quieter voices of women washing clothes.

Much of the terrain was marshland. Flooded rice paddies flanking many of the roads, gave the impression of driving down a narrow peninsula. Dikes dividing the rice paddies were used as paths and in some cases were the only way people could get to and from their thatched homes, perched above the water on wood stilts. Dawson found this beauty and illusory tranquillity remarkably incongruous with the horrors of war,

Passing the airfield, Dawson recognized the building where he had waited for transportation a few hours earlier. They drove by several Army and Air Force commands, and stopped at the entrance to the MCB-10 camp. Clark quickly described its primary construction responsibilities. From there they circled the entire Da Nang Airfield, stopping occasionally, as Clark provided names of many smaller military commands strung out along the runway.

By the time they had driven around the airfield and were headed back toward Red Beach, the sun was resting low on the horizon. When they got to the Red Beach entrance, razor wire barriers had been drawn across the road for the night. The barriers were staggered so the jeep could zigzag between them at low speed after being waved on by the sentry.

Clark parked near the headquarters building, and as they walked to the officer's hooches, he said, "It's time for chow; I'll meet you in the mess after I wash up."

Clark walked to the second hooch as Dawson entered the first one. Retrieving soap and a towel from his bag, Dawson walked to the washroom building between the two hooches. The cool water felt refreshing on his face and neck, as he washed off red dirt and sweat.

When Dawson came out of his hooch, Clark was waiting for him. "Thought I would wait and walk over with you. We can eat together and I'll introduce you to some of the officers." They entered at the corner of the L shaped building. The long room on the right had eight tables, each with four chairs.

The Commodore, seated at the nearest table, said, "Bill, come over here a minute. You haven't met our Executive Officer. Gordon Brooks, meet Bill Dawson."

Commander Brooks stood, extending his hand. His light handshake matched his slight build and easy-going appearance. "Welcome to Red Beach, Bill."

"It's a pleasure, Commander," Dawson responded.

"Our Operations Officer, Tom Ramore, you met earlier," Commodore Rhodes said, indicating the third man at the table. Then he clanged on his glass with a fork until all conversation stopped. "Gentlemen," he said in a booming voice that filled the room. "I want you to meet our newest member, Bill Dawson. He's an old friend to some of us, but to those of you who haven't yet met him, you'll have to do so when you can, as Bill won't be checking in through normal channels. I had him working within an hour of his arrival this afternoon. I'm sure you'll find him a welcome addition to our crew." Then turning to Dawson, he said, "Go ahead, get your dinner before it gets cold, Bill."

Clark was seated at the far end of the room with another officer. Dawson stopped at a table where Lieutenant Case and another LDO, Lieutenant Paul Knight, were seated. "Hi, Paul, didn't know you were out here."

Knight stood, offering his hand. "Yeah, they got me too. Looks like all the LDOs will be out here soon. Good to see you again, Bill."

Dawson looked at the third officer at the table and said, "The face is familiar, but I can't put a name with it."

"Ed Fallon," the other Lieutenant said. "It's been a long time, Bill. The last time we were together was in the Philippines over fifteen years ago. We were both First Class at the time."

"Sure, now I remember. Good to see you again, Ed."

"Sit and eat with us."

"I'd like to, but I think I should sit with Ken Clark. We have more business to discuss. I'll get with you guys after dinner."

When Dawson sat down, Clark said, "This is Joe Markowski, our Supply Officer, and Mess Officer."

They shook hands across the table, and Lieutenant Junior Grade Markoski continued eating. Soon a young Vietnamese woman brought two plates of food to Dawson and Clark.

"This is Fan Ti Wa, our number-one girl. To keep her happy you got to pat her once in a while." Clark reached out to put his hand on her thigh, but she quickly side-stepped, slapping at his hand.

"You dinky dau," she said, marching away, head held high.

Dawson raised his eyebrows, canting his head to one side. "Guess she doesn't like the way you pat her. What was that she called you?"

"Dinky dau? Oh, that means I'm crazy."

"Do the Vietnamese women take the place of stewards here?"

"We have two Navy stewards. They cook and supervise the four girls who serve tables. The only other Vietnamese working for the regiment are the women who clean our rooms."

Later Clark said, "A quick word on protocol: The head table is reserved for the Commodore. The only others who sit there without specific invitation are the

X.O. and OPS. Officer. Other tables are used on a first-come basis. There's little formality. We're supposed to be here at 1830 if we're in the immediate area. If we're away from the camp, it's no problem when we come in late, except the food may be cold."

By the time Dawson and Clark had finished dinner, the other officers had migrated to the bar located in the corner of the L, between the dining area and the lounge. The two officers joined the group at the bar and ordered drinks. Dawson looked down the other wing of the building and saw a lounge area furnished with rattan couches and chairs and coffee tables. Four men were playing ping pong at the far end of the room. Clark took Dawson from one group to another introducing him to the officers he hadn't met.

Dawson finished two drinks during the hour he spent exchanging personal details with Ed Fallon and Paul Knight. When one of the stewards started setting up a projector and screen to show movies in the lounge, Dawson said, "It's been a long day. Think I'll hit the sack early."

"You will have a lot of those around here," Lieutenant Knight said.

"Lot of what?" Dawson asked.

"Long days," Knight said with a grin.

Dawson found Clark before leaving. " I'm turning in early. What's our schedule tomorrow?"

"More geographical orientation in the morning, and in the afternoon you're scheduled for a briefing by the Battalion Intelligence Officer. Reveille is at 0515 and we start work at six. Want me to call you in the morning?"

"No, I have an alarm clock. But 0515! I haven't had to get up that early since I left the ranch. I'll see you at breakfast."

The intermittent "boom, boom" of artillery in the distance caused Dawson an uneasy night, waking him several times. Each time, he was vividly reminded that he was in an active war zone.

After a hurried breakfast, Dawson and Clark headed south on Highway One, going straight into Da Nang. The sun still hid behind the calm, leaden colored sea. Cool, moist air caressed the men in the open jeep.

Thinking of the sniper shot from yesterday, Dawson felt nervous when they left the base, but as they continued on into Da Nang on the well traveled road, he relaxed. As Dawson observed the countryside around Da Nang, he was reminded of Hawaii. Except for the rice paddies it looked much the same. Narrow roads wound through dense foliage, and through clearings covered with grass and fern-type plants growing waist high. In one area, low gently-rolling hills looked barren in contrast with the nearby jungle. The soil contains too much rock for the heavier vegetation to grow, Dawson thought.

Clean, white sand formed a beautiful, picturesque beach. Low rolling sand dunes rose-up close to the water's edge in spots; other places the beach fell gently into the sea, where swimmers could walk a hundred yards out into the water.

Red Beach was centered in a large half-moon bay. The point of the crescent to the north was formed by Hai Vung Pass and the mountains, the southern point was Monkey Mountain.

When they came to the outskirts of Da Nang, Dawson noted the lack of congestion they had encountered the day before. That early they were able to maintain posted speed all the way into the center of town. Clark pointed out the Naval Forces, Vietnam (NAVFOR V) headquarters, the senior command over all U. S. armed forces in the I Corps. Leaving the center of Da Nang they crossed a two-lane, cantilever bridge, with three long spans supported by two massive concrete piers in the Song Han.

"This is the only bridge between Da Nang and Da Nang-East," Clark said. "At times it's hopelessly congested. I've found it faster to take the water taxi that docks near NAVFOR V Headquarters if I'm going only to the Marine headquarters across the river from NAVFOR V.

Studying the map Clark had given him, Dawson noted Da Nang-East was a spit of land bounded by the Song Han on one side and the South China Sea on the other. The end of the spit swelled into a mountain standing like a mute guard protecting the harbor at the mouth of the river.

"According to the map, this river flows down from enemy territory. Doesn't it provide the V.C. easy access to our ships anchored in the harbor?" Dawson asked.

"It would if the River Patrol wasn't so effective. They check out everything that moves on the river. Even fishermen know better than to use it at night. The patrol shoots anything moving after dark.

A mile after crossing the bridge, they entered a base fronting the Song Han. "This is the top Marine command in the I Corps area, the Third Marine Amphibious Force; for short, called III MAF. And, of course, this is who Seabees do most of the work for." Clark stopped the jeep at the end of a street, dead-ending into the sluggish, brown river. He pointed across the river. "There you can see NAVFOR V Headquarters building-that large white one. It's called the 'White Elephant' why, I'm not sure. Possibly the French used it as command headquarters, and look what happened to them."

Next they circled through the main supply yard and then drove to the end of the peninsula, to the dock area where two cargo ships were disgorging tanks, jeeps, ammunition, food, clothing, and other necessities for the fighting troops.

Looking out across the harbor, Dawson counted fifteen ships at anchor. "Are all those ships waiting to unload?"

"Yes. That's one of our major logistic problems. As you can see, there's dock space for only two ships. Landing craft go out and pick up cargo, then they beach and off-load near the bridge. But that's a slow process. One of our hottest projects is another dock, which we'll be starting soon."

Near the dock and cargo-staging area, Monkey Mountain rose up abruptly, about a thousand feet. Clark pointed to it. "Earlier we cut in a road and built a radar site on top for the Air Force. We have no work in progress up there now, but we'll go on up anyway. You can get a good panoramic view of the entire Da Nang area from there. It might help you get oriented."

The narrow, red, dirt road spiraled the cone shaped mountain, like stripes on a barber pole. But instead of red and white stripes, the road wound through lush green vegetation smothering the entire mountain. A four-foot lizard crossed ahead of the jeep, and scrambled awkwardly up the steep bank on the left. It reminded Dawson of the giant lizards in the Philippines.

Faint-hearted sightseers wouldn't drive up Monkey Mountain a second time. The road was perilously steep. In places there was barely room for two vehicles to slowly ease by each other. The remainder was a single-lane road with a high-cut bank on one side and an unprotected drop-off on the other. The drop-off, on Dawson's side all the way up, made him wish the jeep had a roll-bar. With the dense jungle there, at least we shouldn't fall far if we go over. Sure glad there's not much traffic on this road, he thought.

They met only one truck before their laboring jeep reached the summit. The clearing had two small buildings and four radar antennae. The view was spectacular. From a single vantage point the unobstructed view encompassed over 180 degrees. The ships in the harbor seemed to be tethered at the foot of the mountain, looking like a fleet of toy boats on a large pond. Across the harbor to the west, and a little north, lay Da Nang proper. The airfield was more to the north, and yet farther north Clark pointed out Red Beach. It was easy to spot since it was the last military camp visible to the north.

Pointing to the mountains a few miles beyond Red Beach, Dawson asked, "Does Highway One go on over those mountains?"

"Yes, Hai Vung Pass is where it crosses the mountains."

Looking southwest along the Da Nang-East peninsula, Marine III MAF headquarters was visible. Beyond, other military bases, interspersed with Vietnamese homes and shops, lined the main road. Clark pointed out the military hospital area and two construction battalion camps beyond the bridge. Then eleven miles to the southwest, a huge mountain of rock with perpendicular walls jutted up incongruously. It looked as though it had been quarried and then somehow moved from the quarry site to its present location.

"That's Marble Mountain," Clark said. "On top is a Marine outpost. They come under attack daily, but they've never been overrun. The V.C. control the country on three sides of them, but can't get to them in force."

After slowly spiraling down the Monkey Mountain road, they drove past the hospital area and then through two construction battalion camps, which were separated by a few kilometers of sand dunes. They turned around at the entrance to the Army Special Forces headquarters. Clark said that was as far as it was safe to drive without armed escort. Then, looking at his watch, he said, "We'll have to hurry to get back to Red Beach in time for lunch."

Traffic in Da Nang-East wasn't bad until they came to a halt behind a line of vehicles, three blocks from the bridge. Then it was stop-and-go until they got across the bridge and the traffic fanned out into four streets.

Looking to the right, down the main street toward downtown Da Nang, Dawson saw it was clogged with buses, bicycles, jitneys, pedi-cabs, and pedestrians intermingled with military vehicles. "What a mess. Reminds me of Manila fifteen years ago. Sure hope we don't have to go that way."

"No, sir. I know a better way." Clark took a small side road skirting around the center of Da Nang, that was much less congested.

After lunch Clark said: "I'll take you over to meet the MCB-3 Intelligence Officer. The Commodore made arrangements for you to get a special briefing so you can get a quick look at the overall situation here."

The MCB-3 Command Post was one-quarter mile south of the Thirtieth Naval Construction Regimental Headquarters. The small building was half-underground, constructed of heavy timbers, covered with many layers of sand bags. Dawson thought it should withstand all but a direct hit by a time-delay artillery shell. Its one entrance was five steps down, and recessed in an arch of sand bags. A heavy blast-resistant door opened at a right-angle to the entryway.

Stale smoke filled the small, dimly lit, windowless room. It reminded Dawson of an old poolroom in Omaha. Clark led Dawson to a corner, partially partitioned off from the main room, where a lieutenant pecked rapidly on a typewriter.

"I'd like you to meet Lieutenant Dawson," Clark said. "This is Lieutenant Sandovan, MCB-3's Intelligence Officer."

The Lieutenant, with worry-lines etched into his swarthy face, barely glanced up from the typewriter. "Good to meet you. I'll be with you as soon as I finish this report."

"I'm not needed here," Clark said, "so I'll return to the regiment. I have some problems to resolve. Is there anything I can do for you, Bill?"

"Yes, you can get a detailed map of the area. I'd like you to plot on the map all commands of company size or larger. Also note what type of land-line communications they have. If they have a switchboard, how many lines it has, how many trunk-lines, and to what other switchboards they're connected. If the unit has a Communications Officer, list his name."

Clark wrote rapidly in his pocket notebook. "I can get that information OK. Some of it I can consolidate from existing sources, but the switchboards and where they're connected, will take time. I doubt I can have it all this afternoon."

"I realize it's a lot of detail, but it's what I need to figure out how the communications system should be designed. I'll help you when I'm through here."

"Give me a call when you're through and I'll pick you up," Clark said.

Lieutenant Sandovan folded his report, dropping it into the out basket. "I'm ready for you now, Lieutenant. I've been told what your job is, and I don't envy you. I'll give you the briefing VIP's get, plus the one I give the ground-pounders. So it'll take a while."

Sandovan mounted a small platform with maps, blackboard, and projection screen. "Have a front seat, you're my only audience for this one. I'll start with a brief historical background, and give you an overview of the Seabees' mission along with a general, geographic picture of our operating area. Then I'll zero in for a close-up of the Da Nang area, including our present tactical situation and a forecast of what we can expect from the Viet Cong-hereafter referred to as Charley. And that will be about as accurate as a weather forecast."

"In that case I'll always wear my raincoat," Dawson quipped.

"Right. If at any point you have questions, interrupt me and I'll try to clear them up."

Sandovan pulled down a large map of South and North Vietnam. "The Seabees became involved in Vietnam six years ago when the Army Special Forces, Green Beret, came in to show the people in small villages how to defend themselves against the Communist Viet Cong. The Seabees sent in special twelve-man teams, who helped the villagers develop potable water sources and build more durable houses, roads, and sanitary facilities. Their purpose was to teach the natives by demonstration, and then move on to another village. We first came in force with the Marines when they landed near Chu Lai, about eighty-five kilometers south of here. That was over a year and a half ago. The Marines have primary combat responsibility for the I Corps, as do the Seabees for construction."

Dawson interrupted. "Question. I see by the map, South Vietnam is divided into four Corps areas, numbered in sequence starting at the Demilitarized Zone dividing North and South Vietnam. The other areas are called Two, Three, and Four Corps areas. Why is this Corps area, which would logically be the One Corps, called the I Corps?"

Sandovan laughed. "That gets into a discussion on Asian mentality. In Vietnam 'number one' means the best. If this area was referred to as the One Corps area, it would imply that the people up here were the best, which would mean people in other Corps weren't as good-and that would never do. It would cause friction between people from this area and the other Corps areas. So the Vietnamese solved the problem by calling this the I Corps area. Perfect logic, huh? I won't charge extra for that bit of sociological insight.

"Back to the present. Da Nang is the Marines' headquarters, and it's the Seabees' construction headquarters. We have eight Mobile Construction Battalions in-country, and expect to soon have ten. Working from the south up, there are two battalions in Chu Lai, four in or around Da Nang, and two located at Phu Bai, just south of Hue, about eighty kilometers north of here. Detachments from the battalions are scattered all over the I Corps. I'm sure you're familiar with the Seabee command structure, so I won't go into that. The top U. S. military command in Vietnam is MACV. The top command in the I Corps is the Naval Forces, Vietnam, called NAVFOR V, commanded by Vice Admiral Scott. All armed forces in the I Corps report to him..."

"Question. MACV stands for?"

"Military Assistance Command, Vietnam. Continuing: The Army has a small number of troops up here, mostly Special Forces units, and the Air Force has several flight and support units here. But the bulk of American troops in this area are Marines. Many Republic of Vietnam troops are scattered throughout the I Corps. We have all three elements of their armed forces up here: the Regular Armed Forces, the Regional Force, and the Popular Force.

"We also have some small units of Cambodian soldiers, and one company of South Koreans. I doubt you'll have much connection with the Koreans, but you'll learn the South Vietnamese hate and fear them almost as much as the North Vietnamese do. The Koreans don't mess around. If They receive fire from a village, they assume the villagers are their enemy, and treat them as such. They have a reputation of being tough and merciless.

"In your job, as I understand it, most of your work will be with the Marines. The top Marine command is III MAF, Third Marine Amphibious Force, headed by Major General Harrington. He has two divisions in-country, with a brigadier general over each one. The First Marine Division has its headquarters in Da Nang, and the Third Division is located in Phu Bai. I understand Ensign Clark is showing you the location of all commands in the Da Nang area, so I won't cover them in detail. Before I get into the tactical situation, do you have any other questions?"

"At this point only one. Does the South Vietnamese military up here come under Admiral Scott?"

"The answer is yes and no. A Vietnamese general of equivalent rank is supposed to report to Admiral Scott. But he also reports directly to the top Vietnamese general in Saigon; and at times he acts independently. The Marines have problems when they want to schedule an operation the ARVN general doesn't agree with. The ARVN general also sends out troops without the Marines' knowledge. As you can imagine, there's some shooting between our troops and the ARVN units, when we don't know who they are and our operation plans don't show friendly forces in the area. That is a serious problem, and..."

The phone rang twice. "Lieutenant Sandovan." He listened for a few seconds, then responded. "I'm doing a briefing now...Yes, Sir. I'll be there in two minutes."

He consulted his large desk calendar. "Gonna have to break it off now, Lieutenant. Boss wants me ASAP. I still have the tactical situation to go cover. Of course, that's most important to keep your tail out of trouble. I have a tactical briefing scheduled for 0600 one week from today. Can you make it?"

"Sure, I haven't been here long enough to have any other appointments. Ensign Clark will be escorting me, so he should keep me from straying into bad country for the next week."

Dawson briskly walked the quarter of a mile to regimental headquarters. He enjoyed the late afternoon sun, and with long strides, stretched his cramped leg muscles. He thought about the resigned, helpless attitude Sandovan expressed at the end of his briefing. It sounds like another Korean, no-win war to me. But I sure hope not, he thought.

Clark was talking on the telephone when Dawson entered. A large map of Da Nang lay open on his desk, with all bases and commands highlighted in yellow, or written in large black letters. Dawson studied the map in detail trying to correlate it with his tour of the area. Names of individuals, and numbers showing the type of switchboard and number of trunk lines, were written alongside some command designations.

After putting down the telephone, Clark said: "I have about half the information plotted. I'm calling each unit to get the specifics you requested. But I won't finish today."

Dawson looked over Clark's shoulder at a diagram with circles containing the call name and organizational name of each major command. The circles were connected by straight lines showing to which switchboards each command was connected.

"Ken, if you get me one of those diagrams, I'll help," Dawson said.

They both worked steadily, telephoning until dinner time. When they quit and went to dinner, they had collected information on all but six commands.

After dinner, Dawson declined a game of ping pong, picked up a drink at the bar and went to his room to write letters. An hour and two letters later he could hardly keep his eyes open. It was still early and he thought: My system must still be screwed up because of the time change. How many hours does it change from the East Coast? Don't know. Must be at least ten hours.

A loud, warbling siren jarred Dawson out of a restless sleep. He jumped up, grabbed his .45 and helmet and ran for the entrance where he remembered seeing a mortar trench. His thoughts were mixed. He wondered if the base was being shelled, or if ground forces were attacking. He jumped into the mortar trench a few feet from the end of the hooch. Four other skivvi-clad men, plus an inch of the cool rain, were already in the trench.

"What's happening?" Dawson asked.

One of the officers replied, "The Marine unit across the highway has been receiving incoming rounds for the past few minutes. Guess the command thought Charley might lob a few into our camp."

Then Dawson saw two flashes, and five seconds later heard the "whump, whump" of mortars impacting a mile away. Must've been what I heard in my dream and thought it was a door slamming, he thought. Then he heard the Marine artillery's answering fire. In a few minutes two helicopters flew by, headed for the jungle area northwest of camp. From their trench the men watched red streams of tracers flowing like neon lights from the two gun-ships, as they saturated a small area with lead.

In a half-hour, quiet had settled in, and the Command Duty Officer gave the order to secure. After Dawson dried off and got back into bed, five minutes passed before he could stop shivering. He lay awake listening for more incoming. At each distant artillery "pop" his mind compared the sound with the prior incoming mortar explosions. A part of him didn't want to go to sleep, but finally physical need overcame mental anxiety.

The remainder of the week passed rapidly, even with the long work-days. Sunday was like other days for the Seabees, with a full twelve-hours of work. In trying to contact other organizations Dawson learned most support units worked only Sunday morning and had the afternoon off. Clark told him the Commodore said the combat troops fought on Sunday, so the Seabees supporting them shouldn't do less.

Dawson inspected the one central switchboard in operation, and talked with major commands to be serviced by the new system he was designing. The only resistance he encountered was from Major Dibble, in charge of an Air Force maintenance unit, who made it clear he wasn't interested in a new communications system. He provided Dawson with only the information he felt he had to.

"When the new system has been completed it'll benefit us all," Dawson said. "I'd think you would want to help."

Major Dibble growled, "I doubt your system will be an improvement over what we have."

"Well, Major, the Navy has been given responsibility for the telephone system. If I can't get your cooperation, I'm sure my Commodore will be able to."

Dawson and Clark spent considerable time looking at possible routes for the main cables, which might present a major problem for completion of the project. They checked on materials and equipment available at a dozen supply yards. Usually they had to search through row upon row of supplies because inventory cards didn't reflect the rapidly-changing status of supplies. Sometimes they inspected the supply yards over the Supply Officer's objection. In most cases Dawson was told none of what he wanted could be released because it had been ordered for other jobs. He knew acquisition of much of the material he needed would have to be taken up with commanding officers.

Part of a day Dawson spent reviewing lists of construction electricians, in-country construction battalions had in their commands. He listed the chief petty officers and other key enlisted men he knew and wanted to head up his work crews.

Chapter 3

Dawson made an appointment to brief the Commodore a day ahead of his one-week deadline. Lieutenant Dawson and Ensign Clark entered the Commodore's office at exactly 0630 as scheduled. Commodore Rhodes looked up from his early morning review of incoming messages. He pointed to chairs saying, "I'll be with you in a minute." When he had finished the message he was reading, he asked, "Bill, can you wrap this up in half an hour?"

"Yes, sir. My presentation will take less than thirty minutes. But it'll depend on how many questions you have."

"Good. I have a conference with Admiral Scott before eight." Commander Brooks and Commander Ramore came in and took seats. The Commodore gave a get-on-with-it wave.

Dawson stood by an easel supporting a map of Da Nang. "I'll describe my plan, and cover the problem areas I foresee. I'm omitting details to conserve time, and will rely on your questions to cover specifics you want to know about.

"The system will have four common battery switchboards. One exists at NAV-FOR V in the right location, but it has to be expanded. One will be installed here," he indicated with his pointer, "at III MAF. One will be situated near the First Marine Division, and the fourth switchboard will be installed at the FLSG headquarters. Field switchboards serving companies or larger units will be tied in to one of the main switchboards with several trunk lines; in addition, smaller units will have a number of direct lines tied into a main switchboard. Trunk lines will connect all four main switchboards.

"I propose leaving the existing system intact, using transfer switches to switch each board over to the new system. We'll be running some larger cables, and Charley may decide it's worth the risk to put them out of order once in a while. If he does, each field switchboard can switch back to the old system until the trouble is located. This method will also permit us to test the new system, then switch over to it with the minimum of confusion. We'll string approximately sixty miles of cable using 2,000 poles. I'll need 46 men, four line trucks and..."

The Commodore interrupted, "Bill, you can give your manpower and materiel requirements to Commander Ramore later. When can you have the system operational?"

"Four months, Commodore. That's if I get the materiel and people I need, and cooperation from all commands. The major problem I foresee, which I'll not be able to control, is the acquisition of land necessary to build the pole lines. The

Property Acquisition Officer at NAVFOR V, Lieutenant Commander Thornbow, was vague about time but implied it would take weeks or even months to get access to some of the land. Another problem is getting the material. Three switchboards I can get out of the War Reserve Stock at Port Hueneme. Most of the cable and poles are here, but they're controlled by several commands. The only place I didn't gain entry to their supply yard was at the Air Force command. Major Dibble wasn't at all cooperative. So I don't know what they have that we can use.

"By the way, Commodore, that Air Force major was talking about putting in an automatic system. I think he has his head up in the clouds. Automatic equipment would malfunction so much in this environment that we would be worse off than we are now. We can't afford the environmental control necessary for that type of equipment."

The Commodore waved his cigar. "You're right about the Major, except his head isn't in the clouds, it's up his rear end usually. Don't worry about him. I'll get him squared away. Getting hold of the property will be a problem. I'll talk with the Admiral this morning. I'm sure he will be able to get maximum cooperation from both gentlemen concerned. The Air Force wanted this job. They were going to drag in one of their Red Horse units. They figured a year or more to make an automatic system operational. Anything else, Bill?"

Dawson shrugged. "Well, yes sir. Much of the material we need is controlled by Army and Marine commands. I'm going to have to deal with higher command than the Supply Officers."

"Right, I expected that. When you run into road blocks, take it up with Commander Ramore." Looking at Ramore he continued: "Tom, you know the priority of this project. Get Bill what he needs. Pull men and material from projects not in immediate support of combat troops. Bill, I'm going to pass your estimated completion time on to the Admiral. I'll expect it completed in four months, not four months and a day."

Commander Ramore stood, saying: "Let's go over to my office, Bill. We can work out the details there."

Dawson spent an hour and a half with Commander Ramore, who took the list of equipment and said he would screen battalions to see who could spare the line trucks and splicing trucks needed.

"The three chiefs I listed are critical to the project," Dawson said. "I've worked with them before and know they can do the job."

Ramore took the list of key supervisors saying he would arrange for their detachment to the regiment. He assigned a project number, and said, "The project should have a name for easy identification and reference. Any ideas, Bill?"

Dawson cocked his head in thought for a few seconds, "How about Simplified Communications?"

"Too long. Let's call it SIMPCOM."

Dawson was standing at the bar after dinner, shooting the breeze and waiting for the projector and movie screen to be set up, when Commander Ramore came over. "The three chiefs you want will report to you in the morning at eight. Sure glad they were in different battalions, or I would've got a lot more static than I did from the battalion commanders."

The movie was a corny western, but Dawson stayed to the end. It provided diversion and a few laughs.

Dawson hadn't had time to check on his mail before dinner, so he checked his box after the movie. He was glad he did-there were two letters from Pat. Her letters always gave him a lift. His first week in Vietnam had been lonely. With the many years he had in the Navy, he felt he should be able to adapt to new surroundings and new people faster. But he found it still took time to get settled in.

The element of danger, the full extent of which Dawson had not yet been able to analyze, added to his need for contact with a saner, more stable world. The unknown was more unsettling to him than the reality of the situation after he'd been there a while. He still had trouble sleeping because of the sharp crack of the 105mm sending out H and I fire during the night.

Dawson put his feet on his bunk, tilting back the metal folding chair. Pat's newsy, cheerful letters took his mind off of war and the day's problems. As he read, warmth and love she'd shown him in past years flooded his memory. He was inundated with longing and desire. You dummy! he thought. Here you are seven thousand miles from home. You could still be there feeling Pat's warm ardent body.

He let his mind wander back to the years following his divorce. Before he met Pat, he'd known a few women, but hadn't let himself get deeply involved. He was afraid to take a chance, afraid of being hurt again. With Pat he lowered his guard-a little. They'd enjoyed all benefits of marriage except children and a marriage license. That was fine with Pat until their last six months together. She wanted children before she got too old, she said, and she wanted a more committed relationship.

She had insisted on marriage. Dawson had refused even when she threatened to move out. Old memories of hurt and betrayal crowded in to dissuade him when he thought of the complete commitment of marriage again. Pat hadn't moved out, but he could tell she wasn't happy. He did love her and at times thought of marrying her. But that love wasn't the same as he had felt for his wife. He was attracted physically, he appreciated Pat's many good qualities, and he enjoyed her companionship. But it wasn't the same as his first love.

Pat's daily letters were long, warm, and supportive. He had written each day since arriving in Vietnam. His letters were usually short and it was becoming more difficult to find things to say-he didn't want to worry her with war stories. He sipped his highball as he read the two letters, and then spent a half hour writing one to her before getting ready for bed. In bed he read her letters through again. They helped block out sounds of Marine artillery firing intermittently a mile away, sounds constantly reminding Dawson he was in a war zone. He turned out the light, curled up on his left side, hoping he could get to sleep early for a change.

An hour later, he got jarred wide awake. An explosion shook his bunk and the building. Dawson's feet were on the deck when the second mortar hit three seconds later, even closer. He slung the webbed belt with his .45 over his shoulder, grabbed his helmet and ran to the nearest end of the hooch. He followed Roger Case into the mortar trench as another shell hit and lit up the area near the camp's west perimeter. Dawson felt the pressure as the concussion enveloped him.

Four men hunkered down in the trench, in their skivvies, waiting for the next shell. The two-foot wide by ten-foot long trench was deep enough for a man to defend his position with a rifle, while standing. So to keep their entire bodies below ground level, the men had to squat.

"Charley can't get me up in the bad-lands, so now he has to try down here also," Case muttered sardonically.

This was too new and unnerving for Dawson to crack any jokes. But from the other end of the trench, Ken Clark mumbled, "If that's why we get shelled, I'm for getting the Commodore to leave you up north and call in your reports."

There was no more incoming, so after five minutes the men stood up in the trench. After fifteen minutes the all-clear sounded and the men returned to their bunks. There were no casualties from the three mortars rounds, but Charley accomplished his purpose-he deprived over a thousand men of at least an hour's sleep.

Dawson learned that sleep does not come quickly after sudden exposure to danger. In his bunk, his thoughts drift back to the day he told Pat he was going to Vietnam. He could still hear her words when he told her he had sort of volunteered.

"You mean you weren't ordered to go, you volunteered because some captain asked you to?" Pat asked, tears glistening in her eyes. "You must be crazy! Don't you think I deserve to be consulted before you agree to something that important? I am not your wife, but I thought you loved me enough to consider my feelings."

When he pulled her into his arms, she remained stiff, unyielding. "Honey, it's not that I don't love you. I felt I had to give him an answer right then. The Captain was right when he said I would be going over there when I finish this tour of duty. Remember, I told you when we first met, the Navy-my work comes first. I really want that communications job. I do love you, Pat, and I don't like hurting you like this. I'll only be gone a year.

"A year!" Pat pulled away from his embrace. "When do you leave?"

"A week from tomorrow."

Pat Russel and Dawson had lived together for the past four years. The issue of marriage had cooled their relationship in the past few months. Several times he had tried to figure out why he resisted. Finally, he concluded, his reluctance was mostly due to the hurt his wife had caused him.

Dawson and his wife were both under twenty when they had married toward the end of World War II. It had lasted a little over three years. He was out in the Pacific on Guam when he received the "Dear Bill" letter. She had met someone else and wanted a divorce. The deep hurt he felt caused him to go around like a zombie for a month. He spent the nights trying to drink local bars dry, and during the day he performed his duties haphazardly. He had loved her so much, and thought nothing would ever separate them.

Now, flipping over on his other side didn't bring sleep any faster. Dawson recalled his last weekend with Pat. They took a three-day weekend at a New Jersey shore resort where they lay on the beach and took long walks, spending as much time together as possible. Pat tried to understand, but Dawson knew she really didn't. She couldn't entirely disguise the resentment she felt. With a twinge of guilt he had wondered, If I really loved her would I be doing this?

Pat drove him to the Baltimore/Washington International Airport. He could still hear her parting words, "You bring my Sailor back to me all in one piece."

The next morning, immediately after chow, Dawson drove to the Battalion Intelligence Center. In the dimly lit room he greeted three newly arrived battalion officers he had met in the Officer's Club.

Lieutenant Sandovan pulled down a map marked "Secret." "May as well get started," he said. "This morning I'm going to give you an overview of the tactical situation. The city of Da Nang is considered secure and safe most of the time. That means there are no enemy forces present in strength, other than some snipers, who operate mostly at night. Sniping incidents have been few lately. But, as Lieutenant Dawson can tell you, they also happen in the daytime. So you need to be on guard at all times. The lightly shaded areas on this map denote areas considered safe.

As you can see Highway One going into Da Nang is safe. It's risky at night, but we use it when necessary.

"The cross-hatched areas are usually safe in the daytime but not at night. Note that those areas lie mostly on the perimeter of Da Nang and between our bases. Whether or not they're safe, even in the daytime, changes from day to day. You should check on their current status each time you go into one of those areas. The roads are swept for mines each morning, so don't try to use them too early. Sometimes you may have to wait for the Marines to clear a particular road.

"Areas circled in red are where Charley is known to move in and out regularly, or are villages known to give support to the Viet Cong, like An Cu five clicks north of us. Our camp forms part of the northern defensive line around Da Nang, so consider anything to the north of us as 'Charley Country.'

"This isn't a conventional war. There are no battle lines as such, no major offensives. It's a war of hit and run tactics. Marines send out daily scouting patrols looking for Charley, and scouting planes search from the air. Charley moves in small units, mostly by foot-and usually at night in terrain too rough or with jungle too dense for mechanized equipment to operate. He moves in, fires a salvo of mortar rounds or rockets and moves out before our artillery can locate him and return fire. In the Da Nang area we seldom get incoming artillery rounds. It's too much trouble for Charley to drag artillery pieces through the jungle. Up north along the DMZ and to the west along the Laotian border, it's a different situation. Charley has artillery, larger troop concentrations; and there we sustain much heavier casualties.

"Another thing we do to counter Charley's mobile forces is put out a lot of harassment and interdiction fire, called 'H and I' fire. That's the firing you hear day and night. We fire at random times into areas or trails we know Charley uses. It keeps them on their toes and makes it risky for them to move large numbers of troops.

"The tactical situation here reminds me of two boxers dancing around the ring, first one and then the other rushes in, throws a punch, and then dances back out of range. They keep on sparring, never staying in close enough to force the fight to a conclusion. Once in a while we locate a large enemy force, but they're usually near one of the borders, and withdraw back into the sanctuary of Laos or north of the DMZ before we can do them much damage.

"Charley harasses us by planting mines in the roads, sniping at us, and shelling us. Frequently he launches an attack against one of our small, isolated units. Sometimes he overruns a camp, not to gain territory, he just wants to inflict as much damage as he can. Then he fades back into the jungle before morning. This is a frustrating war; especially for the generals and admirals who have the responsibility of fighting the war, but must limit their actions to pacify the politicians."

"I would think a situation like this would be rough on morale," Dawson commented.

"Well it's not my job to comment on that, but between us, troop morale would be a lot better if they knew their lives weren't put on the line by politicians who know nothing about fighting a war." Sandovan shook his head in resignation, putting down his pointer. "That's it, gentlemen. Any questions?"

"Is this where we get briefed when we're going to take a work-crew out of the Da Nang area?" One of the battalion offices asked.

"Yes. If I don't have the latest info., I'll refer you to a Marine command that does. Anything else?"

"There's a flock of questions flying around in my mind, but they have little to do with my work here, so I won't take more of your time." Dawson said. "Thanks for a bird's eye view of our situation."

When he got to his office the three chiefs were waiting. Dawson had served with them at various times in the past twenty years, when he and they were young enlisted men,. When Dawson entered the office, Chief Perod jumped up and met him with a crushing handshake, saying in his usual loud boisterous voice, "Good to see you old buddy. You must have some hot project to get us all together."

Dawson frowned at the familiarity, thinking, I wonder if I made a mistake selecting him-but he is the best line construction foreman I know.

"Good to see you again, Chief Perod, Chief Skinner, Chief Wilson." He shook hands around and spent a few minutes reminiscing. Then Dawson explained the project in detail. He showed them on the map where the cables were to be strung, and where the switchboards would be located.

"Chief Perod, you will run the line construction. You'll have four line trucks, so you need enough men for four crews."

"Can I get who I want?"

"Well, within reason-if they're in-country.

"Chief Skinner, you will supervise the cable splicing and switchboard installation. I figure you'll need enough men for four cable crews and two inside equipment crews later."

"I know which battalions have the men I want," Skinner said.

"Good. And Chief Wilson, you will expedite material. Most of it's available in the Da Nang area. Here's a list of major supply requirements, and a list of where some of the material is located. Work out immediate requirements with Perod and Skinner. With your reputation for scrounging and trading, I'm sure you already know the location of anything we'll need, not shown on the list."

Wilson smiled at the reference to his unorthodox methods of obtaining supplies.

"The first thing I need is a list of men you want for the line crews and cable crews." Dawson continued: "I want those lists before you secure this evening. I made arrangements for office space on the first deck. Follow me and I'll show you where it is."

The next day Dawson took the Property Acquisition Officer from NAVFOR V around, showing him the cable routes. All morning Lieutenant Commander Thornbow was stuffy and distant. He resented being directed to drop other work and give priority to a project headed by a mere lieutenant. While eating lunch at the Officer's Club in Da Nang, they put aside business and exchanged personal information. After lunch Thornbow had thawed a bit and was more cordial.

That afternoon while examining more cable routes, they came across the first cemetery, a small family cemetery with each grave mounded up in a circle. Near by, a thatched hut perched on stilts some distance from the road. A dike, separating rice paddies, led to the cemetery; an island surrounded by flooded rice paddies. The house, cemetery, and dikes were on the same level-and all surrounded by water. Thornbow told Dawson many families had their own burial plots, and those areas would be the most difficult to obtain permission to work in. Dawson assured him none of the graves would be disturbed. The poles would be spaced to insure that.

"It will be difficult to get permission for the cable to even cross over the graves," Thornbow said. "The Vietnamese are a superstitious people. They may think evil spirits will bother their ancestors if a cable hangs above the grave. One thing for sure, it'll cost us plenty to get access to the land. Every time we work near a burial plot it's costly. Some people insist we pay for the relocation of their ancestors. So you see it's best to go around a burial plot whenever possible."

The next day they came across two other burial plots the cable would pass over. About half of the cable could parallel existing roads or was located on military installations, which presented few acquisition problems. The other half ran through the small plots of farm land of dozens of individuals. When possible the route was established so the pole line could be built along the dikes surrounding each rice paddy.

Dawson stood on the beach one evening after dinner, looking at the calm emerald sea, with the sun setting behind him. As he listened to the rhythmic slap, slap, slap of gentle waves on sand. He thought, What a beautiful setting Red Beach would be for a resort hotel. He could see glistening bodies stretched out on towels far down the beach, and swimmers bobbing in gentle swells. He could hear laughter of men and women at play blending in with the singing surf. Large and small sail boats would tack back and forth in the gentle breeze, that brought the sea smell of cool salt air to Dawson's nose. But the daydream ended when his glance dropped down to double rows of concertina wire between him and the sea.

He skipped a flat rock across the green sea. Why don't the Viet Cong go back to their country in the north and leave these war-weary people alone, he thought. Then we could withdraw our troops, and some entrepreneurs could invest capital to develop this country. What a difference that would make.

His dreams were nice, but the concertina wire was reality.

Two weeks after Dawson's arrival in Vietnam, crews were organized and ready to start work on the pole line. For security reasons two crews were to work in the same area, always within sight or sound of each other. The danger of their being attacked was minimal in populated areas, but the more remote the area the greater the danger.

Dawson's primary concern was that his men would relax their guard too much. Due to his years working as a lineman, he was well aware of their nonchalant attitude. They were used to working high up on poles with only two small, steel gaffs keeping them from a sudden, deadly encounter with the ground. Young, efficient linemen were inherently risk takers; if they couldn't handle risk, they washed-out as linemen. The morning before they started construction of the pole line, Dawson assembled the men between their hooches.

"Many of you have been here several months, and may be used to the incoming Charley harasses us with frequently. On this project you'll be working outside military bases much of the time, which will expose you to a much higher level of danger." Dawson paused, letting that sink in, deliberately scrutinizing the men's faces. "You must constantly keep in mind that you're not building a telephone line across the plains of Montana or the swamps of Florida. Just because you have worked out there for a week or so without Charley shooting at you, doesn't mean he won't. You must keep in mind at all times that you are in a war zone." The excited look of being selected for a special job disappeared from the men's faces, replaced by a more somber look, as Dawson's words penetrated their young minds filled with immortal expectations.

"We have an important job to do, and we have a short time to get it done. But that doesn't mean you should take unnecessary risks. Remain alert at all times. Periodically scan the area around you, especially you linemen, who will have a good viewpoint. When we finish this job, I want to see all of you back here in one piece."

Each morning Dawson attended an intelligence briefing while the chiefs got their crews squared away with material and equipment for the day's work. The briefings covered a summary of Charley's activity throughout the I Corps and details of his activity near Da Nang.

The report of mined roads discovered the previous day was included, along with reported sniper attacks. The briefing officer also gave an estimate of Charley's activity for the day, and identified areas being patrolled by Marines.

Dawson passed on pertinent information to his crew chiefs. At times he had to change the work schedule, deferring work in an area where Intelligence thought Viet Cong might be operating. One morning the Intelligence Officer said they suspected the V.C. might still be in the area between the Marine Tank command and ammunition storage area. Remembering the sniper, Dawson thought, Right! I know that road. He and the chiefs agreed they could avoid that area for the day.

It was a fortunate decision. Shortly before lunch, the Marine patrol flushed ten V.C. hiding in a bush covered draw. The results were: 8 V.C. KIAs and two prisoners, and two Marines wounded. The fire-fight took place very near the road the line crew would've used. Quite likely the V.C. would have ambushed the Seabees.

Commodore Rhodes had a briefing scheduled every Sunday morning at 0700. The four Project Liaison Officers responsible for coordinating all work assigned to the mobile construction battalions, and Lieutenant Dawson briefed the Commodore, the Chief of Staff, and Operations Officer on the previous week's progress. They also used this time to alert the Commodore to potential problems and delays on major, critical projects.

At the third Sunday briefing Dawson attended, there was general concern about the V.C. increasing their activities around Da Nang. For the past week Intelligence had been reporting a larger number of V.C. troops in the Da Nang area.

"The battalion will start repair and maintenance work on that gravel road north of the First Marine Division," Lieutenant Fallon said, after reporting the status of his other projects. "That area is quite remote from friendly forces, so I've held the battalion back from working on it, hoping Charley activity around there would slow down. Well, it hasn't, so we'll have to get on it now, otherwise that road will be out of service once the rainy season gets here. We'll start this coming week so we can finish it before the heavy rains arrive. That's it for me, Commodore, unless you have questions."

"No questions, Ed. But I agree on getting the road work done. It's vital for that road to stay operational. You're next, Bill. How's your project coming?"

"We're a little behind schedule, Commodore, but we can make it up. We are learning to have alternate locations to work when we can't get into the area we had scheduled. I have a line to build along the road Ed's battalion is going to work on. I didn't intend to start it for another month, but it'll be much safer for my men if other Seabees are near by."

Ed Fallon interrupted. "Sounds good to me, Bill. The more men we have in the area the less danger they'll get jumped. The road crews and your men can provide security for each other."

"Speaking of security," Dawson continued, "I'm really worried about my crews. They're working in some very isolated areas. They are small crews, and I think, quite vulnerable. Is there any chance of getting Marines for security when needed?"

"The chance is zero," the Commodore answered. "All of our Bees face a security problem in most of their work. But you can talk with Commander Ramore about that later.

Dawson followed Ramore to his office after the briefing. "Commander, the Commodore didn't sound very encouraging on the subject of security for my men. I haven't been here long, so I don't know what other Seabee units are doing about this problem. But I'm concerned about my men's safety."

"Bill, the Commodore's right. There's no chance of getting Marine security for your work crews. You're working in the Da Nang area, which is considered relatively safe. We have problems getting a Marine escort when we need to get to one of the outlying camps and have to travel through country the V.C. control. The Marines have their hands full already; they don't have enough men in-country to provide security for us."

"I understand, Commander. I guess that's why we get combat training and the Seabee motto is 'We Build. We Fight.' My concern is that much of the time my men aren't able to defend themselves from the top of a pole." Dawson paused for a few seconds and then shrugged. "Well, so far we've had no trouble. Maybe I'm being overly pessimistic."

Dawson divided his time between property procurement SIMPCOM, exerting pressure to obtain necessary material, and working out details of the new system with some larger commands. Major commands were worried about not having direct communications with subordinate units, especially their line units. Sometimes Dawson had to present the same assurances and explanations to three different levels within the same command. He constantly used the P. R. approach, selling them on the value of the new system, the reduction of time contacting their units, and the greater reliability of the new system. Only when he met what he considered unyielding resistance did he resort to the force-feed approach. Then he evoked the Commodore's name, General Harrington's name, or whoever he thought would have most effect on his listeners.

The Executive Officer of the Army Special Forces in Da Nang-East, Lieutenant Colonel Fellows, told Dawson, "Our communication system is adequate. I don't see the need to disclose the details of our system to you."

After lengthy discussion, when Dawson realized he wasn't changing the Colonel's mind, he said: "Well, Colonel, if I can't get the information I need, I'll exclude your units from the main system. That's what will be reported to Admiral Scott next week."

Fellows' eyes said he didn't like being pushed or having to back down. Finally he replied: "I wouldn't want to cause the Admiral concern over such a small matter. You can check back with my Communications Officer. He'll provide what you need."

The Chief of Staff called a meeting one Friday morning shortly after breakfast to announce a "dining-in" Saturday evening.

Dawson was surprised, thinking, Not out here in a combat zone! He was used to formal dinners back in the states where all officers in the area were expected to attend. Those traditional dinners were usually in honor of a visiting admiral or other dignitary, and required everyone be in formal dinner-dress uniform.

Commander Brooks noted the surprise on Dawson's face. He continued in his slow, easy manner, "Now gentlemen, don't get excited. You don't have to go out and buy dinner-dress uniforms, and you can't take the day off to fly back to the states to get one. Dinner-dress greens will be the uniform. They will be starched and pressed, and boots will be shined. You're all expected to be there-and on time. Admiral Scott, General Harrington, and the new Third Marine Division Commander, Brigadier General Brock, will be with us. You can even knock off work fifteen minutes early tomorrow to get spruced up."

After Commander Brooks left, Dawson asked Case if this was a routine occurrence. "Oh, we've had the big dinner twice before, when some new top-brass arrived. Don't sweat it. We have to listen to a couple of speeches, make a few toasts, and spend a couple of hours at the table. One disadvantage is, no flick that night. But we do get better chow. Oh, one more thing, we'll all get tapped for a larger mess bill next month."

Before hitting the sack, Dawson checked his locker. He was relieved to find two sets of starched, pressed greens on the shelf. Laundry service was better than he had expected in a war zone. Some enterprising Vietnamese did their laundry, picking it up once a week and bringing it back the following day. Dawson was amazed that it cost only ten dollars per month.

In his travels to locate telephone construction material, Dawson had managed to "cumshaw" a second pair of combat boots. Getting ready for the dining-in Saturday evening didn't require much work, only a quick buffing of his new boots. To get the ones he wore for work ready would've taken an hour to clean off the mud and polish them.

The long narrow dining room was impressive even with its rough unpainted interior. The tables were set end-to-end forming a banquet table forty-two feet long, down the middle of the room. Navy embossed silver was in formal array on linen table cloths with matching napkins. Water decanters and wine bottles were evenly spaced down the center of the table. The Vietnamese girls were dressed in their best ao dais, their long hair in simple rolls at the back of their heads instead of hanging loose down their backs as usual.

Fan Ti Wa's floor length ao dai was light blue and almost as tight as a sheath dress. The split on the left side stopped mid-thigh. Two of the girls wore white, another wore red. The girls were excited, their voices sounding happy as they chattered and moved quickly about their tasks. Fan Ti Wa was much in charge that evening. She stood proud and commanding, the majordomo of Red Beach.

Some junior officers assembled around the bar a half-hour early, trying to down enough booze to anesthetize themselves for the long evening. They viewed dining-in much the same as they did dress inspections or reviews. They griped about having to do it and probably wouldn't, voluntarily, but their griping wasn't a genuine dislike. Inspections, parades, and dinings-in were something to talk about disparagingly, but deep inside was a pride of participation. It's the type of event that sets the military apart from civilians, an element of military esprit de corps not readily recognized.

When the Chief of Staff entered two minutes before the hour set for dinner, he announced, "Gentlemen, take your places behind your seats. You may take your drinks to the table."

Although there were no name cards, officers were to be seated according to rank, and when of the same rank, according to date of rank. This "pecking order," if not already established, was determined by simply asking. Dawson knew he was behind Lieutenant Case, but wasn't sure about Fallon, who had lined up next to Case. After checking, Fallon moved down one chair and Dawson, as the second-senior lieutenant, stood between him and Case. In less than two minutes the two dozen officers arranged themselves in proper order. When the Admiral and two generals entered with the Commodore, the Chief of Staff called, "Attention!"

The Commodore left the officers at attention while the senior officers found their places at the head table. He introduced the three guests and then said, "Seats, gentlemen."

Dinner was excellent: served in courses starting with French onion soup, followed by thick slices of roast beef, potatoes with rich brown gravy, corn soufflé, and creamed broccoli. The dessert was flaming plum fluff. A lettuce salad was served last. Officers at the junior end of the table didn't eat the salad, and quietly harassed Lieutenant Junior Grade Markowski, the Mess Officer, for serving salad after the meal. He insisted it was the proper sequence for a formal dinner. But plates of salad all ended up clustered around Markowski's plate.

Brandy and cigars were served as Commodore Rhodes rose and gave a short speech providing background on General Brock and then made a toast welcoming the new general. General Brock made a few routine comments, then more toasts were presented by some of the senior officers. General Harrington gave the principal address, commending the cooperation between Seabees and Marines and praising Seabee units for their excellent work. He made general comments on the war's progress, and overall plans for pursuing the war in the I Corps area.

General Harrington's commanding voice matched his appearance. He captured the attention of every officer in the room. No one sipped his brandy, cigars smoldered in ash trays, sending spiraling ribbons of smoke to the ceiling. He was a powerful looking man with a square, rugged face. His blue eyes issued a challenge. Every inch of him was Marine. His tough appearance was softened by compassion and understanding his words and eyes at times projected.

When he had finished speaking, the Commodore announced there would be an "open bar" for the evening. Roger Case seated to Dawson's right muttered, "There goes our mess bill again." As a non-drinker he resented having to foot the bill for other's drinks.

When Rhodes introduced Dawson to General Harrington, Dawson's first impression of the man was reinforced.

Harrington acknowledged the introduction saying, "I've been briefed on SIMPCOM and am happy to meet the man who's going to straighten out our communications mess. I want to stress the importance of your task. In this war, even more than others, rapid communication is vital to its progress. Hundreds of hours are wasted each day waiting for a clear line, and then having to start over because of being disconnected. The faster you can solve that problem, Lieutenant, the faster we can resolve this war, God and politicians willing."

After the "Brass" left, many of the officers remained in the bar and lounge area drinking. Roger Case went to his room to write letters. Dawson continued socializing with some of the battalion officers who had been invited to the dining-in. He played a couple of games of ping pong and continued drinking moderately till 2200. By that time most of the officers were feeling their drinks. The noise got too much for Dawson, so he walked to his hooch.

When he entered, in the dim light he saw someone nailing something on the wall at the far end of the hall. As Dawson continued down the hall, he saw it was Case nailing a sheet of plywood over the entrance to Ensign Carl Havner's room, two doors down from Dawson's.

"What the hell you doing Roger?" Dawson asked.

"Fixing a surprise for our young friend when he staggers in tonight."

Case had a reputation for being the regiment's practical joker. This was the first Dawson had seen of it. "It should be a surprise all right," Dawson said. "But how do you expect him to get to bed?"

Case laughed as he drove in another nail. "That's his problem. I'm trying to cure him from getting drunk all the time."

"Well, I guess I may as well read," Dawson said. "No sense in going to sleep. There's going to be a lot of noise when Red comes in."

Ensign Havner was called "Red" for good reason. His hair was a fiery red, but he didn't have a short fuse like some red heads. He was exceptionally easy going. Dawson wondered if he got drunk most evenings trying to blot out the war. As Administrative Officer, Red did his job surprisingly well considering how much he drank.

The hall running the length of the building was four feet wide and eighty-feet long. Because of low generator capacity it was lighted with only two 15-watt bulbs. Before Case went to his room he removed the bulb near Havner's boarded up entrance. From the end of the hooch facing the officer's mess Havner's room was fifth on the right, and got very little light from the one bulb remaining.

Dawson hit the sack and turned on his improvised reading lamp-a pig-tail socket with pull-chain, spliced to Romex cable stapled to the wall. He opened the paperback he had started reading the evening before, and settled down to read and wait. Two other officers living in the hooch came in and were in bed by the time Dawson heard Havner stumbling up the short flight of steps leading to the hooch. He was trying to sing a sailor's risqué version of "Bless 'Em All." Case and Dawson turned off their lights before Havner opened the hooch door.

He staggered down the hall bouncing from wall to wall. He stopped when he thought he was at the entrance to his room, and then went on to the next opening, which was to a vacant room containing only a cot and bare mattress. Havner came back into the hall muttering, "Wrong room." He wandered back and forth along the hall, pausing at each room.

"Must be drunk. Maybe in the wrong hooch," He mumbled, as he weaved his way back to the entrance with considerable difficulty, and went outside to look at the number over the door. When he came back in he said, "Got the right hooch, just gotta find my room. I know it's here." He started down the hall feeling along the right side and counting when he came to an opening. "One, two, three..." He wandered a little way into Dawson's room before regaining his balance, then continued, "four, five. I've found you now!" He entered, felt around and came back into the hall cursing.

He came back down the hall to where his doorway should have been, and this time he felt the plywood nailed over the entrance. He cursed some more as he tried to pull the plywood off with his hands. After a few minutes he gave up, went into the empty room and flopped down on the bare mattress.

A little while later Case got up and covered him with one of his own blankets.

The next morning when Case awakened him, it took Havner a few seconds to get his bearing. Then he said, "You did it didn't you, Roger?"

Case was the picture of innocence. "Did what?"

"Nailed up my room so I couldn't get in."

Case laughed. "It wasn't me. You must have some other good buddies around here."

Line construction was going slower than Dawson had expected. Waiting for Marines to sweep roads for mines often caused work crews dead-time. Charley activity in some areas, caused delays and rescheduling of work. High humidity was hard on men doing physical labor in the direct sun, but the sun was good for the construction schedule. Dawson had been advised there was little time left before the heavy rains started. He knew he had to get the maximum out of his crews if they were to complete SIMPCOM on schedule.

Early Sunday morning Chief Wilson came into Dawson's office steaming. "Lieutenant, that Air Force Major lied to me. Instead of letting me in to see what he has in his supply yard, he had me give him a list of equipment and material we need. He had his men check off what they had, which was little. Remember I told you trenchers were hard to come by?"

"Right. We have only two available."

"Well, the day before yesterday the Marines reclaimed the one they had loaned us and flew it to Chu Lai. They said it was for combat support. So we couldn't stop it. We need one for the airfield section, so yesterday I checked with that Air Force command again, and the Major said they didn't have one and not to bother him about things on the list I had given him, that he hadn't checked. One of our boys from MCB-10 said he thought he had seen one in the back of the Air Force supply yard. So last night we dug under the fence and got into their supply yard. Sure enough there it was. Never been used, covered up with a tarp."

Dawson hit his open left hand with his right fist. "I'll get his tail in the ringer for that! The Admiral will be all over him. We'll get that trencher. But nuts! It'll take at least three days by the time I go to the Commodore, and he reports to the Admiral, and then it works it's way through the Air Force commands. We're scheduled to start on the underground section near the airfield tomorrow, and I sure hate to postpone it."

Chief Wilson scratched his head and said in his slow southern drawl: "Well, boss, I know a faster way. The Air Force supply yard backs up to MCB-10's heavy equipment yard. A crane could pick up that trencher as easy as whistlin' Dixie and put it right down in the equipment yard. I need you to pave the way with MCB-10 so they won't worry about what I'm doing with one of their cranes."

"I like the idea, Chief, but Air Force people working in the supply yard are sure to see you unless you do it at night. And that's too risky. Someone could get shot."

"Not if we do it today. The Air Force doesn't work on Sunday. There's one man on duty in their supply yard; and he's always goofing-off in the bunker at the entrance to the yard, reading a book or something."

"OK, Chief. Do it. But don't put anyone in jeopardy."

Monday morning, when Dawson arrived at the runway, the trencher was digging steadily and cable was going in right behind it. It was painted Seabee-green. None of the Air Force-yellow showed through. A little mud had been splattered around to age it. But up close it had a distinct new-paint smell.

When Dawson arrived back at his office Tuesday evening, he found a note telling him to call Major Dibble. It took him five minutes to get connected to the Major's office. "Major, this is Lieutenant Dawson returning your call."

"I want my trencher returned immediately."

"Don't know what you're talking about, Major. The last I heard from my Chief, he said you told him you didn't have any trenchers."

"Never mind what I told your Chief. It's none of his business what I have in my supply yard. One of my men said he saw a trencher, he thinks is ours, near the runway. I want my trencher returned today or someone's tail is going to be in a sling."

"Good luck, Major. It's been my experience, fooling with someone's tail can get messy if you are not sure what you're doing." Dawson hung up before the Major could respond.

Late Wednesday afternoon Dawson dropped by to check his crew's progress at the airfield. They were almost at the location where they could bring the cable out of the ground and start stringing it on poles. He was in his jeep about to leave when Major Dibble pulled up beside him.

"Afternoon, Major. Can I help you?"

"Yes, Lieutenant. You can return my trencher immediately."

"I don't know what you're talking about, Major. As I said yesterday, I was told you said you didn't have a trencher."

The Major's face turned red, his eyes narrowing as he pointed. "That trencher is what I'm talking about. I had one in my supply yard, and it was stolen. That one has new paint on it, and I don't think it'll be hard to prove it belongs to the Air Force. If it's not back in my yard by tonight, I'll start an investigation that will probably result in your court martial."

Dawson's smile was that of a poker player who lays out a bet knowing he has a cinch hand. "Easy now, Major. I don't think you can afford an investigation. I have a piece of paper with your initials on it indicating you didn't have a trencher. If you did have one at that time, the Admiral might consider your not showing it on the list you gave me, as being direct disobedience of an order. Matter of fact, if I had the time, if completion of this project wasn't vital, I would singe your tail feathers so bad you couldn't sit down."

Major Dibble blustered and sputtered, his face growing even redder, "You can't talk to me..."

"I am not finished, Major," Dawson interrupted, leaning closer. "I'm out here to do a job. It is a small job but it's part of a much larger one-the same one you're supposed to be a part of. I intend to do my job as good and fast as I can. If you get in my way, I'll go around you, under you, over you, or right straight through you. I suggest you join the team. There's only one objective out here. To win this war. As for your trencher, write it off. You'll never get it back. But it'll be doing its job out here whether you are or not." Dawson drove off without hearing the Major's reply.

The officer's washroom at Red Beach was a small hooch with an entrance in one end, located between the two officer's barracks. Four wash basins with mirrors over them were mounted on the wall, inside the door to the left. Plumbing was in for two toilets on the right side, but the fixtures weren't there. In a separate room, with a concrete floor sloping to the center, hung four shower heads that gave only cold water, since there was no water heater.

The day was especially hot and humid. Sweat glued the dirt to Dawson's face and clothes until his uniform was more red than green. He'd been looking forward to a shower all afternoon. Now he, Red Havner, and two other officers were showering, getting ready for dinner, when suddenly there was a loud clattering on the corrugated tin roof right over their heads. Someone out side yelled, "Mortar attack! Mortar attack!"

Dawson dropped his soap and ran toward the door, mentally debating whether to stop for a towel or run for the mortar trench as he was.

"Relax, Bill," Havner said. "It's our old buddy Roger having his fun. He must've just got back from up north."

Dawson's thumping heart dropped back down where it belonged as he got back under the cold water to finish his shower.

In the hooch Dawson called into Case's room: "You almost had me streaking out of the shower. Don't you know you can give a man a heart attack scaring him like that?"

Roger stuck his head in, with one of his lopsided grins. "Just want to keep you guys on your toes. Got to have a drill down here once in a while so you'll know there's a war on."

As Dawson drove from one job site to another, day after day, he observed the Vietnamese people more and more. He continued to ponder the expressions on older Vietnamese faces that had perplexed him on his first day in Da Nang. One afternoon it finally dawned on him what he was seeing. It was a look of resignation. They no longer cared because it did them no good to care. There had been fighting in their country for over twenty-five years. Since World War II the Viet Minh or Viet Cong had been trying to force Communism on them.

They don't have the will to resist any longer, Dawson thought. And that's why we're here. He remembered in a briefing before leaving the States, he was told that if the United States hadn't sent troops into South Vietnam when they did, the North Vietnamese would've taken over the country within six months. Now, seeing their look of resignation, Dawson believed that assessment to be correct.

Vietnamese in the country lived a simple life, or at least tried to. As Dawson watched them walk slowly along dikes bordering their rice paddies, he thought: How unfair the war is to them. They're not interested in more territory, more power, more wealth. More food would make them happier, and they would welcome freedom from fear, decades of war has imposed on them. They don't want to make other people conform to their ideology-or any other. All they're concerned with is their families, and satisfying the basic needs of life. Dawson felt sorry for them as he realized their helplessness. They don't really know what the Communists are trying to do to their country. They don't understand, they have no control. But they can pay. They can die.

Most of the time SIMPCOM crews were working in uncontrolled areas. Vietnamese civilians were around them and passing by constantly. Prostitutes, always present around the Vietnamese Army, increased considerably with the arrival of American troops. American servicemen were paid much more than Vietnamese soldiers. So the law of supply and demand functioned here too. The greater demand and higher prices caused a rapid increase in the number of prostitutes.

Girls in tight short dresses and gaudy makeup hawked their wares constantly along roads where Seabees were working and traveling between work-sites and Red Beach. The girls called and teased the men while they worked. Some girls in their heavy make-up, with exaggerated lips and too red cheeks, resembled little girls who had gotten into their mothers' make up. But that illusion was quickly dispelled by their suggestive gyrations and vulgar gestures.

Soo Tu, a petite girl with lighter complexion than most of the street women-who Dawson guessed was no older than fifteen, had taken a liking to one young Seabee. He was a tall blond Construction Electrician 3rd Class named Beleu. Soo Tu seemed to always be across the road from where Beleu was working. One morning Dawson sat in his jeep watching as line crews prepared to sag-in a long run of messenger cable. The young lineman, Beleu, was belted-off thirty feet up on the pole closest to Dawson.

Soo Tu, standing across the road, called out, "What's a matter, blond boy? You no like Vietnam girl?"

Beleu continued working, sagging-in the messenger cable. He gave a quick glance over his shoulder at the pretty girl in a low-cut blouse and mini-mini-skirt.

Striking a provocative pose, she taunted him. "Maybe you no like any girl. I think you maybe like boys."

This time Beleu glowered at her. But he set his jaw without replying.

Soo Tu tried again. "Marine boy friend say Seabee no-can-do. I think maybe you no-can-do."

The Seabee on the pole one span to the north called out, "Beleu no-can-do," and the man on the pole to the south picked up the chant, "Beleu no-can-do." It was repeated on down the line like an echo.

Color flushed Beleu's face. He half turned in his lineman's belt. "If I come down from this pole I'll show you what I can do. Go away. Don't bother me. Go find your Marine boy friend."

The girl shook her head. "Me no-can-do."

"Why?" Beleu asked.

"He dead." Soo Tu said in a subdued voice and then slowly walked away.

Dawson mused on the subject of servicemen's morals as he listened to other girls and some of the men on down the line calling back and forth. Previously he had observed that a war environment seemed to erode men's morals, especially those concerning sex. Temptation was there every day. And it grew stronger as time passed. Some men who wouldn't even consider being promiscuous in a more stable environment, readily availed themselves of sex in a place like Vietnam. And their consciences didn't seem to prick them very hard.

I wonder why? Is it because a man's life is in greater jeopardy out here, and so he's willing to take other risks too? Does war change his values, his moral outlook, so his conscience doesn't bother him? Or were the moral values he subscribed to at home simply a facade to be discarded when with strangers less likely to be critical? Well, whatever the reason, it's a fact.

Dawson had heard rumors that some men were slipping off to meet with girls in the bushes, or stopping off at their shacks on the way to Red Beach. He told the three chiefs to bring the men in fifteen minutes early one Monday evening, and to muster them between their two living hooches.

Chief Martin finished calling role and reported, "All men present, sir."

Dawson put the men at ease. "I hear scuttlebutt that some of you men are spending much longer in the bushes than necessary, unless there's an epidemic of constipation going around. Female voices have been heard coming from those same bushes. I've also heard there are men here who pass up lunch for a "nooner" with one of the local lovelies. The scuttlebutt is that there may be a few really simpleminded Bees who slip out and stay overnight. Now these are only rumors as far as I'm concerned. But I want to remind you of some facts, in case the rumors are true.

"I am not a chaplain, so I'm not going to talk to you about the morality of supporting the local prostitutes. If your own moral values don't keep you from patronizing them, then I doubt I can change your values at this late date. But I am going to talk about three important subjects: regulations, VD and death."

Dawson paused letting that sink in, then continued. "You've all heard that as Americans we're protected from double jeopardy in our legal system. The way I see it, if you go out with these Vietnamese girls, you're putting yourselves in triple jeopardy. First, you all know about the regulations against fraternizing with Vietnamese. If you're caught you'll be subject to courts-martial. Second, the odds are heavily in favor of you catching VD. The women aren't inspected, and some of them are running around with a 'full-house.' The doctors say some women have 'non-specific.' It's called that because they don't know what type of VD it is-and worse, they can't cure it.

"Third, you may not live through that short period of pleasure. You don't know these girls. You don't know, they may be working for the V.C. Even Intelligence isn't sure who is on our side and who isn't. They do know there are plenty of enemy agents around. Aside from all other considerations, if you're tempted to indulge, think ahead. Think how vulnerable you are at times. I doubt any of you would take your rifle to bed and lie there with your finger on the trigger. Remember, they don't give medals for dying with your pants down.

"Personally I don't think it's worth the risks. If you do, and are caught, don't expect help from me. I'll tell them to throw the book at you, and in the same breath ask for your replacement. To summarize my little talk, I leave you with a saying I learned in boot camp many years ago: KYPIYP. If some of you younger sailors don't know what it means, ask your Chief."

Chapter 4

Dawson shivered in the cool November drizzle, realizing the rainy season had started. He was watching Chief Perod's crew set a 60-foot pole in a rice paddy adjacent to the main road leading north from Da Nang. There was no bottom to the rice paddy. Men had to dig the hole inside a 50 gallon oil drum with both ends cut out. As they dug inside the drum they let it sink, and then welded another one onto the one in the quagmire. They had three drums in the ground, the line truck had set the pole inside the drums and was holding it vertical with the A-frame. They were ready to start pouring concrete around the pole when the line truck's rear wheels started sinking. The men quickly steadied the tall pole with pike poles so the line truck could release the pole and pull up onto solid ground. All the men including Perod were busy at the base of the pole trying to steady it and get the concrete chute in place.

Dawson, standing in the narrow road to stop traffic and pedestrians, was watching the pole when it started to fall.

Perod yelled, "We can't hold it!"

It was leaning toward the road, and Dawson figured it would hit about 10 feet from where he stood. Then out of the corner of his left eye he saw a figure on a bicycle coming from behind him, ignoring his outstretched arms, riding directly into the path of the falling pole. The bicycle passed close enough for Dawson to reach it in one lunging step.

His momentum carried him and the rider to the ground. Dawson was on top, tangled up with the bicycle and a young girl. She struck him with her small fists and her feet, screaming at him, mostly in Vietnamese. He understood one phrase in English, "Stupid American pig."

The pole hit the road with a "splat" five feet away. Dawson got untangled from the bicycle and the screaming, thrashing girl as quickly as he could. Scrambling to her feet, she picked up her bicycle and rode off, still yelling at him. He shook his head, laughing, as he brushed off the mud and retrieved his hat.

"Guess she thought I was trying to attack her," Dawson told the Chief, who had rushed over to help.

The next day Dawson was back watching the crew reset the pole. This time they added another oil drum and used a line truck with a greater outreach. Dawson was leaning on the hood of his jeep watching the concrete being poured when he became aware of someone behind him. He turned and there was the girl of small fists and fast feet standing beside her bicycle.

"May I speak with the Lieutenant?"

Dawson raised his eyebrows in surprise at her soft pleasant voice, her excellent English, and the realization she definitely was not a little girl.

"Sure. But I want you to know I'm sorry I had to knock you down yesterday to..."

The young woman interrupted, "No. Please! It is I who must be sorry. I think you saved my life and I am most grateful. I am sorry I said bad things to you yesterday. When you ran at me and knocked me to the ground, I did not see the pole. I thought you meant me harm. I was frightened and hurt, that is why I screamed and struck you. When I got up and saw the pole, I was so confused and embarrassed I continued screaming at you. I am sorry."

While speaking, she looked directly at Dawson, then bowed her head when she finished. The contrast of her directness and demureness he found very appealing. "It's OK, I understand," He said. "I wondered if you were hurt. You were going quite fast when I hit you."

She looked up again with a smile. "I hurt a little. My leg hurts, and up higher here." She placed her hand on her hip and then looked down embarrassed.

"Well, I'm happy you weren't seriously injured. My name is Bill Dawson. What's yours?"

My name is Lati Noi." She gave a half curtsy. "I am honored to meet you, sir. Is it proper for me to address you as Mr. Dawson or Lieutenant Dawson?"

"You can call me Bill. All my friends do."

"Thank you. I would like for us to be friends. But I will call you Lieutenant Dawson. That is more proper."

Dawson studied her as she spoke. She wore no makeup. She didn't need any. A natural beauty radiated from her fine featured face. He decided she wasn't strikingly beautiful, but she was very lovely. Her lips weren't painted to accentuate her small mouth that seemed to invite a kiss. Natural eyebrows framed her warm dark eyes, with soft curled eyelashes devoid of mascara or liner. He thought she looked warm and lovely and cuddly. She seemed to have some inner beauty, not visual; something Dawson couldn't quite define. She was only five feet tall, and petite. She looked delicate, but remembering yesterday he knew she was stronger and tougher than she appeared.

"Is Da Nang your home?" He asked, after what seemed like an awkward pause.

"No. My home was in the north part of Vietnam, but it is no more. All that is left of my family is my grandfather and me. We live in what Americans call Refugee Village. Now there are only the two of us, my grandfather and me are close. He was angry with me when I told him how I acted yesterday. I told him about the big pole falling and that it would have hit me if you had not stopped me. My grandfather instructed me to tell you of his appreciation for saving my life. He would like to thank you himself but he does not speak English. And he is ashamed of where we must live. He said it is not fit for a person of your station to see."

Lati Noi was dressed in an ao-dai, the type of dress most women in Vietnam seemed to wear. They reminded Dawson of women's pajamas with a long top. Yesterday the one she wore was black. The blouse part ended considerably below her waist. Today the ao dai was plain white. The top part extended down over her pants almost to the ground, with both sides split up to her waist. Dawson wondered if it might be her best ao-dai. And I wonder how she keeps it clean in this dirty environment.

"Tell your grandfather I accept his thanks, but tell him it wasn't necessary. Having the pleasure of speaking with a woman as lovely and gracious as his granddaughter is more than enough thanks."

Lati captured the right side of her lower lip between her teeth, plainly embarrassed by Dawson's flattery. Color flowed into her cheeks as she looked down. "I..., I must go to work now."

As she rode off on her bicycle, Dawson said, "I hope we can talk again sometime."

December arrived with incessant rains, the weather changed from cool to cold, and eight weeks of the SIMPCOM construction schedule had passed. Along with the rain and cooler temperature came problems. Setting poles and stringing cable became more difficult. Trucks got stuck frequently and at times mud slowed or stopped construction. Now, instead of being able to splice the cable from an open platform, a tent had to be installed over the platform.

Because of the weather less air reconnaissance was possible. American and the South Vietnamese forces, relying more on mechanized equipment and air support to fight the war, were slowed down. But the Viet Cong took advantage of their greater jungle mobility; relying on muscle, they continued to move supplies, ammunition and equipment down the Ho Chi Minh Trail. Charley stepped up his attacks on smaller isolated bases. They could also better afford to attack larger bases when there was no danger of Americans getting planes in the air. All around Da Nang Charley harassed the many bases and outposts with increased sniper fire. He planted more mines in road beds and at night increased his mortar and rocket attacks.

Snipers were of most concern to Dawson. Although his crews had full battle gear, it was their own option whether or not they wore the steel helmets and flack-jackets. Most of them didn't. Men on the ground were required to keep their rifles within reach while working, but men working on poles were defenseless. They couldn't climb with helmets and rifles and heavy awkward flack-jackets.

Dawson was discussing material delay with Chief Perod near a section of line running parallel to a narrow gravel road, where two crews were working,. Across the road and set back 30 yards were three native huts with the jungle a short distance beyond. On the side of the road where the cable was being strung, flooded rice paddies stretched for two hundred yards. Beyond that thick jungle grew, jungle so dense a person could stand within three feet of the edge and not be seen.

The men were laughing and joking, calling back and forth to each other from atop the poles. One Seabee called out, "Beleu no-can-do," and the chant echoed down the line. The men had been razzing Beleu since his encounter with Soo Tu.

When the single shot rang out five linemen were in the air. Four were belted off working on separate poles. The fifth man was working on a platform suspended from the messenger cable. He didn't bother to get over to the pole to come down. He swung out on the hand line, used to hoist materials up to him, and dropped rapidly to the ground. The other men on poles unbelted, took a couple of long steps down and then cut out, dropping free the last ten or twelve feet. Men working on the ground grabbed their weapons and hit the deck.

As they lay in the mud one stocky lineman called Blinky, with a nervous laugh said, "Sure glad he was a lousy shot."

A new "grunt" in the crew said, "Now I know I don't want to get promoted to lineman. I'll stay a grunt and live longer."

There were no more shots. No one could tell where the single shot came from. That was typical of Charley, they would learn-take one shot and then disappear. But sometimes he would wait a few minutes and then crank off another round.

The Seabees quickly formed two squads of four men each and started a clockwise and counter-clockwise sweep through the jungle and huts near their work site. Lieutenant Dawson went with the squad searching the area around the huts. From what the Marines had told him, they would find nothing. The sniper would be far back in the jungle. But they had to go through the motions, otherwise the sniper might hang around to take another shot. And Dawson knew the hour his men spent looking for the sniper would help allay their fear and give them confidence that the sniper was gone, enough confidence and nerve for the men to climb back up the poles and continue work.

After completing their fruitless search and returning to the work-site, Dawson waited around a few minutes. He noticed the crew chief, a first class construction electrician, had difficulty getting the men back up the poles. They spent more time than usual putting on their climbing gear, checking their safety belts and fiddling with other tools they normally wouldn't bother with.

Blinky seemed to blink his eyes faster than usual. "Sure wish we'd found that dude and put him out of action," he said.

Johnson, the crew chief said, "Oh that bugger only wanted to give you men some experience going up and down poles. He was probably a mile away when he cranked off that round. Now let's get hitched up and hit those poles."

From his jeep Lieutenant Dawson could tell they didn't want to make themselves targets again. And he didn't blame them. As he drove away Dawson thought, I know we're due for more of this. Maybe Charley got the word on what we're doing. As many agents as intelligence says there are in Da Nang, the word must've filtered into their ranks by now. They probably know exactly what SIMP-COM is all about-and they don't like it. Well, Charley accomplished his purpose. He stopped nine men from working well over an hour.

Dawson drove to one of the First Marine Division Company offices. He had met Captain Sam Arnold his first week in Da Nang, when he was planning the telephone system. Captain Arnold commanded a company of Marines, commonly called "Grunts" because they did the hard work, they chopped and grunted their way through the jungle. Dawson felt fortunate at finding the Captain in his office. Usually he and his grunts were out on patrol.

"Hi, Sam," Dawson called as he entered the small hooch furnished with four packing crate desks and metal folding chairs. In a corner an operator manned a field switchboard.

"How's the grunt business?"

Arnold looked up with a quick smile of recognition. "Business is too good. We got back this morning and have to go back out and make another sweep tonight."

Dawson pulled up a chair from the next desk. "Sam, I have a problem with snipers. This afternoon one of my line crews received sniper fire."

Arnold shrugged. "They tell me that's what war's all about-people shooting at each other."

"Don't waste your sympathy on me, Sam. All I want is a little free advice. My men hang up there on poles like dangling ducks in a shooting gallery. They're completely defenseless. With the increase in sniping activity, I believe my men are going to be subjected to more and more of it. I want to get patrols out around the areas where they're working, but I need some numbers before I talk to my boss."

Arnold frowned, then asked, "How many areas are you working in each day?"

"I have eight crews working all over the Da Nang area, from Red Beach to Da Nang East. But two crews work together, so it would be four areas to patrol."

"How far are the men in each area spread out?"

"They're usually working within three to four hundred yards of each other. But sometimes they get spread out over a half mile of line."

"Well, I'll tell you, Bill, if you had a regiment out beating the bushes you couldn't eliminate all sniper activity. If you had a platoon of grunts distributed properly, you could worry Charley enough so the sniping would be cut down a lot. I don't know how many of your Bees it would take to do the same job since they don't do much of the grunt's kind of work."

Dawson got up saying, "You've told me what I need to know. I intend to try to get Marines for the job. So I'll use your estimate of one platoon."

Arnold shook his head. "Man, I don't think you have a snowball in hell's chance of getting Marines. With Charley's increased probing, and overrunning some of the smaller units, like Deo Dai they hit last night, every Grunt is committed. We had eight Marines KIA and thirty two wounded last night. We've got every ground pounder out on patrol or making large-scale sweeps. I wish you luck, but remember, I warned you."

Dawson went straight to Commander Ramore's office when he got to Red Beach. He reported the sniping incident, and said: "I realize the Marines are busy, but considering the priority of SIMPCOM, isn't it possible to get some security for my crews? I'm afraid my schedule will slip, and worse-I may lose men."

Ramore slowly shook his head. "Bill, I'm sure it wouldn't do any good to even try. You hear the reports at intelligence briefings. Charley is causing everyone more headaches. You heard at the briefing this morning. Deo Dai was hit hard and Tan An was overrun last night. When relief got in to them this morning, of course, Charley was nowhere around. The casualty report shows six of the Special Forces Team killed along with 26 RVN troops. Two of the Seabees in the detachment working there were killed too. I don't know yet how many were wounded. But you can see why I wouldn't feel right about exerting pressure to get fighting troops, to protect your men, when they're needed so badly at other places."

"I understand, Commander. And I wouldn't ask except men working on the poles are so defenseless, so vulnerable. I need to try to do something. Sir, who were the two Seabees killed?"

"They were with an MCB-6 detachment, drilling a well and hardening up some defenses." He took a clipboard off the wall, and studied it for a few seconds. "The men killed were Construction Driver Second Class Richards, and Constructionman La Porte."

Dawson had held his breath, waiting for the names. He exhaled with relief. He didn't know either man. Then immediately he was angry with himself, and ashamed. *So I didn't know them. But why should I feel relieved?* He thought. *If they were someone I knew I would feel more sadness, grief, sorrow. But those two men I didn't know, so I'll forget about them in a few hours. Or a few days. Or a week or two. War! Nuts! It gives men calluses on more places than their feet.*

Ramore's voice broke through his thoughts. "Is there anything else, Bill?"

"Oh! No, sir. I was thinking about the men who were killed. I guess we'll get along without Marine security."

Lati Noi stopped and talked with Dawson every day or so. He learned she worked as an interpreter in the headquarters building called the "White Elephant." She came along the road each afternoon on her way home, a road where the line crews had nine miles of poles to set and cable to install. Dawson didn't consciously acknowledge it, but he scheduled his inspection of this area late in the day, ever since meeting Lati. That placed him on her route at the time she went home.

Sometimes Dawson had to be some place else at that time of the afternoon. On those days he realized he missed seeing Lati and talking with her. Their meetings were brief, and their conversation light and casual. After a half-dozen brief rendezvous, Dawson decided there was definitely mutual attraction. Not the slightest verbal intimation had been uttered. But he could see it in her eyes, could hear it in her voice and could feel it within himself.

When he analyzed his own feelings Dawson had to admit he was strongly attracted to Lati, and not only physically, although she was sensually attractive. The way she moved and walked, her gestures, her soft, warm voice were provocative-but not by design. It was her natural warmth showing through more and more as they became better acquainted.

One afternoon when Lati stopped to talk, Dawson felt a current of excitement of expectation in her voice, her looks, her actions. She nibbled on her lower lip, seeming to be on the verge of asking him something several times, but instead spoke of something else.

Finally, she said: "My grandfather would like to thank you in person for saving my life. He would like for you to come and have tea with him." After a brief hesitation she looked up at him shyly. "I would like it also."

The pressure of desire had been building higher in Dawson each time they met. *If I go, I wonder what the chances are of us being alone.* He shook his head to clear it of the fleeting, unbidden thought. "Thank your grandfather for me. Tell him I would enjoy having tea with him, but I'm afraid I can't make it. I work every day; there's just not time."

Lati looked down at her hands resting on the handle bars. "It would not take much time, and my grandfather would be pleased. He is very old and does not get out much. He said he was ashamed to ask you because our house is such a poor one. It is put together from scraps. But I told my grandfather you would understand. Now he will know he was right, that you will not come to such a poor house."

"No, Lati, that's not the reason. We have orders forbidding us to be with Vietnamese women. If I go to your house I'll set a bad example. Then my men will think they can go out with the street women. It would make things very difficult."

Lati's eyes registered hurt for a second, then anger as she tossed her head and mounted her bike. "I am not one of those women." She pointed across the road where two young girls sat in front of a shack, looking for business. "I do not invite you to my house for that reason. You shame me with your thoughts." She rode away before Dawson could answer.

He started to get in his jeep and follow her. But he knew some of his men were watching. They had teased him about her a little already. If he was out in the field away from the road and they saw her coming, one of the men would call down from the top of a pole, "Lieutenant, your girl friend is coming." Dawson wished she had let him explain instead of riding off so abruptly.

The next day while Dawson was on the road observing the work, some of the Bees started calling out, "Beleu can-do, Beleu can-do." Dawson considered talking to Beleu, assuming he had been in the bushes with So Tu, but then decided it would be better for the Chief to do it.

That afternoon, Lati rode by on the opposite side of the road. She didn't even slow down. When he called to her, she didn't look up or answer. She'll get over it in a day or so, Dawson thought. Then I can explain what I meant.

Chapter 5

Rain was drumming on the metal roof of the Officers Mess hard enough that diners had to speak louder to be heard across the table. At dinner the four LDOs, Roger Case, Ed Fallon, Paul Knight and Bill Dawson sat together, as they did frequently. Some junior officers called it the LDO table. Dawson sat quietly, enjoying the good-natured banter flowing back and forth. During a lull he said: "I hear we're getting a new Operations Officer, Commander Padelford. Any of you know him?"

Ed Fallon glanced up from his food, a frown creasing his forehead. "I had a tour of duty with him a few years back-Stateside. I was happy my tour finished a short time after he arrived. We didn't get along well."

"Tell us about him," Case said as he wound spaghetti in his spoon. "What's his problem?"

"Look fellows, I don't want to stack the deck against the Commander. It may've been only a personality clash between Commander Padelford and me. But unless he's changed, I think we have trouble. All I'll say now is, don't let him get behind you."

Dawson noted how tense Fallon had become and wondered what he wasn't telling about his experience with Padelford. That's all we need, some do-it-by-the-book, ineffectual OPS officer to screw-up a smooth running organization.

"I've heard scuttlebutt the Commodore tried to block his orders," Knight said. "But the only way he could do it was by holding Commander Ramore over till the Detailer could get another Commander worked into the pipeline. That would've taken three months. The Commodore didn't think it was fair to Ramore, so he agreed to our new OPS Officer. All I can say, gentlemen, is, if the Commodore doesn't want our new boss out here, there must be something wrong with him."

Before Commander Padelford arrived, Dawson considered the 30th NCR an efficient, smooth flowing command. From his observation, Seabee commands that operated best, living up to the "can do" motto, and maintaining high morale were those with Commanding Officers and Executive Officers of dissimilar personalities. The C.O. can be a hard-nose and the X.O. easy going. Or the C.O. can be the public relations type and the X.O. the disciplinarian. Not that they can be in conflict or work in opposition; their efforts must be coordinated. But if they're both rigid do-it-by-the-book officers they will be alienated from the enlisted men and junior officers. If they're both "good guys," discipline is lax, personnel problems abound, and efficiency falls off.

At Red Beach Commodore Rhodes was the prime mover. He was tough and direct. If he was angry it was evident. If he thought you did a good job you knew it. Dawson smiled, remembering third-class electrician, Johnston, who got drunk after work, "borrowed" a jeep without permission and got it stuck in the sand. One of the Battalion ensigns put him on report for unauthorized use of a vehicle, operating a vehicle while intoxicated, plus other charges.

When Dawson read the report slip he thought, That ensign must have studied the Uniform Code of Military Justice for an hour to find all of these charges. As the man's division officer, he went to Captain's Mast with the petty officer. Before the Mast started, Dawson went in and talked with the Commodore. He explained that Johnston was an excellent lineman and recommended a Warning. Johnston was called in and stood at attention in front of the Commodore, who gave him a hard look and then glanced down at the report slip.

In a deep booming voice he slowly read all six charges, then looked at Johnston. "How old are you, sailor?"

"Nineteen, Sir."

"There are enough charges on this sheet to refer to a General Court-martial. Do you realize they could sentence you to years in prison?"

"Yes, Sir."

"You have any idea how many man-hours a General Court-martial would waste?"

"No, Sir."

Dawson, who stood to the left and behind Johnston, didn't quite manage stifling a smile. He could see the young man's legs shaking and hoped the Commodore would end it quickly.

"Lieutenant Dawson says you are a good worker. Considering that, and not wanting to waste nine officer's time in a court-martial, I am awarding you two-weeks restriction. Lieutenant Dawson will explain what you can and cannot do while restricted. Dismissed!"

Dawson followed Johnston out, and took him to his office. There he explained the restriction meant Johnston could leave Red Beach only when working, and he could not use the enlisted men's club for the next to weeks.

A week later Dawson overheard a Seabee make a comment critical of the Commodore. Johnston responded immediately, telling him that Commodore Rhodes was the best C.O. in Vietnam. He ended with, "Don't ever bad-mouth the Commodore around me."

When Dawson's attention returned to the conversation at the table, Case was saying, "...maybe the Commodore will give Padelford the X.O. job. He couldn't cause as much trouble there."

Dawson didn't respond, but thought: Case is right, the X.O. would make a good OPS Officer. But Commander Brooks complements the Commodore's method of operation too well. He won't want to lose him from that position, even considering the importance of the OPS Officer.

The Operations Officer was the Commodore's right hand man when it came to manpower, supplies, and project completion. Commander Ramore did his job well. He worked closely with the eight battalion commanders and the commands wanting work done by the Seabees. That left the Commodore time to deal with the Admiral and Generals who wanted twice as much work done as the Seabees had manpower and materials available.

"Guess we'll have to wait and see what we get with the new Commander," Dawson said, joining the conversation again. "If he's too bad, we should be able to straighten him out." He pushed back his chair and stood. "Enough doom and gloom, who wants to get beat at Ping-Pong?"

Commander Padelford, prophetically, arrived on a nasty day in a rain storm, stomping into the headquarters building at Red Beach, soaked. When Dawson met him he felt sure it wasn't only bad weather that put the sour expression on the Commander's face. He doubted Padelford used muscles for smiling often.

The new OPS Officer was five-feet, nine, and weighed 200 pounds Dawson estimated. The spare tire stressing his belt indicated very little of his bulk was muscle. He tried to hide his bald spot in front by letting the hair in back grow long and combing it forward. But it actually drew attention to his baldness. He would be better off letting the bald spot show, Dawson thought. People would've gotten used to it and after a while not even noticed. The long hair he frequently patted and arranged called attention to his baldness and the fact he was trying to hide it.

His eyes were hard and distrusting. They were constantly searching, probing for something out of order, something he could criticize. His mouth was a thin straight line cut into a fat round face. If he had lips they weren't visible.

I'll bet he would've been right at home in the days of flogging and keel hauling, Dawson thought at their first meeting. I hope this is one time my first impression is wrong.

Padelford didn't make many changes for the first two weeks. He had a week overlap with Commander Ramore, and spent most of his time in briefings and getting familiar with the local commands. The second week he was out in the field, all over the I Corps, wherever the Civil Engineer Corps and the Seabees had projects underway.

After his orientation tour to Chu Lai with Lieutenant Knight, and to the Phu Bai, Hue and the Dong Ha area with Lieutenant Case, Padelford wasn't anxious to get out into Charley country again. In the two days he was in the Dong Ha Area they had incoming artillery four times. Roger Case said the Commander wanted to leave long before they had covered all of the major projects in that area. The frequent shelling made him so jumpy he couldn't keep his mind on the information Case was giving him. He also didn't like flying in helicopters or small planes to Seabees work-sites.

Dawson had returned to his office a little early Saturday evening to prepare notes for the Sunday morning briefing. His part usually didn't take long. He gave status reports on different phases of his project, he also mentioned any unresolved bottle-necks. Dawson valued sitting in on the remainder of the briefing by the Project Liaison Officers because it helped him keep up with major projects in progress. Some of them affected his line construction, and he was able to better coordinate his work from the information he learned about other construction work being planned.

Commander Padelford called from his office, "Lieutenant Dawson, I want to see you."

Dawson wasn't invited to sit so he stood in front of the Commander's desk. "Yes, sir."

He looked up with mirthless eyes. "I want you to brief me on the SIMPCOM progress. I'll brief the Commodore tomorrow. You won't need to attend the briefing."

Dawson frowned. "Why? Is there something special you need me to do early tomorrow morning?" he asked.

"No, you can go on about your regular work. Your project really isn't large in scope. There's no need for you at the weekly briefings.

"Commander, I don't think that's a good idea, there..."

Padelford interrupted, "Lieutenant, I didn't ask for your opinion. Get me the details on SIMPCOM. No further discussion is necessary. I'll expect you back in ten minutes."

When Padelford briefed the Commodore the next morning on Dawson's project the Commodore asked, "Where's Bill Dawson? Is he sick?"

Padelford replied, "No, sir, He's not sick. I can handle his briefings. His services can be better used out in the field."

The four LDO's sat at their regular table discussing the newest problem. "That sour faced Commander is going to be almost as much trouble for us as the V.C.

He hasn't done much to affect me yet, but I recognize trouble when I see it," Paul Knight said, shaking his head.

Case gave a short laugh. "Guess I'm lucky having the north territory. I used to think I got the dirty end of the stick being up there where I was getting shot at all the time. But now I don't know. The new Commander can't bug me much when I'm up there making my rounds. If he makes things too rough down here I can always spend more time up in Charley country."

"Well, Ed, it looks like you and I are stuck with the problem," Dawson said. "We can't get away from him. Has he been on your tail much yet?"

"Well, he's been nosing around a lot. He made some stupid suggestions which I ignored. For example, he told me to cut roads through berms around each tank in the new tank farm by the airfield. He said it would be easier for workers to get at the tanks. When I told him, 'And easier for the fuel to get out in the event of a rupture,' he didn't insist on the roads. So far he hasn't really interfered, but he will. He hasn't appreciated my ignoring his suggestions. He'll be on my back before long. By the way, Bill, the Commodore didn't look like he agreed with you not being at the briefing."

Dawson had been busy with construction problems near the air field for the past two weeks and had seen Lati only twice. She rode by without speaking even when Dawson called to her. The third time, he waited a few minutes after she had gone by, and then followed in his jeep. He caught up with her two miles down the road in a sparsely populated area. Dawson stopped ahead of her, then stood in the middle of the road as she approached.

Lati maintained her speed and Dawson thought she was going around him. But as she got closer, she slowed down and then stopped in front of him. "I do not want to talk with you. You think I am one of those, those prostitutes. But you are wrong. That is not why I asked you to my house."

Dawson stepped forward, placing one hand on the handlebars. "Lati, I don't think that of you. You misunderstood me. I meant if I come to your house and my men know of it they will think of you as a prostitute. Most men visit Vietnamese women for sex, so they would think that's why I went to your house. That would be bad two ways. They would think badly of you-I wouldn't like that. Then they would use my actions as justification for them to visit the street girls. Now do you understand?"

The defiant look on her face softened. "I am not sure I understand. You say your men would think me a prostitute. They are soldiers-you are a soldier. Why do you not think as they do?"

Dawson reached out and placed his other hand on hers as she gripped the bicycle handle. He felt an unexpected pleasant current flow from her through his body. "The answer is simple. Other men see you from a distance. They see you as a woman like the street women, more lovely and desirable than the others, but still as a woman to sleep with. They put all women over here in one category because that's the way they want to view them. I don't think of you like that because I know you and like you."

Lati's first reaction when Dawson's hand covered her small one was to jerk hers back. At that moment he could tell she was still a little angry with him. When she didn't obey her first impulse he thought that she enjoyed the feel of his hand on hers. It was their first physical contact since he had knocked her to the ground.

"I think I understand now," She said. "I do not care what other soldiers think of me. Vietnamese soldiers think of women in the same manner, but I am happy you do not think badly of me. I was sad when I thought you believed I am like those women who sell their bodies. I could never do that. Not even to save my grandfather's life. Where I work, American officers offer me much money to sleep with them. But I will not."

Dawson released her hand. "I'm glad we're friends again. I love talking with you. But it's always too brief. I want to know more about you, and talking in the middle of the road is difficult. I have an idea! We could eat lunch together. What time do you get off for lunch?"

"I have lunch at twelve O' clock. I bring my lunch and eat in a little park two blocks from my work."

"That's perfect. I'll have lunch there with you tomorrow. I'll bring the food. The park where you eat, is it the one along the river?"

"Yes. Where I eat is down the river two blocks, close to the boat landing."

"I know where the landing is. I'll see you there at noon tomorrow. "

That evening Dawson was cleaning up some paperwork when Chief Perod stomped in. "Lieutenant, you got to do something about those snipers. They shot at two different crews today."

Dawson looked up with a concerned frown. "Anyone hurt, Chief?"

"Yes, sir. Not shot, but might as well have been. One of my best linemen's out of action. His last step down the pole was too long, about 15 feet. The doc said he broke both heels. Another man burned a pole and got a chest full of splinters and creosote. It's getting harder and harder to get men to go back up on the poles."

"OK, Chief. I'll try again. You know the situation around here. The Marines are spread out awfully thin. But I'll try."

Dawson caught Padelford in his office before he went to dinner. He explained what had happened. "We're behind schedule now," Dawson said. "Unless we can do something about the snipers, I'm going to get some men killed, and the project will slip more behind schedule."

The two men's dislike for each other had already been established. There was no warmth or cordiality in their voices. "The project will be completed on time if it means your men working longer hours to do it. If you utilized your men better you wouldn't have trouble meeting the schedule. When I've been out on your jobs I see men standing around on the ground looking up at one or two men on the pole. You need to keep your men better occupied. As far as your men getting shot at, well they have to take their chances like the rest of us."

Dawson gritted his teeth, took a deep breath and swallowed, trying to contain the anger boiling up inside. He only partially succeeded. "Commander, have you ever climbed a pole? Have you ever worked on a line crew? Have you even directly supervised a line construction job? I doubt it or you would understand what the man on the ground is for."

The Commander started swelling up like a horned toad, his mouth working but no sound coming out. Dawson continued, not giving him a chance to break in. "There has to be someone on the ground to send up tools and equipment to men on the poles. At times he isn't busy, when he's waiting for the men on the pole. What would you have him doing? Picking up water buffalo chips in his spare time?"

Padelford came out of his seat like a spring, his face red with anger. "You do not talk to a commander in the United States Navy that way. You're being disrespectful and insolent. You are required to respect me. And I warn you against further insubordination."

Lieutenant Dawson leaned across the desk, keeping his voice low. "My apologies to the Commander. But you're wrong. I am not required to respect you. I'm required to respect the uniform, your rank. I don't need your OCS lecture on Navy regulations. Now let's knock off the crap and stick to the issue. I want some additional Seabees to act as a defensive force for work crews. I know Marines aren't available, but..."

The Commander's face was almost purple when he interrupted Dawson: "You do not tell me what to do. I tell you! Get out of my office now. That's an order. Now!"

Dawson did an about face and stomped out of the office. He went directly back to his office and typed out a memo to the Operations Officer. He requested sixteen additional men to function as security for his work crews. He went out to the administration area and had the yeoman burn him two copies. Then he dropped the original in Padelford's incoming basket. By that time he was late for dinner, so he hurried over to the Officer's Mess.

"What did you do to our Commander, Bill? Fallon asked. I knew he was nasty and quiet. I didn't know he had an explosive nature too."

Roger Chase said, "I got back from up North this afternoon, but it sounded more dangerous here in my own office. I may have to go back to Dong Ha for some peace and quiet."

"Don't you guys give me any crap," Dawson grumbled. "I've had enough of that today. Let me enjoy my meal."

"He's been leaning on me too," Ed Fallon said. "He has interfered on two different projects. But I chopped his legs out from under him when I briefed the Commodore. He didn't like it, but I got my projects back on track. I don't think he likes LDO's. He thinks we're morons or something. One thing I've noticed-he doesn't go out of the controlled areas to nose around my jobs. Guess he puts a high priority on personal safety."

"Some people call it being chicken," Dawson mumbled.

Case laughed. "I guess that's one advantage of having the North country. He hasn't been up there since the orientation tour I gave him. He didn't like being shelled. I arranged it so we had an extra day up there just for him. He wanted to come back after the first day. But I told him there were other projects we should see. I hadn't really intended to inspect them on that trip, but after meeting the Commander, I figured he needed the additional exposure. He was plenty nervous up there in Charley country."

Dawson's face lit up with a smile. "That gives me an idea. I'll bet I can cure the Commander from messing around my project so much."

Ensign Clark shook his head and said, "I think I'm in bad company. This war is bad enough, but you gentlemen make it sound like there's a revolution brewing too."

After dinner, the officers migrated to the bar. "Have you fellows heard of the trouble Ensign Halter, in MCB-10, is having trying to marry that Vietnamese girl?" Fallon asked.

"I've heard about it," Clark said, "and I don't see why they're giving him such a hard time."

"It's against Navy policy." Fallon replied. "While the orders over here don't say 'thou shalt not marry one,' they do forbid fraternization, and I assume he did a little fraternizing before he decided to marry her. I don't know that they can stop him if he's determined, but he'll likely ruin his chances of having a Navy career."

"Yeah, I know two officers who are married to Orientals, and they realize they'll never get promoted above Commander, Dawson said. "It doesn't seem fair to cut short a man's career, but I think I understand the policy. It's primarily to protect the young inexperienced boys. I've seen them in the Philippines and on other Pacific islands-it's their first time away from home, they meet a dark skinned girl who gives them food, a place to sleep and lots of lovin'. All of a sudden they're madly in love and want to get married."

"Right," Fallon interrupted. "And they don't consider the problems they'll face when they bring a native or Oriental back to their home town to live. It usually doesn't work out. Ken, if they didn't discourage servicemen from marrying these girls, there would be ten times as many doing it."

"Nine out of ten of those marriages would last only long enough to produce a house full of kids," Dawson said. "The American taxpayer would end up picking up the tab and the kids would end up on the street. I don't think we need to import trouble, we have plenty of homegrown problems."

The next morning Dawson told one of the stewards he would be away at lunch time, so the steward prepared sandwiches, potato chips, a thermos of coffee and some fruit to go. On the way into Da Nang, Dawson stopped where Chief Perod and two of his crews were working. He called the Chief aside and talked with him in private. Perod nodded his head and smiled broadly.

Rain had been intermittent all morning, making Dawson wonder if he and Lati would be able to have lunch together. It was overcast, but not raining when Dawson drove to the park and found Lati sitting on a piece of plastic under a large tree. Her lunch consisted of a bowl of rice with a little fish in it, some home-made bread that looked like hardtack and a jar of tea. He gave her one of his sandwiches and she gave him part of her rice in another bowl she had brought. Lati offered him a small bottle of what she called Nuoc-Maum. "It is for the rice," she said. "It is very good."

Dawson made the mistake of smelling it. It smelled like rotten fish. He almost gagged, but couldn't figure a way to avoid using it without hurting her feelings, so he poured it on sparingly. He took the first bite with reservation, but the Nuoc-Maum tasted quite good, like a soy sauce. He tried not to smell it as he was eating.

Lati seemed to enjoy the roast beef sandwich. Dawson wondered how long it had been since she had eaten any beef. After he finished the rice, Dawson asked Lati, "What is Nuoc-Maum made from?"

"Fish seasoned in the sun."

Dawson wished he hadn't asked. "That's what it smells like," he said keeping a straight face. "Tell me about yourself. Where was your home? Do you have brothers and sisters? Where are your parents?"

Lati smiled, looking directly at Dawson. She seemed pleased that he wanted to know about her. "My home was in a small village south of Hanoi. My grandfather and my mother's family had a large farm there until the Viet Minh took control of the area, after the French left and our country was divided into a North and South Vietnam. My father and mother and two brothers were killed when they tried to keep the Viet Minh from taking over our farm. They killed them all and had other people take over the farm. I do not know why they did not kill me. I guess they thought I could cause them no trouble. They let my grandfather live because he was too old to fight them. They let him stay in a small house on the farm, but he had to give the Viet Minh most of the crop he grew. My grandfather has taken care of me for these past years."

Dawson had kept his eyes on Lati as she talked, which seemed to make her nervous, and she looked down as she talked. "Don't you have other relatives? Aunts, uncles, cousins?"

"Yes, but they shunned us when Grandfather became part of the underground resistance. He provided food for them until about a year ago when we learned the local officials were about to arrest us because they suspected he was not giving them all of the crops he was supposed to. Someone told them my grandfather was not loyal to the Viet Cong. You see, some of the people living there did not like my mother's family because they were of pure Chinese ancestry. I was disliked even more because I was not a Buddhist and was part Caucasian. The Chinese have invaded and occupied Vietnam several times over the past centuries. Because of the occupation many Vietnamese have Chinese blood, but others do not like the Chinese. Even though my family has Lived in Vietnam for over two hundred years, they kept their blood line pure. Many Vietnamese considered us foreigners and resented us because we were wealthy and Chinese."

Dawson sipped his coffee slowly, with his back against the tree, watching Lati as she talked about her family. She sat cross-legged in front of him, her hands moving gracefully as she painted word scenes with them. Her dark, almond shaped eyes were sad when she spoke of her family. She seemed so natural and guileless. He smiled as her face turned pink, when she looked up and found him studying her.

She looked at her hands again and continued: "When we learned the Viet Cong were going to arrest us, the underground helped my grandfather and me get out of the North and relocate here. We left with few possessions and little money. The Viet Minh had confiscated all the money my family had, when they took over the country. Now we have nothing. But it is better living in the Refugee Village than it was in North Vietnam for the past years. At least we do not live in constant fear and we are free to come and go from our house when we want."

"How did you learn to speak English so well?" he asked when she had finished speaking.

"My father was a missionary from America. I attended school at the mission and grew up speaking English and Vietnamese. It was a much better school than what the Communists provided. All the Viet Minh taught in their schools was why one should work for the Communist cause, and how bad Americans were. You know, the Communists really want people to remain ignorant so they will work for the State and not question why they are treated like cattle."

"Your father's last name was Noi?"

"Oh, no. He was not Vietnamese. His name was Baker. That is the name I went by for many years, until my father was killed. I think he knew it was coming. They had two reasons for wanting to kill my father. He was the head missionary and also a member of my grandfather's family that had much land. A short time before he was killed he told me that if anything happened to him, he wanted me to take my mother's family name. Otherwise the Viet Cong would treat me badly.

"I really do not know why they permitted the missionary school to continue so long after the Viet Minh took over the country. They were cruel to the missionaries, and made life difficult for them. They pressured them to leave. But my father and two other Americans had been in Vietnam for so long they considered it their home and the Vietnamese their people. So they would not leave. They continued teaching and helping people. It was five years ago the Viet Cong killed my family. The other two missionaries disappeared. I am sure they were killed too. So you see I have lost all of my family except Grandfather. But what my father taught me did not die. It lives on in my heart and in my mind."

Dawson wanted to take her hands in his or hold her in his arms. She seemed so alone. "I'm sorry you've had so much sadness in your life. I wish I could promise you a happier future, but I'm afraid there's a long way to go before your land will have peace. Lati, do you mind telling me your age? Age is a sensitive subject with some American women, so I hesitate to ask."

"No, I do not mind. My age is what it is. By your calendar I am twenty-six. But what of your life? Are you married? Do you have many children?"

"I'm not married. I was once, but we divorced many years ago. There were no children. My family had a farm in Nebraska, which is in the center of the United States."

Lati nodded her head. "I know of Nebraska. It grows much corn. I studied much geography of America."

"We didn't have a large farm, and were actually poor most of the time. But we had enough to eat, even in the Great Depression. I left Nebraska many years ago and have been in the Navy since you were a small girl. The Navy has sent me to many countries which I've enjoyed seeing. Most of all I've loved meeting people with different customs and ways of thinking. I'm sure I would enjoy being here if it weren't for the war. War destroys all beauty. I doubt that I'll get to know the people here very well, since you're the only one I've been able to talk with. But I'm sure I would love your people if they are all like you."

Another flush surged into her neck and face as she smiled and averted her eyes. "You are kind with your compliments. I have enjoyed talking with you, but I see by your watch it is time for me to return to work. Before I go I must speak for my grandfather. He said to tell you that you will do him great honor if you will visit his humble abode. I know you work every day, and it is not safe for you to be out at night; but next week is Christmas and American forces, not actually fighting, will be given a holiday for that afternoon. Is it possible for you to visit us then? It is not only my grandfather's wish. I too would like for you to come."

Dawson frowned. "Oh! I haven't heard that before. There's been no announcement about us being off Christmas afternoon. Who told you?"

A quick look of apprehension appeared on her face, and she nervously nibbled on her lower lip before replying. "I am sorry. I have told you something I know from my work as interpreter for Admiral Scott. He told this to the Vietnamese General through me. Please believe me, I never speak of what I hear at my job. I would not tell you of the holiday, but I was afraid I would not see you again before then, and I wanted to ask you to come to my house. I do not even tell my grandfather of what I know. You must not tell anyone because the Admiral does not want it known in advance. He is concerned that the Viet Cong may become more active if they know the American forces will be on holiday."

Dawson thought her habit of biting the right side of her lower lip when she was nervous was cute. It was such a lovely mouth, so sensual, so kissable. He shook his head, purging his mind of such intriguing thoughts, as he rose to his feet, extending his hand. "Don't be concerned, I'll not tell anyone. I understand why you told me."

Lati was still seated, looking up. A smile came into her eyes, as the worried look changed to one of trust. When she gave him her hand, as he helped her up, it lingered in his after she was on her feet. A current of understanding and affection flowed between them in those brief seconds.

Reaching into her ao dai, Lati pulled out a small paper and handed it to Dawson. "Here is a map to help you find my house. Can you understand my directions?"

Dawson looked at the map briefly. "Yes I can find your house and I'll be there if possible."

The weather turned colder and heavy rain at times became a deluge. All Seabee construction jobs bogged down. The men were working wet and cold half the time. Equipment got mired in the red mud. Tempers flared as men were thwarted in their attempts to accomplish too much work in too short a time, in miserable conditions. Dawson's men had to do more and more work by hand because equipment couldn't get into areas to dig holes and set the poles.

Damp cold soaked into the men's bones. The actual temperature wasn't so low, but with high humidity and the temperature staying about 50 degrees for days on end, it felt much colder. The men never got warm and dry because none of the buildings were heated. They were built for tropical use, with louvered vents near the floor and window openings covered only with screens. Dawson couldn't get warm, even at night. His bedding was damp and cold. The two blankets allotted didn't keep him warm, so he spread his poncho over the top. That helped, but still didn't really warm him.

Perod and Dawson were standing alongside the road talking when Commander Padelford arrived in his pickup. Dawson said quietly, "Now would be a good time, Chief."

The Chief said, "Yes, sir," and strode rapidly to where part of his crew was setting a pole three spans away.

Padelford made his way carefully around the deeper mud holes to where Dawson stood in the mud, a few yards from the road, looking at a map of the area.

Padelford returned Dawson's salute. "I got your memo, Lieutenant, and the answer is still no."

"I wanted to go on record. It's your responsibility if one of my men gets killed," Dawson replied.

They were in an uninhabited area, where the jungle came up to within a few feet of both sides of the narrow gravel road. Padelford asked about progress in different areas of Dawson's project. Chief Perod was headed back their way when the Commander started to leave. Dawson detained him with, "Sir, before you go I want to mention that I may need your help to get two graves in another area moved."

Perod gave a snappy salute. "Good morning, Commander. Lieutenant, my man the third pole thought he saw some movement out in the bush. I'm going to take the men out and sweep the area."

"Hold it, Chief," Dawson said. "I don't think that's necessary. There's been no report of Charley activity in this area today. You know how jumpy the men have been lately. We can't afford the time. We're behind schedule now."

Perod saluted and replied, "What ever you say, Lieutenant," and turned to walk away.

Three shots in quick succession rang out. The Chief yelled, "Snipers! Hit the deck!"

Padelford responded immediately flopping on his belly in the mud. Dawson, Perod and the other men on the ground squatted in the mud. The men on the poles came down at a leisurely pace.

"Guess your man was right, Chief," Dawson said. "Make up two recon-squads. You want to come with us Commander?"

Padelford got up, muddy from head to foot. "No. I have other things I should be doing," he said, and hurried to his pickup parked across the road.

After Padelford disappeared down the road, one of Chief Perod's men came out of the jungle grinning. All of the men laughed and went back to work.

Dawson said, "That was excellent timing, Chief," then got in his jeep and drove away.

The following day at dinner, Paul Knight said quietly to Dawson, "I hear you gave our Commander a baptism under fire."

Dawson gave a knowing smile and said, "Not me. Charley did. But I will say it couldn't have happened to a more deserving fellow."

At the movies Padelford glowered at Dawson. By now he knew what had happened but couldn't prove it. Dawson's smile confirmed the scuttlebutt going around about the sniper attack was correct.

It had been a week since his memo requesting more men to use for security, and no action had been taken. Padelford refused to discuss the subject further. Dawson considered going over Padelford's head and talk with the Commodore, but he procrastinated, hoping Padelford would change his mind.

Dawson was at the work-site of two crews setting poles and stringing a lateral cable in a sparsely populated area. The jungle growing very close to the road made Dawson apprehensive. Seabees working on the ground as well as the four linemen belted-off on poles didn't laugh and joke as usual. Frenchy said, "Charley could have a whole company close enough to spit on us and we wouldn't know it."

After watching them sag-in six spans of messenger cable, Dawson was about to leave when a shot rang out. Everyone on the ground hit the deck. The men on the poles dropped down in long steps. Dawson, squatting between two of the vehicles trying to figure where the shot came from, realized the lineman on the pole ten feet away hadn't come down. Looking up, he saw the lineman hanging limp against the pole, both gaffs cut out of the pole. The only thing that kept him from dropping thirty feet was his safety belt snagged on the through-bolt.

Chief Perod saw him at the same time. He looked at the three linemen, who had run from their poles to the vehicles for cover. "One of you get up there and bring Relonni down." No one moved. "What the hell you gonna do? Let him hang there till they shoot him again?"

Dawson was standing now. "You've been trained in pole-top rescue, haven't you?" The linemen didn't reply. He gave them a hard look, then pointed to the closest one. "Give me your hooks and belt. I haven't climbed in years, but I'm not leaving him up there."

"It's not your job, Lieutenant. I'll do it," Beleu, the young, blond linemen from Tennessee said, and ran to the pole. He climbed rapidly and belted off under the unconscious lineman, positioning himself so he could place Relonni astride his safety belt. Perod grabbed a hank of half-inch line from the nearest line truck, and heaved one end to Beleu. He looped it over the messenger cable, and secured it to both "D" rings on Relonni's belt. "Take a strain," he yelled, as he worked himself higher, lifting the unconscious lineman, trying to get the strain off of Relonni's safety belt. He unsnapped Relonni's safety belt, then dropped down three feet, and swung around the pole so he wasn't under Relonni. Two men on the ground tending the line, let it run through their hands until Relonni was in the arms of Perod and a lineman.

Beleu unbelted and as soon as Relonni was clear of the pole, he dropped down the pole in three long steps. He cut out with both gaffs, dropped eight feet, cut back in to break his fall, then immediately cut out again, and back in eight feet lower and then cut out, dropping to the ground. It was a dangerous way to come down a pole, but not as dangerous as giving Charley another shot.

They laid Relonni on his left side. Dawson heard a sucking sound with each labored breath. Perod ripped off the right side of Relonni' shirt exposing an entry wound in his right chest, and a larger exit wound in his back under his shoulder blade. From the first-aid kit he got 4 X 4 bandages, placing them over both holes. "I want you to hold pressure on both dressings," he told the lineman.

"Lay him in the back of my pickup-two of you in with him," Dawson ordered. "There's a Marine company and doctor three miles from here. Chief, may as well clear out for the day. You can help the other crews working near the runway."

When the doctor saw the chest wound he had one of the corpsmen locate the chopper pilot. "Have to get him to the hospital ASAP. Get an IV started now and occlusive dressings on entrance and exit wounds."

Dawson waited with the unconscious man until the chopper took off five minutes later. "How does it look? Think he'll pull through?" he asked the doctor.

"Hard to say till they get inside and assess the damage. I've seen men survive with a lot worse looking wounds."

Heading out of Da Nang toward Red Beach, Dawson was angry with himself for not taking action Sunday. After the briefing session Dawson had asked Case, "Did Commander Padelford mention my request for men, or that increased sniper activity is making it difficult to keep SIMPCOM on schedule?"

"Nope. Didn't mention a word about more men. From what he told the Commodore your project is going along fine, right on schedule."

Dawson slammed his hand on the desk. "That does it! This week I'm going to talk with the Commodore." Dawson had been reluctant to go over the Commander's head. Even though Commodore Rhodes had said his door was always open, Dawson was supposed to go through the Operations Officer. Navy regulations decreed going over your superior's head was a breach of military conduct.

Now, he was angry at himself. If I had taken action Sunday I might not have one man wounded, he thought as he parked the pickup in front of the Regimental Headquarters building. Dawson knocked on the door jam of the Commodore's office. Commodore Rhodes looked up from the papers on his desk. "Come in, Bill. Haven't had a talk with you in a while. I've missed you at the briefings. Have a seat. You look like a man with a load on his mind."

"Yes, sir. I have a problem I'm not able to resolve. Commodore, you've known me for a long time. I think you know I believe in Navy regulations, protocol, and all that. It bothers me to go over Commander Padelford's head, but I just had one man wounded, and can't wait any longer."

"How bad is the wound?"

"Don't know yet, sir. Sniper got Relonni, one of my linemen, in the chest. He went to the hospital by chopper. I'll check on him later and keep you advised. Commodore, I believe my men's lives and the completion of SIMPCOM are more important than worrying about chain-of-command. That's why..."

"Bill, I don't question your motives. Get to the point. What has you so riled up?" Commodore Rhodes' face was lined with concern.

Dawson handed the Commodore a copy of the memo he had given to Padelford. "Have you seen this, sir?"

The Commodore scanned the single page rapidly. "No, I haven't seen this memo."

"Commander Padelford refused to consider my need for more men for security. When I pressed the issue he ordered me out of his office. That's when I wrote the memo."

The Commodore finished reading, a frown wrinkling his brow. "But I've been told you're staying on schedule. Why in hell haven't you been in to see me before?"

"Well, sir, it's hard for me to break years of military training and violate Naval custom. It was difficult..."

The Commodore broke in with a wave of his hand. "I'm not in the least interested in namby-pamby rules and customs if they're going to put our men in more danger or cause us to fall down on our mission out here. We must have discipline here as well as on the parade field. But the pomp and polish some people indulge in won't win this war. Bill, you'll get your men. You're right in your memo-no Marines. I wouldn't feel right trying to get Marines who are needed worse in many other places. But you will get more Seabees."

"Thank you, Commodore. I'll do my best to keep SIMPCOM on schedule."

"Bill, I have confidence you will complete the project on schedule. I want you back in the briefings every week from now on. I'll work it out with Commander Padelford. I'm aware of the dissension since he arrived; been trying to resolve that problem, but I'm sure you realize it's a delicate situation. I'll appreciate it if you'll do all you can to get along with the Commander."

Dawson stood up and headed for the entrance. "Yes sir. I'll do my best."

"Oh by the way, Bill. I've heard scuttlebutt about the Commander's mud bath. Personally, between the two of us, I was glad to see a little starch taken out of his uniform. But officially I must warn you, that if he can prove the rumors I've heard, the Commander could bring you up on charges."

Dawson smiled. "I've heard some strange scuttlebutt too, but I'm not worried. My fatigues are clean-you know how Seabees like to talk."

The Commodore called to his yeoman as Dawson left his office. "Sampson, I want to see Commander Padelford."

The next morning , when Dawson passed his office, Padelford called, "Lieutenant, I want to speak with you."

Dawson entered the office and stood at exaggerated attention in front of the Commander's desk. "Yes, sir?"

"You are to attend weekly briefings from now on," Padelford said, rancor plainly evident in his voice. "Why didn't you tell me about your man being injured?"

"Didn't think you were interested, sir. Last time I tried to discuss my problems you ordered me out of your office."

Padelford glared at Dawson, hardly able to talk. Then he spoke very low so his voice wouldn't carry beyond his office: "You violated Navy regulations going over my head. I don't like that. Apparently you have an 'in' with Commodore

Rhodes. If it weren't for that I would already have you up on charges. I know the sniper incident was staged. If I can prove it I'll have you court-martialed. Let me assure you that you won't be promoted beyond lieutenant. I'll see to that when I fill out your fitness reports-and if I have the opportunity I'll take more severe action."

Dawson, remaining at attention, gave Padelford a tight smile. "Commander, your threat of blocking my promotion is wasted on me. Even if you can accomplish that it won't bother me much. When I came in the Navy my goal was to make Chief. I'm way past that. So if I must retire as Lieutenant I'll be content. Speaking of promotions, if you'd stay out of the way and let others do their jobs they might help you get promoted to Captain."

Padelford's eyes blazed. His voice rose to a higher pitch. "Out! Get out of my office!"

Chief Wilson did his job well. Seldom was SIMPCOM held up due to lack of supplies. If he couldn't get what was needed through requisitioning, Wilson borrowed it. If he couldn't borrow it, he traded for it. And it wasn't always like items that he traded. A bottle of whiskey helped a supply sergeant locate a reel of cable urgently needed for SIMPCOM. A Seabee jacket and combat boots uncovered a pile of telephone poles.

Once Wilson found a reliable interpreter and got plugged into the South Vietnamese Army "informal chain of command" his trading market expanded. He couldn't get anything through official channels, but through bartering anything was possible. The Vietnamese Forces had considerable supplies and equipment lying idle, sometimes because they didn't know how to use it, sometimes because they had no need for the material. They relied on the American forces to do the major construction and maintenance work. But they still kept supplies and equipment, provided by the U. S., in their yards.

The Vietnamese enlisted men were paid little and were accustomed to the barter system. Because supplies were free to the Vietnamese their methods of accountability were informal at best. Inventory control was non-existent. In this environment Chief Wilson's horse trading talents were much more effective than going through normal supply channels.

Wilson also had excellent contacts on Guam and Okinawa. So when he had exhausted his sources locally he flew to one of the bases on those islands. Dawson assured Wilson's "combat priority" for his flight space and cargo shipment. At times he wondered if the trips to Okinawa were absolutely necessary, since it was a good place for R & R. But the requests always seemed justified and the supplies arrived when they were needed.

Three of the four switchboards required for SIMPCOM were on hand. But they hadn't been able to locate the fourth one through normal supply channels. Chief Wilson told Lieutenant Dawson, "I think I know where there's a switchboard not in use, on one of the bases on Okinawa. I'll need authorization to make some long distance calls to be sure."

"That's great, Chief. I'll get you clearance to make the calls."

Later in the day Wilson located Dawson at one of the work sites. "I found a switchboard, Lieutenant. I'll have to go pick it up, and it's going to cost us two cases of jackets. I wouldn't even bother you, but I can't get that many foul-weather jackets on my own."

"Wait a minute, Chief. Why should we have to give anyone jackets? You located the switchboard, now let me handle it. Tell me where it is and I'll go through official channels to get it. You said it's not in use, so it should be easy enough to get through a property transfer. If they balk, I'll get the Commodore to exert pressure."

"Well, sir, it isn't quite that simple. The switchboard is on a base the U. S. abandoned and turned back to Okinawa. I'm negotiating with one of my old friends, an Okinawan supervisor in charge of the buildings where the switchboard is located."

Dawson gave a resigning shrug. "OK, Chief. You make the flight arrangements through personnel. I'll locate the jackets. We may have that many here in regimental supplies, but I don't dare requisition them because Commander Padelford would probably find out about it. He's just waiting for me to step over the line. He would have me charged with misappropriation of government property. I'll try to locate the jackets at one of the battalions."

"No sweat, Lieutenant. I know where some jackets are. I just can't get at them. MCB-10 has more than two cases. If you can, get all small size."

Arriving at the MCB 10 camp, Dawson located the Operations Officer who fortunately owed him a favor. He explained the problem, what the jackets were for and why he couldn't get them from the regiment. The Operations Officer said he had enough jackets, but he might need them before he could get more from the States. "You can draw them from the Regiment if you really need them," Dawson told him. "But if you get to that point be sure and let me know so I can cover the trail to keep Padelford from learning about it."

One week later the switchboard was in the 30th NCR supply yard. What a way to have to do things, Dawson thought. But if we went by the book some things would never get done on time. Sometimes our own system strangles us.

Sixteen additional Seabees provided for security had the desired effect. Sniping incidents dropped off considerably. Two men were assigned to each work crew, with orders to stay together and stay on the move. They worked their way through the jungle making large circles around the work area. SIMPCOM men's morale improved and production increased, despite the rain and mud.

As they got more and more cable strung on poles, sabotage became a serious problem. Charley climbed poles and either cut a small section out of the cable or drove nails into it. Because they were difficult to locate, the nails caused more trouble than a cut cable. The nail shorted out several wires and later rain soaked in grounding out the entire cable.

Chief Martin had all of his men trying to locate one wet spot in a cable. They became irritable at having to waste time, and they became frustrated working in the steady downpour, unable to find the trouble.

Frenchy grumbled as he climbed a pole he had hiked earlier in the day. He examined the cable a second time, finding nothing. He was about to come down when he ran his hand over the cable out three feet from the pole. He shouted, "I've found it. Those dirty gooks stuck a pin in our cable."

Dawson had figured the cable would be subjected to some sabotage. But he hadn't thought it would be as bad as it turned out. He realized the problem would continue after the system was put in operation and something had to be done about it. He called his three chiefs together and asked if they had any solutions.

"We could put metal guards around each pole like rat guards they use on the lines tying up a ship," Chief Martin said. "The V.C. must be shinnying up the poles, since they probably don't have climbers. The biggest problem with that idea is our men would have to take the guards off when they want to work on the cable."

"How about embedding pieces of glass or sharp nails in the poles?" Wilson asked. "That should discourage them after the first time."

"That would be rough on the maintenance men who will have to work on this line," Chief Perod replied. "I know a way to stop Charley. And it might increase the body count too. All we have to do is string a single phase of primary voltage right below the cable. There's no way for Charley to get past that. When our men want to work on the cable they'll have to be sure the power on that circuit is off."

Dawson listened to the three men as they discussed the advantages and dis-advantages of various deterrents. Finally he said: "I like the high voltage idea. It seems the most foolproof. All it'll take is some bare wire and insulators. We can tap the primary side of transformers in different areas to get the juice. If we sectionalize the system, it'll be easier to kill when we want to work on it. Chief Wilson, can you have some wire and insulators ready by tomorrow?"

"Sure, Lieutenant. There's plenty of that available."

"Fine. Now, I want you to put all splicing crews and line crews to work installing the hot wire on poles we've already set. Charley is causing us too much rework. We'll string the hot wire on new poles as we go. Better get some 'High voltage' signs to tack on the poles."

Chapter 6

Christmas Day at 0530 Dawson walked from his hooch to the officers mess in a steady cold rain. Warming his hands on a second mug of coffee, he wondered how the men would react to working on Christmas in the damp cold. They will probably like it as much as I do, he told himself.

Line crews started work, without adequate light, at 0600 as usual. When Dawson stopped where a crew was framing up a corner pole, he watched the lineman halfheartedly climb the pole. He cut out twice because he hadn't planted his gaffs firmly enough in the pole. Good lineman, Dawson thought as the man cut back in both times without falling. The grunt on the ground, in his poncho, set about making up the down-guy automatically, showing little interest in his work. He shivered once in a while, having not put on enough clothes under his poncho. The men's spirits matched the weather not the season. It would've been better had they not known it was Christmas.

As noontime approached, although the weather remained dismal, the Seabee's spirits brightened. The usual ribald comments were exchanged, enthusiasm and camaraderie became evident as they anticipated Christmas dinner and their first afternoon off.

Dinner at the officer's mess was a full banquet. The smell of turkey and dressing and ham with pineapple sauce filled the room. Sweet potatoes with browned marshmallows on top, mashed potatoes with brown gravy, peas and green beans and tossed salad filled out the menu. Wine was served with dinner, cigars and brandy followed the pumpkin pie and savory mincemeat pie. War and the damp cold were camouflaged by a festive mood in the bar area and dining room. The stewards and Vietnamese girls had worked hard to make it seem like Christmas. The girls were dressed in their best ao-dais and chattered excitedly.

Food at the enlisted mess was essentially the same as at the officer's mess, but instead of being served at a table men stood in line and were served by mess-cooks. The head cook stood back of the mess-cooks, arms folded over a substantial paunch, looking as proud as if he were a chef at the St. Mark. A two-hundred pound Seabee shoved his plate back across the steam table. "Put more ham on my tray. You'd think you're paying for it." The mess-cook shrugged and gave him another slice of ham.

Instead of sitting at tables for four with white table cloths, they sat at long mess tables with benches attached. No wine or brandy was served in the enlisted mess. Still the atmosphere was charged with a festive spirit, with men horsing around and calling back and forth to each other. After dinner most of them spent the afternoon at the enlisted club where they played games, relaxed, or got drunk.

Most of the officers drifted into the bar area after dinner to play acey-ducey or Ping-Pong, or to reminisce about home. Dawson had a couple of drinks, chatted for a while and then walked to his hooch for the gifts he had bought for Lati and her grandfather.

The main road going toward Da Nang was deserted except for old people and children. His attention was drawn to one boy who looked to be about eight with dirt streaked face. He carried a bundle of cardboard and boards much too big for his small body. I wonder if the boy's parents are alive, Dawson thought. Wonder what he had for Christmas dinner, or if he had dinner.

The old people trudging along with booty scavenged from the dump didn't look up. Dawson slowed the jeep, considering their plight. I wish I could help them, he thought. But what can I do? One frail looking old woman, face furrowed by years, privation and sorrow, limped along dragging a pair of combat boots, some pieces of torn uniforms, collapsed cardboard boxes and tar paper on a tattered scrap of tarp. After a few steps she stopped to rest. Dawson doubted Christmas had any joyous meaning for her. She is probably concerned with keeping dry and warm and alive.

Hoa 0, south of Red Beach was a small village of a half dozen old wood and masonry buildings lining the highway, residences and shops combined. Dawson wondered what the shops offered. He couldn't tell from the road, except for the one where gaudy women lounged enticingly under a covered porch.

The sight of the prostitutes gave Dawson a twinge of guilt. As he made plans to visit Lati, he had let one part of his brain convince him it was simply a friendly gesture. His intentions were pure. It wouldn't really be considered fraternization-which he had warned his men against. After all, he could say it was the grandfather he went to see. The other part of his brain told him: Oh, sure! That's a good story if you get caught. Dawson rationalized his intentions enough that the nagging thought, do-as-I-say-not-as-I-do didn't linger long in his mind.

In the almost flat sand dune area, on both sides of the highway, the hobo-looking shacks surrounded the village. Gently rolling sand dunes with scattered patches of green shrubs extended a thousand yards to the sea. If he hadn't looked at a map, Dawson would never have known the village, Hoa 0, had a name other than Refugee Village. That's what Americans called it.

A high arch rose on masonry columns north of where the cardboard and ply-wood tin-covered shacks began on the east side of the highway. The arch looked out of place standing there alone, the nearest building fifty yards away. Dawson had seen it before and wondered why it was there. He speculated that it was the entrance to an old estate no longer in existence. Now he turned, drove under the arch, and stopped in the sand to look at the map Lati had drawn for him. She indicated a road going alongside the first irregular row of shacks.

It wasn't much of a road, only a pair of sand-packed tracks made by vehicles. Looking across the sand Dawson understood the purpose of the arch entrance. About three hundred yards from the highway was a small red, green and black Buddhist temple. Following tracks in the sand almost to the temple, which was on his left, Dawson turned right into a cleared area between shacks. The sand became less firm, so he stopped before he got in where even his four wheel drive wouldn't get him out. He felt relieved when he saw his jeep was obscured from the road.

He walked to the third row of shacks, following the map. It led him right to Lati's home. Vietnamese faces appeared at windows, scrutinizing Dawson as he made his way through the loose sand. The shacks were curious looking. Some were built side by side, each leaning on the other. Others had a foot or two separation between them. Some leaned precariously, others were almost plumb. Some had doors with rope hinges, others had no doors, only cloths draped across the openings.

Lati, who had been watching for Dawson, opened the door as he approached. "Come in. I was worried you would not come."

Dawson's concern about where he was and what he was doing was forgotten when he saw Lati in her pale yellow ao dai. Her long dark hair, pulled back, hung to her waist. She looked so small, but well proportioned. This ao dai seemed more form fitting than others. It emphasized her well shaped body and Dawson couldn't keep from staring. He thought, I'll bet she would look great in a sweater.

The shack was made with scraps of plywood and rough lumber. Dawson wondered how it remained standing. It had no wall studs. Each piece of plywood somehow clung to and held up the next. The only vertical supports were 4 by 4's at each corner and 2 by 4's on either side of the door. A few horizontal 2 by 4's kept the sheets of corrugated metal roofing from falling down. The slightly pitched shed type roof sloped to the front. The shack was only ten by fourteen feet, Dawson estimated. Good it's no larger, he thought. If it falls down, it's so small it probably won't kill them.

The only light came from the one three-foot square, plastic covered window two feet to the right of the door. Seated on a stool at a small home-made table, the frail looking old man smiled. Lati said, "This is my grandfather, Chin Ling." She finished the introduction in Vietnamese. The old man nodded in recognition and spoke a few words.

Chin Ling's very wrinkled face reflected his age. The few white hairs hanging from his chin made his face look even longer and thinner. The very old round, cloth hat of black brocade denoted a Chinese man of importance. But his eyes were what held Dawson 's attention. They were alert, and intelligent looking.

Lati interpreted, "My grandfather welcomes you to his humble abode, and asks your pardon for not rising to greet you, but his arthritis makes it painful for him to stand at times. You do him great honor to come in the rain and to enter such a pitiful house. He asks you to please be seated."

Dawson thought of bowing, but since the old man couldn't get up, he extended his hand to Chin Ling who gripped it lightly. "Tell your grandfather it is I who am honored by his invitation. I think houses do not matter much. It is the people living in them who are important." Dawson removed his raincoat and sat on the stool opposite Chin Ling.

Chin Ling nodded in appreciation of the compliment. He pointed to the bottle of wine and two glasses on the table and spoke.

Lati poured the wine and seated herself on another stool. "My Grandfather offers a toast to your good health and long life. He thanks you for saving the only thing that matters to him, the only one left to care for him in his old age. If this were in times past when we had wealth, you would be well rewarded."

"Tell your grandfather I am rewarded by being of service and my reward is multiplied each time I see you."

In the dim light Dawson saw color flow into her face. She looked down, embarrassed, as she spoke to her grandfather. He thought, She must not be accustomed to getting complements, but I don't know why. Still not looking up she said, "I think it is more difficult to be an interpreter for personal matters than it is when I am working."

They continued talking as they sipped the wine. Chin Ling spoke of Life in the North before the Viet Minh. His face saddened and looked older as he spoke of his wife and children dead; his farms and possessions confiscated. His words betrayed no bitterness. He spoke with sadness and regret of the waste of lives that had produced nothing but a harder life for everyone, including the peasants, who, according to the Communists, were the ones to gain by the bloodshed, the revolution, the dispossession of their overlords.

"But they only acquired new masters with different titles. They have to work harder and receive a smaller share. Their young men are taken off to fight and die. Their children, taken by the State, are taught to hate their parents, to distrust and to spy. The young are purged of human feelings. Pride and love of family and home are squeezed from their hearts, their minds, their very souls. Machines replace their minds. Pumps replace their hearts. In place of their souls are voids. They become puppets."

There was a long silence as the old man paused in thought. "You have very lovely hands, Lati. I love the way you move them when you're talking," Dawson said looking directly into her eyes. Bright color flowed into her face, and she looked down at her hands.

Eager to change the subject, Lati asked, "What did your base do for Christmas?"

"We had the standard Christmas dinner, much like we would have had at home." "We had...." He started to elaborate, but stopped when he thought about the meager rations Lati and her grandfather must have had. The smell of fish and Nuoc-Maum still lingered in the room. "It was very good, considering we're in a war zone," he continued.

Chin Ling cleared his throat. "The Communists have controlled the North for so long, there are not many who try to resist them any longer. Those who would resist have not the resources; and they are being rapidly eliminated. I have talked with many Vietnamese here in the South. They do not have the will, the determination it takes to win the war here either. They have been fighting for so long they are weary of it. Now the United States has entered the war, the Vietnamese think you will win it for them. You represent great power. You have unlimited resources and weapons.

"But they are wrong. I do not think you will win this war. I want you to understand, I am most grateful for your country coming to our aid. If you had not, South Vietnam would have been under Communist domination now. But the reason you will not win this war is because your politicians do not let the generals run the war. Your tactics are not aggressive enough. You follow the same methods used in Korea. You let the enemy come down here and attack, you fight back, but you do not go to the source of his power and eliminate it. Bombing alone will not defeat the Viet Cong. They will continue to be supplied by the Russians. They do not care how many men they lose. They will continue to inflict casualties on you until Americans demand an end to the killing of their sons."

The old man sipped his wine and seemed lost in thought. "The paper your grandfather was reading when I entered, is it a Da Nang paper," Dawson asked.

"No, it is from Saigon. It is the one luxury we indulge in. I buy one almost everyday for grandfather. He has me buy it a day late, so I get for half-price. It is good for him to be able to know what is happening in the world. He has nothing else to do."

Dawson glanced at another paper at the other end of the table. "Do you read the 'Stars And Stripes' to him?"

"Yes. The Admiral gives it to me when he has finished with it. I think my grandfather regrets not learning English. He does not like waiting for me to read to him."

Chin Ling raised his hand, and then continued as though he had not paused. "Even now your Communist inspired dissidents riot against this war. The Viet Cong see this and know all they need do is continue their hit and run tactics. The American public will demand your withdrawal after many thousands of men have been killed and you are no closer to winning than when you started. Only this time when the United States withdraws its forces the results will be worse than in Korea. The Viet Cong know the South does not have the will to resist. They will not live up to their promises, and they will conquer this country in a very short time. I hope, Lieutenant Dawson, that you will not be one of the useless casualties. I know and your military leaders know the only way to win is to carry this war into North Vietnam. And I do not believe that will be done."

Dawson listened to this grim prediction, being relayed to him by Lati, with some skepticism and disbelief. But the sincerity of the old man's pronouncement caused a feeling of fear and dread to flow through him. He didn't want to argue with Chin Ling, so all he said was: "I sincerely hope you're wrong, sir. I believe we will win this war, at least to the extent that South Vietnam will be left alone to determine its own form of government."

Chin Ling looked tired. He smiled and shrugged, saying, "Only with the passing of time will we know truth."

Dawson smiled and nodded, looking from Chin Ling to Lati. The old man's predictions dampened his spirits as they sank in.

Then Dawson remembered the gifts he had brought and welcomed the distraction. Time to change the subject, he thought. He pulled the pound can of tobacco from the sack he had put on the floor and extended it across the table to Chin Ling. "I thought you might like some American pipe tobacco. I saw your granddaughter bringing tobacco home, so I assumed you smoked a pipe. I see I was right."

Chin Ling felt the can with both hands. "It has been many years since I have had this much tobacco at one time. A thousand thanks to you."

Dawson handed the other package to Lati. She opened it to find a bicycle light with spare batteries, that Dawson had Chief Wilson buy on his last trip to Okinawa.

Lati's dark brown eyes lit up like a small child's. She looked from the light to Dawson, her eyes sparkling with excitement. She spoke to her grandfather, holding the light out for his examination. Her entire face radiated her thanks to Dawson. The look was as warm as an embrace. "It is the best possible thing you could give me," She said. "Sometimes I must come home late and it is difficult on the dark streets. Thank you. My grandfather and I both thank you. You are a most kind man."

The smile on Lati's face brought a lump to Dawson's throat. I wish I could do something to make her look that happy all the time. Such a lovely, innocent face.

Chin Ling opened the tobacco, loaded his pipe and sat smoking with evident pleasure. "It is excellent tobacco. Since the French left I have not had such good tobacco." The mild Turkish tobacco filled the room with a pleasant aroma.

Dawson savored the smell of fresh tobacco. It brought back strong memories of the days when he smoked. Times like now I would really like to have a smoke, he thought. But I sure wouldn't want to go through the struggle of quitting again. He sat silent sipping his wine. He found it awkward conversing through an interpreter.

Chin Ling finished his second glass of wine and said, "It is painful for me to sit very long. If you will excuse me I will lie down now."

In evident pain and with help from the table, Chin Ling got to his feet and limped the short distance to his cot at the side of the room. The old man lay down on his cot with a sigh and then released the cloth curtain so it dropped to the floor, giving him some privacy.

"My grandfather will rest now. He is old and tires easily. The pain from his arthritis consumes his strength making him spend much time in bed."

Dawson openly studied Lati, while she glanced around the room, with a quick glance or two at him. She's nervous now that we're alone, he thought. Alone? He smiled, thinking of her grandfather only four feet away with a thin cloth separating them. I wonder how she would look with out the ao dai. Sure would like to find out. But it's not going to happen today. Have to figure out how we can be alone.

Finally, Lati said, "I would like some tea." "Will you drink some if I make it?"

Dawson nodded, with a slight smile, keeping his eyes on Lati. It was obvious that made her more uneasy. He didn't want to make her feel uncomfortable, but he continued studying her. It was hard for him to believe a mature woman could get so flustered by a man's attention. Could it be an act, he wondered.

As Lati busied herself lighting the two burner kerosene stove Dawson examined the room in more detail. It was one room where they cooked and ate and slept. It had a faint musty smell, but was as neat and clean as a room with a sand-packed floor can be. Along one side were two narrow cots built up off the floor with rough lumber. They were against the wall, end-to-end and divided by a hanging light green cloth partition. A wire was strung near the ceiling with the light green material hanging to the floor, separating the cots from the rest of the small room and from each other. It gave each of them a separate compartment of about three feet by six feet.

Dawson watched Lati in the back of the room, where she leaned over a kerosene stove setting on wood boxes. He noted storage shelves were wood boxes stacked one on another. There's no counter or sink. Of course! What good is a sink without water? What luxury we enjoy in the United States, and most Americans don't even realize it.

Lati gracefully carried a small metal pot of tea and two cups to the table and sat down. After she had poured the tea, wisps of steam rose and the smell of light Chinese tea replaced the fading tobacco smoke and musty smell.

Watching Lati in silence for a few moments, Dawson sipped the tea, reflecting on what Chin Ling had said. "Your grandfather is old but his mind is quite active. He seems sure of what he says. I hope his predictions are wrong."

"My grandfather is a very wise man. He understands things others do not. When we lived in the North many people came to him for counsel on business and political matters." She hesitated, thinking. "I believe my grandfather is correct. At my work I hear much that supports what he said. Vietnamese generals want the Americans to go into North Vietnam with ground forces. American generals would like to, but cannot. They speak of winning the war by bombing and wearing down the Viet Cong. I think they know it will not succeed. But they have no choice, they must obey orders."

Dawson frowned, his voice filled with concern. "If you really believe the Viet Cong will eventually take over, it must make you anxious. Don't you worry for your own safety and your grandfather's? I think it'll be worse than when you were in North Vietnam-there will be no place to go."

Lati tilted her head to the left, then shrugged. "I do not think of it often. I cannot change what is coming, so it makes no sense to worry. My grandfather says he will not live much longer, that he will not be here when the Viet Cong take control. For myself I do not worry because I have an inner peace that cannot be destroyed-I am a Christian."

Christian! Her declaration quelled his amorous thoughts. It reminded him of his mother, of the holy-roller churches he had attended as a boy, and the pressure on him to become a Christian. He hadn't liked it then and now he thought, What's so important about being a Christian. To change the subject, he asked, "Do you want me to help you put the light on your bicycle?"

Lati nodded her head, with a shy, grateful smile. "I would appreciate that. "I am not so good with things mechanical."

She didn't have a screwdriver, so Dawson used his utility knife. While attaching the light to the bike, he thought about Lati and her situation. He visualized what it would be like for her after her grandfather died and then much worse if the V.C. took control. A deep pang of fear for her suddenly shot through him..

Finishing, he stood up and smiled at Lati, standing within arms reach. What would she do if I pulled her into my arms. I wonder what she wears under that thin ao dai. Her small mouth with full lips looks so inviting. The urge to kiss her was almost irresistible. He didn't have the nerve, with Chin Ling only a few feet away. Placing a loose-clenched right fist into his left hand, he exerted pressure, cracking the knuckles of all four fingers. Dawson felt his face flush when Lati glanced at his hands without saying anything. "I think I should go now. It's getting late," he said, after a prolonged silence.

"I would like for you to stay longer, but I understand you must go. Please promise you will come again soon. It is better talking here than standing on the road with people watching and thinking bad things. My grandfather and I would like for you to visit us again. Thank you for the presents. The tobacco will give my grandfather much pleasure and the light will keep me safe at night."

He welcomed the wind blowing through the jeep as it cooled his desire. The war, his work, had no place in his mind that was filled with Lati. He thought of how her body would feel through the thin ao dai and wondered how she would respond to his kisses. Is she as cool and composed as she appears? he wondered. But is sex all I want from her? That thought slowed his racing mind. He didn't recognize another feeling trying to insert itself into his thoughts.

Dawson shook his head and changed the subject in his mind. He pondered Lati's simple, trusting attitude. Amidst the bloodshed and chaos of war, she seems to possess some inner strength, like a coat of armor giving her protection and comfort. He told himself, be careful, don't get in too deep.

Chapter 7

With the new year came cold rain in an endless downpour. The monsoon set in with the sun not showing itself for days at a time. Even in his foul-weather jacket, with its cotton inner lining, Dawson felt cold as he looked at the Vietnamese in their light clothing. It's a wonder they aren't down with flu or pneumonia most of the winter. The women's ao dais and the men's trousers were of thin cotton; certainly not heavy enough for winter wear. Their jackets were light and not at all warm looking.

As the weather made it more and more difficult for air attacks to stem the flow of supplies down the Ho Chi Minh Trail, the attacks around Da Nang increased. The dense jungle and incessant rain were Viet Cong allies. American forces were more and more restricted in their search and destroy missions. Night rocket and mortar attacks became more frequent and American forces spent more time in mortar trenches and bunkers.

Seabees built underground bunkers for Marine commands and other fighting forces around Da Nang, but they hadn't diverted the manpower needed to provide better protection for themselves at Red Beach. Seabee officers at the regiment ended up wet and cold in their open mortar trenches night after night.

Following Christmas, Seabees were given Sunday afternoons off. The Commodore concluded the time off added more to the morale of the men than it cost in lost production. One Sunday afternoon Lieutenant Chase organized a working party for the officers to build a bunker during their time off.

With a borrowed front-end-loader they dug a large hole in the sand between the two officer's hooches. They filled sandbags and built walls with them. At ground level they placed heavy timbers, with plastic over the top, then placed several layers of sandbags over the plastic. A narrow opening in the south end provided access. The sandbagged roof would give them some protection even from a direct hit. It was large enough to permit all of the officers to crowd-in. And it was dry! It made nights more bearable. Sitting on sandbags, some slept while waiting for attacks to end.

It took a week for Dawson's crews to string the high voltage line on poles they had already set. Safety rules were established for working on poles with the hot wire on them: One of the men went to the transformer providing power for the section to be worked on, and opened the switch. He padlocked it open and hung a sign, "Do not energize. Men working." After they were sure the circuit was dead, the work crew installed a ground wire using a "hot-stick," a ten-foot insulated pole one and one-half inches in diameter, that permitted linemen to work high-voltage lines without being electrocuted. The ground wire provided protection in the event someone cut the lock and energized the circuit while men were working on the poles.

The second morning after the high voltage system was in operation, one of Chief Martin's splicing crews found a Viet Cong dead at the bottom of a pole. Dawson received the report in his office and immediately drove to the scene. By the time he arrived a Marine Intelligence Unit was there to take charge of the body and try to determine the man's military unit. Dawson winced at the sight of the man with hands charred black, mouth open in a soundless scream. It brought back memories of a friend who had been electrocuted by a circuit he thought was dead.

"Either he couldn't read or he didn't believe the sign," Chief Martin said. "Anyway, that one won't cut any more cable. They're not sure whether he died of the shock or of a broken neck when he hit the ground."

The next morning Dawson went with Perod and two of his crews to an area where they had been setting poles and stringing cable. They had hit a snag. Chief Perod didn't think they would be able to set the poles along the route specified. The route shown cut across a field that had been dry when the drawing was made, now it was flooded with a foot of water. It was impossible to get equipment in to work. Perod wanted to follow the road, which would add a quarter of a mile to the line, but would be faster than working through the marshy area. They finished checking the proposed new route and were back where one crew was busy setting a pole. The other crew had gone back down the pole line to splice cable on poles they had worked on the day before.

One of the linemen yelled down the road, "Hey! We got another one."

Perod and Dawson jumped in his jeep and drove four spans down the road. A bare wire hung down from the high voltage line, with a Viet Cong still clutching it, curled up in the grass.

"That would've been a neat trick," Perod said. "But the dumb bugger shouldn't have held on to it after he threw the other end over the hot wire. I bet this'll cure them from messing with our cable."

The day after the second Viet Cong had been killed Padelford called Dawson into his office. It was the first time he had bothered Dawson since being chewed out by the Commodore. "Have you seen what Chief Perod has painted on the door of his pickup?"

"No, Commander, I didn't know he had anything painted on it except the vehicle number."

"Well, he has a drawing of a man labeled 'V.C.' and two marks under it. It's crude and sadistic to advertise the number of men killed by your hot wire."

"Nothing to get excited about, Commander," Dawson answered calmly. "He's only keeping score like they did in World War II on the sides of planes and ships showing the number of planes shot down or ships sunk."

Padelford became more excited. "I won't have it. I want you to have it removed. Today!"

"I think it would be better to leave it. It'll be good for morale. My men get shot at and they don't get a chance to shoot back. That symbol will help them feel they're participating in the fighting more directly rather than being only support forces. Most men risking their lives would rather be able to shoot back. I think their little V.C. score board will help them psychologically."

"Lieutenant, I'm telling you to get those marks off that pickup."

"Before I do, sir, I'll see the Commodore and explain my position."

"You stay out of the Commodore's office. I'll talk with him about this; I'm sure he will agree with me. That's all. You're dismissed."

Nothing more was said about removing the score tally on the pickup door. Men talked about it throughout the camp; it gave some measure of prestige to the men working on SIMPCOM. They joked about it and other enlisted men ridiculed it. But it showed they had done more than just plant poles and string telephone cable. It also eased the frustration the men felt as sitting ducks for V.C. snipers.

Charley quit cutting telephone cable and punching holes in it, so there was less rework and more effort was concentrated on new work. Sniper activity had dwindled considerably since the Patrols started. Construction in the swampy area was completed; now the pole line construction was concentrated in several sections of hilly terrain away from the sea and rivers. Most of the soil contained shale, making it more stable, and vegetation was sparse on the rolling hills. But it gave Dawson something else to worry about. Charley moved in and out of the hill area regularly, where there were countless draws large enough to hide a squad. The Seabees set up direct radio communications with the nearest Marine unit. They realized the new danger and remained on a high level of alert while still doing their work.

Even with the continuing heavy rain, their equipment managed to get the job done. The shale on the higher ground made it easier to work than in the rice paddies. In places, the hills were red gumbo mud and at times the heavy line trucks bogged down to their axles and had to be dug or pulled out. But the trucks were able to dig the holes and the men rapidly set the poles.

It was 0800 when Dawson drove through the First Marine Tank Command toward one of his crew's construction area. He stopped at the check point as he was leaving the Tank Command.

"Some of your men ran into trouble down the road," the Marine guard said. "I told them the road hadn't been swept and they should wait, but they didn't. So they hit a mine."

Two miles down the road Dawson found Chief Martin with two of his cable crews unloading equipment and material from a line truck which would never see service again. The entire rear end of the truck had been demolished.

"Anyone hurt, Chief?" Dawson asked.

"No, sir. We were lucky. Must've been a pressure mine. It didn't detonate until the heavier rear wheels were on in. If it had gone off under the front wheels I would've lost three men."

Dawson gritted his teeth to control his anger, as he glared at the chief. "The Marine guard said you came on through before they had swept the road. You know my orders. You're supposed to wait until the road has been cleared, anytime the Marines say it hasn't been swept. You can get court-martialed for this."

"Let me explain, Lieutenant. We were waiting at the check point like we're supposed to when Commander Padelford came up behind us. He asked what we were waiting for and I told him. He said that he hadn't received any report of Charley activity in this area last night. He told me we were wasting time and that we should go on through."

"Didn't you tell him I had given specific orders to wait until the road was clear?"

"Yes, sir, I tried to argue with him. I told him, 'It's against Lieutenant Dawson's orders.' He said: 'I am giving you new orders, Chief. I'm ordering you to move your men out now.' I considered refusing to obey his order, but I figured I would end up in the brig. I asked him, 'Commander, would you like to lead the way?' He said, 'If you don't get in your vehicle immediately, I'll have you up on charges for insubordination.' So we drove on; and this is what happened. The Commander was behind us when we hit the mine. As I was checking things over he came up to me and said, 'I guess we should have waited.' I didn't even reply. I did an about face and got away from him so I wouldn't be on report for striking an officer."

"OK, Chief. I understand; you didn't have much choice. I'm glad all we lost was a vehicle," Dawson said as he patted him on the shoulder by of apology. "You'll need another line truck, see Chief Wilson. He may know the location of one we can get right away. I'll take care of that Commander. Where is he?"

"He turned around and went back. He was real shook up when he left."

Dawson made the ten minute trip back to Red Beach in five minutes. He stomped into Commander Padelford's office and leaned forward on the desk. The threat of physical violence was so evident the Commander pushed back in his chair.

"What do you..."

Dawson leaning even closer, interrupted. "Did you order my Chief to go down that mined road after he told you why they were waiting?" The question shot out like venom. He could almost feel his fist smashing into the fat round face.

"Yes. But I didn't think it was mined and there were nine men sitting there doing nothing. I was trying to help you get your project done on time." Padelford's face was red with anger, but he remained seated with his chair pushed back against the wall.

"You almost killed some of my men. You are the sorriest excuse for a Naval Officer I've ever met. I'm going to do my best to correct that blight on the Navy." As Padelford started blustering, Dawson did an abrupt about face and stomped out. He marched rapidly to the other end of the building and into the Commodore's office.

Commodore Rhodes looked up, visibly annoyed. He wasn't accustomed to people coming into his office uninvited or unannounced. "Bill I'm very busy right now. You must have a problem to burst in here like this, but can't it wait?"

Dawson stood at attention in front of the Commodore's desk. "No, sir. It can't wait. I need to talk with you now!"

The Commodore gave an exasperated sigh and leaned back in his chair. "OK, Bill. I'll give you a few minutes. It must be pretty important to get you all steamed up like this. What has our good Commander done now? Sit down. Don't stand there like a stick of dynamite about to explode."

Dawson sat but didn't relax. His jaw muscles flexed, his hands were clenched as he explained the circumstances causing the truck to run over the mine, and then said: "Commander Padelford almost got some of my men killed. I want to bring him up on charges for countermanding my orders without justification, and for unnecessarily endangering the lives of my men."

"Bill, you're right. The Commander could be brought before a court-martial. He probably would be convicted and then reprimanded. He wouldn't be promoted, and in three more years he would be forced to retire as Commander. But that would use up many man-hours that should be devoted to fighting this war. I can solve the problem in a much smoother way."

Anger started building up in Dawson again, he clinched his teeth and his face got red. He thought the Commodore was about to suggest sweeping the incident under the rug.

"Now calm down, Bill, and listen to me a minute. Commander Padelford has been passed over for Captain once. He requested this assignment because he thought combat duty would help his chances for promotion this next year. I had reservations about his coming out here and started to block his transfer. But I was told I should give him a chance. Well, he's caused more problems than he has resolved since he arrived. I've been quietly working through Washington to get a replacement for him.

But with this incident, I'll see to it he gets a set of immediate orders back to the States, with or without a replacement. I guarantee his career is finished. He'll be put in one of the retirement graveyards and in three years he'll be permitted to retire as Commander. So you see the end result will be the same without a lot of friction and wasted manpower. This way he'll be out of our hair in a week. In the meantime I'll relieve him of his duties as Operations Officer so he won't cause more problems. That agreeable?"

Lieutenant Dawson got to his feet. "Yes, sir. He really deserves a court-martial. But you're right, it would waste a lot of man-hours."

"Fine. As you go by his office tell the Commander I want to see him."

A message was sent out to all battalions that Commander Padelford had been relieved as Operations Officer and Lieutenant Knight would fill the position until a new Operations Officer was on board. Details of the mine incident ran through the enlisted ranks like a brush fire. Dawson knew how such an incident could get blown out of proportion and effect morale. He hoped, with the commander being relieved of duties, everything would calm down again.

By the evening meal it had filtered up to the other officers. As they were eating, Lieutenant Fallon asked: "Is what I hear on the grapevine about the mine true, Bill? Is that why the Commander was relieved of his duties?"

"I imagine what you heard is pretty close to fact. The Commander screwed up and he'll be leaving us soon. I think that's enough said. The more talk there is, the more the whole incident will grow in people's minds and the more it will hurt morale. So let's not add more fuel to the fire."

"Seabees are like other military men in their reaction to orders from their officers," Case said. "Many of the management and operating decisions we make don't please all of the men. Some changes do adversely affect a small number of the men-or at least they think it has hurt them. But if there's good logic in the action, the bitching and griping of a few isn't picked up by the majority, and it soon dies out."

"Yeah, but if the officer giving the order is in error or acts capriciously, the response from the entire group can be dramatically negative," Fallon added, looking at Dawson. "When your crew was ordered to proceed before the road was cleared of mines, the men knew their lives had been put in jeopardy unnecessarily. If they were civilians and a supervisor gave them such an order, they would've told him to shove it. But because of military regulations and their training, they had to obey the order."

"And when something like that happens, a deep hatred is developed for the officer giving the order," Dawson said. "There are rumors going around that if Commander Padelford goes out alone on one of the back roads he might not return. I'll be glad when he is gone."

Fortunately Commander Padelford remained within the camp confines, spending most of his time in his quarters. Everyone was relieved when he received his orders and flew out of Vietnam four days after the incident. With him gone the Bees could look for something else to bitch and gripe about; something else to divert their thinking from the terror of war.

Everyone had just secured from work. Six officers were in the washroom. Dawson, in his hooch getting ready for dinner, was thinking of the good progress his men had made that day. It had been the first day without rain for two weeks. He was combing his hair when he heard the first "whump" in the distance. It didn't sound quite the same as a mortar exploding. While his mind was trying to decide what it was, there was a double "whump, whump," followed by the Red Beach alert siren.

Ten officers crowded into the small bunker facing south toward Da Nang and watched flashes of small explosions near the airfield.

Someone asked: "What the hell are those? Sure aren't mortars. Are they artillery rounds?"

"Nope," Case said. "Those are some of the new rockets Charley's been using up along the DMZ for the past two weeks, compliments of Russia. They have a longer range and pack a much heftier charge. Intelligence up North reports the V.C. have mobile launchers for them, launchers that men on foot can move around through the jungle."

The rockets continued pouring in, sometimes three or four impacting almost simultaneously. Two jets scrambled before the attack had become too intense; they streaked toward the hills northwest of the airfield.

Suddenly a huge orange ball lit up the entire horizon west of the airfield. "Man!" Fallon said. "They must've got a direct hit on the ammo dump." Hundreds of smaller explosions continued from the same area as one pile of explosives detonated the next one. Shock waves from the concussion rolled over Red Beach thirty seconds after the explosion. A continuous red glow came from the direction of the ammunition storage area as it burned. Bombs and rockets and mortar rounds cooked-off with increasing tempo.

"As heavy as the concussions are here, I can't imagine what it's like near ground zero," Dawson exclaimed.

Smaller steady glows lit up several areas around the airfield from fires. They provided a red backdrop for the continuing hailstorm of incoming rockets. A large cargo plane, a DC-4, passed overhead, lumbering at low altitude in the direction the jets had taken.

"There goes 'Puff the Magic Dragon,'" Case said. "He'll get them."

"Where did a name like that come from?" Dawson asked.

"Puff gets its name from the fire and destruction that spews from its side," Case said. "In the large cargo door opening in the side, a battery of rapid firing machine guns is mounted. When the suspected enemy location is identified, the slow flying plane circles the target and literally saturates the area with lead. Puff spits out thousands of rounds per minute. At night the multiple streams of tracers resemble a rain of fire. I've seen Puff in action several times up north."

The attack on the airfield lasted a half-hour, but the fires raged for several hours before they were all extinguished. Sporadic explosions from the ammunition dump continued. The smaller caliber ammunition went off like a dozen machine guns firing and then were periodically drowned out by larger projectiles exploding.

Men at Red Beach had a late dinner that evening. But at the airfield and surrounding area men dealt with more serious problems.

In the morning as Dawson visited job sites, he saw the extensive damage done by last night's attack. The ammunition storage area was now stable, and demolition men were busy removing live ammunition. They had plenty of work to do clearing the runway and roads littered with unexploded projectiles and bombs. Dawson's crews were already busy replacing several spans of cable in the ammo area when he came by.

A large two-story barracks the Seabees had recently completed for an Air Force jet squadron was flattened. It had received a direct hit at one end, and looked like it had been smashed by a giant hand. Half of the ammo storage area had gone up. Earth berms around each pile of ammunition was the only thing that kept the entire dump from blowing. Several planes were destroyed. Over twenty buildings were demolished or severely damaged. As Dawson looked at the damage, he thought the casualty list would be large.

That evening an unofficial report placed American casualties at twelve KIA, and Vietnamese civilian fatalities at about the same number. The mortar trenches really do a lot of good, Dawson thought. Most of the men were probably in trenches after the first rockets hit, otherwise hundreds would've been killed.

None of the line crews were working along the main road between Da Nang and the Refugee Village, so Dawson didn't get to see Lati when she rode home from work. He had lunch with her once but hadn't been able to visit at her home because of work. Although the Bees were supposed to have Sunday afternoon off, there always seemed to be problems that required Dawson's time.

His feelings were mixed and more than a little confused. Pat occupied less and less of his thinking and Lati more and more. Dawson began to realize the real reason he had resisted marrying Pat, when he compared his feelings for her with his feelings for Lati.

He found Lati very desirable and wanted to make love with her-he thought of that often. He certainly needed some physical love; although he knew it wouldn't be only physical between them. A deeper more enduring feeling, they both recognized, already existed. It was that deeper feeling of love, of respect that kept him from aggressively pursuing his physical desire.

Other factors also troubled him. He wondered if she would be receptive; and the right time and place hadn't presented itself. But if those were the only inhibitors, he would've found a way around them, or at least he would've made a strong attempt. The moral issue was what really held him back. And that, he thought, was strange since he hadn't let moral constraints hold him back in the past. When he thought about the situation, he wasn't at all sure his desire wouldn't override this unfamiliar moral restraint.

Four weeks after his first visit, Dawson knocked on Lati's door early Sunday afternoon. When she opened the door and saw Dawson, color flowed into her face as she brushed loose hair back. "Oh, it is you! I...I, aah, please come in."

"I'm sorry to come unannounced. But I have the afternoon off and want to see you. There wasn't any way to contact you, so here I am."

"Oh it is all right. You are welcome in our home anytime. If I had known you were coming I would have made myself presentable."

Dawson stepped inside, taking her right hand in both of his. "You're always presentable to me," he said smiling and looking into her flushed, upturned face.

Chin Ling was seated at the rough, clean table reading in the dim light. As he looked up and spoke in greeting, Dawson thought how old and tired he looked. Much more so than on his previous visit. Lati took Dawson's poncho, and spread it on a box in the corner to dry.

The two men talked of war, of the weather and of the dissident college students in the United States. Lati voiced no opinion of her own, she only interpreted for the two men.

Chin Ling said, "You see how well the Communists work? First they capture the young minds. They give them a cause and then goad them into action. That presents a great problem for your President. That is the way the Viet Minh came to power in my country after the great war. They prey on young minds open to new ideas and filled with ideals. The Communists exploit the ideals to their advantage. They preach a social reform that young, unseasoned minds quickly embrace. They do not detect the lies, the distorted logic until too late."

Dawson listened more than he talked. He could tell the old man enjoyed talking on world matters to someone whom he believed could understand what he was saying, which did not include his granddaughter, who was only a woman. Dawson enjoyed watching Lati as she interpreted. She had tied her long dark hair back with a simple white ribbon. Her lovely, enticing mouth moved fluently as she spoke Vietnamese, and it pursed with hesitation at times, on some English words.

The more Dawson studied her face the more beautiful she seemed. Her mouth and eyes were delightfully expressive as she tried to impart meaning along with the words. A few times Dawson smiled at her as she faltered, searching her mind for the right English word. His smile brought a bright flush to her face and she became flustered.

After a while Chin Ling excused himself and hobbled over to his cot. Dawson wondered if it was really because of the arthritis or if it was to give Lati and him some privacy-what privacy possible in a ten by fourteen-foot room with a cloth partition.

As they sat at the table talking, Lati seemed to get embarrassed easily. She avoided direct eye contact, when Dawson took her hand in his. She didn't resist or withdraw her hand, nor did she respond, other than nervously biting her lip.

"We could...I mean ..." Her face lit up again. She closed her eyes and swallowed before gently, slowly withdrawing her hand. "I will make tea for us."

Lati had her back to Dawson as she prepared the tea at the stove. He watched her in silence, desire flowing through him like a warm flood. Quietly he came up behind her. His heart hammered louder and faster as desire increased. When his hands encompassed her tiny waist, she started in surprise with a quick intake of breath. Then she froze, not even breathing. Dawson gently turned her by the shoulders. She didn't resist. She looked up into his eyes with one quick glance and then looked down. She was stiff and frightened.

With one hand under her chin he gently tilted her face up. Her eyes were filled with anxiety. She frowned questioningly, helplessly, like someone looking for a way to escape. He gently kissed her closed lips. Then looking into her large brown eyes, he said quietly, "Don't be afraid, Lati, I won't hurt you." A quick frown crossed her face again as Dawson pulled her closer to him and kissed her again. This time he covered her lips with quick, soft kisses until her mouth lost its immobility and became alive. She relaxed in his arms as he drew her close. He could feel the quickening of her breath and the warmth of her body through thin cotton material.

Now the fear was gone. Her eyes were filled with warmth and wonder. Her mouth parted, inviting as she placed her arms around his neck drawing herself up to meet his lips. Her body trembled against his and she pulled herself closer. For a few minutes they forgot the old man lying on the cot a few feet away.

Then Lati pushed back, her hands on Dawson's chest. Her eyes mirrored the passion he felt. She shook her head slightly to bring herself back to reality. He tried to draw her closer to kiss her again. But she said, "No. Please! We must stop. I am afraid of what will happen."

"But I don't want to stop. I want you now."

She shook her head, her eyes pleading for understanding.

Dawson wanted her so very much and he thought she felt the same. Even when he remembered her grandfather, his passion was flowing so strong, he wanted to make love to her there and then. But as his thoughts cleared and he looked at her cot end to end with her grandfather's, with only cloth draped between, he knew he couldn't do it, even if she was willing. When he released her, she quickly busied herself with the tea.

As they sat at the table quietly sipping tea, Dawson reached across the table and took her small hand in his, studying her open trusting face. Now she didn't avoid his gaze. As he looked into her eyes, he wondered how this lovely woman had managed to work her way into his heart. No words seemed necessary. Their eyes communicated better than words. Lies can be formed with words, but what they saw in each other's eyes left no doubt of the truth. A mutual feeling of love, respect and passion flowed between them.

Dawson leaned across the narrow table and pressed his lips softly, quickly to hers. "I love you, Lati Noi," he said smiling, the tenderness he felt apparent in his voice. "And not just with my body. My body desires you and needs you. But..." he paused trying to sort out his feelings. "My heart and mind also feel a different love."

The shyness she had shown previously when their talk became personal, had diminished. Her face radiated happiness, eyes glistening with wonder and joy and love. "I have had strange feelings for you since we first talked on the road. I do not understand these feelings. I have not experienced this kind of love before. I have loved Father and Mother and Grandfather for as long as I can remember; it has been a special feeling of love and respect and affection. But this new feeling in me is almost frightening. It is so new, so wonderful, I feel as though I cannot contain it. I have read much of love between a man and woman, but the thousands of words I have read seem inadequate."

"Have you never loved a man before? Didn't you have a childhood sweetheart?"

Lati gave a helpless shrug. "There was a family arrangement when I was very small. But he was killed by the Viet Minh before I was of age to marry. My feelings for him were that of a friend. He came to our home many times as a guest, but we did not speak of love. I was only a child and knew him as a kind man whom my family said I would marry when I was old enough."

"Surely there've been other men in your life since then. I'm amazed you weren't married long ago. With your beauty and temperament, there must've been many men wanting to marry you."

Lati smiled shaking her head. "You do not understand the situation in North Vietnam. First, the many years of war; then when the Viet Minh took control, years of persecution of people who would not accept their way-accept Communism. My family were considered subversives. And I was an outcast because of being a Christian, and Amerasian.

"Oh there were men who wanted me; Viet Minh, or Viet Cong as they are now known, but they wanted only my body. They had no respect or compassion or love; they wanted only to use me as a thing, to degrade me and destroy my beliefs. I could not accept any of them as a husband and would not agree to their demands outside of marriage. Please, let us not speak of the bad things of my past. Too many sad memories intrude on the wonderful feelings you have awakened in me.

"You know much about me, but I know little about you. You speak of love; do you not have a woman in America whom you love? I do not think you are a man to live a solitary life for the many years since your divorce."

Dawson took a sip of tea, trying to decide what he should share with this woman he knew so little. "Well, I have known many women since my wife..., and I've loved some of them-it was a love driven by passion and desire. Nothing permanent developed. I have a girl friend in the States who wants to get married, but I don't. I guess that's because I'm not in love with her." Dawson paused, as those words, now spoken, registered deep inside him. "She doesn't cause the same feelings in me that you do."

Lati canted her head with a questioning look. "I am not at all sure of your meaning when you talk of your love for a woman, but then say you are not in love with her. I have not considered that before. I must think on your words and try to understand what you mean. If your girl friend wants to marry you and wants to have children, which is the natural thing, I think she must be unhappy because you do not. That is sad. What will you do when you return to America? Will you marry her?"

"Now we're getting into a subject I'd rather not talk about. I don't know what I'll do. I like talking about us, and what we're going to do. Now that I know how warm and loving, and passionate you are, I want more of you. But with your grandfather present, what can we do?"

She looked toward her grandfather's cot, secluded by the drop cloth. "I cannot deny what you say. I feel something very strongly when we kiss. The feeling is new to me, a feeling I have only read about until now. My heart and mind do not know how to cope with it. I know what I want to do, but that conflicts with what I think I should do-what I know is right. Lati stood and then said: "I must be by my self to think on this-this inner confusion. I do not mean to be inhospitable, but I need to be alone now, to try and sort out these conflicting thoughts and emotions."

"I don't really want to leave," Dawson said touching her cheek gently. "But if you want me to, I will."

When she handed him the poncho, he drew her close with one arm and kissed her gently. As he was leaving Lati asked, "You will come back soon?"

"Yes, when I can. I'll see you along the road or in the park this next week."

Driving to Red Beach, with the wind pulling at his cap, Dawson's mind replayed Lati's question, "What will you do when you return to the States?" Good question. What am I going to do about Pat? He shook his head impatiently, indecision gnawing inside him.

Chapter 8

For a change, the officers had a class "A" movie most of them hadn't seen and there was no rain on the tin roof to compete with the sound. After the movie Red Havner remained to close up the bar as usual, and Case and Dawson went to their hooch. Dawson was in his room writing to Pat when he heard hammering down the hall. He found Case in Havner's room nailing his combat boots to the floor.

Dawson shook his head. "You really work at it Roger. I ought to tell Red who the gremlin is."

Case laughed. "He knows who to blame. He can't catch me at it that's all. I have to give him something to gripe about once in a while or he'll think I don't like him."

"Some day, Roger, he's going to return the favors." Dawson had no idea how prophetic his statement was.

The next morning Red cursed loudly as he tried to put on his boots. He came down the hall and stopped at Case's room. "You did it again, didn't you, Roger?"

Case turned and looked with mock surprise. "What're you talking about, Red? Did what?"

"You know what I'm talking about. You nailed my boots to the deck. I need to borrow your hammer so I can get ready for work."

Havner came in a few nights later-sober, and looking into Roger's room found him sound asleep. Dawson was reading when Havner entered his room and asked, "You want to help me fix up our good buddy across the hall?"

"What you got in mind, Red?"

"I've had a man in the warehouse saving Styrofoam packing liners for the past month. There's a whole pickup load now, and I'm going to fill Roger's room with them. You know how soundly he sleeps, nothing bothers him. So if we're careful he won't wake up."

Dawson smiled and got up. "Sure I'll help. He deserves some harassment."

The two men loaded a pickup with Styrofoam pieces of every imaginable shape and size. They started stacking pieces right next to Case's bed. They had just got started when one of the other officers came in slamming the entrance door. Dawson and Havner froze where they were. Case grunted and turned over facing the wall. The two men continued stacking Styrofoam from floor to ceiling, filling every cubic foot of space in the room except the 30-inch by 6-foot area occupied by Case's cot. To complete the job and fill the room to the entrance, they had to get another partial pickup load from the supply yard.

When they finished, Havner admired their work. "That was more fun than getting drunk. I wish I could see his face in the morning when he wakes up. In the morning when he starts yelling, don't help him. Don't even answer. I want him to dig his way out if he can."

The next morning Dawson got up extra early and woke Havner so they could enjoy their night's work. While shaving, his mind drifted to Lati, as it did more and more lately. He remembered the feel of her body pressed against his, and her warm trusting eyes. How am I ever going to get her alone? Could send the old man to the store for something. Sure, with his arthritis! He felt ashamed for the desperate thought. He cupped his hands under the faucet and splashed cold water on his face. That cooled him off.

Red was sitting quietly with Dawson in his room when Case's alarm clock went off. He kept it under his cot on the floor, and couldn't reach it because of the Styrofoam. They heard him grumble, "What the...? What in bloody blue blazes is going on?" He tried to push the white wall out of his way, but it was a cube of Styrofoam 7-feet high, 8-feet wide, and 7-feet thick going toward the entrance.

"Hey! Get me out of here. Anybody out there?" Case yelled. "All right you clowns. I know you're out there. But I guess the game is for me to get myself out." He started stacking pieces of Styrofoam, first placing them on his cot, and then stacking them behind him as he made a narrow corridor to the entrance.

Havner and Dawson slipped out quietly before Case reached the hall. They laughed and congratulated each other all the way to the officer's mess. When Fan Ti Wa brought their breakfast, Dawson told her Lieutenant Case would be a little late and to save him something to eat.

Case finally got to the hall, then he had to pull out the Styrofoam and stack it in the hall so he could open his locker to get dressed. He emptied his room lining one side of the hall with packing material. By the time he got to the officer's mess everyone had finished eating and were sipping on their last cup of coffee before going to work.

Case had a glint in his eyes as he approached the table. "Red, no doubt that was your little prank."

Red shrugged, looking innocent. "I don't have any idea what prank you're referring to. Do you know what he's talking about, Bill?"

"Sure don't, Red. He must've got up on the wrong side of the bed this morning."

"OK! OK! Don't give me that innocence crap. So you were in on it too, Bill. You can both stand by. You have one coming from me. And it'll be a good one. Don't turn your back or close your eyes. You never know when the phantom will strike."

Lieutenant Knight filled in two weeks as Operations Officer. The new OPS Officer, Lieutenant Commander Eduardo Sanchez, arrived none too soon to suit Knight. He was having trouble keeping his own projects on-track as well as doing the OPS Officer's work.

Case and Dawson were trying to hurry with their showers. "I can't decide whether the water or the air is coldest," Case said. "Wonder if we'll get a water heater installed before I leave?"

"Well, one thing for sure, this unheated building and cold water discourages frequent or long showers," Dawson replied as he shivered and hurriedly rinsed off. "What do you think of the new OPS officer?"

"Looks like he will be a great improvement. He spent two days up along the DMZ with me this week, and strikes me as being very sharp. Seems to grasp things quickly. Should fit in nicely with our group. No pomp and polish. I like him."

"He rode around with me today," Dawson said. "I took him to most of my work sites, and he doesn't mind getting his boots muddy with the rest of us. He seems to have a practical outlook on things. In my book, he's a vast improvement on the last OPS officer. He let me know he was here to help in any way he could. That's a welcome change. He even told me an off-color Mexican joke. I think it was to let me know he isn't sensitive about being Mexican."

The next time Dawson visited Lati she seemed withdrawn. It appeared she didn't want to be alone with him. Her grandfather didn't go to his bunk, he sat and talked a while and then read. Knowing the old man didn't understand English, Dawson tried to not let his presence bother him as he talked with Lati.

"Lati, I've thought about you a great deal since we were together last, and I've missed being with you very much." After a few seconds of silence, he asked, "Do you think of me when you're at work?"

She only glanced at him quickly and then looked down. "Well, a little. But mostly I think about my work." Then she changed the subject. "I try to not discuss anything classified with my grandfather. But he is constantly talking about how the war is going. He thinks the Viet Cong are going to build up their forces more; and from what I hear discussed at work, the generals and admirals believe the same."

Dawson couldn't understand her cool attitude. He tried to think of what he had done to cause her act so remote. He shrugged when he couldn't figure it out. "I hear and see enough of the war every day. When I'm with you I would like to talk about something more personal-like how I want to take you in my arms and kiss you.

"My grandfather would not consider that at all proper."

"I am not asking what your grandfather thinks. I'm asking about you. Don't you remember the last time we were together? I thought it was a very special day."

Chin Ling cleared his throat, looked up from his paper, and then continued reading. Dawson guessed Lati had asked her grandfather to remain up so she could avoid physical contact with him.

Her hands were in her lap, fingers nervously fiddling with each other. "Of course I remember. The day was special for me too. But I do not know how to manage the new feelings you cause within me."

Every time Dawson got the conversation on a personal vein, Lati changed it. He became frustrated when she refused to talk about them. After two hours of small talk and three cups of tea, he said: "I thought you wanted me to visit you, but now I'm not so sure. Would you prefer I don't bother you any more?"

Lati's eyes showed alarm at his question. After a short pause she said: "I do want you to visit me again. I don't know how to explain my thinking now. Things are confusing, troubling in my mind. When you come again, my thoughts will be clear. I promise."

He wanted to hold her close, but knew she would not like that, in front of her grandfather. So he told them both good by and left, very confused. Maybe she doesn't want us to have a deeper relationship, he thought. And exactly what is it I want? More than just getting her into bed? He shook his head in exasperation as he headed toward Red Beach.

At a Sunday morning briefing early in February Dawson reported: "Commodore, tomorrow we'll start cutting over to the new system. The switchboards are in place and have been tested, all of the cable has been installed. Now it's a matter of connecting all field switchboards and telephones to the central switchboards. We'll start with the major commands, and work our way out to the smaller units. I expect the cut-over to be completed in about a week. In most cases we'll leave the old system intact, to function as a back-up in the event of major problems with the new system."

The Commodore interrupted, "Do you anticipate problems with the new one?"

"No, sir. But if Charley should knock out one of the main switchboards, or do extensive damage to some of the main cables, we can switch back to the old switchboards and cables while the new one is being repaired. If everything goes smoothly, we should have the new system in operation one week ahead of the deadline. I figure it'll take another week to work out some minor bugs, then as far as I'm concerned the project is finished. I'll return the men to their battalions, and MCB-6 will take over the maintenance and operation of it."

The Commodore nodded approval. "Fine, Bill. I'll be happy to report to the Admiral and Generals that the system will be in operation on schedule. I want you to stay after the briefing, and we'll talk about your new assignment."

After the other officers had left, Commodore Rhodes said, "Bill, I want you to know I personally as well as officially appreciate the work you've done here. I realize you had some unnecessary problems. But you were able to proceed with the job despite them. The new communications system will be of great value and help us get the job done here. Now as to your new job: I'm sure you know Roger Case has received his orders, and you may've already figured out you're to be his relief. I know you'll do as good on that job as the one you're completing. Any questions?"

"No, sir. Roger and I have discussed his work some. I assumed I would get his job since I'm winding up my project about the time he's due to leave. I think it'll be an interesting job. Roger's going to leave a gap that will be hard to fill, but I'll give it my best effort."

Sunday afternoon following the completion of SIMPCOM, Dawson visited Lati and her grandfather. Lati seemed more cordial and open than last time. Chin Ling welcomed Dawson into his home and sat talking for a few minutes before he crawled into his bunk and pulled the curtain-that's what it reminded Dawson of, a shipboard bunk hung from the bulkhead.

"The way you acted the last time I was here, I wondered if you were angry with me. I even wondered if you wanted to stop seeing me," Dawson said, looking directly at Lati with disappointment in his eyes. "I don't understand what made you change."

Her lovely child-like face held a sad, concerned look. She quickly reached out placing her hand on his. "No. Please do not think I do not want to see you any more. I know I acted terrible the last time you were here. My grandfather told me that too. I was not angry with you. My thoughts, my feelings were very confused." She paused for a few seconds, her eyes on his, pleading for understanding. "I was angry with myself because of my confusion and fear. I was afraid to be alone with you, afraid you would kiss me and cause those disturbing feelings to bubble up inside me again."

He squeezed her hand and smiled. "Are you not afraid now? I still want to kiss you and hold you tight in my arms. But I won't unless you want me to."

"Yes, I am still afraid. Not of you, but of my own emotions. One part of me is afraid, another part wants you to kiss me. The other part, my desire, is stronger now I believe." Her smile was shy but inviting, as she glanced up with her head tilted down.

Dawson kissed the palm of her right hand he was holding. Then he leaned over and kissed her gently, lingeringly on the mouth. Her lips, warm and pliant at first, quickly became mobile and inviting. Pulling her to her feet, he drew her close. She stood on her toes, her mouth seeking his. As they kissed and Dawson caressed her petite body through seductively thin, satin-like material, the old man lying six feet away was forgotten. The metallic "tat-tat-tat" of rain on the tin roof was drowned out by the increased tempo of two hearts. The damp chill of the room was replaced by a warm glow.

When Dawson's hands moved down over her buttocks, Lati's arms tightened around his neck. The tremor he felt ran through her body, added more fuel to his excitement. Then Lati pushed back, but Dawson's hands held her tight at the waist. She leaned back, breathlessly pleading in a trembling whisper, "We must stop now or I do not know what will happen."

"I know. I know," Dawson whispered, still holding her tight against him at the waist. "But I want you very much, and you feel so good in my arms. I... I know we can't do anything-with your grandfather right over there. I want to so much, but I realize we can't make love here, now."

She relaxed against him as he held her quietly, one hand low on her back and the other high. Realizing she wore no brassiere aroused him more. As he felt her firm breasts pressing against his lower chest, he desired her more than he could remember ever wanting a woman before.

With her head pressed against his chest, she said, "I think it is good my grandfather is here." Disengaging his arms, she stepped back. "I will make some tea."

Dawson could hear in her voice, the passion she felt. It was husky and soft at the same time. Not only does she have bedroom eyes, she has a bedroom voice too, he thought as he reached out caressing the side of her face. "But I want you, not tea."

She raised her eyebrows and tilted her head with a "me too" look. "The tea will calm us and make us warm," she said.

"You warm me more than all the tea I could ever drink."

"But I cannot calm you like the tea," she said, turning to the stove.

He watched her body move under the thin loose ao dai. He visualized what she would look like without clothes. If only we were alone, he thought, shaking his head, trying to clear delicious images fueling the raging fire inside.

As she carried tea to the table, her eyes met Dawson's. The look was warm and affectionate. Her small, full mouth formed a revealing smile, making him wonder if she could ever be anything but honest. He doubted she even knew how to act coy. Her direct innocence stirred feelings within him, unrelated to passion-unexpected feelings.

They talked for a long time, with periods of silence when they simply enjoying looking at each other and the touch of the other's hand. They both felt the physical effects of tension caused by the unfulfilled passion that had enveloped them. While the tea calmed them, loving looks and soft words soothed their stifled desire.

Holding her hand, Dawson looked deep into Lati's eyes. "I may not get to see you as much from now on. I finished the SIMPCOM project and have been assigned a new job, working with our battalions in Dong Ha and along the DMZ. I'll still be in Da Nang part of each week, but I don't know how much time I'll have or what my schedule will be. I'll come to see you when I can."

Her eyes clouded with concern, her hand clasped his. "I am sad because you must go to that area. It is much more dangerous than here. I shall be very happy when I see you and know you are safe."

"Don't worry. I'll still be in construction. My job won't be as dangerous as a combat soldier's. I'll spend much of my time traveling to job sites, mostly in controlled areas. So there's nothing to worry about."

"You will be in my prayers," Lati said, as Dawson was leaving. "I will pray for you every day. Only God can insure your safety."

Dawson paused at the door for a moment. He really didn't know what to say, so he gave a small shrug. "Thanks. I guess prayer can't hurt."

A few days before Dawson completed the SIMPCOM project he received a letter from Pat Russell that really bothered him. She had been writing regularly, and even though Lati had been occupying more and more of his thoughts, he looked forward to Pat's letters. They kept him connected to the civilized world. Her letters gave him something to look forward to. Her words of love and encouragement gave some meaning to the chaos surrounding him. They made the incessant rain, the cold, the ever present danger more bearable because he knew there was someone to go back to. At least they did until he started seeing Lati. Since then, they added a new element of chaos in his mind, along with pangs of guilt.

When Dawson got his mail after he knocked off for the day, he was wet, and cold, and tired. As he walked in the rain to his hooch, with Pat's letter in his hand, his mind dwelt on this new dilemma. What kind of jerk am I? Here I'm supposed to love Pat, but I find myself thinking more and more of Lati. How would I feel if Pat was messing around with some guy while I'm over here? A month ago it would have made me angry. But now? I really don't know. Guess I've been drifting along with the tide, not thinking about where I'm headed. That isn't good.

He opened Pat's letter in his room, after he had spread out his poncho to dry.

Dearest Bill,

Writing a letter like this to you, considering your present circumstances, may seem cruel and heartless. I'm sorry, for it isn't my intent to hurt you or add to your troubles. But I think I would be unfair to you if I continue to let you believe you can return, and we'll go on as before. I can't live like that any longer.

I want you to know I love you as much as ever (and that is very much). Nothing has happened to change my love for you. If anything, it has deepened with the loss and longing I feel since you left. We have discussed this several times, and you've always managed to talk me into accepting your point of view.

You know I want to have children while I am still young enough, and I won't have them outside of wedlock. You have resisted the idea of marriage. You haven't said "not ever," but you keep putting it "on the back burner," as you say. Well, the back burner doesn't work now. So we need to bring it forward in our relationship, and decide what we are going to do. I want you to understand that when you return our situation will have to change.

I have presented the problem directly (and you have always been one to get right to the point). With your love of logic, the prior paragraph should make my position clear. I would like for you to think it over for the next few months. I'll not bring the subject up again because I want to be as supportive as I can be while you're overseas. But when you return, either we will be married, or we'll go our separate ways and each make a new life.

Please don't be angry with me. Know that I love you. Believe me when I say this is the most difficult letter I've ever written. I had to write this because it would be more unfair to let you believe that when you return things between us can go on as they have been. I know it seems as though I'm issuing an ultimatum, but please don't consider it in that light. Think of it in terms of my having to make a very difficult decision. Now you have a decision to make.

During our relationship I've felt you held back a part of yourself. That makes me wonder if you truly love me-as more than a bed-companion. Because it takes much more than sex to make a marriage work.

As you consider what I've said, remember, I love you more than anything else on this earth. So please think on this for a while and try to understand my position. Don't reply in haste or anger.

I pray for your safety daily as I go about my work. And I look forward to your letters.

All my love,

Pat

Dawson sat quietly, in deep thought for a long time. He was content to leave things as they were. He loved and appreciated Pat. But he didn't want to make that commitment again. He didn't want to get married. In his mind, it made him vulnerable, open to be hurt again. Well, I can understand her point of view, he thought, as he paced back and forth in the small room. She may be right. Maybe I don't really love her. At least not enough for a permanent relationship.

Finally, he put her letter in his locker and got ready for bed. No sense in worrying about it now. I have plenty of time before I go back. Maybe things will become clear by then.

Chapter 9

A 0640 Case stuck his head in Dawson's room. "Saddle up and let's go. Can't mess around or we'll miss the Phu Bai/Dong Ha "milk run," as some of the regimental officers jokingly called his trips up into Charley country.

Dawson stuffed his shaving kit into the small bag, picked up his battle gear, and they piled into the jeep near the front door. The young driver popped the clutch, scattering gravel behind them.

As they drove into Da Nang, Case asked, "You ever do any hitch hiking, Bill?"

"Yeah, quite a bit when I was a kid bumming around the Mid-west."

"Good. Then you should feel at home with this job. Only most of your hitch hiking will be done by air. This morning we're going to catch a C-130 at the Marine Air Freight Terminal. They usually have one going up north in the morning at 0730. I try to get there around 0715 or earlier because they don't hold to a tight schedule. They leave when the plane's loaded. You can't make reservations, but I rarely have trouble getting on the flight. We have a priority designator, so we can get on ahead of everyone except top brass and combat troops.

"If the Marines don't have a flight scheduled, or you can't get there in time, I've found two other places with flights going fairly regularly. The Green Beret headquarters in Da Nang-East has choppers going up north to service their teams almost every day. We don't have any priority with them unless they ask us to look at a job they want done. Otherwise you'll have to check to see if they have a chopper headed where you need to go, and if they have room for you.

"They're good about making room if they can. We do a lot of work for the Special Forces, as you'll soon find out, and they really appreciate our services. The other place is a small Army airfield in Da Nang-East. They fly eight or ten place jobs, Otters, I think they're called. That's usually my last resort because they don't have a regular schedule, and we don't have any pull with them."

"I remember you mentioning the Special Forces projects at briefings, but do we really do a lot of work for them?" Dawson asked.

"Well, Bill, not in volume, but what they want us to do usually has a super high priority. Anyway, that's how you get up to the area near your projects. Sometimes you have to catch a hop to Phu Bai, and then hang around till you find a plane going to your destination. I usually stop in Phu Bai for one day and then go on to Dong Ha. But as you heard at our last briefing, they're moving more Seabees into the Phu Bai Combat Base, and are going to split the territory. Since you'll have all projects north of Phu Bai and Hue, you won't have as much need to spend time in Phu Bai. So you'll have to change your schedule to suit yourself."

When they checked into the Marine Air Terminal, the Corporal behind the counter scanned their orders and gave them boarding numbers. The big awkward-looking C-130, even with four engines, didn't look like it would fly. The tail ramp was down and the air terminal personnel were loading the last of the equipment aboard when Case and Dawson got to the group of men waiting to board it. Most of the men were Marine medical returnees, and R & R returnees. In the group were two Marines with muzzled German shepherd guard dogs, three sailors, a few Air Force officers and enlisted men. After the equipment was secured, the men were loaded by number.

Canvas bucket-seats ran the length of the plane on both sides, facing inboard. Cargo and equipment was strapped down in the center on loading tracks running the length of the plane. Room barely remained for legs and feet on either side.

Case and Dawson were loaded early and got seats near the front of the plane. Directly in front of Dawson was a large stack of boxes tied down with heavy web straps. He read on the boxes, "Combat Boots, Size 12" and thought, The people needing them probably have size 10-feet. Two jeeps were on the plane, and the remainder of the cargo was boxes of ammunition. Dawson was amazed at the amount of gear crammed on the plane.

The four engines with their tremendous thrust, were deafening on take-off. As they climbed and banked sharply, Dawson looked at the pile of boxes leaning, straining against tie-down straps. He felt nervous, thinking what would happen if the straps broke. Once they got up to cruising altitude and power was cut back on the engines, noise in the plane was cut down to a loud roar. Then it was possible to talk and be heard, if you yelled.

After a three-bounce landing, Case and Dawson disembarked at Phu Bai. They spent the morning talking with several officers at the Third Marine Division Headquarters. The Third Division had only recently moved to the Phu Bai combat base, 75 kilometers north of Da Nang, and most of them were living in tents. All around the tents, Seabees were busy building hooches for living quarters, mess halls, and offices. They passed a dozen metal Butler buildings being built to store supplies, for cold storage, and one for a morgue. Near the airfield, Bees were building a large helicopter pad with adjacent maintenance buildings.

Two mobile construction battalions were busy in Phu Bai. Newly arrived Lieutenant Jake Thurman, had already relieved Case of his duties in this area; and Case was to assume responsibility for all construction north of Phu Bai. In addition to building for the Marines and the Army, Seabees were busy building their own camps. Seabees were well named; the entire area was a beehive of construction.

Heavy equipment was tearing up the natural terrain in every direction Dawson looked. A concrete deck was being poured for one building, next to it another one was being framed. Runway matting was being laid, and a short distance away, a well drilling rig was searching for fresh water. Like a swarm of bees, Dawson thought.

By noon Case had finished introducing Dawson to staff officers he would be dealing with. As they ate lunch in one of the Marine tent-mess halls, Dawson thought: Sure a change from Da Nang. This entire area seems to be on a more alert status. "This place as hot as it looks, Roger?" he asked.

"Compared to Da Nang, it's hot. But the troops in Dong ha consider it a place for R and R. You'll see tomorrow."

After lunch, they went back to the airfield looking for a ride to Dong Ha. Nothing was scheduled, but the man at the flight shed said they could wait around, that there was usually something unscheduled going to Dong Ha. Case called the helicopter squadron and the Special Forces command to see if they had anything going north, but didn't make out. They waited around until 1700 without getting a flight, then caught a ride over to MCB-42, and checked in to stay the night.

They ate dinner in the battalion officer's mess-a tent with a wood deck. After dinner, Case and Dawson stayed in the mess drinking beer. They were studying maps of the area Dawson would take over, when a heavy explosion rocked the deck and ripped the tent. Before they got to the mortar trench waves of concussion rolled over them. After they dropped into the trench, two more explosions followed.

A battalion officer in the trench said: "Those aren't mortar rounds. Sounded like artillery coming in. But I didn't know Charley had any close enough to reach here."

After the five explosions there was an eerie quiet. Then Dawson heard a faint call: "Corpsman. Corpsman. We need a Corpsman."

Looking in the direction of the first explosion, they saw one living quarters tent demolished, about one hundred feet down the road. Four corpsmen were working over Seabees, and more men were headed in that direction.

"They don't need our help," Case said as he walked back to the officer mess tent. Inside they found everything blown off the table. After they picked up the maps and work orders, Case said, "Bill, you wipe off the table and I'll get us new beers."

Dawson looked around and shook his head. There was one large rip in the tent caused by the concussion. He saw several small holes. Must be from shrapnel, he thought. "It's a good thing we were seated. Have you noticed those smaller holes about even with your chest, Roger?"

"Yeah, I see them. We were lucky. And we haven't even got to the hot area yet. If Charley has artillery down in this area, then Phu Bai is going to get as hot as Dong Ha. May as well finish the briefing, Bill. Spread out the area map, it's the only one we'll need."

Dawson shook his head thinking, Business as usual. But he's right. What else can we do.

"It's better to finish giving you an overview of your territory now, than to wait till we get to Dong Ha. We have the time here and we might not up there. The field commands the Marines have north of here are all under the Third Division, now. So when you run into problems like who gets what done first, you'll have to get with the Division here in Phu Bai. As you can see, Dong Ha is about forty miles north of here. Your territory extends from the mouth of the Qua Viet River, nine miles east of Dong Ha, to Khe Sanh, thirty miles to the west." Case ran his finger from the China Sea west along the blue wandering line indicating a river.

"I see the river is called Qua Viet where it runs into the sea," Dawson said, "but at Dong Ha it's named, Song Bo Dieu. Why?"

"I really don't know, but we usually refer to it at Dong Ha as the Qua Viet. If you follow it on up west toward the mountains, you'll see its name is changed twice again in the next ten miles. Enough geography. Back to our job: Marines you'll work for are spread out over about forty miles. That doesn't sound like much to cover, but it may as well be four hundred miles for the time it takes to get where you have to go. Much of your time will be spent waiting for a plane, or boat, or convoy going to your destination."

"Looks like I'll get to see a lot of the country on this job."

"Yeah, Bill, probably more than you'll want to see at times. One thing to remember is, up in that area, you're in Charley country when ever you leave one combat base to go to another."

Before Dawson and Case finished their beers, two battalion officers entered. The ensign was pale and shaking. He collapsed on the bench at the next table. The lieutenant got two beers from the refer, opened them both and set one in front of the ensign, who had his elbows on the table, head between his hands.

"Andy," Case asked the lieutenant, "have they figured out where those shells came from?"

The lieutenant took another long drink of beer before answering. "Yeah we know where they came from." His voice projected loathing and sorrow. "I don't even like to say it, but it was friendly fire. We lost one man, have several who are critical and more with shrapnel wounds."

"Friendly fire?" Case asked. "Where did it come from?"

Andy shook his head and shrugged, looking at his beer. "Came from a Marine 105 battery south of here."

"They couldn't have five short rounds, so how could they drop them in this area?" Case asked.

"We have only a preliminary report. A patrol spotted V.C. a half-mile outside our west perimeter, and called for fire. Don't know who screwed up the coordinates. There were five people in the chain to the sergeant who issued the command to fire. It will probably fall on the officer in charge of that battery. He should have recognized our coordinates."

As they walked to the tent where they were to sleep, Case said, "What a horrible error! That's going to trigger one hell-of-an investigation. This is the first time Seabees have been hit by friendly fire."

Dawson didn't say anything, but he thought: What a terrible thing for someone to have on his conscience. Aside from the legal ramifications, living with the knowledge you killed one of your own men, will be rough.

The next morning Case and Dawson were at the Phu Bai air terminal shortly after breakfast. They got a ride on the first flight to Dong Ha on a C-123, a plane much smaller than the C-130, and so noisy it was impossible to hold a conversation while they were in the air. The flight took less than thirty minutes. On this leg of the journey Dawson could see the ground through the small window by his seat. As they started losing altitude, Dawson saw the small village of Dong Ha, a cluster of huts and buildings along the south bank of the Song Bo Dieu.

Just south of the village the Dong Ha Combat Base was being built. Twelve square miles of rolling hills, denuded of most vegetation, now lay red and bare. Roads under construction crisscrossed the area to service the commands already established in clusters of tents dotting the barren landscape. The perimeter of the base was well defined by concertina wire, machine gun bunkers, and mortar trenches. And all around was "Charley Country."

Ugly, desolate, and deadly, Dawson thought. The only thing of beauty was the Song Bo Dieu snaking its way through lush green jungle to the low lands and flowed slowly to the sea. Some places it was no more than two hundred yards across, but when it changed to the Qua Viet, it spread out until it was over a half-mile wide, and a muddy brown.

Until a month ago Dong Ha had been only a beefed-up Marine outpost where everyone lived on the ground in tents. Then the brass decided to make it a forward combat base. Previously the Seabees had only a detachment of men from one of the Phu Bai battalions working in Dong Ha. Two weeks ago a full battalion of Seabees flew in fresh from the States. They were still in the process of developing roads and drainage on the hill assigned them. The red gumbo mud every where made a real slippery mess. Seabees worked in ankle-deep mud, getting forms set for a concrete pour for their mess hall, and for a shop building. A few hooches for office space were being built to replace the tents.

Seabees had recently completed the tactical runway at Dong Ha. The surface was AM-2 aluminum planks, a much improved version of World War II Marston matting. The ten-foot by 16-inch wide by one-inch thick planks were surfaced on both sides with sheet aluminum; in between the sheets corrugated aluminum was welded on edge. All four edges were designed to interlock with other planks. When laid over well compacted base materials, they formed an extremely strong, durable runway with great flexibility. As the heavy plane roared down the runway on landing, Dawson listened to the clickety-clack of aluminum planks flexing and moving under stress.

They hitched a ride with a Seabee driving a dump truck, who dropped them off at the MCB-21 equipment compound. As yet there was no building for the mechanics to work in, so they worked in the open or under tarps supported by four poles to give them protection from the rain. Case led the way to a beat-up looking weapons carrier parked in a corner of the compound. The three-quarter-ton weapons carrier looked like an oversized jeep. But it was much more of an all-terrain vehicle, with its large tires, high freeboard, and four wheel drive.

As he climbed in beside Case, Dawson said: "Man! This looks like a real dog. Is it our regular vehicle?"

Case laughed as he started the "weaps." "That's what everyone thinks. But this is a Roger Case mobile special. I got this rather than a jeep because it can go places jeeps can't. I went through the bone yard at the regiment and found this baby. It had been junked because it was old and beat-up, and it had a blown engine. I got a mechanic, an old buddy of mine, to work it over. He reconditioned the running gear, got an almost new motor out of a weaps that had hit a mine, and put in a new transmission. Under this beat-up body is a new vehicle. This thing looks like it may fall apart at any minute, so none of the battalion officers bother it. If I had a new looking vehicle it would never be here when I need it. The only ones who know its value are the mechanics. I told them if they kept it in good shape and kept their mouths shut, they could use it when I'm not here."

"It had better be in good running order," Dawson said. "There must be a ton of sand in here."

"This thing is as mine proof as you can make it. In addition to sandbags on the floorboards and in the bed of the truck, I got them under the seats also. The country we move around in up here is a lot hairier than the Da Nang area. I've seen too many jeeps and their riders blown into scraps. These sandbags will absorb a lot of energy, and can stop most chunks of metal before they get to my tender posterior. So you see, old buddy, I got things fixed up nice and comfortable for you here."

"Right, I'll do my best to not get spoiled by these luxuries."

Dawson recognized the value of the weaps in the first hour. They slued through deep mud three times, where a jeep would've mired down all the way to its ball joints. They checked in with the Commanding Officer, Commander Richard Benson and the MCB-21 Operations Officer, Lieutenant Commander Darrell Grady, both of whom Dawson had met when they were at the Regiment for an arrival-briefing. Case reviewed the major projects ready for MCB-21 to work on. He upped the priority on two of them, and told Grady they had to be started this week.

Grady, young, cocksure, and filled with importance, blustered. Dawson could tell he didn't like having a mere lieutenant telling him what to do. "I'll try to get them started, but I'm not sure I can," he replied. "We're still trying to get settled in camp, you know."

The tone in Case's voice hardened. "You will find, Mr. Grady, the rules of the game out here are-customer work comes first. Much of your own camp improvement work is going to have to take a back seat. When I tell you these two projects must be started this week, I'm passing on to you an order from the Commodore."

After they left the OPS Officer, Case said, "I can tell he's going to be a cry baby. You're going to have trouble with him. My recommendation is, don't give him one inch of slack. You will find one bad aspect of this job is you have the responsibility to see that jobs get done, but you don't really have any authority. So, if someone balks, like Grady, you have to remind them that you represent the Commodore."

They drove around the perimeter of the MCB camp checking their defenses on the west and south which faced Charley country. Concertina wire was in place, defensive mortar trenches were dug, and machine gun emplacements had been built up with sand bags. Two observation platforms had been built on tripods of fifty-foot poles set in the ground. Overall, their defenses looked good. The north and east boundaries weren't fortified since they joined Marine camps.

The camp covered one-half square mile, sitting up on a knoll overlooking rough, uninhabited terrain on the south and west, and fell off into a ravine before joining a Marine camp on the east.

Driving to an area where a rock crusher was being set up, Case said, "This rock crusher is the only job in the Seabee camp with top priority. Sand and gravel for concrete, and rock for roadbeds is going to be one of your major problems up here now. Building has been minor compared to what has to be done, and the detachment from the Phu Bai battalion has been using river-run sand and gravel. But it's a problem even getting that. It has to be hauled about ten miles through Charley country. And the quarry site isn't accessible during the rainy season, which, fortunately, should soon end. I had the detachment stockpile a lot of river-run before the rains really set in. That's what MCB-21 is using now for concrete, but as you can see it's getting low."

"How long do you think this pile will last?" Dawson asked.

"Hard to tell. My guess is three weeks. The rains are slacking off, and soon the river will be down enough for us to get back in to work on the sandbar; that is, if Charley lets us. We really need crushed aggregate for roadbeds and better concrete. Good rock exists up in the mountains, but not where we can get at it. I worked up a contract with the Vietnamese to haul it for us. They're supposed to stockpile it at the crusher site. As you can see they haven't got much yet. We'll have to check on that too."

The remainder of the morning they drove around the rest of the combat base, checking on jobs the Seabee detachment had started and MCB-21 had taken over. When they stopped at an area with concrete decks already in place, Case said, "This is the hospital complex, it has top priority too, and look at the work force; only a half-dozen men. I'll talk with Grady about this one!"

"I see from the drawings that the main part of the hospital is 'T' shaped. What are those leveled areas behind? They aren't on the drawings."

"They're for hooches that weren't part of the original project. They'll be used for recuperation by men with minor wounds."

Case and Dawson inspected the cold storage facility being built for the Marine Supply, and a 500 man mess hall under construction a hundred yards away. They inspected five concrete decks that had been poured for the metal elephant huts, and were walking toward the weaps when a mortar round hit two-hundred yards to their left. No mortar trenches were near, so they flopped flat on their stomachs in a drainage ditch near by, just before the next round hit a little closer, as the combat base siren screamed a warning.

Case raised his head up from the mud, looking at Dawson. "Welcome to Dong Ha. They must've known you were coming and are giving you a welcome. This is something you'll have to get used to. Charley throws in a few rounds to keep everyone on his toes and nervous. Sometimes we have several attacks in one day."

"Our helmets and flack jackets don't do us much good in the weaps. Guess we should wear them," Dawson stated tentatively, not wanting to seem like a nervous Nelly his first day in Dong Ha.

"I don't when I'm within the base parameter. You do as you like. Our Bees can't work in such cumbersome gear very well. That's why I don't wear it around here."

Two more rounds hit in quick succession in the Seabee base on the hill directly in front of them. One explosion did no more than dig a large mud hole. The other one hit a tent and demolished it completely. A few seconds later two more rounds hit off in the distance, near the runway. After fifteen minutes of quiet, the siren sounded the "All-clear."

After getting up they scraped what mud they could off their uniforms. Dawson thought, lucky the ditch had rock in it. We didn't get very wet, and the mud wasn't gooey.

"They screwed-up when they started this job," Case said. "No mortar trenches. The rule of construction up here is: dig a mortar trench first at every job site. MCB-21 had better learn fast. Since the Marine regiment moved up here, shelling and mortar attacks have increased. I guess the V.C. figure they have a lot more to shoot at now. Their ten-ring has been enlarged a hundred times. They can blindly lob them in now and figure on hitting something."

After lunch Case said: "We'll go to Camp Carroll, about eight miles west, this afternoon. They want us to build some more gun decks. If we're lucky we can catch a Marine supply convoy or a patrol going up there."

They checked with two Marine commands and neither of them had anyone going near Camp Carroll. Case asked a company of Grunts if they could provide a patrol. But the Captain said all of his men were out in the bush. No one expected to have anything going up there on the next day either.

Case gave a resigned shrug. "Well, this is where we really earn our money. That's the way it works most of the time. Places I have to go, Marines won't go without a well armed escort. Seldom will you find they can provide an escort, and if you wait until they have a convoy going, you'll never get your job done. I usually go on my own. So far I've been lucky. I hope your luck holds out the same."

Driving through the only gate out of the combat base, in a short distance they were on Highway One. Dong Ha village was considered "friendlies." But, of course, Viet Cong spies had infiltrated, like they had in most South Vietnamese communities. Highway One continued north across a steel bridge spanning the muddy Song Bo Dieu. Short of the bridge, Case turned left onto Highway Nine, the road running parallel to the east flowing river. Dong Ha village stretched out for a half-mile with huts and shops on either side of the road. Most buildings on the right, backed up to the river.

Case pulled off on the shoulder of the gravel road before leaving the village. "Now's the time to wear your flack jacket and helmet. At least I do. And I recommend it. For the next eight miles there's no military; a couple of small villages, and lots of Charley country."

They each chambered a round into their 45's, put the safes on and holstered their pistols. The gravel road was in good shape considering heavy rains; a tribute to the French, who had built good secondary roads. Early morning rain gave a fresh smell to the vegetation, as sunshine warmed the men. The terrain started getting rougher a short distance from Dong Ha. Jungle closed in tight to the road on the left. On their right flowed the Song Bo Dieu which was now called Song Hieu Giang. Sometimes they bordered the river, other places rice fields stretched out for a long way between the river and road.

At the first wood bridge spanning a small nameless tributary feeding the river, Case pointed to a muddy bypass going down into the stream and back onto the road again. "That's one reason we can't get gravel during the rainy season," he said. "These wood bridges weren't built for heavy loads, so we had to scrape out bypasses. But they can't be used when it's wet. We'll pass five of these before we get to Cam Lo."

The river narrowed, flowing faster, and was now called Song Cam Lo. The road became more winding and steep as they entered a canyon. A road branched off to the right, which Case said went to the Cam Lo quarry site. They came to Cam Lo Village, only a wide spot in the road, where Dawson saw his first Montagnards, the mountain people of Vietnam. Their skin color was much darker than most Vietnamese. They were small, but wiry and strong. Dawson watched four women with their colorful print, turban style headdress, carrying woven baskets three feet long and two feet in diameter. The baskets were carried on their backs by means of shoulder harnesses, and were filled with long pieces of wood extending four to five feet over their heads. Their wide, bare feet looked like tough leather. Their smiles showed teeth stained dark red from chewing betel nut.

Dawson felt more apprehensive when the jungle closed in on the road. He strained his eyes looking for some evidence of Viet Cong around each curve. He couldn't decide which worried him more, the Viet Cong or Case's wild driving. But he sure didn't want him to slow down and present a better target. Fortunately, they met only one small Vietnamese vehicle. As they passed, Dawson was sure there was no more than an inch between vehicles.

When they turned left from Highway Nine onto a heavily rutted road, leading to the crest of a hill cleared of jungle, and now bristling with huge guns, Dawson relaxed. The defensive perimeter was a welcome sight with its concertina wire, rows of claymore mines sticking up like harmless road markers, another row of concertina, and then the actual defensive positions.

On the knoll stood eight 175mm cannons, each mounted on a large wood plat-form. Their long barrels pointed threateningly to the north, like eight giant arms pointing out objects in the sky. Nearby, a huge pile of shells was stacked like cordwood, and off in one corner of the compound lay a pile of expended powder cases.

"We completed those gun decks a few weeks ago," Case said. "From what I hear they're really giving Charley fits. They can reach many miles into North Vietnam and Laos. Really keeps Charley on his toes as he trots down the Ho Chi Minh Trail, northwest of here. They tried shooting one of those long toms from its regular stand, but after a few shots the carriage was buried in the mud. So the Bees designed platforms for them. All we have to do is build it like we're building a bridge for tanks to use."

The Marine major commanding Camp Carroll said he had six more guns on the way, and showed Dawson and Case where he wanted the gun platforms built. "No sweat. We can build them," Case said. "It's a question of when. If you want them built soon, Major, you'll have to get an A-1 priority assigned. We have our work force stretched too thin now, and the only suitable material in-country is already allocated to bridge construction. And you know how hot bridge work is now."

"Yeah, Yeah. I know all about that crap," the Major grumbled. "But my Reg-imental Commander said this has the highest priority, I need it done now. Those guns will be here in two weeks."

"OK, Major, don't get hot at us. We're not fighting you on this," Case said. "All of our customers want everything done now. My priority comes out of Da Nang. You get on the horn to your boss and have him get the general to give my boss a good enough priority, and we'll fly the material in and start work next week."

"Fine. You'll have triple A priority on this when you get back to Da Nang. And if you need unskilled manpower, my grunts can help."

As they drove back down the hill to Highway Nine, Case said: "There's your first work order to write up. I'm sure the Major will get his priority. When we get back to the battalion I'll let you work it out with Grady. Tell him the timbers will be up by plane next week. Have him pull men off his camp construction, not some other customer project. He'll cry and scream, but you may as well get used to handling him because it's going to be your baby from here on. Tell him the paperwork will be here next week."

When they got to Highway Nine, Case turned west instead of heading back the way they came. "I want to show you where there's plenty of good rock."

Dawson thought, Just tell me. I really don't need to see it. All he said was, "How far is it?"

"A couple of miles. We haven't been able to set up a quarry because it's definitely V. C. territory. But if the Marines ever get the area secured, it's something you should keep in mind for the future."

If it's definitely V.C. territory, let's not go there, Dawson thought. Well, Case has survived for a year up here, so he must know what he is doing. No wonder he considers Da Nang such a tame place.

The road grew steeper and more snaky as they followed the fast flowing river. After they had gone about two miles, Case stopped on a point overlooking the river. A mile away granite cliffs rose up from the riverbed. At the base was a perfect spot for a quarry operation.

Case pointed off to the north about a quarter of a mile from the proposed quarry site to a granite mountain with perpendicular walls on three sides rising up over five hundred feet. "That's called 'The Rock.' The Marines wanted it for an observation post. They lost many men getting control of it and keeping it. It's one of the most desolate places Marines have set up permanent housekeeping. The Rock will probably go down as another Tripoli."

"I wonder if Marine historians will pick up the Rock in their list of glorious achievements?" Dawson asked. "But what do they want it for?"

Case shrugged. "Observation, I guess. They have to supply it by helicopter. When you sit in on the local intelligence reports, you'll hear 'The Rock' mentioned regularly. Charley tries to take it almost every night. Bad place, in my book."

"Speaking of bad places," Dawson said. "Aren't we inviting trouble, sitting here sightseeing?"

"You're probably right," Case said, as he scattered gravel making a U-turn, and headed back toward Dong Ha.

By the time they got back to the Seabee camp the sun had dropped behind the mountains. Blue sky framing scattered clouds, tinted red and pink by the setting sun, was most welcome after weeks of gray overcast. Dawson met the other battalion officers as they stood in the temporary officer's mess drinking beer before dinner.

Dawson and Case sat on either side of Lieutenant Commander Grady at the long mess hall table. Dawson outlined the new project for Camp Carroll, and told him: "It has to be started next week. You can borrow from the bridge project if the timbers aren't here in time."

Grady blustered. "We don't have any men available without stopping some other job."

"Pull men off camp construction. That's your lowest priority," Dawson told him.

Grady didn't finish his beer. He got up grumbling, "I'll work it out somehow."

"Don't take men from customer projects," Dawson told him.

"By the way, Darrell," Case said, "when we inspected the hospital complex, there were only a half-dozen men at work. I told you two weeks ago it has top priority. At least three times as many men should be working if it's going to be completed on schedule. You don't have any hold-up on materials do you?"

Grady gritted his teeth. "I'll get it done as soon as I can. I'm trying to get my people settled in. I want to get them up out of the mud and in more comfortable quarters. I can't get everything done at once."

Case looked at him with eyes of cold steel. "While you're getting your men comfortable, Marines are dying because they don't get better medical care. If I can't get your assurance you'll go full-bore on the hospital, I'll talk with your C.O. If that doesn't do it, the Commodore will talk with the C.O."

"I'll get more men on it in the morning," he said through clenched teeth and stomped out of the tent mess hall.

Dawson finished his second beer and told Case, who was playing darts, "I'm going to turn in early." He felt extra tired from the tension of driving around in Charley country all day. Shortly after midnight the Combat Base went on alert after receiving incoming artillery rounds. The men shivered in the mortar trenches for an hour before the all-clear sounded. Dawson lay on his canvas cot for another hour wondering if there would be more incoming.

The next morning immediately after breakfast Dawson and Case drove to the material staging yard south of the bridge spanning the Qua Viet-alias, Song Bo Dieu. It was about two acres fenced in, fronting the river where LCM's unloaded cargo they had picked up at the mouth of the river.

"A lot of the material never gets to its destination unless there's a supply representative present when the boats arrive," Case said. "The Seabees keep one man here to guard their material until it's hauled to their supply yard; if they didn't, a Marine would take it for some boondoggle project."

They climbed aboard the first "Mike boat" (LCM) going down river. The slow, muddy Song Bo Dieu divided at several points, making islands, as it meandered to the sea nine miles away. Several rivers and smaller streams fed into it as it wandered through the low lands providing transportation for small fishing villages scattered along the river banks.

Fields of rice bordering the river were surrounded by broad grass pastures where small boys and girls herded water buffalo. Sampans chugging up and down river were the primary means of transportation for people in remote villages; and the only means of getting their produce and fish to market-other than packing it on their backs. Large fishing boats were powered by sail or motors, with smaller ones being sculled or paddled.

Half way down the river a Mike boat was beached, unloading a squad of Marines. "This area is relatively safe in the daytime because Marines and the RVN have patrols out beating the bushes regularly," Case said. "But at night it's Charley's ball game. He moves in from the dense jungle you see in the distance. They plant crude mines in the river which have wiped out two of our boats. Now and then a sniper harasses the boats from the cover of large clumps of grass."

The trip from Dong Ha to where the Qua Viet emptied into the South China Sea took one hour. Two LSTs, their bows rammed up on the south bank of the river, were busy disgorging cargo. The beaching area was 250 yards up from the mouth of the river. A dredge was sucking up sand from the bottom of the river, and pumping it over to the beach, so the channel would remain deep enough for the LSTs.

Loose white sand on the beach caused vehicles to mire down easily. The off-loading and staging area had been covered with Marston matting, where six rough-terrain fork lifts scurried in and out of the ships. Mike boats were nosed-in to the beach, with their bow ramps down, on both sides of the LSTs. Some cargo was moved directly from an LST to a Mike Boat, and some of it was stacked at the rear of the staging area.

"MCB-21 has a fifty-man detachment working and living at the Qua Viet," Case said. "Our primary work here is building a quay wall, concrete ramps for LSTs and to replace this matting with a concrete staging area. We're also building some hooches for the Navy command here and for the Marine tank and amtrack command who provide security for this area. Naturally, this is a rush job because of the heavy Marine buildup at Dong Ha. This is the only means of getting supplies from Da Nang up here, other than by air."

They located the chief in charge of the detachment and discussed the progress of his projects. Hooches and other buildings under construction were on schedule. They had started the soil-cement work for the staging area, scheduled to be done in four sections so it wouldn't interrupt off-loading operations.

The most important project was stalled because the pile driver had broken down, with only half of the pilings for the quay wall in place. The Chief said he hadn't been able to locate a part to make repairs, and it looked like he would have to send back to the States for it. Case said he would try to get one from RMK, a large contractor, who had pile drivers working in other places in Vietnam.

Case and Dawson rode back up the river on a boat carrying gasoline. The Mike boat had large rubber bladders almost filling the well-deck. The bladders were filled with fuel and then at Dong Ha it was pumped into tank trucks that delivered it to the combat base.

As they churned slowly upstream picking their way around sand bars, Dawson said, "I really don't care much for riding on this boat. Sure hope he's a careful driver, wouldn't want to hit a mine with this load."

"Don't sweat it. The odds are with us. One consolation is that if we hit a mine, we won't know what happened, and we won't have to spend a long time in a hospital. You gotta keep alert to see the hidden benefits of this job," Case said with a humorless laugh.

Right! Dawson thought. That does a lot to calm my nerves.

Dawson and Case were seated on the deck with their backs against the dog-house, a rectangular enclosure of heavy gage metal protecting the coxswain, when a shot rang out. The projectile splattered on the plate steel directly over their heads. They scrambled into the well of the LCM, dropping into the narrow space between the gas bladder and the side of the boat. They drew their .45s, each chambered a round and peered over the side.

The coxswain yelled, "Incoming," as he shoved the throttle to flank speed.

"Must have come from there," Case said, pointing to a dense clump of foliage three hundred yards off the port side. "Too far for these pistols to do any good."

Another shot sounded. The lead ball made an indentation six inches below the coxswain's head, which was the only part of his body exposed. Two Marines in the front of the boat returned fire with their M-16s, firing blindly into the clump of foliage. They each emptied a clip and reloaded. They continued firing as the LCM pulled away from the sniper location. The sniper fired once more, hitting the rear end of the boat a foot above the water line.

"Makes me wish we had rifles," Dawson said.

"There are times when they would come in handy, Case said, with a shrug. "But mostly they would be in the way, with the traveling we do."

"The men running these boats must feel like ducks in a shooting gallery," Dawson commented, thankful he didn't have to ride these boats every day.

The Mike boat beached at Dong Ha just as incoming mortar rounds were heard impacting in the combat base a half mile away. The red alert siren sounded as the men looked for shelter. There were no mortar trenches so Dawson followed Case to a Marine machine gun position built of sandbags. A few more rounds hit in the main part of the base, then after a half hour lull the "all-clear" sounded. Driving back to the Seabee camp, Case said: "Charley has to keep messing around. I guess he can't stand to see me leave in one piece. Well, he'll have to improve his aim real soon, 'cause I'm not going to give him many more shots."

When they got back to Da Nang, Dawson and Case were busy from dawn to dark going over dozens of projects in various states of planning and processing. Some hadn't received final approval, some were awaiting material, others were awaiting manpower because they had a low priority. Case spent time introducing Dawson to special contacts he had developed in other services headquartered in Da Nang.

Dawson planned to visit Lati Sunday afternoon, but he worked late into the evening arranging for the heavy timbers for gun platforms to be flown up to Dong Ha. Everything going to Dong Ha had high priority. A dozen different military commands were up there now, all needing a myriad of supplies-food, ammunition, housekeeping supplies and men, to perform their assigned tasks. So getting some non-essential looking timbers pushed in ahead of other urgently needed supplies took much convincing, coercing and threatening.

That night reading didn't put Dawson to sleep as usual. After he turned out the light, he lay awake much too long. He couldn't get Lati out of his mind. His body ached for her. Desire permeated his entire being as he thought of Lati in her white ao dai-with nothing on under it. "You're stupid," he told himself, as he reach up and turned on the light. He read until his eyes wouldn't focus any longer, and thoughts of Lati couldn't command his brain.

Monday at dinner, Case said: "We get whirley-bird limo service in the morning. A Special Forces chopper will drop in early to pick us up. They got a hot job for us in Lang Vei. You'll learn all work we do for the Green Beret is hot. One bonus is that you will usually get door-to-door chopper service."

"What's the hot job?" Dawson asked, trying to remember where he had seen Lang Vei on the map

Case shrugged. "Not sure. The major said the camp got overrun and now they want us to build concrete pillboxes. Pack your diddy bag and I'll get them to drop us off at Dong Ha when we finish at Lang Vei."

Tuesday morning the Huey Gunship, machine guns bristling from both sides, dropped in on the Red Beach helicopter pad. The pilot didn't even bother to wind down the rotor. Case and Dawson ran through the strong down draft to the port side. The major motioned for Case to take the one vacant canvas bucket seat beside him in the compartment directly behind the pilots. The gunner, in the side compartment, motioned for Dawson to sit by him.

He climbed in and was barely seated when the chopper lifted off. He was still trying to get his seat belt fastened as they flew over the regiment headquarters building. I sure won't complain about not getting to see the scenery on this trip, Dawson thought.

The day was sunny and warm, with air temperature comfortable even at a thousand feet. The gunners left the large sliding doors open, ready for action. Dawson had a breathtaking view, with no obstructions. The seat belt gave him some sense of security, once he got used to the strong rush of air, and having nothing between him and the ground but space. They headed north and inland a little to the west. Their destination, Lang Vei, was a Special Forces, Green Beret camp located in the mountains in the extreme northwest corner of South Vietnam.

In the low lands rice paddies encompassed small villages. Their centuries-old burial sites, with perfectly round mounds of red dirt, made a sharp contrast with the carpet of green surrounding them. The mounds were grouped into small family graveyards. Some families, Dawson thought, have more land devoted to graveyards than to growing rice.

Most of the terrain, as they left the lowlands, was impenetrable jungle of various shades of green. Shell and bomb craters made garish pockmarks of brown and red in the thick green carpet. The reddish brown scars were scattered out randomly for the most part. Dawson thought, must be from H and I fire. Several times they flew over areas devastated by artillery and air strikes. Then for a quarter-mile area there was more red earth than green jungle.

On his prior flight to Dong Ha, Dawson had passed directly over Hue, the ancient Vietnamese capital, but he couldn't see it from the C-130 since he wasn't near a window. Now as the helicopter flew a little to the east of Hue, he got a complete panoramic view of the city. He decided it was the most beautiful city, from the air, that he had seen in Vietnam.

The view was spectacular as they flew northwest at an altitude of one thousand feet. The streets were wider and the central part of the city didn't look as crowded as Da Nang. Many large, old stone structures gleamed white in the bright sunlight. But the most impressive sight was the moat and stone wall surrounding the ancient city, with stone towers still on guard.

The water, a brilliant green, was contained by perpendicular banks made of stone. Sections of the moat ran straight for some distance, and then made precise angular changes. At each point, where the moat changed direction, stood a massive stone defense tower. Some of the towers were now only huge piles of stone, others still stood like mute guards. The configuration of the moat around the citadel must've been of some significance to the ancient architect, but Dawson couldn't determine what the shape was supposed to represent.

Past Hue they headed more west until they came to Highway Nine, then flew due west. As they paralleled Highway Nine, Dawson spotted the big guns at Camp Carroll. This sure beats driving on that road through Charley country, he thought. The chopper continued west past Camp Carroll, flying over mountains that became more and more rugged. The road, looking like a red string, wound along beside the silver ribbon of river.

Five minutes after they left the river, Dawson spotted a small airfield and base scratched out in the red mud, a mile to the north. He leaned over and yelled in the gunner's ear, "What base is that?" The noise of the engine made it impossible to be heard without yelling in the other person's ear.

"The Marine base, Khe Sanh," the gunner yelled back.

A mile short of the Laotian border, they approached Lang Vei. The pilot made a counter-clockwise circle around the camp looking for V.C. snipers. When the chopper heeled hard to port, suddenly Dawson was facing down, with tops of trees zooming by close enough to touch. His heart raced and felt as if it would choke him, as gravity pulled him hard against his seat belt. This is better than a roller coaster ride, he thought, as he swallowed his fear and sought a hand hold. As they circled he studied the layout of the Special Forces camp, perched on the crest of a hill that dropped off steeply to the south and west. Highway Nine passed to the north of the camp, and on the other side of the road was the small Montagnard village, Lang Vei. The chopper landed on the dirt helicopter pad fifty yards east of the camp entrance.

Before the rotors had stopped, the men stepped out of the chopper into swirling dirt. When they got clear of the rotor turbulence, Case introduced Dawson to Army Special Forces Major Milinsky. The major was a huge man, six-foot two and about 250 pounds. He would've been right at home on the L. A. Rams front line, Dawson thought.

Milinsky extended his hand, and appraised Dawson with hard gray eyes as he clamped down on his hand. Dawson returned the grip with all of his strength, barely able to not flinch. Finally Milinsky smiled and released Dawson's hand. "How did you like the side-saddle chopper ride?"

"Can't complain about the view, Major," Dawson responded as he flexed the fingers on his right hand. Sure glad he didn't squeeze any harder, Dawson thought. Guess he wanted to test me a little.

As they walked up the rutted road to the camp entrance, Dawson noted their perimeter defenses looked more impregnable than any other he had seen. First were double coils of concertina, then a fifteen-foot wide area with pressure mines. Next a row of claymore mines stood on foot-high stakes, looking like convex reflectors, the 700 steel balls glistening brightly in the sunlight. They were backed up by two more coils of concertina razor wire. The defensive positions were a short distance back from the last concertina wire, with additional claymore mines in front of the fighting trenches and machine gun bunkers.

Walking beside the Major, Dawson exclaimed, "Man! This place is really fortified."

"It better be," Milinsky said. "Cause they're all on their own up here. This is our most remote camp. There's a twelve-man U. S. team and 250 ARVN soldiers here. The only help they can get is from the air, and then only when it's clear enough to fly. Much of the time this camp is socked in, making air strikes impossible. So these men have to hold out against what ever Charley throws at them. He mortars them every night, and probes their perimeter several times a week. The V.C. overran the camp two nights ago. They knocked out machine gun positions on the south and then came right through. We lost four men and twenty-two friendly gooks before the V.C. pulled back."

Dawson cringed, thinking, I wonder if he disrespects the ARVN as much as "gooks" imply. "Gooks" is used all the time for the V. C. But for our allies?

Milinsky continued, "The camp has a 10 KW generator for a few lights, freezer, refrigerator and two way radio. Their food supplies are brought over from Khe Sanh, eight miles to the east." At the entrance a lieutenant met them. "This is the U. S. Camp Commander, Lieutenant Kingston." Milinsky said. Meet Lieutenant Dawson, from the Seabee regiment."

Lang Vei Camp was about 100 yards wide by 150 yards long. To the north and east there was plenty of clearing beyond the defense perimeter, for good fields of fire. But on the south and west sides the hill dropped off at a 45 degree angle. Thick jungle came up to within a few yards of the perimeter, so mines and wire weren't as effective as on the other sides of the camp.

"Here's the problem," Kingston said, standing in one of the machine gun positions, looking down the steep hill. "At night Charley gets up close enough to lob in grenades before we even know he's there. That's what he did the other night. They knocked out three of our machine gun positions and threw a wave of men against our wire in one section. After we fired our claymores, they sent another wave of troops right on into our camp. We can't develop wider fields of fire, so what I need are five concrete machine gun bunkers that won't be affected by grenades. They should have slits for machine guns to fire through, but no way Charley will ever throw a grenade inside."

"We can build them," Dawson said looking at the indicated locations. "But only if we can get sand and gravel. Can't haul it up from Dong Ha, with highway nine closed."

Major Milinsky shrugged his tank-wide shoulders. "We can tell you what we need, how you do the job is your problem. If you tell me you can't do it, I'm going to recommend we abandon this camp."

"The only solution I can think of is to use river-run sand and gravel," Case said. "Is there a stream close by that we can get equipment into?"

"There's one beyond the village. Let's check it out and see if it's what you need." Kingston got the camp interpreter, and the five men piled into a jeep and drove into the Montagnard village. Stopping at one of the dozen thatched huts built on stilts, Kingston said, "I'll talk with the 'Yard chief, and let him know we won't screw up their drinking water."

The cluster of huts making up the Montagnard village was set back from the road one hundred feet. The natives were totally self sufficient. They grew some vegetables, but mostly grubbed for roots, and got other edible food from the forest. The men hunted with bows and arrows for meat to eat, and skins to trade. The Americans called the Montagnards "Yards."

The Chief came out of his hut and talked with Kingston and the Major via the interpreter. The Chief's face resembled tough, weather-beaten leather. His dark eyes darted from man to man. Dawson guessed he must be at least sixty. His legs, visible beneath a breech cloth, were gnarled and bowed. Even at five feet tall, he looked fierce. Dawson doubted he would back down from anyone or anything.

After a few guttural sounds, the chief, bow in hand, led the way back of the village, to a stream fifty yards from the huts. They located a sandbar accessible to equipment, where Case and Dawson probed with sticks to determine the depth of the sand and gravel. They let the sand and gravel flow through their fingers underwater, and decided it was clean enough to use for concrete.

Kingston explained that the Seabees would have to drive through the village, and would tear up a little of the jungle getting to the stream. He offered the chief two bags of rice for clearing a wide path to the stream. The chief nodded and grinned, showing his red betel nut stained teeth.

Don't think I'll start chewing betel nut, Dawson decided. As they walked back to the jeep he asked, "How far can you trust these people?"

"All the way. If a 'Yard makes a commitment, he'll keep his word even if it costs him his life." The major pointed to the chief walking ahead. "That scrawny little devil will walk any of us right into the ground and still be going at full speed. They're a very proud people, and loyal. We use them for scouts when we go out on patrol. I'd rather have a squad of 'Yards than a whole company of ARVNs. In a tight situation they'll fight until the last man drops. I've never heard of one of them turning tail, and that's a hell-of-a-lot more than I can say for the ARVN."

"If they're such good fighters, why don't they have them in the South Vietnamese Army?" Dawson asked. "I've never seen one of them in uniform."

Milinsky laughed. "I wish they would, but no way. We've tried to get the South Vietnamese to let 'Yards in the army, but neither group will even consider it. The South Vietnamese despise 'Yards, who they consider subhuman; and they treat them worse than they do their dogs. It's been like that for centuries, I guess. The 'Yards hate the South Vietnamese almost as much as they do the V.C. It's so bad that, unless an American leads the patrols, the 'Yards won't scout. They won't go out with the ARVN no matter how much we offer to pay them.

"The 'Yards like Americans-I guess because we treat them like humans. They really give the V.C. a hard time. They won't fight for them, they won't work for them and they won't provide them food. If he has a chance the 'Yard will destroy his food rather than let the V.C. have it. The only way the V.C. can control the 'Yard is to kill him. As far as I'm concerned, they are our best ally in this stinking war."

Back in camp they ate lunch with the Special Forces team. Hot beans helped the C-rations go down easier, and the beer cooled off the hot sauce in the beans.

"You got the picture now, so how soon can you get our bunkers built?" Milinsky asked.

Case frowned and shook his head. "Our north battalion is stretched too thin now. We have all our men on top priority jobs. I doubt we can get at it in less than a month, and maybe more."

"Damn!" The Major slammed his hand down on the rickety table making cans of beers jump. "We can't wait. We'll lose a lot of men. Roger, I know you've always stretched things as far as you could on other jobs for us, which I appreciate. I hope I won't step on your toes if I go to high command and try to get this done sooner."

"Nope. Won't hurt my toes one bit. If we get the word to pull people off other jobs and put them on this one, we'll do it, no sweat. Bill will be working with you from here on, and he doesn't have soft toes either. So put on all the pressure you want."

The three men were twenty-five yards from the chopper when the mortar round hit fifty yards the other side of the helicopter that had its rotor idling. They sprinted to the chopper and jumped in as the rotor responded to full power. Dawson wasn't seated by the gunner when the chopper lifted off. Three seconds later a second mortar hit ten yards from the helicopter pad.

On the starboard side the gunner spotted the mortar site when Charley fired the second one. He directed the pilot on the intercom to a jungle clearing where four V.C. were scrambling for cover. At three hundred feet elevation, the pilot heeled the chopper sharply to starboard. The gunner raked the area with machine gun fire. Three of the enemy dropped to the ground and didn't move. The chopper circled the area looking for the fourth man, who had made it to the cover of the jungle. Then the pilot took a heading for Dong Ha. After a half-hour tree-top flight, the chopper dropped Dawson and Case off at Dong Ha.

They inspected the projects at the combat base until time for evening chow. As they relaxed with a beer before dinner, Grady told them the timbers for the gun platforms had arrived, and that a crew was up there working. Charley shelled the combat base only twice, both times in the day. So the men in Dong Ha got a full night's sleep for a change. The following day Case and Dawson checked out the Qua Viet projects, then headed back to Da Nang late in the afternoon.

They arrived in Da Nang late in the evening. Dinner was almost over when they got to Red Beach. Ensign Clark stopped at their table and told Dawson, "I was on duty yesterday and received a call from a woman who asked for you, Bill; said her name was Lati Noi. She asked that you see her when you return. I offered to fill in for you but she wouldn't have any of that. She has a lovely voice, what's she like?"

"Like her voice, Ken. Thanks, I'll contact her when I can." A twinge of guilt ran through Dawson's mind. No one had said a word about his visits to see Lati. Wonder if anyone even knows? Well, at least now that I'm not supervising work crews, I won't be telling a group of men one thing and doing the opposite.

Dawson thought of calling Lati where she worked, but remembered she said they wouldn't permit Vietnamese to receive personal calls. With Case leaving on Saturday, Dawson was busy trying to catch up on small details before he left. So he didn't get to see Lati until Sunday.

When she opened the door, Dawson knew something was wrong. Lati's face was sad. She didn't smile when she asked him to come in. She went to the table and fidgeted with an ao dai she had been sewing on. She didn't look at Dawson.

"What's wrong, Lati."

She didn't look up or answer, as she bit her lower lip. By now Dawson realized it was something she did when tense or worried.

"Where is your grandfather?" he asked stepping closer to her.

When she looked up, the tears she had been holding back welled up in her eyes. "He is dead," she said in a small, forlorn voice.

Dawson took her in his arms. "I'm very sorry, Lati." As he held her, head tight against his chest, quiet tears turned onto sobs that shook her body. He held her for a long time, caressing her gently. "I know how much you loved your grandfather, Lati. Is there anything I can do?" She shook her head, pulling tight against him.

Finally her sobbing stopped, and she could speak. She drew back a little, but kept her head down. "I am sorry. In my family we are taught not to cry, and I promised grandfather I would not cry. I held it back until now."

Dawson tilted her head up and kissed her gently. "Don't be sorry. I think it's good for you to cry rather than to keep the sorrow bottled up inside."

"I have not been able to sleep much since grandfather died on Tuesday. He was buried Friday. Now I am very tired. Maybe that is why I cry."

Dawson sat down and pulled her onto his lap, cradling her in his arms as he would a child. After a while she relaxed, and from her breathing Dawson knew she had dozed off. He held her gently, for a long time.

Deep feelings of love and compassion rolled over him, feelings he hadn't experienced since his divorce. Then he thought of Pat and his feelings for her, or rather his lack of feelings. As he compared the love he felt for Lati, he realized he didn't have those deeper feelings for Pat, feelings that reached beyond the physical. Dawson hadn't specifically responded to the letter of ultimatum from Pat. He had agreed with her that they should wait, and he would think on what she had written. Now he knew he had to write to her soon and set matters straight.

When Lati awakened, she said, "I am sorry to sleep when you are here. It is not polite, but I do feel better. I will make us tea."

Dawson's thoughts drifted to the two empty bunks; the fact that he was alone with Lati and wanted her. Nice going, Dawson, he thought. Here she is grieving over her grandfather, with no one else to turn to, and you're thinking about getting her into bed.

Lati gave him a cup of tea and a small smile.

"What will you do now?" Dawson asked as they sipped their tea, and he stroked her hand lying on the table.

"Tomorrow I will return to work, and continue living, doing what I did before."

"You will continue living here?"

"Of course, where else can I go?"

Dawson gave a small shrug realizing it was a dumb question. He didn't have any other suggestion. He knew what he wanted to do. He wanted to protect her, to make her happy again, to ensure she had adequate food and a better place to live. He didn't stop to analyze where those type of feelings could lead.

The sun had set when Dawson said, "I'm sorry, but I must go now. It's not good for us to be out at night. If I could, I would stay here with you. But I would be in trouble if I got caught. Then I wouldn't be able to see you for a long time."

"You go. I will be all right. I feel much better now. You will come to see me next Sunday?"

"Yes, I'll be back next Sunday if possible. I miss not having lunch with you. But with my new job, everything is urgent; I never get caught up."

When Dawson returned from the next trip to Dong Ha he was loaded down with problems. Case's shoes where getting harder and harder to fill. Saturday morning right in the middle of a discussion with a Marine light colonel about citing funds for some priority jobs already approved, a vision of Lati in her thin ao dai invaded his mind, making him miss the colonel's decision to shift funds from one project to another. He shook his head, clearing Lati from his mind. Then Dawson had to ask the colonel to repeat the project number again.

Sunday morning Dawson spent locating the part RMK said they had sent up for the pile driver at Qua Viet. It had gotten pushed back in the corner of their own Da Nang warehouse. Once that was resolved, the morning was shot. Reviewing what he had left to do, he could see that most of his afternoon would be used to untangle a holdup on material for the hospital complex. He felt as if he was operating at half speed while the sun raced toward the horizon at double speed. Then he felt guilty for being concerned about personal matters.

During the past week Lati invaded his mind often. Part of the time he was concerned about her welfare now she was alone, but frequently desire crowded out noble thoughts as he remembered how her body felt pressed against his. When he saw her last, compassion kept his sensual feelings in check. Since then he thought about being alone with her. With no one else there, they would have nothing to hold them back. With that thought, desire built up in him until he could hardly stand the pressure of wanting her.

By the time he got to Lati's shack it was 1600. He was angry with himself for not being there earlier. When Lati answered his knock, she threw herself into his arms as soon as he had closed the door. With her arms around his neck she pulled herself up, her mouth seeking his. They kissed for a long time, and their bodies responded to the passion building inside. How does an ao dai come off? Dawson wondered. He hadn't seen any buttons, and didn't feel a zipper.

When his hands slipped up under the loose top, making contact with soft, warm skin, Lati responded with a quick intake of breath. Then she drew back, her breath coming as rapidly as Dawson's. He wanted action, not talk. But Lati braced both hands against his chest and said: "I have been so worried. I was afraid something had happened to you. Afraid you were not coming to see me today."

Reluctantly, Dawson withdrew his hands from under her ao dai. "I'm sorry to be so late. But I had much to do today." When he tried to pull her close to kiss her again, she resisted. Her face looked sad and lonely. Under her eyes dark circles told of a lack of sleep. Dawson felt ashamed of his desire, when he thought about how she must feel, with the grief of her grandfather's death fresh in her mind. He resolved that he would contain his passion until later, after she had time to adjust to her loss.

"This past week I have been more lonely than I have ever been before," Lati said. "When my parents and brothers and sisters were killed, my grandfather comforted me. Now I have no one. You are the only one I can trust. But you cannot be here all the time. I am beginning to really realize, I have no family. I am all alone now."

He reached out, gently caressing her neck. "Not alone. You have me. I know I can't be with you much, but remember, I love you and will do what I can to help you."

He stayed as long as he dared. Before he left, they kissed and held each other tightly for a long time, neither wanting to let go.

With her heart and feelings exposed, Lati said: "Please come back to me. I love you and need you."

"If possible, I'll be back to see you next Sunday. But if something happens to keep me from coming, don't worry. Remember, I'll return when I can."

Chapter 10

As the rains abated, the nights lost their bone-chilling effect and became just cool enough to make sleeping under a blanket feel good. The mornings were brisk and beautiful. By midday it was hot, but not uncomfortably so. It was balmy tropical weather.

In Dong Ha Grady really got up tight when told the Commodore had given top priority to the concrete bunkers at Lang Vei. "Another top priority job! Hell, that's all we get up here. I don't have any men to put on it now," he told Dawson.

"You just finished the gun platforms. Put that crew on the bunkers." Dawson suggested firmly.

"Can't do that. They're already on another job. I won't be able to start the Lang Vei job unless I pull men off of another top priority job," Grady said, slamming the file drawer closed.

Dawson clenched his teeth for a second, and glared at Grady who was looking at job orders on his desk. "If that's your final word, I'll talk with your C.O."

"Fine with me. He's the one putting pressure on me to get a million things done in our own camp. He wants the Command Post underground bunker completed, and the one for our sick bay. There's no way I can get everything done now."

The battalion C.O., Commander Benson, bowed his neck a little when Dawson told him the problem. He said he needed to get his men up out of the mud and living better, for the sake of their morale. Dawson reminded him of the mandate the Commodore had laid out on the battalion's arrival. He made it clear the Commodore would have to be notified if the work schedule couldn't be resolved between the Battalion and himself. He didn't lean hard on the Commander, wanting to give him enough room to change his decision without a direct threat of the Commodore intervening. Commander Benson got the message. He said he would see to it Grady got men on the Lang Vei job right away.

At lunch, Grady told Dawson the Third Marine Division had called and wanted Dawson to go to Gio Linh and see the camp commander about a "combat-immediate" problem he had.

"He didn't give you any more details?" Dawson asked.

"No. He said the camp commander would brief you. I can see it now-another top priority job," Grady said with resignation.

"I'll go right after lunch. Can you give me directions?"

Grady shrugged. "Well, I've never been there. But from what I've been told, you go north on Highway One, across the bridge and in about six miles you'll come to the camp. It's right up against the DMZ. From what I hear it's all Charley country from the bridge to the camp. If I were you I would get a Marine escort."

Dawson checked with Marine commands that might have business in Gio Linh, but none of them had a convoy going; and none of them could spare a patrol to escort him. He considered waiting till the next day, then remembered it was designated "combat-immediate," which was the highest priority. Marine Intelligence said they had no report of heavy V.C. activity in that area in the last two days, so he decided to go on his own.

He stopped when he left the combat base and put on his helmet and flack jacket. He chambered a round into his .45, then clicked the safe on. After he crossed the bridge and went through a small section of village that was part of Dong Ha, Dawson put the accelerator on the floorboard thinking, the faster I go, the lousier target I make. Highway One was flat and mostly straight. The jungle receded from the road about a half-mile beyond the bridge. Stretches of sand, and a few rice fields bordered the road.

As he approached a cluster of native huts, Dawson slowed to 25, thinking there might be children around. As he got closer, he thought it strange; there was no one in sight. When he was even with the third hut, at the moment he pressed the accelerator to the floorboard, a shot rang out. It came from his left, immediately followed by a "thunk" on the side of the weaps directly behind him. One more shot rang out, as he gained speed. He slouched down in the seat as low as possible and still see to drive.

Dawson stayed in the middle of the paved, pockmarked two-lane highway. He had to move to the edge of the road only twice for oncoming Vietnamese vehicles. The center of the road was much safer. If the V.C. mined the road it would be at the edge where they could burrow under the asphalt and bury a mine without it being seen.

Shortly before he got to Gio Linh, the flat land gave way to gently rolling hills. In the distance Dawson saw the Gio Linh outpost dug into the crown of a larger hill.

Dawson's fear hadn't really registered until he stopped at the gate and asked for directions to the C. O. The he noticed his hands were shaking and his voice wasn't quite steady.

At Gio Linh there was no foliage. It looked as though a colony of human moles had burrowed into the hill and made their home. The area of the camp was a half-mile long by one-quarter mile wide. The red clay road had a high crown to shed the water and keep it from becoming a quagmire. By American standards it was barely a one lane road. When two vehicles met, they eased by each other slowly, both drivers keeping their eyes on the deep ditches to their right.

Looking across the camp Dawson saw the barrels of large guns protruding above their sandbagged revetments. Mounds of sand bags formed roofs for underground bunkers and mortar trenches. The concertina wire entanglements had several more coils on the side facing the DMZ. At the north east corner he saw what was left of a forty-foot tall, three-legged observation tower. The platform now sagged on the two legs remaining in the ground. The tower looked much out of place in this land of moles.

Also visible were several tanks parked at strategic points throughout the camp, backed into three sided sandbagged revetments. Parked alongside the one road that made a circle through the camp were half a dozen trucks and other military vehicles, each backed into a little niche of its own, protected by sandbags. Around the entire perimeter was a mortar trench, connecting heavily fortified bunkers every thirty yards.

It was too quiet for a military camp. A feeling of dread was evident. Men moved about, working quietly, not talking. Fear and weariness etched deeply into their faces, matched their resigned movements. As the men worked at their various tasks, they reminded Dawson of dogs with ears pointed, listening for a strange sound. They all knew that if the V.C. massed an attack across the DMZ, they were the first line of defense, and because of their isolated location, expendable.

They would function as the warning gun, the buffer to slow the enemy force down while heavier defenses were formed in Dong Ha. If the attack came with bad weather, they couldn't even expect air support. They were a small pocket of men all on their own with only a ribbon of road connecting them to the main force six miles to the south.

Living with this threat week after week, and with the dozens of rounds of incoming artillery they received day after day, had etched the deep lines on the men's faces and added the droop to their shoulders. The one thing they looked forward to was the end of their three month tour when they would be moved back to the rear forces for three months-and maybe they wouldn't have to return to Gio Linh.

Dawson drove half way through the camp to the C. O's bunker. He saw that his hands didn't shake, and he felt calmer. He walked down six sandbag steps then made a ninety-degree turn to the left before finding the door to the bunker. The ninety-degree offset functioned as a blast barrier for the door.

The bunker, dug into the ground, had six feet of sandbags on the roof. Inside the command post, Dawson hunched over because of the low overhead. The room was five feet wide by twelve feet long. It had two bunks, end-to-end, placed along one wall, with a tactical radio and field switchboard at the far end. The major was seated on one of the cots eating a can of beans.

"I'm Lieutenant Dawson. I understand you have a hot project for the Seabees."

"I'm Major Lott. Have a seat." He didn't offer his hand, just pointed to a wood crate with his spoon, in between bites of beans. "Got another can of beans if you want some lunch." He was a short man with a good build, red hair, deep circles under blue eyes, and too many lines for a face so young.

"Thanks, Major, but I'll pass on the lunch. The message I got didn't give any details. What do you want?"

A muffled "whump" came from above and the command post shook from the explosion. Then excited voices right over the command post shouted, "Incoming! Incoming!"

Major Lott smiled and shrugged. "That'll teach them to listen." Two more shells hit in quick succession quite close to the command post. The entire underground structure shifted, Dawson almost fell off his box, sand drifted through the heavy timbers overhead. The Major continued talking and eating his beans as though nothing had happened.

"The Seabees put up an observation tower a few weeks ago. Yesterday Charley got a direct hit, and chopped off one of its legs. We really need that tower to keep track of what Charley's doing out there in the DMZ. Otherwise he might give us a real surprise. All we want you to do is set another pole and rebuild the platform at the top."

"Fine, from what you say, it should be no sweat. I'll have a crew up here tomorrow with a line truck and a new pole."

The Major shook his head. "No line truck. Those dirty buggers zero in on any large piece of equipment they see moving up here. And where your men will be working is on the brow of the hill facing the DMZ. I guarantee they would be in a trench more than they would be working; and you would lose one line truck."

"Well, that's going to make it more difficult, it may take a little longer, but we can do it. Now I need to take a look at the tower up close."

Major Lott told the private with the radio, "Tell Sergeant Jones to report to me on the double."

"On the way up here, Major, I was shot at from one of the huts in the last group along the road. Sounded like two rifle shots. Any chance of getting some of your men to check it out?" Dawson tried to sound casual about being shot at.

"Sure, some of my boys need the exercise."

When Jones stuck his head in the door, the Major said, "Take the Lieutenant out to the observation tower. And when he finishes take a short squad to those huts down the road. The Lieutenant can show you where the fire came from."

"A crew will be up here first thing in the morning," Dawson said. "If they need a little help, can you provide some manpower?"

"Sure thing. Have them see Sergeant Jones. He'll get them all the men needed. By the way, Lieutenant, come back up and visit us anytime. I don't get much company up here."

Dawson smiled at the Major's indirect reference to his reaction when the shells hit almost over their heads. "Thanks, Major. I appreciate the invitation. But I'll be back only if it's necessary."

Outside, the Marines were working around the camp filling sandbags, rebuilding walls and roofs over their bunkers, and doing other camp chores. But there was an eerie quiet. The men didn't laugh and joke as men working together usually do. Dawson climbed in his weaps and motioned for the Sergeant to get in. "May as well ride," he said.

"No thanks, Lieutenant. I'll walk. When the V.C. shoot at us from across the DMZ, we can hear the pop from the artillery three seconds before the shell arrives. In that vehicle you'll never hear the pop, which is about as loud as a kid's popgun. You can drive if you like; just follow me. If you see me dive into the ditch, you have three seconds before the shell hits."

"Thanks, Sergeant, but you have changed my mind. I'll walk too."

The tower was less than a quarter-mile, but it seemed much farther to Dawson as they walked along in silence, him wondering when the next shell would come in. When they were almost to the mangled tower, Sergeant Jones yelled, "Incoming" and flattened himself in the ditch alongside the road. Dawson was less than a second behind him. He hadn't heard any pop. But the Sergeant wasn't wrong; two shells hit and then two more within thirty seconds. Dawson was glad he had his helmet and flack-jacket on, and that the ditch was dry. He pressed himself into the bottom of the ditch as hard as he could as the shells hit near by. The concussion felt like a giant hammer. The Marine's 105mm sent out answering fire for about five minutes.

Lying in the ditch Dawson asked, "How many incoming rounds do you get on an average day?"

"I guess it's about seventy-five or eighty, on the average. The most we got was 412 about a month ago. That was a bad day, we had low clouds, no air cover, and plenty of rain. We had fifteen KIA that day."

About a minute after the Marines quit firing someone blew a whistle, and everyone came out of their holes and resumed what they were doing. Dawson looked closely at the two remaining poles to be sure they were still sound. They had small pieces blown out at many places, and shrapnel sticking in them, but they were structurally sound. The platform on top was sagging badly without its third support.

Jones said, "I have to round up a squad. Can you make it back by yourself?"

"Sure," Dawson said. But he didn't feel the assurance he voiced.

"Fine, sir. Have your crew ask for me when they get here. I'll give them all the help I can. I'll meet you at the gate."

Dawson jogged back to his vehicle. Since he hadn't heard the other pop, he was worried about hearing the next one, so he kept his eyes on the men working outside. He got his weaps turned around and drove as fast as was safe back to the barricaded camp entrance. After weaving through the barricade, Dawson waited until Jones, with a jeep load of men pulled up behind him.

When they were within sight of the huts, Dawson stopped and the jeep pulled up beside him. Dawson pointed out the hut where he thought the shot had come from, and the jeep took off ahead of him. The six Marines fanned out and were advancing on the huts as Dawson passed.

Back at the MCB-21 Camp, Dawson found Grady in the Operations Office. He explained the problem and said the observation tower had to be repaired the next day. Grady started blustering and sputtering before Dawson had finished.

"Let's not go through that not-enough-men routine again, Commander. A crew of only four men can do the job. I know you don't have a job order; I'll write one as soon as I get back to the Regiment. Don't send a line truck; Charley will use it as a target. I suggest you send a weapons carrier. It can pull a small pole trailer, and the wench can be used to set the pole. Tell your linemen to take a block and tackle with plenty of line so they can use an existing pole as a gin-pole."

Grady got puffed up and red in the face. "Not only do you tell me when to do the job, now you want to tell me how to do it. You may as well take over my job completely and I can go back to the states."

Dawson shrugged. "I don't mean to tell you how to do the job. I was only trying to save time and manpower. If you want, go up there yourself and look at the job. I really don't care as long as the work is done tomorrow morning."

The next morning going down the Qua Viet, cool air bathed Dawson's face seductively, blotting out the war, attuning his senses to the peaceful looking green fields bordering the lazy river. On the LCM, he leaned against the doghouse. He was talking with the coxswain of the Mike boat, a lean, clean-shaven sailor of about twenty, with the self-assurance of a man of thirty.

As they cruised down the river at full speed, the coxswain searched for sandbars ahead as he talked. "We lost a Mike boat late yesterday afternoon when it hit a mine. We'll be coming up on it around the next bend. One of Charley's UDT men placed a charge on the bottom of the dredge last night-I got that on the radio this morning. Didn't sink it though. Dumb V.C. didn't know what he was doing, or he would've put the charge back about fifty feet and blown the fuel tanks."

Rounding the bend they passed close to the LCM resting on the sand bottom, only about a third under water. Another boat was tied alongside, and men were working on the disabled LCM.

"Will they be able to salvage it?" Dawson asked.

"They think it can be fixed," the coxswain said. "Probably have to haul it up on the beach and shore it up to work on the bottom. The mines the V.C. make are kind of rinky-dink. They don't do much damage. But it's a good thing that boat wasn't carrying fuel or ammo."

At the mouth of the Qua Viet, construction of the hooches was progressing rapidly. The pile driver was rhythmically hammering steel pilings into the sand. But the docking facilities were behind schedule because the pile driver had been out of service for two weeks. Commodore Rhodes had told Dawson to take a hard look at the dock work, and see if it could be accelerated.

The Chief in charge and Dawson spent two hours going over the project in detail, looking for ways to speed up completion; but for much of the pending work, one step had to follow another. They decided if more men and equipment were brought in they would be in each other's way. The Chief agreed to try working a second shift on the pile driver. He said they had tried working at night before, but sniper fire from across the river was too heavy. Now that the days were getting longer, and the heavy rains had stopped, the V.C. weren't quite so bold. He would get the Navy to park one of their boats in front of the pile driver, to shield the men working there. If the second shift worked out, Dawson figured the project would be back on schedule in about two weeks.

By late afternoon he was ready to go back to Dong Ha. A boat loaded with ammunition was about to leave-the last one going back upstream for the day. Looking at the tons of ammunition, Dawson had a strong urge to stay overnight at the Qua Viet camp. Nothing but his fear justified staying-and he had plenty to do at Dong Ha. So he pushed aside his fear and boarded the boat.

As they cruised up the Qua Viet, Dawson tried to read his pocket book. It didn't work. He couldn't concentrate. His mind was on the tons of explosives-and the possibility of the boat hitting a mine. He marveled at the nerve of the young men who made this trip day after day. The coxswain whistled and appeared as casual as if he were piloting a pleasure cruise to Dong Ha. The deck-hand lay asleep on the deck behind the doghouse.

It must put them under tremendous mental strain, even though they act very casual, Dawson thought. I sure wouldn't want their job. Guess I could do it if I had to, but I doubt I'd ever get used to it.

Sitting with the book forgotten in his lap, Dawson realized that he was slowly, methodically cracking his knuckles. He smiled as he remembered getting his hands rapped with rulers when teachers caught him doing it. Then, he hadn't tried to stop. Now he wished he had. It embarrassed him when people heard the "pop, pop, pop," and looked at him. He knew that since arriving in Vietnam he had been cracking them more frequently, as fear and tension wore on him. He shrugged, thinking, If cracking makes them larger, I should have knuckles the size of oranges by the time I leave Vietnam. Then he continued pulling and twisting each finger until all knuckles had popped.

Not able to concentrate on reading, Dawson stood up and scanned the banks of the river for snipers. He mentally helped the coxswain steer the boat around sand bars. Dawson strained his eyes trying to spot mines in the water ahead, even though he couldn't see more than four inches into the murky water. He worried the boat right into the landing at Dong Ha, and breathed a big sigh of relief when he disembarked and drove away from the deadly cargo.

On Sunday the weather in Da Nang was perfect. The sky was cool, azure and cloudless as Dawson drove to Refugee Village. How easy it would be to forget there's a war on a day like this, he thought.

Lati greeted him with joy and excitement in her eyes and voice. She wrapped her arms around his waist and squeezed hard. In between kisses she said, "I missed you so much." She pulled him over to the table. "Please sit. I have tea already made. And you can tell me about your trip to Dong Ha."

Dawson handed her a package of cookies he had bought at the PX. "These should go good with tea. What do you want to know about my trip? There's nothing to tell about except war and problems, and today is too beautiful to even think about such things."

When Lati insisted, he did tell her some about his last trip. He tried to play down the danger so she wouldn't worry more than she already did. They sat sipping tea, holding hands, and talking. After a while they stopped talking and sat looking into each other's eyes with unspoken love and desire. Finally Lati got up. "I'll get more tea," she said trying to pull her hand out of his.

But Dawson didn't let go. He stood up saying, "I've had enough tea. What I need and want is you."

Her face registered wonder, desire, and reluctance as he drew her into his arms. She didn't resist, but neither did she respond. Dawson kissed her lightly on the mouth and then on her neck and ear.

"You look especially beautiful today, Lati," he said holding her out at arms length and deliberately studying her from head to foot.

She had on a sexy ao dai. Sexy. Right! Dawson thought. Anything she wore would look sexy to me, now. He pulled her back to him, running fingers of his right hand through her long black hair. It felt damp. He savored the fresh soap smell in her hair. As he tilted her head back, the look on her face was that of a frightened child.

He kissed her gently, teasingly for a few moments, and then more demanding as her lips responded to his. Suddenly she was no longer passive. Her arms wrapped tightly around his neck pulling herself up to him, molding her body to his. They caressed and kissed until they were breathless. Dawson found a zipper and started unzipping Lati's ao dai on the side. She drew back, stopping his hand. "No! Please!"

"Lati, I want you. I want to make love to you. Now! Unless you were pretending, I believe you want me as much as I want you. You do want me, don't you?"

Lati captured one of his hands in both of hers. "You can tell. You know I desire you too much. But I cannot make love with you."

"Why not?"

"It is not right for me to do that."

"Right! What is right?" Dawson asked, sarcasm showing through his desire. "This war isn't right. It's not right your people and my people are killed every day. For you and me to love each other totally, completely, who's to say that's not right?"

"God said it. He said it is only proper between a man and wife. You see, I am a Christian, and I try to live according to those principles. Are you a Christian?"

Dawson was nonplused by her question. He stopped caressing her and sat down. At first he felt angry. Then he felt the same resentful defensiveness building up inside that he always felt when people tried to discuss religion with him.

He buried the resentment inside as he said: "Oh, I don't know. I believe there's a God, some Supreme Being who created everything. It's not something I worry about. I don't really think much about things like that."

"Maybe you should," she said softly.

Dawson felt uncomfortable. He wanted the focus of the conversation off of him. "You may be right. One of these days I'll have to really think it through. But what about your grandfather, was he a Christian too?"

Lati's face became sad as she poured two more cups of tea. "No, he was a Buddhist. He wanted me to be raised as a Buddhist too. But I accepted Christ when I was eight years old. I tried to witness to my grandfather. It was a difficult thing for me to do because of our custom-the young do not teach the old. The young go to their elders for instruction and advice. My grandfather would not consider a change in something so important as religion because of what I said, when he had not listened to my father whom he respected very much. Even though my grandfather was very wise and a good man, he would not accept advice from me being so young-and a woman.

"When I told him I had accepted Christ, he was disappointed. In some Vietnamese or Chinese families my mother and I would have been cast out for denying Buddha. My grandfather told me that if it was my sincere belief, it was all right with him, but I was not to mention my religion to him again. I tried over the years, but he always silenced me with his forbidding look. Now I am sad because we will not spend eternity together. And I wonder what I could have done to convince him."

Dawson sipped his tea in silence. The hot flood of passion had drained from him. He didn't know how to counter her refusal. She was so direct, so sincere. No matter how much he desired her, he knew he didn't want to hurt her in any way. He was thoroughly confused and didn't know what to do.

Finally he said: "I don't agree with the way you believe. I know we need each other, and I know it would be right to make love. I could understand it if you didn't feel the same way about me. But I don't understand how you can let words from a book written two thousand years ago, tell you what you can do."

She smiled, putting her hand on his. "It is not 'a book,' it is the Book; and the words came from God who is eternal. His commandments for how we are to live apply forever. But I do not want to argue with you. I think it does no good to argue religion. It must be a matter of individual conscience."

Dawson smiled and tried to shift things into a lighter vein. "You're right. Let's discuss something we can control, like when you're going to let me make love to you."

"Nothing will change with more discussion. The answer will still be no. Now I remember something else I need to tell you. I may be leaving my job soon."

"Why? I thought you liked your work, and from what I hear, the Admiral thinks highly of you. So why do you want to quit?"

"Well, it is a problem with a colonel on the Admiral's staff. He has been after me for a long time, and now that he knows I am alone, he has become more insistent. He wants me to move into his apartment. He said he has a house on the beach that is well protected, and I would be happy and safe there. I tell him no, no, no, but he does not quit. He frightens me. I do not know what else to do."

Dawson reached across the table caressing her cheek and neck. "Very simple solution, Lati. Tell him you already have a boy friend, and he will leave you alone."

"But I cannot tell him a lie."

"I have a simple solution for that too. If we were lovers, then it wouldn't be a lie. Do you want to start right now so you won't have to lie?"

Lati smiled and slapped his hand lightly, realizing he was teasing her. "Since I will not do that, what else can I do but quit?"

"Seriously, Lati, there is an easy solution. The next time he bothers you, tell him if he doesn't stop, you'll quit and will tell the Admiral why. I guarantee he will back off."

Lati shook her head, looking down. "Oh, I could not do that. He is a very senior officer. I could not talk to Colonel Satour like that."

"Well then, I'll talk to the Colonel. I'm coming up to the White Elephant to-morrow anyway. So I'll talk with him then."

Lati frowned. "I am afraid you might get in trouble because of me, and I would not like that."

"Don't worry about it. I won't have any trouble. Trust me. He won't bother you any more. Now I'd better go, unless you want me to stay all night with you."

Lati smiled, shaking her head. She put her arms around him and pressed her head against his chest. "I am sorry I cannot do what you want me to. Tell me you understand. I do not want you to go and be angry with me."

He stroked her back gently. "I think I understand, Lati, but I don't agree with you. I'm not angry, only disappointed. I love you too much to be angry with you." He tilted her head back and asked, "Does your 'no, no' mean you don't want me to kiss you either?"

She stretched up and kissed him hard and long. "Does that answer your question?"

"Yes. Do it again and I for sure won't leave."

She pushed away from him. "You are impossible!"

As he turned to go, she asked, "You will be back to see me won't you?"

"Of course, as soon as I can. But I must warn you, I'm not giving up. Maybe you'll change your mind and me let make love to you."

Lati shook her head with a smile. Then as he walked away from the shack she said, "I love you very much."

That night Dawson laid awake for a long time. Confused, conflicting thoughts wouldn't let him sleep. Pat Russel kept popping up in his mind. He tried to an-alyze his reluctance to marry her. He thought he loved her, but there seemed to be some elusive ingredient missing. Now, his feelings for Lati seemed to have that ingredient. It was the first conscious thought Dawson had given to Lati and marriage. That idea was troublesome enough to keep him awake, considering the talks he had given men working for him, against marrying natives.

Something inside said, But this is different. His prejudice against marrying out of his race didn't seem to apply to Lati. In addition to the physical desire, a strong heart-felt love seemed to grow within him the more he was around her. He wanted to protect her, to make life easier for her. A part of Dawson couldn't believe he was really considering marrying a Vietnamese, but then another part of him seemed to accept it as natural. She's one-half English, he rationalized. He didn't resolve that matter before falling asleep, but he decided what he had to do about Pat Russel.

The next morning on the second floor of the White Elephant, Dawson was directed to Colonel Satour's office. He knocked on the door jam. The middle-aged, pleasant looking Marine colonel, who was shuffling a stack of paper, waved for him to enter.

"Colonel Satour?" Dawson asked, standing in front of the desk.

"Yes, Lieutenant. What Can I do for you? Have a seat."

"I'm Lieutenant Dawson with the Thirtieth Naval Construction Regiment. I would like to talk with you about a Vietnamese employed here."

"You have the wrong office. I don't have anything to do with personnel."

"Well, sir, it's about one of the interpreters working here. Her name is Lati Noi."

The Colonel gave Dawson his full attention at the mention of her name. "What about Lati?"

"Lati and I are good friends. She confides in me. She tells me you've been trying to get her to move in with you, and that you won't leave her alone. I think..."

"Just a damn minute, Lieutenant! I won't tolerate such accusations."

"Colonel, if you let me finish, it'll be easier on both of us. I'm not here as a jealous boy friend or anything like that. I want to help Lati, and possibly you. Are you aware that she's thinking of quitting her job?"

"No. Why hasn't she said anything about that to me?"

"Well, sir, she's too shy to speak with you plainly. That's why I came over this morning. When she quits she'll tell the Admiral you are the reason, that you bother her all the time. I told her to hold off until I had a chance to talk with you. I felt sure you wouldn't want to be blamed for the Admiral losing a good interpreter. Colonel, can I tell Lati you won't bother her any more?"

For a few seconds Colonel Satour blustered, red flooding his face, his eyes angry. Then shrugging, he smiled and said: "No problem, Lieutenant. If she had told me she already had a boy friend, I wouldn't have bothered her. I sure wouldn't want her to quit, she's a good worker, in addition to being a fine looking girl. When I see her later this morning, I'll let her know everything is OK. No hard feelings, Lieutenant?"

"Not at all, sir. I'm glad things worked out with no problems. Good day, Colonel."

Chapter 11

Ensign Johnson from MCB-21 contacted Dawson by radio. He said he had been designated Project Officer for the Green Beret base, at Lang Vei, and that men and materials would be at Khe Sanh on Wednesday. Dawson agreed to meet him at Khe Sanh, accompany him to Lang Vei, and show him where the bunkers were to be built.

The C-130, loaded with ammunition and other supplies, strained and shuddered as it finally lifted off the runway at Da Nang. With each trip Dawson made he was more and more impressed with the amount of cargo the C-130 could carry. Looking at the supplies piled almost to the overhead, he wondered if anyone really checked the gross weight, or if they simply loaded supplies until the plane was full.

Seated by a window, as they flew along the coast, Dawson saw a large bay called Dam Cau Hai, where fishermen had fish traps that looked a mile long. From the air they resembled huge brown arrows floating on the emerald water.

The flatlands, the rivers, the jungle, the mountains streaked by as they turned inland toward Khe Sanh. The small, tactical runway and Marine base was perched on a small plateau sandwiched between two mountain ridges. Dense green jungle stretching for miles in every direction, made the area look peaceful and quiet. Then Dawson remembered the latest briefing: the V.C. had twenty thousand men in the mountains around Khe Sanh.

A beautiful waterfall tumbled down the face of the cliff near the east end of the runway that began on the plateau above the falls. Fifty yards before the beginning of the AM2 matting, the sheer cliff dropped off a thousand feet to the floor of the canyon and stream below. At the west end of the runway a jungle covered hill rose; so all landings were from the east. Planes also took off to the east, providing a spectacular, breathtaking view as the ground disappeared when the plane reached the cliff.

Ensign Johnson had his twelve-man crew, two dump trucks, a portable cement mixer, a front-end loader, and a D-6 bulldozer ready to roll when Dawson arrived. Johnson said the Marines had cleared the road of mines earlier, but they couldn't provide an escort to Lang Vei, nine miles away. They recommended that the Seabees wait till the next day, then they could go with the mine sweep detail. Dawson decided to go without escort, since he had to be in Da Nang the following day. He obtained a radio from the Marines so he could maintain contact with their command post. If they were ambushed, the Marines would respond immediately.

The single lane dirt road leaving Khe Sanh was bordered by thick jungle, with no more than twenty feet from wall to wall of green. Their progress was slow, with the bulldozer in the lead setting the pace. In about a mile, the jungle on the right gave way to a clearing, where a well maintained masonry house was set back from the road a hundred yards. The tea plantation had been developed by the French when they controlled Vietnam. A Frenchman, who still owned it, waved as the Seabees went by. Dawson wondered how he had been able to exist with the V.C. controlling the countryside all around him. He must've reached some accommodation with them or he would've been killed long ago. Beyond the house Dawson saw many acres of well kept tea trees.

In another mile the slow convoy came to Highway Nine, the narrow paved road winding its way up from Dong Ha to the east, and continuing west to the Laotian border. Turning right on Highway Nine, they weren't boxed in quite so tightly by the jungle, which made Dawson feel relieved. The jungle wall started some ten to fifteen feet back from each side of the road giving better visibility ahead-but little more protection from possible ambush.

Two miles down the road they came to a single lane wood bridge. After close examination, Dawson and Ensign Johnson agreed the bridge wasn't strong enough to support the bulldozer. So the operator made his way down the steep bank, through the small stream, and back up the other bank. The dozer almost got stuck coming up the steep slope, but the Seabee operator demonstrated much skill as he carefully and slowly worked his way up the steep slope and back onto the highway. They encountered one more bridge, which was also bypassed without a problem.

For the entire forty minutes it took them to reach Lang Vei, all of the men were on edge. With their weapons at the "ready" they constantly scrutinized the road ahead, trying to visually penetrate the jungle. They all breathed easier when they arrived at Lang Vei. Dawson called the Marines at Khe Sanh by radio, reporting their safe arrival. He then located the Special Forces camp commander, Lieutenant Kingston, who had one of his men show the Seabees where they would bunk. Dawson showed Johnson where the concrete bunkers were to be built, then they went through the village to the site where they would get their river-run sand and gravel. The Montagnard Chief came out of his hut and smiled broadly, pointing to the wide path, cleared to the stream.

Johnson scratched his head looking at the sand and gravel. "I've never used river-run before. Sure hope it's clean enough to make good concrete."

"It looks pretty good to me," Dawson said, letting sand run through his fingers. "I've made concrete with a lot worse material than this. It'll have to do the job; that's all there is."

One of the dump trucks and driver belonged to the Seabee detachment working at Khe Sanh. That was Dawson's ride back. The young, brash Seabee was an excellent driver. Dawson wanted to close his eyes several times as they sped along the single lane road, going around blind curves. He comforted himself with the thought, The risk of a collision isn't as great as the V.C. getting a good shot at a slow moving vehicle. The Constructionman and Dawson arrived at Khe Sanh in less than half the time it took to get to Lang Vei.

A C-130 was off-loading when they arrived at Khe Sanh. Dawson checked with a crewman who said the plane was returning to Da Nang as soon as it was unloaded. He returned the radio to the Marine command and walked back to the supply staging area. He was less than fifty yards from the plane when the first mortar hit near the runway.

Dawson followed the Marine ahead of him into the nearest mortar trench. The second mortar hit as Dawson dropped into the trench. The third one hit a few seconds later, very close. The V.C. were walking their mortar rounds right down the taxiway toward the C-130 still half loaded with supplies. The roar of the plane's four engines surprised Dawson. He looked over the side of the trench in time to see the remainder of the supplies on pallets come tumbling from the rear of the plane.

Now I understand why they have rollers on the decks and loading ramps of those planes, Dawson thought.

The plane looked like it might become airborne as it taxied at high speed to the runway. The pilot gave the huge plane full throttle while he was still turning to line up with the runway. The plane used only two-thirds of the runway before lifting off. Then, it tucked its wheels in its belly and headed for Da Nang.

More rounds came in, impacting closer and closer to the trench. Dawson pressed himself against the side of the trench as did three Marines. He felt his own fear increasing and could see it in the faces of the other men. But Dawson kept telling himself it would take a direct hit to get them, and the odds were long against a direct hit.

One Marine tried to make a joke about Charley being a lousy shot, but his joke was cut off in mid-sentence when another round exploded near enough to shower them with dirt and rocks. When Marine gunners located the mortars and returned fire, incoming rounds stopped. The "all clear" sounded five minutes later.

Dawson knew he was stuck at Khe Sanh for the night. The sun was setting and no more planes would be in until the next day. Chief Kerns, in charge of the Seabee detachment at Khe Sanh, got an extra cot so Dawson could sleep in the hooch with the Seabees. But he may as well have saved his energy. Charley threw in another short barrage of mortar rounds as Dawson and Kerns sat down to eat.

When they got back from the mortar trench the food was cold and tasteless. An hour after "lights out" the camp was splattered with a heavy barrage of shells from 122mm artillery located in Laos. Several shells hit close to the trench Dawson was in, the concussion driving him into the wall of the trench.

He tried to keep his fear under control by telling himself over and over: They won't get a direct hit in my trench. They won't hit my trench. They won't hit my trench. The odds are against it.

Khe Sanh was on "alert" for the rest of the night. Dawson remained with the Seabee detachment who defended part of the south perimeter. Charley sent in a few rounds of artillery or mortar intermittently all night. Dawson along with all the camp residents, huddled in trenches, got less than two hours sleep that night.

A heavy barrage of incoming mortar and 122mm shells started at 0415, with one of the mortars hitting the trench fifteen yards from Dawson. Concussion and damp earth covered him like a blanket. At the call, "Corpsman! Corpsman!" Dawson crawled down the dark trench to see if he could help. He felt the body crumpled in the trench, but couldn't see who it was until another flare lit up the area. Dawson could barely recognize Chief Kerns who had the right side of his face and right arm blown off.

A corpsman, stopping massive bleeding on a young Seabee a few feet away, asked, "Is he alive?"

Dawson knew the answer before he checked the left carotid artery. "There's no pulse," he said.

He helped the Corpsman lift the injured Constructionman out of the trench so other corpsmen could get him to the field hospital. Then he returned to his post, fighting wave after wave of nausea, realizing there was nothing to be done for Chief Kerns other than put him in a body-bag.

At 0435 the Marine positions on the north and west perimeters started taking small arms fire. The first wave of North Vietnamese assaulted the north side at 0445, getting through the outer concertina wire, but were stopped in the mine fields. Base command moved in reinforcements for the north and west sectors before the next wave of North Vietnamese attacked. A mortar barrage preceded the second attack, causing heavy casualties in the Marine trenches.

Machine gun and rifle fire increased as the attack intensified. The Viet Cong swarmed through the land mine area after their first squad had been sacrificed to the mines. But when the Marines fired the Claymore mines, killing seventy men at once, the charge halted, and the enemy retreated under heavy fire, disappearing into the jungle. The next volley of flares illuminated a field of fire devoid of movement, covered with bodies and silence. By dawn the V.C. were hidden again under the heavy jungle canopy.

The first plane arrived at 0930. It unloaded men and cargo and headed back to Da Nang at 1000. Dawson was relieved to be up and away from Khe Sanh. The ceiling was dropping, and it was questionable if anymore planes would be able to land at Khe Sanh that day.

Dawson looked at the six body-bags and wondered which one held the remains of Chief Kerns. One night is enough, he thought. Guess I could stick it out like the poor buggers on duty there, but I'm glad I don't have to. Now I understand why their faces have such a haggard look. Chief Kerns-I wonder if he had a wife and children. It sure makes the war seem deadly and personal when someone you know is killed only a few feet away.

After dinner at Red Beach, Dawson had two drinks and then decided to skip the movie. He had been putting something off; but procrastinating didn't make it any easier. He had his bourbon and seven refilled, took it to his room, got out pen and paper, and then sat at the desk for a long time before beginning the letter.

Dear Pat,

I have thought a lot about what you said in a letter several weeks ago. I know you're right. We can't go on as we have, or at least we shouldn't go on. What you said didn't make me angry. It made me do some serious thinking. This place is conducive to introspection. The danger and death all around has made me dig down below surface feelings and examine our relationship-more specifically, examine my feelings for you.

We've had a good physical relationship. I believe you do love me very deeply, as you've said. I've loved you, and do love you in a way, and not only sensually. I have enjoyed being with you, enjoyed the many things we've shared together. A multitude of pleasant recollections are stored in my mind. But as you said, I've always held a part of myself back. I couldn't give you complete commitment. I guess that's because I haven't loved you completely, without reservation.

It bothers me to put these words on paper, because it seems I have cheated you. I didn't mean to. I wanted to be with you and have a good time for however long we could. Now I wish I had realized my lack of deeper inner feelings a long time ago so our situation could have been set straight and you could have gone on to a more complete and satisfying life.

Dawson paused. He thought about putting the letter aside and finishing it the next day. This was such an irrevocable act, and a part of him didn't want to eliminate Pat from his life. Come on boy, he thought. You're only trying to postpone a difficult job-and it won't be any easier tomorrow.

He continued writing.

What I'm trying to say is, we can not look forward to marriage, not because you've done anything, but because I don't love you enough to want to establish a permanent tie. I feel strongly about marriage, and believe it should be as permanent as life. Now I know if I agreed to marry you it would be a charade; I would be acting out a lie, because my love for you is not of the quality on which to build a marriage.

So I think we should end it now. I see no reason to wait until I return to the States. I too want to be as straight forward as possible, and think you should know my feelings now. I wish you all of the best in life, and hope you will find complete happiness with a man deserving of your love. You will always occupy a very special place in my heart and mind.

Love,

Bill

Sunday wouldn't come fast enough. Dawson's mind was clearer than it had been for many weeks, and he was very anxious to see Lati. She greeted him at the door with a warm smile, and pulled him inside before she offered her lips and arms. They kissed and caressed until they were breathless.

Lati, with her head pressed to Dawson's chest, said: "The neighbors talk about us. They think I have taken you as my lover now grandfather is gone. I correct them when they speak of us that way. But it does no good. They think that all women who see American military are sleeping with them."

"We can very easily correct that erroneous thinking by making it come true," Dawson replied. "Then you wouldn't have to worry about what nosy neighbors are thinking."

Lati slapped playfully at Dawson. "No, I prefer facing them with a clear conscience. They may never believe me, but I know the truth."

As they sat at the rough table sipping tea, Dawson asked, "Has Colonel Satour bothered you since I talked with him?"

Lati smiled shaking her head. "No, he has been very kind to me. He treats me as though there had never been a problem between us. You were right about what to do. Thank you for talking with the Colonel."

"Now your grandfather is no longer with you, have you thought about finding a husband?" Dawson asked.

She frowned, shaking her head. "No, I am not looking for a husband. I do not know any Vietnamese whom I would consider marrying."

"But won't life be more difficult for you living alone? Even as things are now, with the South Vietnamese in control, it's not very easy for a woman alone. If the Viet Cong take over some time in the future, as your grandfather thought they would, things will go badly for you having worked for the U. S. Military."

Lati pursed her mouth for a few seconds. "I do not let myself worry about that. There is nothing I can do about such things. What they do to my body will not really matter except for the pain, because Christ lives in my heart. When my body dies, my spirit will live forever with God. So you see there is no need for me to worry."

After he left, Dawson pondered her words in silence for a long time. She made it sound so simple. He marveled at her uncompromising stand and quiet faith. And he wondered how one so small and fragile looking could have so much courage and determination.

Chapter 12

From the air Dong Ha looked like a huge dried-up wheat field in Kansas. The wind blowing red dirt, that was mud a month ago, now covered the entire combat base. Most of the vegetation south of Dong Ha village had been scraped off for roads, building sites, open storage, or living areas. The constant dust seemed as bad as the mud was before. It stained the men's sweat drenched shirts red. But at least the machines don't get stuck all the time, Dawson thought.

He had gotten an early flight to Dong Ha, then caught a Mike Boat and reached the mouth of the Qua Viet River by 1000. Work there was progressing well, although still a little behind schedule. With Charley's increased shelling and sniping, not much else could be done to increase productivity. Dawson would be able to report that the pile driver was driving piles rapidly; the dredge was keeping the mouth of the river open; the concrete crews had the staging area almost finished; and construction of hooches was nearing completion.

The LCM taking Dawson back up the river to Dong Ha, carried a tank and a few crates of supplies. Three miles from Dong Ha, where the river made a large "S," a smaller river joined the Qua Viet in the upstream curve. After they rounded the first curve, a large sampan was visible backed into the far bank 500 yards in front of the Mike boat. Suddenly bullets were ricocheting off the water around the boat. Three punctured the hull and made dull thud sounds when they hit the tank. The sound of a machine gun accompanied the bullets across the water. Everyone but the Coxswain running the boat dropped down into the well of the boat.

A Marine sergeant in the tank yelled at the coxswain, "Keep the bow pointed straight at 'em and drop the ramp. I'll give them a big surprise."

When the ramp lowered, Dawson was standing behind the tank. He quickly discarded the idea of using his .45, at that distance. Another machine gun burst came from the sampan and ricocheted off the tank. Sure glad we aren't carrying ammo or gas, Dawson thought. The gunner fired a round from the tank cannon two seconds after the ramp dropped. The shot was short, spraying the sampan with water.

Peering around the tank, Dawson watched the V.C. scramble to get the sampan away from the bank and headed toward the small stream. They were ten feet from the bank when the second shell found its mark, blowing the sampan to bits.

The water was too shallow for the Mike boat to get to the sampan, but there was no sign of life. The Coxswain reported the attack on the radio, which would get one of the river patrol boats dispatched to investigate, to look for survivors and to get a body count.

Back in Dong Ha, Dawson inspected the many construction sites. With the arrival of hot, dry weather, the tempo of construction had increased. Concrete was in big demand, but a steady source of rock to feed the crusher hadn't been found. The Vietnamese contractor was very slow delivering rock. So the Bees were still doing most of their concrete work with river-run sand and gravel from Cam Lo. The sandbar they had been dredging was depleted, so the crane and drag-line had to be relocated. Getting the new location adapted for efficient loading of trucks had slowed down sand and gravel production. Dawson drove out to inspect the new site. It looked good, enough accessible material existed to last till the next rainy season. Maybe by that time, he thought, we'll have a reliable source of rock.

Driving back to Dong Ha, Dawson was fifty feet ahead of one of the huge Euclid dump trucks when he heard an explosion behind him. Looking through the rear view mirror, he saw smoke coming from under the dump truck. He turned around and went back to help the driver who was shaken, but uninjured. The right rear dual tandems had been blown off by a mine.

"Must have been a pressure type mine set for a heavy load," the driver said. "Otherwise it would've gone off when you drove over it, Lieutenant."

"Good thing I didn't have enough weight to set it off. It would've done a lot more damage to my weaps, and probably me too," Dawson replied. "Hop in. I'll take you to the base so you can get someone to bring in your truck."

For the rest of the drive to Dong Ha, Dawson was more cautious, although he tried to not let his apprehension show. He drove a little slower, and searched the road edge for signs of fresh digging that would indicate a mine. Since Charley had become expert at planting mines and covering his tracks, they were hard to detect.

After dropping off the Seabee driver at the MCB-21 equipment yard, Dawson drove to the officer's mess, where he got a cup of coffee. The strong, stale, black liquid calmed his nerves after the mine incident. Don't know what I'm so jumpy about, he thought. It's the dump driver who should have been shaken.

After a few minutes of quiet, he drove across camp to inspect a new warehouse the Bees had started. When Dawson was about fifty feet from the building, an artillery round hit, only thirty yards behind him. The explosion beat on his eardrums. Concussion squeezed every square-inch of his body. Panic flooded through him. The weaps wouldn't stop fast enough. The ignition switch eluded his fingers. Seconds seemed like minutes. Panic grew when his feet hit the ground and he realized he didn't know the mortar trench location. This feeling of complete terror was new to Dawson.

Spotting a Seabee running from the building, Dawson dashed after him. Before he got to the trench, another shell exploded, closer. To Dawson it was like a bad dream in which he tried to run from some overtaking danger. His legs wouldn't move fast enough. They seemed to move in slow-motion. In reality he was running as fast as he could, but didn't seem to be getting to the mortar trench fast enough.

After dropping into the mortar trench his fear and panic didn't subside. In previous attacks, Dawson felt fear, but never debilitating terror. He knew he usually had a few seconds to get in a trench before the next round hit. Before, when he got below ground level, his fear subsided because he believed the odds of Charley hitting close enough to kill him were one in a million.

But this time panic distorted his logic. He was sure each incoming shell was aimed at him. He pressed tight against the earth wall, keeping his back to the other men in the trench so they wouldn't see the panic in his face. Six more shells hit more distant from the mortar trench. When the "all clear" sounded, after fifteen minutes of silence, Dawson didn't really want to leave the trench. He was sure another round would hit at any second. But he had no choice. When the other men climbed out and went back to work, he had to get out too.

Dawson made a quick inspection of the building, then drove back to the main part of the camp. Most of the shells had hit within the Seabee camp. One living hooch was completely demolished. The south end of the mess hall, which was used for storage, was a tangled mess of metal and wood.

It was almost time for evening chow, so Dawson went to his hooch across the road from the mess hall. He lay down on his cot trying to relax and calm his continuing fear. When it came time for dinner he didn't want to go. He didn't feel hungry, but finally forced himself to walk to the officer's mess after reasoning it was as safe there as in the hooch. After dinner Dawson went back to his hooch rather than sitting around swapping stories and drinking beer.

Mobile Construction Battalion Twenty-one had improved on the standard hooch. Two mortar trenches were dug and then hooches built over them. Inside, hinged trapdoors were installed in the plywood deck so the men could roll off their bunks and quickly drop into a trench. The trapdoors, kept closed during the day, were opened by the men when they turned in for the night. When Dawson got to the hooch he opened the trapdoor by his bunk and lay down to read, trying to blot out his fear. It did little good. He found himself dreading the next incoming round.

Tossing the book aside, unable to read, he tried to understand what was happening to him and why. Maybe it's because of the machine gun attack, or the mine incident returning from Cam Lo and then the mortar attack, and my not knowing where the mortar trench was located. Maybe it's too many dangerous incidents in one day, he thought.

In the past, when men were reported to have battle fatigue or be shell-shocked, Dawson had thought they were trying to take an easy way out of a combat zone. It was all in their minds, and they could control it if they tried. Now I understand, fear can't always be controlled.

His thoughts were interrupted by a new barrage of incoming artillery. Dawson was down in the trench within two seconds of the first shell impacting. Panic enveloped him again. He fought a crazy urge to bolt from his trench and run. Alone, he huddled against the end of the trench waiting for each shell to hit him. Even though he knew the shells were impacting a half mile away, he couldn't calm his fear. When the "all clear" sounded, he remained in the mortar trench for another half-hour. Finally, he climbed back into his bunk and tried to read until "lights out." Then he lay in the dark trying to force himself to sleep.

Shortly before midnight more incoming arrived. When the "all clear" sounded this time, Dawson pulled the mattress off his bunk and lay on it in the trench. He decided the spiders and scorpions living in the trenches were more tolerable than the near panic he felt when in his bunk. He was glad the other officer who lived in the hooch was gone with a detachment. He managed to doze off a few times, but got very little sleep even though there were no more incoming.

The next day Dawson had planned to fly to Khe Sanh and then drive over to Lang Vie. He felt relief when told that Khe Sanh was socked in with low clouds, and they didn't expect to have any planes going up there until the next day. Dawson contacted Ensign Johnson by radio, who reported work was progressing on schedule. They were having no trouble getting the river-run sand and gravel for the concrete bunkers.

By noon Dawson had taken care of all the business he could at Dong Ha. Since he couldn't get to Khe Sanh, with much relief he boarded a plane to Da Nang right after lunch. He breathed a sigh of relief when the plane lifted off the runway. Leaning his head against the webbing, that formed the back to his seat, he let the vibration and roar of the engines put him to sleep.

In between catnaps Dawson thought about the pervading fear he had felt last night and all through the morning, even when there was no ongoing danger. He convinced himself it was a temporary thing, and he would be over it by the time he had to return to Dong Ha.

Back in Da Nang a day earlier than usual, he made good use of the extra time. Supply problems abounded, and several pending jobs needed to be discussed with headquarters commands. Too many people wanted too many jobs done immediately. Activity along the DMZ had picked up, and the Marines were moving more and more troops into the Dong Ha area. That meant more wells, roads, storage, mess halls, more of everything. The manpower in MCB-21 was stretched thin. Some work would have to be deferred and that was sure to make the top brass unhappy.

In his last briefing Dawson told the Commodore, that MCB-21 was getting overloaded with what customers said were top priority jobs, and in fact they were. Most jobs were for direct combat support. Few requests were for what Dawson considered frills.

"I understand the problem, Bill, but we're in the same position throughout the I Corps area," the commodore said. "We have no extra Seabees to move up there. You'll have to be blunt with the Marine commanders. If they want a new project started immediately, ask them which job in-progress they want stopped so we can start the new one. If you get too much flack about which job in different commands has priority, we'll have to push the problem right on up to Third Marine Division. But keep the lid on things as long as you can before we have to go that route."

The relative quiet and safety of Da Nang area seemed like heaven to Dawson. At night when Red Beach went on alert because a nearby Marine command was being mortared, he didn't experience fear and panic as he had in Dong Ha. Of course the rockets and mortars were impacting two or three miles distant. So far the V.C. had attacked the Seabee base at Red Beach only once. Dawson rationalized that the shells weren't aimed at his camp, so he was able to control his fear.

Several times during the week he had been tempted to stop and see Lati. He had been up in the White Elephant twice, but both times with another officer, and they had urgent matters to resolve. At night Lati occupied more of his thinking. Unbidden, his thoughts converged on marriage more and more. He vacillated. A part of his mind wanted to ask her to marry him, another part argued against it. By Sunday afternoon when he went to see Lati, Dawson hadn't resolved that ambivalence.

For a brief time, holding Lati in his arms blotted out all fears, all other thoughts. He was aware only of her lips and her warm supple body pressed against his. Her welcome was so warm and passionate that for a while he thought she had changed her mind about making love. He found out he was wrong when his hands started wandering into off-limits territory. She pulled away from him and captured his hands. Lati stood shaking her head even though her face was flushed with the same desire he felt.

Dawson smiled and said, "Remember, I said I wasn't going to quit trying."

"I know. But please do not get angry with me for doing what I must do. It is very difficult. When I see you, I want to kiss you and have you hold me in your arms and feel the warmth of our bodies together. Then it leads to this situation. It causes me much distress to push you away, to tell you to stop. Please, will you help me to control this problem?"

Dawson gave her a teasing smile. "Don't you see, Lati, we would have no problem if you relaxed, then we could do what is very natural between a man and woman. If we make love like we both want to, there would be no problem."

Lati moved away shaking her head. She pointed to a stool at the table inviting him to sit. She sat opposite him, taking one of his hands in hers. Her face grew calm and serious. "Please," she implored. "You tease me when I tell you no. I think you do not understand how difficult it is for me. Please be serious and listen with your heart as well as with your ears. At times I think of not meeting with you again, but I love you too much.

"I cannot tell you to go away. So I lose that battle. I tell myself I will be calm and very proper when you come, that I will sit across the table as we are now. Then we will not get the passion flowing that is so hard to control. But I only fool myself with those plans. When I see you I do not remember what I tell myself in private. The desire to kiss you and feel your arms around me pushes out all other thoughts."

He started to speak, but Lati said, "No, please. Let me finish. Your kisses and caresses build such great desire in me that I would like to let you make love to me even if it meant the end of life for me after you leave. My love and desire for you is that strong. But I know it is not proper. Not only because my father was a missionary and taught me that, but I know it is morally wrong.

"My compassion, my love for you makes me want to give you joy and happiness. It makes such an impossible situation for me that I do not know what to do at times. I am afraid you think me cruel for coming to you and yielding to you for a few minutes, but then pushing you away when our passion is high."

Dawson pushed aside his own feelings, his desire, as a strong feeling of empathy grew within him. He listened, really listened to what Lati was saying, as she continued. "I think I know how to make you understand the importance of my moral convictions. I am sure you are quite patriotic. Suppose you possessed some important information, something if disclosed to the enemy would do your country harm. If I told you I was an enemy agent, and that if you gave me the information I would make love with you, would you do it?"

Dawson frowned. "I couldn't do something like that no matter how much I love you and desire you."

Lati gave a little smile, with both hands turned up, extended toward Dawson. "Then you know why I cannot give in to my desire and do what you want. My Christian convictions have even stronger control over me than patriotism."

He took her hands in his, slowly shaking his head. "Lati, you've made your point totally, completely. I'm ashamed for taking your feelings too lightly. To me, making love seems natural because I love you. I've not really considered it from your viewpoint. I'll try to be more considerate of your feelings in the future, I promise. It won't solve the problem, but it'll make it easier for you."

Lati came around the table to Dawson. Then she hesitated. "May I sit on your lap without causing too much problem?"

He smiled, pulling her on to his lap. "You may. I'll use superhuman control and not let it bother me-I think."

Lati kissed him lightly on the lips. "You are a kind and gentle man, and I love you very much."

"Enough to marry me?" The question seemed to pop out of its own volition. Dawson could hardly believe he had asked it. Silence filled the room for a long time, as Lati searched his face for evidence she had heard correctly.

"You are teasing me! You truly want me to marry you?"

"Yes."

She looked at him. Waiting. Expecting more enlightenment. "I do not know what to say. I..., I cannot give you an answer. I am overwhelmed with surprise."

Dawson stroked her hair gently. "Haven't you even considered the possibility of our being married?"

Now Lati dropped her gaze. "Only as a fanciful dream. I never seriously considered it because I did not think it was possible. I cannot give an answer now. There is much to consider."

Even with her head bowed, Dawson could see that she was nibbling on her lip. "When will you give me your answer?" he asked in a subdued voice.

"I do not know. Will you be back next Sunday?"

"If possible."

"I promise to give you an answer then," she said getting up from his lap.

Before he left, Dawson kissed her gently. When he drew back, Lati didn't let him go. She held him with her face only a few inches away. She looked long into his eyes. It was a questioning look filled with love and wonder.

Driving back to Red Beach Dawson thought, I really did it! In a remote part of my mind I've considered it for a while, but I sure didn't plan to ask her today. Wow! A gigantic step. Of course, Lati may not accept my proposal. And there are problems I haven't really thought through. Getting approval from the Navy will be a big problem-then there's this religion thing. Difference in ages-that's a big consideration. The racial difference and its effect on my Navy career is another problem. A lot seems to be against it and only one thing in favor-our love for each other. I wonder if that's enough to overcome all of the problems.

After dinner, as Dawson joined other officers in the lounge to watch a movie, his mind dwelt on returning to Dong Ha the next day. Dread started building within him. He didn't want to go back up there. He even tried to think of reasons why he shouldn't go. Then he reminded himself that while he might be able to invent work to justify staying in Da Nang for another day, eventually he would have to return to Dong Ha. The movie did little to ease his mind.

Dawson hadn't bothered wearing his steel helmet or flack jacket in the combat base on his prior trips, but this time he had them on when he got off the plane. He needed as much of a security blanket as he could get. The days dragged by slowly as he forced himself to go to all of the places necessary. But the two nights Dawson stayed in Dong Ha were worse. Those nights he slept on a mattress in the mortar trench under the hooch. Again he was thankful there were no other occupants to see his fear.

The only place he really felt safe in Dong Ha was in the MCB-21 underground Command Center. The Command Center was constructed of heavy timbers, with six feet of earth covering them. In the C. P. were two bunks, which the Commanding Officer and the Operations Officer used. Dawson wanted to take his mattress and sleep in one corner of the C. P. But he couldn't. He felt ashamed and disgusted with himself when he thought of the men who were based at Dong Ha and endured the danger day after day for weeks on end. They didn't have the relief of going to Da Nang to get away from the horror.

Wednesday afternoon Dawson hitched a ride on a Special Forces chopper directly to Lang Vie. There, construction work was almost complete. The five-sided concrete bunkers, with slits for firing, made the camp look formidable. The camp commander was well satisfied with the bunkers. Johnson said he would pull his men and equipment out in the next day or two.

The supplies for Lang Vei had been off-loaded by the time Dawson had finished his inspection. Then the chopper pilot agreed to take Dawson directly back to Da Nang, letting him off at the helicopter pad on Red Beach.

Lati had crept into Dawson's thoughts all during the week. At times it was difficult for him to concentrate on material shortages and the need to constantly shift material from a job that wasn't quite ready for it, to another project that was ready, but whose material hadn't yet arrived. Later he had to sweat out the arrival of supplies to repay the job he had borrowed from. The part of his job Dawson found most difficult was constantly having to change priorities and schedules. He always took heat from the people whose jobs got pushed back.

Suspense built all week for Dawson. The more he thought about being married to Lati the more he liked it. Sunday seemed as if it would never arrive-and with it Lati's answer. He decided to discuss potential problems with Lati before she gave him an answer. He didn't want to put obstacles in their path, but he knew they were topics that had to be considered.

Dawson intended to take Lati some flowers, but didn't get into downtown Da Nang on either Saturday or Sunday. So he took her a box of candy instead. When Lati opened the door, Dawson stood in the opening and whistled. She was dressed in a new yellow ao dai that complimented her light coloring. Her hair was done up in a roll at the back of her head, making her look older and highlighting her graceful neck.

"You are exceptionally beautiful today," Dawson said as he stepped into the shack and closed the door.

Lati made a quick curtsy, and said, "Thank you. You are most kind," before she came into his arms.

After a long kiss that left them both breathless, Lati took him by the hand and said: "Come. Sit. We have much to talk about, and I can not talk or even think while we are kissing."

Dawson pulled the candy from the paper bag and handed it to Lati. "I wanted to get you flowers, but I didn't have a chance. That's a new dress, I mean ao dai, you're wearing, isn't it?"

"Yes, I just bought it. And Yesterday was the first time I ever went to a beauty salon. I told the madam in charge of the shop I wanted my hair done up for a special occasion. Do you like it?"

"Yes, very much. It brings out another quality for me to love."

"Do you want tea before or after?" Lati asked.

"Before or after what?"

"Before or after I give you my answer."

"Later," He said. "We need to discuss some things before you give me your answer."

Lati sat across from him, some of the excitement and radiance leaving her face.

"Lati, I know your age, but do you know how old I am?"

"No. But that will make no difference."

"I am fifteen years older than you. That's not a problem now, or even in the next few years. But in twenty years, our difference in ages could cause serious problems. Then our needs and wants will differ greatly.

Lati smiled. "That is not much of a problem. The Chinese and Vietnamese women marry men as much as twenty-five years older than they are. So you see, fifteen years is not much difference."

"OK. I just wanted you to know how much older I am. Another consideration is our racial difference. In the United States you won't be accepted by some people because you're part Oriental, although the majority will accept you. Sometimes you may get your feelings hurt by unkind people, so you need to know what to expect in advance."

Lati shrugged. "Because some people do not want to accept me will not matter. That is the way of the world, I think. One race does not accept members of a different race. If we were married and lived here, some Vietnamese would not accept you. Do you have more problems to give me?"

"No, not now. We need to discuss other things, but they can wait until after you give me your answer." He paused, waiting. The silence felt heavy, even though Dawson thought he could read the answer in Lati's eyes.

Finally she bowed her head. "I will be most honored to be your wife."

Dawson leaned across the table, tilting her face up and kissed her.

Lati drew back. "Wait. There are other things I must say to you. Vietnamese custom is for the father of the bride to give a dowry, but I must come to you without one. There is no one to give a dowry even if there was something to give."

"Your marrying me will be more important than a thousand dowries. In my country the dowry was done away with many years ago."

Lati continued: "One other thing I wonder about is whether the military will permit you to marry me. The American admirals and generals are not in favor of men marrying Vietnamese girls. In my work I have seen many cases when permission to marry was not granted."

"Yes, that may be a problem. I'll start work on it as soon as I get back from Dong Ha on Thursday. Don't worry, it'll work out OK. Now if you come over here and sit in my lap we can celebrate."

They kissed and caressed for a long while. Lati was flushed and breathless. Dawson felt as though he would explode with desire.

"Now that we're going to be married I think it would be all right for us to make love. What...?""

"No, she interrupted. The Bible does not sanction intimacy because we are betrothed. We must be married for our union to be blessed by God. Do you want me to show you in the Bible?"

Dawson held up both hands. "No. No! You don't have to show me. I'm sure you're right. But I don't see what difference a little piece of paper can make. Guess I should have known what your answer would be even before I asked. Maybe you should make some tea to cool us down."

They talked and planned their lives for a long time, until shadows grew long. They decided to get married as soon as possible. He agreed with Lati continuing to work, since she liked her job and there would be little for her to do while he was gone.

Lati asked about his work. He told her a little about the different jobs, where he had to go and how he got to the many bases.

After a long pause Dawson said: "I didn't intend to tell you about this, but I need to talk with someone, and I can't tell the men I work with. They would consider me weak, a coward. Maybe talking about it will help to diminish my fear."

Lati studied Dawson's face intently, realizing he was sharing something of great concern to him. Her face showed her desire to understand and help.

"Until two weeks ago I had my fear under control when I went up to the Dong Ha area, and other more dangerous places. Sure, I was afraid at the instant of danger, but my fear subsided along with the immediate danger. I didn't constantly worry about the next time we would be shelled. I was able to convince myself Charley wouldn't hit me.

"Now I worry all of the time I'm up in the hot areas. When I'm down here in relative safety, I don't want to go back to Dong Ha, or the Qua Viet, or Khe Sanh. I dread going back up there. I have to use much will power to force myself to go. But that's my job and I must do it."

"Maybe you can get assigned to a job not so dangerous. I would like that too," Lati said. "I worry about you up in those bad places. I hear at work how much fighting there is north of here each day, and I worry."

"I considered requesting a different job this past week. But I can't do that, it would be cowardly. Someone must do this job, and it was assigned to me. When I think of the little danger I face compared to what the men out on patrol endure every day, I'm really ashamed. I don't like feeling like a coward, but I seem to have no control now. Tell me truthfully, Lati, do you think less of me now that you know how much fear I have?"

"Of course not. I love you more and want to protect you, but I can do nothing but pray."

166

Later, when Dawson was ready to leave, Lati came into his arms and after they had kissed she said, "I will pray for you every day. I will pray for your safety and your peace of mind."

"Thanks. I can probably use your prayers."

In Dong Ha, Dawson found his fear hadn't lessened, if anything it was worse than before. He wore his helmet and flack jacket all the time, hot and uncomfortable as they were. The OPS officer's comment, "Looks like Dong Ha is getting to you," made him feel more uncomfortable. The helmet gave him a headache, and the twenty pound flack jacket made him hot and sweaty and tired. But they provided a small measure of security.

The second shelling of the day started when Dawson was washing off the sweat and grime, getting ready for dinner. The camp remained on alert for an hour with 122mm rounds coming in every few minutes. By the time the "all clear" sounded, Dawson had no appetite. He went to chow, but only poked at his food as he drank beer to calm his nerves. *Now I understand why some of the men out here drink so much.*

After making his bed in the mortar trench, he slept only fitfully. Lying awake at different times during the night, he berated himself and tried to rationalize the situation. *Why am I such a chicken? What if I had to stay up here twenty-four hours a day, seven days a week like the men who live here? What would I do then?* But rationalizing didn't help, it only made him feel worse; in addition to his fear, he felt the guilt of not measuring up.

The next morning at the MCB-21 Battalion Command Post the action report was grim. In addition to casualties from incoming rounds, sniper fire, and the V.C. probing the defensive perimeter, a Marine company out on a search-and-destroy mission had been ambushed by a North Vietnamese Army battalion. Bravo Company suffered extremely heavy casualties. They couldn't get air cover to assist them because of the low ceiling. The V.C. had them surrounded when they sprung the trap, and then they stayed in such close contact the Marines couldn't call in artillery without endangering their own positions. As the battle raged through the night, Marine casualties mounted, and the V.C. kept pressure on them.

At 0400 the Company Commander realized he couldn't hold out, that what remained of his company would soon be overrun, so he gave his own coordinates and told the 105mm Battalion six miles away to start firing. The first salvo of shells were off target, so the C.O. gave them a correction. That brought the shells in all around and on top of them.

The Marines who were still alive had dug slit trenches during the night, and were somewhat protected from the shrapnel from the shells. The heavy shelling broke the V.C. attack. They suffered heavy casualties before withdrawing and fading into the endless jungle. The Marines lost one-third of Bravo Company.

Dawson had seen a few V.C. bodies in the field where they dropped, he had seen bodies of Marines brought back from patrols-they were usually in body bags on their way to the morgue. He had ridden on planes laden with coffins, that marked the beginning of the final journey home for many men. He had not gotten used to being in close proximity to the dead. Now it didn't bother him as much as it had at first, and seeing the enemy dead didn't seem to bother him as much as seeing American dead. But Dawson was not prepared for the sight he encountered the morning after the Bravo Company ambush.

A new Marine battalion had set up camp about a half-mile from the Seabee camp, where they were still living in tents. One of their responsibilities was to process all American bodies in the Dong Ha area. Dawson had been to the Battalion Commander's office to discuss the Bees building a mess hall and living hooches. As he drove back to the MCB-21 camp, he passed a tent with a sign in front that read, "morgue." He had been by there before and had seen a few bodies in bags lying near the tent. Now as he drove by, out of the corner of his left eye he caught a glimpse of an unusual looking pile. From the quick glimpse out of his peripheral vision, his mind wouldn't accept what his eye told him it saw.

Dawson braked to a stop, and looked back to see what the pile was. Immediately he wished he hadn't. Piled five feet high were Marine bodies. Heads and arms and legs pointed out in every direction. The pile was predominately green from their uniforms. Contrasting patches of stark white or black skin stood out in the sun, with the red of their blood superimposed on the green and white and black. About fifty bodies, or parts of bodies, were in that pile.

Two men came out of the tent and dragged one of the bodies off the pile, carrying it by hands and feet into the morgue tent. To Dawson, the men handled the body like they would a mannequin, not like they should handle a flesh and blood human, whose life had very recently departed.

When Dawson's mind finally accepted what that inert pile was, he felt as though someone had hit him in the stomach. He felt dizzy, and wanted to vomit. After regaining some control, he drove off, relieved to get the pile of bodies out of his vision. But driving away didn't remove it from his mind's eye.

It was lunch time when he got back to camp, but Dawson couldn't eat. He went to his hooch and lay on his cot trying to read, trying to blot out the sight of those bodies, stacked up like fire wood.

That night was worse than previous ones for Dawson. Fear seemed to bore into his bones. They received more incoming rounds at dark. He pressed himself against the end of the trench under his hooch until the "all clear" sounded. Then he went to the underground command bunker on the pretext of discussing work with the Operations Officer. His fear subsided in the bunker even though they received more incoming while he was there. Finally, at midnight, Dawson couldn't think of a good reason for staying in the bunker any longer. By the time he got back to his hooch, fear had closed in on him again. He slept fitfully in the mortar trench for the remainder of the night.

Back in Da Nang Dawson could breath easier again. He didn't realize the effect constant fear was having on him physically until he observed his haggard face while shaving. He had lost weight too. He could tell by the loose fit of his uniform.

His second night back in Da Nang, after dinner, Dawson went to the headquarters building and had the duty yeoman get the MACV rules and regulations out along with those of the Regiment. He spent two hours looking for regulations on Americans marrying Vietnamese. Although they said no fraternization, MACV didn't forbid marriage, but they instructed the lower commands to strongly discourage it. They did require the approval of the man's commanding officer.

Sunday, after the Commodore's briefing, Dawson hung back when the group of officers had been dismissed.

The Commodore looked up. "You have something else on your mind, Bill?"

"Yes sir. It's a personal matter, a request. I want to marry a Vietnamese woman, and I need your permission. Do I need to give you the request in writing?"

Commodore Rhodes put down the letter he had been reading. He looked into Dawson's gray eyes for a few seconds, and then said: "Sit down Bill. We'd better talk about this one. It isn't as simple as it may seem. You're sure? You're really serious about this?"

"Yes sir. I've found the woman I want to be with for the rest of my life."

"Well, I'm not going to give you a lecture. You're old enough to know what you want to do. I'm sure you've read the MACV regulations on this, and know COs are to discourage such marriages. That order was set up primarily to protect our young impressionable boys. The General in Saigon has put more teeth in it verbally. He told all troop commanders not to approve such requests. So for sure I don't want you to put in an official request."

"Commodore, are you saying I can't get married?"

"Officially, yes. And officially telling you if you put in a request I'll have to disapprove it."

Dawson could feel himself getting up tight. He knew his face was red. "What happens if I go ahead and get married without permission?"

"Officially, I must tell you not to. Unofficially, I'll tell you there's nothing we can do about it once you're married. Oh, I will probably be told to reflect the violation of command policy in your next fitness report. That's one suggestion I assure you I'll ignore. By the way, Bill, as far as I'm concerned this conversation never took place. I have no knowledge of your plans."

"Right, Commodore. It never happened, and, sir, thank you."

That afternoon when Dawson went to see Lati, the first thing she said was, "Do you still want to marry me?"

He started to laugh. Then he saw she was serious. "Of course I do. Why do you ask such a question?"

"I am sorry." Lati hugged him tight, pressing her supple body to his. "You will think me a silly girl. I had a strange dream, and since then I have worried that you changed your mind. Do you forgive me?"

"OK, if you promise to ignore bad dreams from now on. Now let me tell you what I've found out. My Commanding Officer can't give me permission to get married. So we'll get married without permission. I've been assured it'll be all right, even though not approved."

Lati frowned. "But will it cause you trouble later?"

"No, the worse that will happen is I'll get chewed out. It must be a quiet wedding. Don't mention it to anyone, since we must do it without the military knowing about it. I can't get one of the military chaplains to marry us, so it'll have to be done outside of the military. Do you know of a minister in Da Nang who could perform the ceremony?"

"No, but a friend at work married a sergeant. It was done very quietly. None of the officials know it yet. She can tell me where she was married."

"Fine. Let's meet in the park by the river during your lunch hour on Thursday. If I'm not there Thursday it'll be because I don't get back in time."

Lati softly stroked his face, and ran her hand through his close cropped hair. "Was it difficult for you in Dong Ha this time?"

"Yes. Worse than before. This unreasonable fear is really getting to me. I've been able to do my job, but just barely. I find myself letting the level of danger, I perceive, determine where I go and what I do at times. That's not good, but I haven't been able to overcome the feeling that every incoming shell is aimed at me."

"I am sorry. I wish I could do something for you. Your face tells of the strain you have been under lately. I think you have lost weight. Is that true?"

He nodded. "It's because of all the tension. I don't eat well, and when I'm up north, I get very little sleep. But let's talk about something more pleasant-us, and our wedding."

Dawson and Lati talked about what they would do after they were married. He made it clear to her that they wouldn't be able to be together much of the time, even when he was in Da Nang. Lati asked if she would have any problem getting to the United States. He assured her it would be worked out. He would start working on that problem next week.

Chapter 13

The night had been pleasantly cool. Even Charley gave the men in Dong Ha a break, the entire night passed without incoming mortars, shells, or rockets. Dawson managed to get a fairly good night's sleep.

The morning in Dong Ha brought a light, cool breeze and red sun on the horizon. Dawson recalled the old sailor's adage: "Red at night, sailor's delight; red in the morning, sailors take warning."

When he first awoke, Dawson forgot his fear. He enjoyed the caress of the cool air flowing over his body, and the fresh, clean smell the breeze brought from the sea six miles away. But by the time he got shaved, cleaned up, and on his way to breakfast, fear was again gnawing at his insides.

At 0700 Dawson was inspecting metal warehouses the Bees had completed in the Marine supply area. He heard the swish of air and the "chooka, chooka, chooka" as the shell passed directly over him. His instant thought was, if you hear it, it won't hit you. He dropped flat to the ground as the shell hit three hundred yards past him, then he scrambled into a nearby trench before the second shell hit.

Dawson was alone in the trench, pressed hard against one corner. Shells continued pouring in. They were impacting between him and the Marine ammo dump, close enough that the concussion squeezed the breath out of him. He wanted to scream. Panic made him want to run. But what rational thought remained told him it was safer in the trench than above ground.

Then there was a gigantic explosion, like a thousand thunderclaps. It made the incoming shells sound like firecrackers. The immense concussion drove Dawson's face into the wall of the trench. It crushed his body with the force of ten earth gravities. Small arms ammunition detonating sounded like a hundred machine guns firing. More thunderous explosions drowned out the machine gun sounds.

It took him a few seconds to realize what had happened, that Charley had made a direct hit on the ammunition storage area, about two hundred yards from his trench. Building earth berms to separate the ammunition into smaller lots was one of the Bees' top priority jobs. It was a job they hadn't yet completed. The last figure Dawson remembered hearing from one of the Marine supply officers was that 20,000 tons of ammunition was stored there.

He remembered the officer's comment: "If it all goes at once it'll have the same force as the first atomic bomb. I sure wouldn't want to be here. It could level all the camps in Dong Ha."

Fortunately, it wasn't all going at once. Almost continuous explosions went on for ten minutes as pile after pile of explosives was detonated by the fire raging through the ammunition dump. Each second that ticked by, Dawson was sure would be his last. He was so tense he felt he would explode inside. The terror that enveloped him made him scream, an inhuman sound swallowed up by the explosions. Shrapnel from exploding shells rained down like hail, littering the trench. Several bounced off Dawson's helmet.

With the one small spark of sanity remaining, Dawson thought of God. The teachings of his mother; the church and Sunday school classes he had reluctantly attended when young, flashed through his mind-along with Lati's serene faith. "God?" he screamed aloud. "I'm not even sure You exist. But I've had it. I can't stand any more.

He looked up into the clear blue sky. If You are there, God, help me. I remember my mother said no matter where I was I could pray and You would hear. I want to believe in You. There is nothing else I can do. I pray that if I'm to die it will come quickly; if not, then calm this fear which seems worse than dying. Lord, I know I don't deserve Your help. I've never done anything for You, and I've done many things the Bible says I shouldn't. But I need Your help now. I don't know where else to turn. So I surrender myself to You."

Although explosions continued, with wave after wave of concussion crushing him, a calm settled over Dawson. He stopped trembling, and began to relax. He became rational. He knew it would be all right. If I am to die, there's not a thing I can do about it; and if I'm to survive this cataclysm, then I have nothing to worry about. As the explosions continued, he remained flattened against the dirt wall. Fear still gnawed at him; not the paralyzing fear as before, but the type of fear that charges muscles with energy for fight or flight.

In between the large explosions, at times an eerie quiet enveloped the area. Then, the impact of shrapnel and bullets and larger shells could be heard as they returned to earth unexploded. During one quiet period, Dawson heard a loud thud behind him. Looking around he saw a 155mm shell, one-hundred pounds of high explosive and metal, lying in the trench six feet away. He didn't know what the odds were of it going off, but he knew if it did, he was dead. He decided he had to get away from it. He looked over the edge of the trench for the first time since he dove into it. He was all set to hoist himself out to look for another shelter, but resting a foot from his face was another unexploded shell.

He saw dozens of unexploded shells, mortar rounds, grenades, and small shells of many sizes, that had been blown out of the ammunition dump. From the flame and smoke boiling up from the ammunition storage area, he knew more was to come. He dropped back down in the trench. Dawson thought of throwing the shell out-if he could lift it high enough; but the little he knew about demolitions made him reconsider. Movement might detonate it. So he decided he would have to share the trench with the shell for a while. He even smiled ironically at his new companion.

As the explosions continued intermittently, and Dawson waited for what seemed like hours, he thought: If I get out of this alive, I'll never let anything bother me again. No matter what the circumstances, if things seem rough, or I get in a bind, I'll think back to this day and know that nothing can be worse than this.

One hour and twenty-five minutes after the first shell hit, the "all clear" sounded. No explosions had erupted from the ammunition dump for fifteen minutes. Dawson hoisted himself out of his trench, and stood looking at the unbelievable destruction. The large metal Butler buildings that had been completed yesterday were now twisted metal frames with missing or distorted metal skin. He stood on a hill that dropped off gently, ending in a small valley before the next rolling hill started.

In the valley were six helicopter pads with earth revetments around each pad. Two helicopters were only smoking piles of aluminum and steel. Dawson thought, Good thing the other four were gone or they would be scrap too.

Across the valley, on the hill where the Seabee camp started, many of the hooches and other wood buildings were completely flattened. Others more distant, or in a more protected location, had one end blown in and the other end blown out by the tremendous concussion from exploding ammunition.

The ammunition storage area which had contained dozens of large piles of shells and mortar rounds, and all types of ammunitions and explosives, now looked like the lunar landscape. Scattered piles of rubble still smoked, and several buildings nearby were aflame.

Across the dirt road, where the Marine's supply buildings had been, Marines were climbing out of their trenches, and doing the same as Dawson. They looked at the, now, unfamiliar landscape in silence and disbelief.

One of the officers yelled at the Marines, "Do not touch any shells or explosives, they could go off with the slightest jar. Demolition men will take care of removing or exploding live rounds."

Dawson carefully walked around dozens of unexploded shells on his way to his weaps parked on the opposite side of the buildings from the explosions. The buildings had protected it from the main force of the concussion. Even the windshield wasn't broken. After removing three pieces of aluminum siding draped across it, he checked for live shells in the vehicle. Finding none, he got in the weaps and very slowly drove toward the MCB-21 camp. He had to weave his way through the unexploded shells, but the farther he got away from the ammunition dump, the fewer shells he had to dodge.

Dawson saw the battalion chaplain entering his hooch. He pulled over and followed him in. "Got a minute padre?"

"Sure, Bill. Have a seat. He pointed to a canvas folding stool. "Where were you when it hit the fan?"

"Too close. That's sort of what I wanted to talk about."

Dawson related what had happened to him in the trench, and how he felt like a new man. "But I don't know what's expected of me now."

The chaplain wrote several lines on a card and handed it to Dawson along with a New Testament. "Bill, when you get time, read the scriptures I have listed on the card. They will get you pointed in the right direction. You may not realize it, but this is a great day in your life."

Dawson checked in with the MCB-21 Command Center. Grady, the Operations Officer, and the C.O., Commander Benson, were listening to casualty reports coming in over the radio and land lines. Most buildings within one-fourth mile of the ammunition dump received heavy damage, and it tapered off from there on out. Live shells littered the runway. That was the area the four available demolition men were clearing, so planes could start landing as soon as possible.

All demolition men available around Da Nang were already on their way to Dong Ha in a chopper. The Army said they would send as many explosive experts from the Saigon area as they could spare. All live rounds had to be removed before the rubble could be cleaned up and rebuilding started.

Dawson had to be in Da Nang in the afternoon, so he spent the remainder of the morning getting a rough estimate of the structures that would have to be replaced. He carefully picked his way through the heavy concussion areas. One Marine unit lost a 500-man mess hall that had been operational only two weeks. The wood building with metal roof was now a large pile of rubbish. Little could be salvaged. It would have to be built again from the ground up.

The abnormal, irrational fear, Dawson had been plagued with for the past three weeks was gone. As he went around making his list, when he did think of the danger at all, it was with a rather detached, objective attitude. He shook his head in amazement at the calm that had settled over him. And twice, as he thought about it, said, "Thank God!"

When Dawson got back to Red Beach, LCDR Sanchez said, "The Commodore wants a special briefing on the damage at Dong Ha as soon as possible, Bill."

Commodore Rhodes waved Dawson into a seat with his cigar. When he finished reading the message, he looked up. "OK, Bill, let's have it. Don't want details. Give us a broad-brush picture of the major damage."

Dawson read down his list: "One 500 man mess hall and fifteen Butler buildings totaled; six Butlers need major repairs. Estimate 125 hooches destroyed, and another hundred need repairs. We had no significant equipment loss. That's it, unless you want details on helicopter losses and such."

"Nope. We don't repair them, so that's someone else's problem. I'm going to shake loose extra material from down here, but can't give you additional manpower. We're starting a cantonment in Da Nang-East; I'll have that material on the next LST going north. You know the mess hall takes top priority-big morale factor."

"Yes, sir." Dawson replied. "When we finish here, I'll radio the battalion to get on that as soon as it's safe to work in the area. They can scrounge material from other jobs until the LST gets up there. A lot of Marines and Seabees will have to move back into tents until we get the hooches rebuilt."

"Right. One more thing before you leave: When you get back up there, tell Commander Benson I don't want to see one of his living hooches replaced until all of the Marines are back in hooches."

The next day, Thursday, Dawson got one of the girls in the mess to make him a sandwich to take along for lunch when he met with Lati. All morning he was snowed under with material problems, and trying to get additional shipping space to Dong Ha. His hot, top-priority items had to compete with ammunition that was filling the C-130s, to replenish Dong Ha's ammunition supplies. His goods didn't have a chance until munitions were restored to a safe level.

Lati was sitting on the grass under the tree where they first had lunch together. She looked worried. Dawson was late. A bright smile lighted her face when she saw him. She got up and gave him a kiss and hugged him tight to her.

"I do not care if people think you are my lover," She said, sitting down and pulling him down beside her. "I have been so very worried since I heard about the big explosion in Dong Ha. Some people said it blew up the entire base there. I could not find out if you were safe. You were not injured? Was it very bad for you?"

"I wasn't injured. And, yes, it was bad for me at first, but later it was OK. I want to talk to you about that, but it can wait till Sunday when we have more time. As far as what the explosion did to Doug Ha; well it did a lot of damage all right, but they exaggerate when they say it almost wiped out the entire combat base. Enough talk about war! Let's talk about something much more pleasant-our wedding. What did you find out?"

"My friend and her sergeant were married by a missionary who runs a home for orphans. He is Reverend Holtz, and is in Da Nang-East. When you cross the river, turn right and stay on the main road for about four kilometers. On the left is a long, two story, masonry building with a large fenced in playground. It is easy to find, with all of the children in the yard."

"Yes, from your description I remember seeing it. I remember the dozens of children. I'll go out there this afternoon. Does it matter to you what date we set for the wedding? I'm in favor of having it as soon as possible."

"If you do not mind, I would like for us to be married after two weeks. I am not going to have a formal wedding gown, but I have a woman working on a very special ao dai. She had to order material from Saigon, and it will not be finished before two weeks."

Dawson patted her hand. "Two weeks is fine. I doubt I could get my R & R before then. Let's talk about where we'll go on our honeymoon-I can take five-days R and R. Because of passport requirements you won't be able to leave this country, so how about Saigon? I've heard a lot about it, and they have some nice hotels I've been told. I'll have to take a military flight there and back, and you can take a commercial flight. How does that suit you?"

"I too would love to go to Saigon. I have never been there. But there is only one commercial plane each day now, and one must have a high priority to get a reservation. The Vietnamese military must approve. One must have official, urgent business or they will not approve."

"Well, I can take my R & R right here in Da Nang. Everyone will think I'm crazy if I tell them I'm staying here. Da Nang-East has a recreation beach, I'll check in there, then you and I can go to a hotel. The Song Han Hotel near the river is very nice. That's where civilian workers stay until they find an apartment. I've talked with some of them, who said the hotel has excellent food. Unless you have a better suggestion, that should be a good place."

"Where we stay I will leave up to you, but I have heard the Song Han Hotel is expensive. We can find a more simple place if you like."

"Oh, don't worry about the cost. I'm sure I can afford that hotel for a few days. Remember this is a onetime event. I don't plan on doing this again, do you?"

Lati bowed her head, embarrassed by his question. "Now you tease me. Of course, I do not expect to be married again. Our marriage will last until we die."

Dawson reached out and took her hand in both of his. "I am glad you're learning when I'm teasing. If I do it too much, just tell me."

Lati looked at his watch. "I am sorry, but I must return to work now." She looked into his eyes. "Bill, it is not possible for you to know how happy I am.

Inside I am so excited, it is difficult for me to remain calm on the outside and continue doing my work. Please come early on Sunday."

Dawson watched Lati walk away. After going fifty feet she turned and waved and gave him a radiant smile. What a beautiful woman, He thought. She seems almost too perfect.

The long, two-story building with many small rooms was very old. Dawson guessed it had been a military barracks. The columns, beams, and girders were concrete, and the walls were of concrete block. The concrete was spalled away leaving reinforcing bars exposed in many places. Dawson told himself the building would've already been condemned in the United States.

Reverend Holtz was a short robust man with a round, pleasant face. Dawson estimated his age in the late forties. His eyes were kind. They looked at the world with compassion and love. He welcomed Dawson into his office furnished with packing crates used for files, a rickety table, and two fruit boxes for chairs.

"I'm Lieutenant Dawson, with the Thirtieth Naval Construction Regiment. I understand you're a minister and can perform marriage ceremonies."

"That's correct. How may I help you?"

"Well, I want to marry a Vietnamese girl. I may as well get it all out on the table at once. I can't go to a military chaplain. They wouldn't perform the ceremony. Matter of fact, the military would try to stop me if they knew about it in advance. Will you marry us?"

"Why do you want to marry the girl?"

Dawson frowned, hesitating. "Well, for the usual reasons."

"Oh, you mean she's pregnant?"

Dawson's voice showed his irritation. "Of course not. I've never slept with her. What I meant was, we're in love and want to be married."

"Aah, yes. That is the very best reason. Your declaration that you have not slept with the young lady is most unusual for this time and place, and I might add, quite refreshing in this world of instant gratification. One other question: How old is the young lady?"

Again Dawson frowned. "She's twenty-six. And yes, there's a bit of difference in age, which we've discussed."

Reverend Holtz held up a hand. "You may think I'm being too nosy, but if she were very young, I wouldn't marry you. Apparently you're both mature enough to know what you're doing. Being of comparable age is no guarantee of a lasting, happy marriage. So, again, given the time and place, yes I will perform your wedding ceremony. If we were in the United States, I would require several counseling sessions before I would marry you. But that is not practical here."

"Could we schedule it for two weeks from next Sunday?"

"That's fine with me as long as we make it in the afternoon. I hold church services here every Sunday morning."

Dawson worked out the other details with Reverend Holtz and told him that he would let him know if they couldn't make the date agreed upon.

Friday morning Dawson sat at his desk mapping out the day's schedule when his phone rang. "Hello, this is Lieutenant Dawson."

"This is Major Milinsky, Green Beret. We almost lost Lang Vei last night. Our camp commander and over half of the American team were killed when it got overrun. I'm going up by chopper in a half-hour. I need you to go along to look at a new site for Lang Vie camp. We'll drop in on your pad in about thirty minutes to pick you up."

"Wait a minute, Major, I'm not sure I can make it. You mean with the new bunkers we just finished, the V.C. overran the camp? That's hard to believe. You talk about a new camp; I don't know when we would ever get to it with all the other work. And I have a dozen hot jobs to work on here today. So..."

The Major broke in. "I know you have your problems Lieutenant, but believe me this has the highest priority. I'll have push all the way from Westmoreland himself. I don't have time to go through channels right now. Take my word for it; this is super hot. I'll see you in half an hour."

Dawson sat shaking his head at the empty line before putting down the phone. He made three quick calls and rescheduled meetings, then reported the call to the Operations Officer, who said he had heard Lang Vie had been overrun and was in bad shape. He agreed that Dawson should go now and get a jump on planning.

When the chopper came in, it was loaded with Special Forces men. Dawson rode side-saddle again, by the machine gunner on the port side. On the flight to Lang Vei he tried to find out more details, but the Sergeant manning the machine gun didn't know any more than Dawson had been told; besides, it was extremely difficult to talk above the roar of the engine. So Dawson sat back and watched the countryside zoom by.

Red dirt boiled up when the chopper landed near the Lang Vei outpost. The passengers disembarked before the pilot got the engine stopped. Dawson could hardly see where he was going for all the dust. They all ran until they were far enough away that the prop wash wasn't blowing dust in their mouths and eyes.

Milinsky, the "Animal," as Dawson had learned the Green Beret men called him, extended his hand. "Good to see you again, Bill. Thanks for coming on short notice. I want you to meet Captain Golder. He'll be the new camp commander. Ralph, meet Bill Dawson."

The men rapidly walked the short distance from the packed dirt helicopter pad to the camp entrance, where a tech sergeant met them. Milinsky said, "This is Sergeant Acker. He's the senior U. S. military here now. You met Lieutenant Dawson when he was up here a few weeks ago, and you know Captain Golder. Let's go in the mess hall and you can brief us."

Walking to the mess hall, they passed rows of American and South Vietnamese bodies along side the road. And then a short distance away was a pile of North Vietnamese bodies. The two jeeps in front of the mess hall were riddled with holes. The buildings had large gaping holes, and countless smaller ones.

The mess hall was a wood frame building with metal roof and walls, 12 feet wide by 32 feet long. As they got their coffee and waited for Acker to start, Dawson shook his head in amazement at the holes in the walls. Light shined in through every square inch. Like being inside a large sieve, he thought.

"Well, it started at two-thirty this morning. It was an inside job," Sergeant Acker said. "The first we knew of an attack was satchel charges going off in four of the concrete bunkers. Some V.C. who were a part of the ARVN troops here, cut the wire on the south side and let the sappers in. After they blew our bunkers, the rest of the V.C. swarmed up the hill and into the camp. We were up to our eyeballs in Viet Cong before we knew what was happening. I was sleeping in the underground CP with Lieutenant Kingston. When we came under attack, he went out to direct our men. He had me stay in the CP and told me to fire the detonator if I didn't hear from him on the walkie-talkie within five minutes.

"Guess I need to back up a little. After we were overrun the last time, we set up claymore mines inside the camp pointing in all directions. Our orders were that if the enemy got inside our compound again, and it looked like there were too many of them for us to handle, someone in charge would give three quick blasts on a whistle, and three seconds later all the claymores would be detonated. As you can see from this place they were very effective.

"Well, anyway, the Lieutenant had been gone two or three minutes when he called in on the radio. He said he had been hit, and that V.C. were all over the place. He told me to count to six slow and then set off the claymores. I believe that's the only thing that kept Charley from wiping out the entire camp."

"The claymores-they made all of the holes in this building?" Dawson asked.

"Most of them," Acker continued. "After I blew them, I came up, and helped wipe out a few V.C. trying to get out of the compound the same way they got in. The gooks who let them in must've forgot to tell them about the three whistle warning. Our troops hit the deck, but the V.C. really got wiped out. The body count is about 100."

"What about Lieutenant Kingston?" Milinsky asked.

"By the time I got to the Lieutenant he was dead; big wound in the chest. Charley had mortars set up on the hill to the northwest of us. He was still pouring rounds in on us as the remainder of the V.C. withdrew. I organized new mortar crews-the regular crews had been wiped out at the beginning of the fight. The rest of the night was just mop up operations. We had a lot of dead and wounded. Eight of our men got it, and seventy-five ARVN were killed. When you finish your coffee, I'll show you the bunkers and where the V.C. came through our wire."

Dawson was surprised at the condition of the bunker as he approached the first one. The walls were intact. The flat concrete roof looked as though it had been lifted off and then set back on crooked, leaving jagged ends of reinforcing bar sticking out. He thought, Well the river-run sand and gravel was pretty good. It made strong concrete.

When Dawson went in the first bunker to see how it held up inside, he almost got sick. The smell of human blood was overpowering. Blood was splattered all over the inside, with bits of skin hanging from the rough concrete. The explosion had literally smeared two men over the inside of the bunker. Dawson wished he hadn't come in. He staggered out, gulping fresh air to keep from vomiting.

"I started to tell you, Lieutenant, that it was pretty bad inside, but I figured you wanted to see how the bunker held up," Acker said. "We can still use them as defensive positions. I'll have some ARVN clean up the mess on the inside before tonight, so men can stand to be in there."

Dawson didn't enter the other three bunkers, he checked the damage from the outside. They were all the same-the tops lifted off. The three officers and sergeant inspected the entire camp. Mortar craters made it difficult to walk through the area. About the only thing that hadn't been damaged was the underground CP, which had taken three mortar rounds, but the earth mounded high over it absorbed the explosions.

Milinsky stood looking at the hill to the northwest a half mile away. "Bill, that's where we want the new camp. Lieutenant Kingston said that's where we should move the camp if we got overrun again, and the Sergeant agrees. It's a little higher than our location, and Charley set up mortars there for both prior attacks when they overran us. We'll go over and take a close look. Captain Golder, I'll want your views after we've had a good look. Since you're going to be Camp Commander, you need to be satisfied."

Back in the mess hall the men drank cool beer from the refrigerator riddled with holes. Sergeant Acker said, "I'll get a squad to go with us." A few minutes later the ARVN Camp Commander, a captain Dawson had seen on a prior trip, came in and said he had ten men ready.

It was evident the Major had little respect for the Vietnamese Captain. He looked out the door at the ten men, and asked the Captain, "Is that the best you can do?"

"Yes, Major. Men all busy with bodies and other work."

"You going with us, Captain?" Milinsky asked.

"No, sir. Have much to do here," the ARVN Captain said, making a quick exit.

Milinsky grunted, "Didn't think he would go. Don't think he has any guts. I see he came out of the fight alive. Probably stayed in his hole all the time. Why in hell couldn't it been him that got it instead of Kingston? Well, let's go."

When Dawson got a close look at the squad going along to protect them if they ran into V.C., his confidence evaporated. They were about the size of the average American ten year old boy, and their faces didn't look much older.

They can't be over fifteen, Dawson thought. If we get jumped out in the jungle, I'm not going to rely on them. I'm going to stick so close to the Major he will think I'm his Siamese twin.

The squad, with Sergeant Acker almost pushing them, led the way out of the camp and down the hill to the main road. They walked west on Highway Nine for a half-mile, toward the Laotian border, which by road was only a mile and a half. Leaving the road, they followed a path through heavy undergrowth to the top of the hill.

The hill covered only with low brush and saplings, jutted out of the surrounding jungle, evidence that it had been cleared. From the top of the hill the view was magnificent. Off to the west the hill sloped gently for a half-mile, then a cliff dropped off into the Se Pone River dividing South Vietnam and Laos. Across the river, the mountains, through which the Ho Chi Minh Trail passed, rose quickly to rugged peaks.

Milinsky lead the way to the crown of the hill, where the V.C. had set up their mortars. He discussed defensive positions with Captain Golder. Once in a while he asked Dawson if his men would he able to build a bunker at that point, or if they would be able to operate a bulldozer on the slope to clear a good field-of-fire.

About half way around the crown of the hill, Milinsky asked Dawson, "Now do you see why this will be a much better place to defend than where the camp is now?

Dawson shook his head. "No, I don't see the advantage. Looks like all you're doing is moving a half mile closer to Laos. Isn't that where most of the V.C. come from up in this area?"

The major swung his arm in a wide arc. "Look at the good fields of fire. You build us concrete bunkers like you did before; here the slope of the hill all the way around is gentle enough for men inside bunkers to see the enemy approaching.

Then if your people clear the ground for a hundred yards out from our wire and bunkers, we can hold off a regiment. Over where the camp is now, on two sides it drops off so steeply the men in the bunkers can't see the ground within twenty yards. Charley can crawl right up to the wire and bunkers without being seen."

Dawson shrugged. "I'll take your word for it, Major. I have no training in tactics. I guess that's why I'm doing the building and you're doing the fighting."

The three Marines, after much discussion, identified eight locations where they wanted primary bunkers. Those eight bunkers to be connected by fighting trenches, with concertina wire and mines beyond that, would form the perimeter of a much larger camp, about one-half mile long by 300 yards wide.

Dawson made notes and rough sketches on a clipboard. They wanted a large underground bunker for a Command Post, sleeping quarters for a dozen men, and first aid station. They finally decided on the size of twenty by sixty feet, all underground with at least ten feet of earth over the top. The camp would require a separate underground ammunitions storage bunker as well. Enough hooches were needed to sleep 300 men, along with separate mess facilities for the Americans and Vietnamese. They wanted fighting trenches connecting the CP, mess halls, and the perimeter fighting trenches.

When they were ready to leave, Sergeant Acker motioned for the Vietnamese soldiers to come in from defensive positions they had established around the crown of the hill. One soldier was making his way toward Dawson, through the brush and grass, when Dawson turned to follow Milinsky, headed for the trail to the road. There was an explosion at the instant Acker yelled "Hit the deck." Dawson felt a blow to his back and was knocked to the ground.

Milinsky dropped to the ground and pivoted so he was facing Dawson and the direction of the explosion, his weapon at the ready. Dawson shook his head trying to clear it. When he tried to get to his knees, Milinsky yelled, "Everyone stay down! Acker, what was it?"

"Bouncing Betty, I think. One of the ARVN tripped it. I yelled when I saw it pop up."

"Anyone wounded?" the Major yelled.

"I felt something hit my back, but nothing hurts." Dawson said. No one else answered.

"OK, everyone get to your feet and stay right where you are," Milinsky yelled.

Everyone except two of the ARVN were in the cleared area at the crown of the hill. Milinsky told the two men to advance to the clearing slowly, looking for trip wires. Acker walked to the ARVN who had tripped the mine and was on the ground not moving. When Acker stood back up, he shook his head. "Back of his neck is gone, severed the spinal cord."

Milinsky checked Dawson's back. "No Purple Heart for you, Bill. Shrapnel just tore up the back of your flack jacket"

Dawson didn't reply, but thought, Fine. That's one medal I-don't want.

"We don't know how many more mines are here, so we're going to leave on the trail we came up here on. Everyone follow me, single file," Milinsky said.

Acker assigned four men to carry the body to the road.

Dawson, who was directly behind Milinsky said: "Bouncing Betty. Isn't that a mine from WWII?"

"Right. The kind that's spring loaded. It pops up in the air before it explodes. Covers more area that way. Must have been put there by the French. Old maps show they had a small camp on this hill years ago."

"You're going to have to get some demolition people up here to clear the hill before we can do any work there."

"I'm way ahead of you, Lieutenant. I'll have a team up here tomorrow. So don't let that slow down your plans."

When they got back to camp they were all hot and thirsty, their shirts soaked with sweat under the heavy flack jackets. In the mess hall Dawson sipped a beer while finishing his list and drawing. When he was through he reviewed the drawing with Captain Golder who made a couple of corrections, and then agreed it was what they wanted.

"This is turning out to be a large project," Dawson said. "It's going to take a lot of material and manpower. If you can get high enough priority to pull men away from other areas, then that part can be resolved. But the one major problem I see is sand and gravel for concrete. It's going to take many yards of concrete for everything you want. And the project officer who built the bunkers up here before, said he had exhausted the available sand and gravel from the stream by the village. So the big question is: Where do we get sand and gravel?"

Sergeant Acker grinned. "I think I have the solution. I told the Montagnard chief we might need more sand for concrete. He said there's a large sand bar in the Se Pone River. A dirt road leads down to it, passing by a small Yard village half way down. I haven't checked to see if it's like the chief said, but we can go now-if the jeeps will run."

Wonder what we'll run into down there, Dawson thought, remembering the blast from the mine.

When one of the other Green Beret men walked in, Acker asked if the jeeps would run. The private said they had started both of them. They had to fix three flat tires, and the windshields were blown out, but he thought they might get down to the river and back.

The Major downed his second beer and said, "Well, let's go."

Dawson had noticed the dirt road as they passed it on the way to reconnoiter the new camp site. Vehicles hadn't used the road in a long time. The natives used it, otherwise it would've been completely overgrown. The road was quite steep going straight down the slope through the village to the river. Most of the Montagnards stayed out of sight, peeking out from their grass huts. Some of the natives, back away from the road, watched the eight men in two jeeps. Their facial expressions showed no interest, possibly a little distrust.

Where the road terminated, a huge sand and gravel bar had built up when the river ran high. Now the river was confined to a narrower channel, leaving the sand and gravel dry and accessible. Dawson got a stick from the river edge and probed the sand. He was able to work the stick in four feet in the half-dozen places he tried.

"There's plenty of sand here, and it can be loaded by a front end loader as long as we get it done before the rains start. The road is steep, but our six-by's can make it up when it's dry. They would go right down to their axles when it's wet."

Major Milinsky asked, "Does that mean you can do the job?"

"Can do, Major. It's still a question of whether I can get the men and material up here anytime soon."

"Let me worry about getting a high enough priority to insure that, Bill. You go with the idea that you'll start the job as soon as possible. Get me your list of material ASAP. I'm sure you'll get authorization to roll on it."

As they drove back to the camp, Dawson thought: Here we're really in the boondocks. The V.C. control this area, and if they decide to ambush us, I wonder what our chance of survival is. If I had done this one week ago, I would've been petrified with fear. I doubt I would have been able do my job. Now, thank God, I can at least control my fear.

When they took off in the chopper, it was well past lunch time. The thought of food fleetingly passed through Dawson's mind, but the highly charged atmosphere, and the rows of bodies quelled his appetite. Dawson sat with the Major in the main compartment directly behind the pilots. Shortly after lifting off, the helicopter banked sharply to the left, passing over a deep ravine south of the camp. Three figures with rifles were running in a small clearing. The machine gun on the port side spit out a dozen rounds, and two of the V.C. crumpled to the ground. The third man reached the cover of heavy jungle.

The "Animal" beside Dawson chuckled. "Charley will have to learn to be more careful in the daytime."

The chopper banked and circled the area for a few minutes, looking for more V.C., then the pilot took a heading to Da Nang. When they set down at Red Beach,

Milinsky said, "You'll have authorization to roll on this before the end of the day, so put some priority on completing that list of material."

Dawson got the Chief in the Planning and Estimating Section to push the new Lang Vei camp in ahead of other work. He said it wouldn't take long since he could use the drawings and material list they had made up for the last concrete bunkers; and he had standard drawings with material lists for underground bunkers and the hooches above ground. The Chief said he would have the package ready the next day.

When Dawson entered the officer's mess for dinner, the Commodore called to him, "Bill, come over here for a moment. You have another super hot job up at Lang Vei. I understand you've already been up there."

"Yes, sir. Special Forces flew me up this morning. What they want us to do will take a lot of material and manpower. I have the P & E Section working on it now."

"Fine, Bill. You were right to jump on this one. I got a call from Saigon this evening-a Special Forces general, forgot his name. He made me understand the urgency of this and assured me that General Westmoreland was pushing it. I told him I would commit the manpower, but the Army would have to provide the material. I know your battalion is hard pressed now, but all of the others are too. MCB-21 will have to pick up the load on this one. Do you see any problems getting the men up there?"

"Well, sir, manpower is a problem, as always, but I think I can handle it. The battalion C.O. may scream because they've really been snowed under since the ammo dump blew. He may want to call you on this one. I'll get on the radio to MCB-21 after dinner and have them get an equipment crew up there this next week."

"Good. If Commander Benson has doubts about the priority, he can call me."

Dawson got LCDR Grady on the land line and outlined the new job. The MCB-21 Operations Officer came up with every excuse he could think of why his battalion couldn't do the work so soon. Dawson told him to pull men off the lowest priority jobs; and recommended that Ensign Johnson be assigned as project officer since he already knew the area and had built the other bunkers. Grady blustered more at that suggestion, but finally agreed Johnson would be best for the job.

Dawson told him, "The initial crew should be small, no more than six men until construction materials arrive. There's no way to get additional equipment up there, so you'll have to pull the equipment away from Khe Sanh. They'll need a dozer, front end loader with back-hoe, two dump trucks, a trencher and a cement mixer. I'll bring you a job order when I come up, and I'll have drawings for Johnson when I meet him up at Lang Vei next week."

"The C.O. isn't here now, but I'll brief him when he comes in," Grady said. "I'm sure he will want to talk with you before we start this project."

"Well, if he wants to gripe, have him call the Commodore, since he set the priority."

Dawson called Milinsky. "I've got the go-ahead on the new camp. We'll have the initial crew up there as soon as they can get transportation. We'll provide the equipment, but I understand the Army is going to supply all material. In the morning I'll bring you a list of what we'll need. Most of it's common building material. First thing we'll need is cement and re-bar. How soon can you have some up here?"

"Should have it in Lang Vei by the middle of next week. I'll pull it from a stockpile that was set up for another job. I'll wait in my office tomorrow until you bring me the material list. So make it as early as possible."

Dawson got permission to take his R & R at Da Nang-East Recreation Center, starting the day of his wedding. Red Havner, the Administrative Officer, told Dawson he was nuts taking his R & R in Da Nang when there were so many good places to go. Dawson smiled, but offered no explanation. He hadn't told anyone about his wedding plans, not wanting to chance the information working up to higher command.

Sunday, Lati was radiant with excitement and expectation when Dawson got to her shack. After a quick kiss and hug, she said, "Tell me. I have been in much suspense since Thursday."

He smiled, raising his eyebrows. "Tell you what? What I'm doing at my job, or where I went Friday?"

Lati looked hurt. "You are teasing me. You know I am asking about our wedding. Did everything go well with Reverend Holtz? When are we to be married?"

Dawson feigned surprise. "Oh! That's what you want to know about. We'll be husband and wife about this time two weeks from today. The wedding will take place at two p.m."

Her eyes and smile expressed her joy, as did her arms when she drew herself tight against Dawson. The kiss started soft and gentle, then grew with intensity as their bodies pressed close responded. The warmth of her small body radiating through their clothes, aroused Dawson rapidly. The love and passion flowing through them drowned out all sounds, leaving them only aware of each other.

It was Dawson who broke off the embrace, his face flushed with desire as he pushed her out to arm's length. "We better stop now, or we won't be able to.

We've waited this long, another two weeks should be easy. Then everything will be proper."

Breathlessly, Lati nodded in agreement. "You are right. It would be so easy to give in to our desire now. But it would not be right. We must help each other be strong.

"My wedding ao dai will be ready before two weeks, and I have already told my supervisor I need to take a week off. Now I can tell him when. Do we need to get our marriage license before the date of the wedding?"

"The Reverend said he has some licenses. We need two witnesses though. I'll bring one of my friends. Can you get someone to come with you?"

"Yes. A friend at work said she will come with me if I need her."

For a long while they sat holding hands across the table, immersed in the aura of love holding them in its embrace. Few words were spoken, they would've been superfluous to the emotion each felt, to the love and understanding their eyes projected.

After a while Dawson said, "Lati, I want to tell you about my last time in Dong Ha. A part of me is reluctant to speak of my experience because it's so foreign to my old way of thinking. But another part of me wants to tell someone, and I know you'll understand. I wasn't far from the ammunition dump when it was hit. I was in a mortar trench, alone. It was the worse explosions I've ever experienced. The concussion smashed my body into the wall of the trench. At times I thought the walls would buckle and bury me. It seemed like the whole world was exploding. Fear smothered me like the concussion. Then my fear turned into terror and panic. I was at the point of running out across the land like a wild animal."

Dawson paused for a few seconds, not sure he could put into words what happened, what he felt. But encouraged by the compassion in Lati's eyes, he continued: "Then a faint rational thought came through the panic, like a wood plank floating by a drowning man. I reached for it, remembering words my mother spoke when I was young: 'God is always there ready to help you. All you need to do is pray; to invite Christ into your life.' I prayed and suddenly the terror left me. The fear remaining was controllable, it permitted logic and reason to function. An amazing calm came over me. I knew everything would be all right."

Lati's face lit up with joy. She hugged Dawson hard. "That is wonderful! What you have just told me makes me even more happy than when you asked me to marry you. I have prayed for you each day, for your physical safety; but even more, I prayed for your eternal security. Now my joy is complete."

"I don't know what God expects of me," Dawson said quietly. "But I will learn. I remember my mother said all we need to know of God is in the Bible. I didn't have one, but later I got a New Testament from the Chaplain, and have been reading some each day. I'm beginning to understand how you can be so calm in this hostile environment, with uncertainty and danger present all the time.

"I have much to learn. And I will learn from the Bible, and from you, how to live a Christian life. It's fantastic, the change that's come over me. I'm able to function much better. When I flew up to Lang Vei Friday, I was calm, even when confronted with some very harrowing circumstances. Had it been a week earlier, I know I would've gone to pieces."

All day Monday and Tuesday morning Dawson had been pushing people hard to get construction material diverted from other projects not quite ready to start, to the rebuilding of facilities at Dong Ha. By begging, cajoling and threatening, he had managed to get a large quantity of material moved down to the LST loading ramp. Then he ran into a brick wall. He couldn't get space for his material on the LST going to Qua Viet on Wednesday.

He talked with the LST skipper and cargo master. They wouldn't budge from their no-space stand. The cargo master had, in the past, made room for small amounts of material Dawson needed in Dong Ha in a hurry, without making Dawson put his material in line with all of the other commands fighting to get their goods moved.

This time the chief said, "Sorry, but I can't give you any space. I have more than a load, and it's all high priority. Talk with my boss, Commander Patranelli. He can override existing priorities, but I can't."

Dawson tried to call Commander Patranelli; finding him out, made an appointment for 1300. He didn't want to call on the Commodore unless he had to. If he could work through Patranelli, it would be faster.

"Afternoon Commander. I'm Bill Dawson, and have a problem you can help me with. I'm Project Liaison Officer for..."

"I know who you are, Lieutenant," the Commander said, extending his large hand across the desk. "You're the fellow who schedules construction work in the Dong Ha area. Right?"

"That's right, Commander."

"First of all, Bill, call me Pat. By the time people stumble through my moniker, they forget what they wanted to say. And second, sit down and have a cup of coffee. You and I aren't going to win this war today."

His appearance matched his name. His talking hands, black hair, and slight accent identified him as Italian, even without knowing his name. He pushed a cup of black coffee across his cluttered desk. "I know what your problem is, Bill. But tell me, who doesn't have problems in this land of chaos? I can help you with your problem, and I'm sure you can help me with one of mine. With a little cooperation we solve two problems and help push this war along to some sort of conclusion. Right, Bill?"

"Sure thing, Commander..., aah, Pat. What's the problem I can help you with?"

"Well, my men at the Qua Viet staging area are still living and eating in tents. It's rough on their morale when they see Marines right down the beach living in hooches. I need only one hooch for a mess hall and two for living. I've had a work order in for over two months now, but can't get high enough priority to get you to start them."

"I remember your work request, and I'm sorry we haven't got to it yet. But I'm sure you understand Marines, the fighting force get first priority."

"Sure, Bill, I understand that. Just like the Marines have the official top priority to get their material shipped up to Dong Ha. But my men feel they're as much fighting men as the Marines. They get shelled and mortared each night right along with the Marines. They could move a lot more material if they didn't spend half their time scratching the sand crabs biting them. So how about my hooches?"

"You have a point, Pat. I could probably divert a little manpower your way, but with the rebuilding to be done in Dong Ha now, I don't know where I would get the material."

"No problem. My men can hi-grade enough material from one shipment, for that little bit of building. So when will you get moving on it?"

"OK, Pat. Let's compromise, I'll get you one hooch built next week, and the other two as soon as the pressure is off from the ammo dump explosion; no later than three weeks from now. But you supply all the material."

"That's good enough for me, Bill. The material you're trying to get up there, will be last on and first off the next LST. See what can happen with five minutes of conversation without all of the rules and priorities to confuse us? Now we got the war back on track again. Good doing business with you, Bill."

The men smiled with mutual respect, as they shook hands, and Dawson said, "Same here, Pat." As he walked to his jeep, Dawson thought: He really set me up for that bit of horse trading. But I don't blame him-he has to look out for his men.

Up in Dong Ha, Dawson got plenty of resistance when he told Grady to up the priority and have his men build one hooch at the Qua Viet for the Naval Support Activity. He explained the whole deal to Grady, and admitted he had stuck his neck out in order to get his material shipped.

Grady swelled up like a self-righteous horny toad. "You tell me I can't use my own manpower for camp work, and then you come along with a pet project of yours and expect me to hop right on it. I don't buy it, and I'll take this one to my C.O. who will talk to the Commodore about it."

"Oh Crap, Commander! You're going to bother the Commodore about one stinking hooch? He has more important matters to keep him awake at night than that. It isn't my own personal pet project. I'm trying to get material up here as fast as I can so you can build things. All I want you to do is pull a few men off the Marine Cantonment at the Qua Viet, and build one hooch for the Navy. The Marines will never know the difference. But if you can't do it the easy way, we'll do it by the book. Since I'm responsible for assigning priorities, as of now the NSA job has triple A priority for one hooch. And if you want to bother the Commodore with something so petty, fine. I'll tell him about it over cocktails the next time I think he can use a good laugh."

"I'll do it," Grady muttered. "But I will bring it to my C.O.'s attention."

Dawson walked away shaking his head. I wonder why he's so obstinate? Maybe it's because he can't do everything the way he wants to.

When light, intermittent rains first arrived, they were welcomed by men tired of red dust that sifted into every crevice, made mud balls in their nostrils, and flavored their food gritty. The cool air accompanying the showers was a welcome change from the enervating heat of the past few months. But the rain was welcome only for immediate physical comfort. Those with experience or foresight knew their troubles and danger would increase along with the rain.

The war ground on in endless, inconclusive gyrations. The Viet Cong stepped up their hit-and-run tactics when the rains started again, which, according to the Vietnamese, were early this year. The low cloud cover protected them against air attacks, and obscured their troop movements through the jungle. They overran outposts, and then melted back into the jungle.

The American and ARVN forces, stepped up their search and destroy missions. But most of their probes into the jungle to hit reported enemy command centers were futile exercises. Usually, all they found were squad or platoon size units, and small caches of food and ammunition.

NSA got their one hooch on schedule. The Seabees worked around the clock rebuilding the part of Dong Ha Combat Base leveled by the ammunition dump explosion. Army demolition men had cleared the new camp site at Lang Vei of mines. The Bees in Lang Vei gladly worked through every hour of daylight without complaining. They wanted to get that job completed so they could get back to the relative quiet of Dong Ha, where the shelling and mortar attacks usually lasted only a few minutes, not the hours they spent in trenches at Lang Vei most nights.

Dawson was relieved when he got word the Lang Vei crew had hauled all the sand and gravel they needed out of the Se Pone River. They had stockpiled it at the new camp site without incurring any casualties-and before the rains made that steep dirt road impassable. Ensign Johnson told Dawson the Special Forces with the ARVNs, gave them good protection while they were working at the river. They had patrols out in the jungle on either side of them all the time. Twice they called in air strikes on the mountains across the river on the Laos side, when V.C. were reported to be setting up mortar positions there.

For a change all of my projects are progressing well, and my wedding plans are going along without a hitch. There must be something I'm missing. Something will go wrong.

Chapter 14

Azure skies and a bright sun greeted the wedding Sunday. Dawson was up early, filled with nervous anticipation. He had told no one of the wedding. When he was preparing for his week of Rest and Relaxation, several officers asked where he was going. When Dawson told them he was going to spend his R & R at the Da Nang-East Recreation Center, they thought he was out of his mind. The R & R trip each man was allowed while in Vietnam was the one pleasurable interlude of the year. They could select where they wanted to go from a list of places that would've made a travel agent envious. On the list were Quala Lam Pore, Hong Kong, Taipei, Tokyo, Hawaii, Australia, Okinawa, and Bangkok. The Air Force flew the men there and back at no charge.

The Armed Forces had made arrangements for Vietnam servicemen to get special discounts at some of the best hotels. Absolutely no one stayed in Da Nang. Only front line troops used the Da Nang Recreation Center, for special week-end recuperation, when they were pulled off the fighting lines for a brief rest.

The officers teased Dawson about having Vietnam fever. They said he liked the place so much he would probably extend when his year was up. He endured their razzing with a shrug and knowing smile.

Ken Clark, who was assigned to take over Dawson's duties while he was gone, drove him to Da Nang-East on Sunday morning. As they crossed the bridge into Da Nang-East, Dawson said, "Turn right here."

Clark turned, then said, "This isn't the way to the recreation beach, unless you know a short-cut I'm not aware of."

"I know, Ken. There's a little business I want to tend to first."

When they got to the orphanage, Dawson told him to turn in. "I've seen this place from the road many times," Clark said. "But I've never stopped here. It's an orphanage from what I've been told. What are you going to do here?"

"Patience my young friend. I have a surprise for you." Dawson found Reverend Holtz in his small sparsely furnished office. "Is everything ready, Mr. Holtz?"

"Yes, Lieutenant. The flowers you had delivered are in our recreation room."

"This is one of the officers from my command, Ken Clark. Ken, this is Mr. Holtz who runs the orphanage. By the way, Mr. Holtz, my friend doesn't know what we're doing here. Let's keep him in the dark a little longer. Is there a place where I can change clothes?"

"Yes, you can use my room," He showed Dawson down the hall to a small room with a cot and a shipping box chair as the only items of furniture.

In order to give credence to his stated plans, Dawson had dressed in regular work greens because that's all anyone wore at the Recreation center. He had brought his dress blue uniform in a garment bag. When Dawson came back into the room in his Blues, Clark shook his head. "What in blazes is going on? I've been trying to imagine what we're doing here. I even wondered if you were going to adopt one of the children, but that didn't seem very likely. Now, in your dress uniform? You really have my curiosity whetted."

"Just be patient. Soon all of the pieces of the puzzle will mesh, and you'll see the big picture. Let's wait out in front."

In a few minutes a jitney drove up and parked beside the jeep. Lati and her friend got out and came up the long walk toward the two men. Lati looked small and lovely and radiant in her white ao dai, the most beautiful ao dai Dawson had ever seen. The top was made of white lace, the bottom of the ao dai was shimmering silk. A white cape rested gracefully on her shoulders. Her head was unadorned except by her hair made into an elaborate coiffure on top of her head.

Dawson stood silent. Spellbound. He knew she was the most beautiful woman he had ever seen.

Clark broke the silence with a low whistle. "That is some beautiful woman coming up the walk. Do you know her?" He looked at Dawson's face. "What...? Oh, no! I hope what I'm thinking isn't true."

"That's right, there's going to be a wedding-and you get to be best man." Dawson walked down three steps and took Lati's hand. "Lati, you look so very beautiful."

She bowed her head, with a shy smile. "Thank you. This is my friend, Tyna Wilson."

"And this is my friend, Ken Clark."

Reverend Holtz had done a superb job dressing up the room in the barren concrete building, giving it some semblance of a wedding chapel. The flowers gave color and life to a gray somber interior. The children were all in attendance, quiet and watching everything with expectant eyes. Twenty of the children stood behind Reverend Holtz, and at his direction sang, "I Love You Truly" in Vietnamese.

The words of the wedding ceremony were simple, standard wedding vows. But as Dawson heard them now, they seemed different than the same words he had heard at a dozen weddings he had attended. They took on a very special, deep meaning.

When Dawson kissed Lati, he was sure he had never looked into more beautiful eyes, eyes that radiated such joy and love. After the marriage certificate was signed and witnessed, Dawson gave Reverend Holtz an envelope with $200. "This is for you and your children with my heart-felt gratitude."

Outside, the jitney was waiting. Dawson transferred his bag from the jeep into it. "Will you take Tyna home?" He asked Clark. "Lati and I will take the jitney. We're staying at the Song Han Hotel. You're the only one who knows where I'll be for the next week, so if something comes up, you know where to find me. Of course I can't think of any reason for you having to contact me. You're also the only one who knows about the wedding. Let's keep it that way for now."

"Don't worry, Bill. I don't want people to know I had anything to do with this. I hope no one can read my signature on your marriage certificate. I would just as soon not share in your future problems. You're too old for me to lecture, and you must know what you're getting into. So I'll wish you and your beautiful bride all the happiness possible. Don't worry about me contacting you unless there's an emergency."

When he made reservations at the hotel, Dawson had asked for the wedding suite. The clerk said they didn't have one, but Dawson was able to reserve a VIP suite on the top floor. It was very nice, for Da Nang, tastefully decorated and comfortably furnished. The sitting room was partially secluded from the bedroom.

When the bellboy left, Lati exclaimed excitedly: "What a beautiful room. The sofa and chair are French Provincial, very much like the set my family had before the Viet Minh came to power. I have never been in a nice hotel like this. It is finished in my favorite color, powder blue. It is elegant! I have never had the occasion to use that English word before. Nothing I have seen before justified such description, but this does. Is it very expensive?"

Dawson drew her close to him, placing two fingers on her lips. "Shh, my lovely bride. Do not be concerned with cost. If I went on R & R to Tokyo or wherever, I would spend much more than we'll spend here. So no more talk about money." He kissed her tenderly at first and then with increasing passion. "You are so lovely in that dress. This smooth silk makes your body feel very sensual," he said, running his hands down her back and over her buttocks. He felt a quiver run the length of her body.

"Thank you for your kind words. My English does not work so good when you are caressing me like this." She looked up at him, biting on her lower lip, then asked, Do you wish to go to bed immediately?"

Dawson smiled at her directness, and the dutiful tone in her voice. "Well, we could, but we have one entire week together, so there's no need to rush. It's past lunch hour, and I thought you might be hungry. I am."

She smiled and reached up, gently patting his cheek. "I, too, am hungry. I was too excited to eat breakfast this morning. Now my stomach is wanting something in it. I am glad you are hungry also."

Their lunch was served on the large terrace overlooking the Song Han. They were shaded from the warm afternoon sun, as a cool breeze caressed them. Dawson had ordered a bottle of white wine along with lunch. He noted that Lati took only a polite sip of her wine when he made a toast.

After a leisurely lunch, he pulled their chairs close, side by side. They sat as close as the chairs would permit, watching small sampans, some under sail, some chugging along with engines, and others being propelled by long sculls working back and forth in their sterns.

Larger fishing boats, with lateen sail rigs, tended their nets all along the river. Fast moving military boats frequently disturbed the serenity of the scene. Passing close, their wake tossed the small sampans about violently, making the oarsmen exert much skill to keep from being swamped.

This is such a beautiful setting. If only there weren't a war, Dawson mused. Why do men filled with greed and lust for power have to ruin something like this? He shook his head to purge such thoughts. Then he pulled Lati closer to him. "Let's pretend all is as peaceful as this river scene. We'll not talk or even think of the war for the next week. OK?" Lati nodded her head in silent agreement.

As he caressed her neck and shoulder, he said, "These chairs weren't made for lovers. We can't cuddle at all comfortably. Would you like to go in now?"

She nodded, with a shy smile. "I think so."

When they entered the bedroom Dawson said, "If you would like privacy when you undress, you can use the bathroom. Or, if you prefer, I'll use the bathroom and you can undress here."

Lati tilted her head in question, then gave a little shrug as she unfastened her ao dai. "That is not necessary for my sake. I am not ashamed of my body. I present it to you unsoiled."

Before Dawson finished removing his uniform, Lati stood before him naked. His quick intake of breath was involuntary, as his eyes told him her small, well proportioned body was as exquisite as her face. He stood, holding her tightly against him, they kissed until they were both trembling, then he picked her up and gently laid her on the bed.

As they lay in bed, Dawson caressing her, Lati said, "I am not afraid, but I am very nervous because I do not truly know what is expected of me, If my husband will be gentle and teach me, I will learn to do what pleases him most."

Dawson was deeply moved by Lati's unreserved love, and silently vowed he would endeavor to be worthy of such trust. "You will please me by being yourself. I think you'll find making love doesn't take much learning."

After they had made love and rested and made love again, they showered and sat watching fishermen returning home, as the shadows lengthened over the river.

Later, after eating dinner in their room, they returned to bed and made love far into the night.

Monday morning, late, as they ate brunch Lati said: "I know nothing of the ways of preventing children. That is not done in this country very much. Will you be angry with me if we have a child soon? I think that is most probable, as much time as we will be spending in bed."

Dawson thought her concern about getting pregnant very charming. "No, my love. Not only will I not be angry, I'll be very happy if we can have a child soon. I would like to have more than one, and I want them to be growing up before I'm too old to enjoy them. So the sooner we get our family started, the better. Would you like to go in and work on that project right now?"

Lati giggled, giving him a shy but enticing smile. "But first permit me to say something from my heart. I am happy you want children, and I will be proud to have your children, as many as you want."

The days and nights passed too quickly as they ate and loved and talked and loved and slept and loved. For more varied exercise, they took short walks along the river. One day, at Dawson's insistence, they went shopping.

"I want you to buy some frilly things women like to buy," Dawson told her.

Lati took him into general department stores. They didn't have nice women's clothes. When he insisted she go to the nicest dress shop in Da Nang, she said it was too expensive. "Lati, I don't mean to push you. I understand you've had money only for necessities. Now I want to make up for that. I want you to have nice things, not only the bare essentials."

Lati looked only in inexpensive shops until Dawson threatened to stop one of the prostitutes and ask them the location of a nice store. Lati frowned at the reference to prostitutes, then shrugged and said, "OK." They walked several blocks and entered what even Dawson recognized was a better shop. It took much encouragement to get Lati to buy a few articles of underclothes. She had never before been able to spend money for things she liked and wanted. For most of her adult life, every piaster spent had to be weighed in terms of survival.

On Friday they looked at the apartment Lati had located the week before. The landlord had said it would be empty and ready for them to move in on Friday. Dawson studied the outside of the old three story building with thick masonry walls. The large house had been an old mansion twenty years ago when the French occupied Vietnam. Situated on about an acre, it had a high wrought iron fence around the entire grounds. They walked all the way around the block-square estate. Then using the large key Lati had been provided when she gave the deposit, they went through the heavy iron gate. Lati waited in front as Dawson walked around the yard.

When he returned, he said, "If the V.C. start making hit-and-run attacks on buildings occupied by Americans, as they're doing in other cities, this fence should make them look for easier pickings. It looks as safe from attack as can be expected. You did an excellent job finding us a safe home, Lati."

Her face brightened with a broad smile at his praise, then quickly turned pink, and she looked at the floor of the porch. Dawson put one arm around her, hugging her to his side. "I didn't mean to embarrass you. Guess you're going to have to learn to enjoy complements because you are going to get plenty."

They walked up two flights of stairs to the three-room apartment occupying half of the third floor, The kitchen, living room and bedroom were sparsely furnished, but clean. The hard smooth tile floor made it seem cold, like a government office building, Dawson thought.

Lati watched Dawson as he looked through the three rooms and bathroom. "Do you like it?" she asked wistfully.

He took her in his arms and hugged her tight. "I think it's great. As difficult as I've heard modern apartments are to find in Da Nang, I'm surprised you could get one this nice so soon."

They hired a jitney, and in one load moved her cooking utensils and clothing. Dawson was surprised at the few things she had to move from the shack she had shared with her grandfather. As they left, Lati looked back from the door as though to impress a picture of the shack on her mind to last all the rest of her life.

Dawson put an arm around her, compassion flowing through him as he realized this was her last contact with her past life. "Honey, I'll try to make you happy and fill the void of having no family."

Lati wanted to move their things from the hotel to the apartment that same day. But Dawson wouldn't agree to it. "No, we'll stay at the hotel until Sunday. I don't want you to be concerned with cooking or cleaning or making the bed while on our honeymoon. I, personally, want all of your attention. When we go back to work, we'll not be together nearly as much as I would like, so we must store up as much love and togetherness now as we possibly can."

Sunday morning, as the lovers ate their last breakfast in the hotel, the rain came down in torrents, as it had done since early Saturday morning. They ate breakfast slowly, postponing their departure. Little conversation disturbed their reverie. Feelings of contentment salved the sadness they felt at having to part and return to the dangers and uncertainties of war.

"I guess we can't put off leaving any longer. I must check in at my command within an hour, and we have to get you over to our apartment. But before we leave here, Lati, I want you to know this has been the happiest week of my entire life.

The love we've shared in this very short time would make life seem worth while, if all other events and experiences were obliterated."

"Words will not come out to describe my feelings, the deepest feelings inside my heart," Lati said. "You know I have not experienced love before. The Bible tells us that in Heaven we shall know happiness far exceeding anything we experience on earth. After this week, it is difficult for me to imagine what greater happiness can be like."

When Dawson checked in at the Regiment, he handed the yeoman his wedding certificate, and told him to change his personnel file to show he was married. "I also want to arrange for an allotment, and an I. D. card for my wife as soon as possible."

The yeoman studied the certificate for a moment. Then he let out a low whistle. "Wow! You were married right here in Da Nang? You married one of the gooks? Uhh, sorry, Lieutenant I didn't..."

"Hold it right there! If you were about to apologize for calling my wife a gook, don't bother. Just because she's my wife doesn't make her any less a gook-if that's the way you think of the Vietnamese. But I don't like that type of reference to any of them."

"Sir, I'm sorry. It sort'a slipped. That's the way we talk about the Vietnamese. We don't mean anything bad by it. I really don't know why we call 'em gooks. When I think about it, Lieutenant, I see how it sounds. You can be sure I won't use that word again."

Dawson smiled. "You're right. Most of the men don't mean anything by it. I can understand calling the V.C. gooks. It sort of makes us think of them as less than human; and it bothers us less to have to kill them. But when that type of thinking is applied to the people we're here to help, it's demeaning to the Vietnamese and doesn't speak well for us as Americans. Do you see any problem in getting my records squared away to show I'm married?"

"No sir. No problem for me, but I think you'll have problems when the top brass find out."

"You're probably right. But I'm sure things will work out."

Dawson spent two hours with Ensign Clark, getting briefed on the past week's events. Clark reported: "The tactical situation around Khe Sanh has worsened considerably. With the heavier rains, Charley has brought more troops into the area. Khe Sanh and Lang Vei are being shelled and mortared more heavily. Work at Lang Vei is going slower because of the rain, as are several other projects around Dong Ha.

"You can keep the North area, Bill. Khe Sanh is bad enough, but that Lang Vei is one hairy place. Four of the Green Beret were ambushed as they were hauling construction material from Khe Sanh to Lang Vei. The Marines rushed a squad in to help them, and then found out they were out-gunned ten to one. The Marines reinforced them with two full platoons. Two of the Green Beret and ten Marines were KIA before the Viet Cong broke off the fight. I read the battle report; according to Marine Intelligence, they were North Vietnamese regulars, well trained and well armed."

"Sure sounds like things are building to a head up there. Have the Special Forces been getting enough material up there so our men don't have to wait?"

"Yes, sir. But just barely, I think that may be a problem in the future."

"Anything else, Ken."

"One other item and probably the worst. When you're up at Khe Sanh next time, take a good look at the runway. The sub-base is getting mushy under the matting. As the rains increase, it can only get worse. I think it's going to become critical. I don't know what you can do about it, but I'm glad it's your problem now."

"Fine, Ken. Guess I'll have to take back my problems now. Thanks for keeping things running smoothly while I was gone. Did Commander Grady give you any trouble?"

"He wanted to change priority on some projects, but I didn't agree to any changes. I put him off, telling him you could decide on that when you got back. All he was trying to do was get more of his own camp work done ahead of re-building for the Marines."

Dawson ate lunch at the Officer's Mess, and then as quick as he could get away, drove into Da Nang to his apartment. Lati greeted him at the door with a strong hug and lingering, passionate kiss. "You have been gone too long. I missed you very much. The few hours we were apart seemed like days. I kept busy, but still the time passed so slowly."

"I came back as soon as I could. I thought it best to eat lunch at the Mess. I missed you too. You've been busy while I was gone, I see. You even put up some cloth from your home for curtains. When you have time, go out and buy some curtains you like. They sell curtains already made up don't they?"

"Yes, but they are expensive. It will cost less if I make them."

"Well, if you want to make them, it's fine with me. I guess you'll have plenty of time in the evenings and on weekends. There's another subject, one of many we need to discuss. My tour of duty will be finished in two months, and I'll be transferred back to the States. We must get your visa as soon as possible. You won't have to come in under a quota because we're married, but it may take considerable time to get all the details worked out. Since the military tries to discourage marriages over here, they may put pressure on the Consul to get him to slow down the paperwork."

"Since I work for the Admiral, possibly he will help see that my papers are processed soon."

Dawson shook his head. "I doubt that. He might be inclined to help you, but he won't like me going against command policy. I've asked one of the yeomen to collect all the forms that have to be filled out. He should have them when I get back from up north.

"Since your father was American, you automatically qualify for citizenship. Do you have any papers to prove who your father was?"

Lati slowly shook her head. "When we found out the Viet Cong were going to arrest my grandfather, we had only a few minutes to collect some valuables and leave. I didn't think of my birth certificate and other papers."

The next morning Dawson got up early enough to drive to Red Beach in time for breakfast. Lati and Dawson kissed and held each other a long while.

"I wish you did not have to go. I know you must, but I wish you could stay."

"I do too. More so now we're married. But I'll be back in a few days-Thursday or Friday, I hope."

Watching him strap on his .45 and put on his coat, Lati said: "I will worry about you, but not as much as before. I will pray for your safety."

"I'll appreciate that. Going to those dangerous places isn't so difficult for me now, except for missing you," he said as he held her close. "The fear of death still exists. But it's not an all pervading fear like before. I'll miss you very much. Keep yourself safe until I return."

After finishing breakfast, Dawson walked over to the Commodore sitting alone at his table. "Commodore, I'm heading up north this morning, and I need to talk with you for a few minutes before I leave."

"Sure, Bill. Have a seat. It's good to have you back. I didn't get heat from anyone, so I guess Ken must've done a good job."

"Yes, sir. He did an excellent job. He's a fine young officer."

"Right. I'm in complete agreement. Now what's your problem?"

"Well, there's no sense beating around the bush, Commodore. I got married while on R & R. I wanted you to know before you hear about it from the Admiral. My wife is an interpreter for him and will tell him today."

"I thought you might have done that while on R & R. I'm glad you told me. Now at least it won't come as a complete surprise from the Admiral. I don't know what will happen, Bill. We'll have to wait and see. I'll do what I can to help you. I hope you have a safe trip up north and back."

Chapter 15

At Khe Sanh the ceiling was 500 feet with a light rain falling when the C-130 landed. The pilot, who knew Dawson by sight from his many trips to Dong Ha, caught up with him as he left the parking apron.

"This runway is getting more and more spongy. We're getting a good sized bow-wave running ahead of the plane on landings. I don't know what you can do, but I thought I'd let you know it's getting worse."

"Right, Major. I had heard it was getting a little soft. I'll look into the problem while I'm up here today."

Dawson located Chief Long, who had replaced Chief Kerns, in charge of the Seabee detachment at Khe Sanh. He was supervising a hooch being constructed. Dawson told him he wanted to take a close look at the runway problem. The two men got in the Chief's jeep and drove to the east end of the runway.

As the jeep drove over the touch-down zone, Long said, "You can feel how the matting gives under the weight of the jeep in this area. There's a cavity under us. Of course this jeep weighs nothing compared to those C-130s. Over here at the edge you can see the mud that's been pumped out."

"I understand you've been replacing the mud with more stable material. Isn't that doing the job?" Dawson asked.

"No. It's only a stop-gap measure, Lieutenant. The soft area we just drove over was mucked out and good material put back only five days ago. You can see the condition it's in now. We're fighting a losing battle, but we might be able to keep it in fairly good shape if they would let us close the runway longer so we can do more work on it."

"How long do you need it closed, Chief?"

"To replace all of the mud under the touch-down area, I need two days, and that's the bare minimum. They let me work on it only when the weather's too bad for flying. Last time I couldn't do the job thoroughly because the weather cleared on the second day, and they ordered me to button it back up and have it operational by noon. I couldn't compact the new material like it should be, so here it is all screwed-up in a few days."

"How long would you need it closed in order to put this runway back in good shape? I don't mean just patching small sections; I mean the whole runway?"

"With the manpower and equipment I have to work with, I don't know. It would take quite a while."

"We aren't going to be able to get additional heavy equipment up here. Charley controls Highway Nine all the way down to the Rock Pile; and from what I hear, the Marines aren't going to open it up soon. But assume you can have as many men as you can use, with existing equipment how long do you need?"

"Two weeks is the minimum, and that's cutting it thin."

"Is that working in shifts around the clock, Chief?"

"No sir. Only working dawn to dark. We've tried working at night. But when we light the work area, my men are like targets in a shooting gallery. The V.C. sit up on the hills and start sniping the minute my men start work. In the day time the Marines zap anything that moves, so we only get occasional sniper fire. But at night the Marines can't see what to shoot at. I really can't get much work done after dark."

"OK, Chief. If I can get them to give you the runway for two weeks, can I guarantee an operable runway through the wet season?"

"No sir! I wouldn't guarantee that at all. It'll last a month or two at best with the rain increasing as it is."

"Wait a minute, Chief. We had the same heavy rain last year and the runway remained in good shape. If we re-do it, why won't the runway last again this year."

"There are two things different, Lieutenant. With all the troops up here now, there's ten times as much traffic as last rainy season. When they put this in before, it was in the dry season. We'll be putting in material that's wet and will never get dried out before they start using the runway again. If you want something that will last, we have to get some rock in there as a sub-base."

"Chief, I'm well aware of what we should have. But I don't see any rock growing on these hills. So we have to use what's here."

"You didn't get the word, Lieutenant? I reported to the Battalion a week ago, that we found some rock. A Marine patrol reported a good source three miles from here. The next day I went out with another patrol to check it out. We can build a haul-road into it, no sweat, but it'll have to be quarried. We'd need a rock crusher for that. With Highway Nine closed, there's no way to get one up here. So we're back to using dirt again."

"I guess the battalion didn't relay the information to the regiment. They probably figured the same as you, that we can't get it crushed. You're right, we'll not be able to get a rock crusher up Highway Nine. I don't know that I can do anything, but I'll explore other possibilities when I get back to Da Nang. But for now run me over to the camp commander's office."

Dawson hadn't met Colonel Richardson, who was busy talking on the field phone when Dawson approached his desk. He was a square shaped Marine with a craggy face and dark hair splotched with gray.

From the strain showing in his face, I'll bet he has many more gray hairs before he's through here. He looks like the type who would rather be out in the field with his men in a fire fight than behind a desk worrying about keeping this place supplied with ammo and food.

When the Colonel put down the telephone, Dawson introduced himself and explained what his job was. The colonel waved him into a canvas stool.

"Colonel, I just inspected the runway. It's in bad shape, needs a lot of work done on it."

"Lieutenant, that's no news to me. Don't tell me what I already know. Tell me what you're going to do to improve it."

"There's not much we can do unless we can close the runway to work on it. To do an adequate patch job, my men need the airfield shut down for two days. Chief Long said the last time he was ordered to put the matting back down before he had finished repairs. Now that section is in as bad condition as it was when they worked on it only five days ago."

"I understand your problem, Lieutenant, but I doubt you understand mine. Are you up on the tactical situation here?"

"No sir. At least not in any detail."

"I have four thousand Marines here, plus a handful of Air Force people, and your Seabees. No supplies can be brought in by road, so all food and ammunition must be flown in. The North Vietnamese have twenty thousand men in the mountains all around us. We think they're waiting for the weather to turn sour, when we can't call in air support. Then they'll pounce, and we'll be all on our own when that happens. I must keep my ammunition supply topped-off, which I can't do with the runway shut down, and my men firing hundreds of rounds day and night."

"I can see why you don't want to interrupt air traffic into here. But have you considered what will happen if a C-130 plows up the runway when the matting fails and comes apart? It'll take a lot more time to get the runway operational then, than to make repairs now."

"Is it really in that bad a shape Lieutenant?"

"I don't know that will happen, but the softer the touch-down area gets, the greater the odds of a big problem. The matting can stand only so much before it fails."

"What's the minimum time your men need?"

"Forty-eight hours, Colonel."

"You can have the runway day after tomorrow. I'll call for more flights tomorrow to carry only ammunition. I should be able to stockpile enough to last forty-eight hours without dipping into reserves. If Charley finds out, he may launch an all-out attack; but if the weather doesn't worsen, I can still get air support."

"I'll tell Chief Long to be ready to start repairs Wednesday morning."

"Lieutenant, if more bodies will expedite things, tell your Chief he can have all the grunts he needs."

"At times he'll be able to use more men to move the matting planks. Who should he contact?"

"Tell him to see my Gunny, Gunnery Sergeant Rust. Will the runway last through the rainy season?"

"No sir. At best only a few weeks. We should take up the entire runway, remove the mud, and put down a good base of rock."

"And how long would that take, Lieutenant?"

"If we can get the equipment up here to do the job, two weeks."

"Two weeks? Impossible! We couldn't possibly last that long without supplies, and there aren't enough choppers in the I Corps to keep us in ammunition alone, much less other supplies. Don't even bother making plans because I'll never agree to that. I can't. It would be suicide for the entire camp."

"I understand your position, Colonel. But I'll have to check out the feasibility of doing the job, and report to my command. Then it'll be up to someone else to decide what to do. Thanks for your consideration, Colonel. We'll do the best job we can with the time and material available."

Dawson intended to drive to Lang Vei. But he changed his mind after talking with G-2. The captain in charge of intelligence said the patrols had been encountering many small V.C. units, and had hard evidence of much larger forces.

"I believe there's at least a regiment-size North Vietnamese unit between here and Lang Vei. You can do as you like, Lieutenant, but I wouldn't try to get to Lang Vei with less than a full company, and then I would want another company in reserve as reinforcements."

"Thanks, Captain. I'll take your advice. It's not my favorite place anyway, so I'll wait for another day to go there."

The ceiling had dropped by the time Dawson finished his business, and he thought he was stuck in Khe Sanh. The V.C. had already lobbed in mortars twice since he arrived. Dawson was well aware that was just a prelude to the nighttime activity. He had finished lunch and was having coffee when he noticed the clouds lifting. Dawson heard the rhythmic beating of a helicopter two minutes before it appeared through the clouds and landed on the runway apron.

The pilot didn't shut down the engine, as three officers got out and ran, bent over, from under the whirling blades. Dawson, ducking down, ran to the open door and stuck his head in.

"How soon you leaving?"

"Immediately."

"Where are you going?"

"Back to Dong Ha. Want a lift?"

"Sure do," Dawson said, climbing in with his small bag.

Dawson had reached the point where he could, at times, view the danger he faced in a rather detached manner. At least he could when he wasn't under immediate fire. As the helicopter flew out of the clouds and Dawson watched the brown and green of land and jungle rush by, he breathed a sigh of relief.

Strange how one's thinking can change, he mused. When I go from Da Nang to Dong Ha I become more anxious; but when I go from a place like Khe Sanh to Dong Ha, I feel relieved, at least until the next attack. There just aren't as many bad scenarios possible in Dong Ha.

After dinner at the officers' mess, Dawson sat with Grady drinking a beer. "The Khe Sanh runway's in bad shape. We're going to have to do major work on it soon, I believe," Dawson said.

Grady frowned. "Sounds like you don't think our maintenance crew can do the job. Chief Long reports that it's in bad shape, but that's because the C.O. won't let him close it down long enough to make repairs."

"Your men are doing a good job considering what they have to work with. But putting new earth under some sections won't last for the rainy season. That's what your chief thinks, and I agree with him. The entire runway is going to have to be mucked-out and new material re-compacted, and if possible, rock instead of earth put back in."

"Bill, I think you're overreacting. That runway will survive as it did last year; and about the rock, well, you're really dreaming. Just because they found rock doesn't mean a thing. We don't have any means of crushing it."

"The rock problem is mine. I'll work on it when I get back to Da Nang. I'm trying to alert you in advance that you may have to send more men to Khe Sanh."

"Like hell! I'm not sending another man up there. You know the workload here. We can't afford to pull men from any projects to send to Khe Sanh."

"Hold on. Don't get all bent out of shape. I'm sure more men will be needed up there, and I doubt the Commodore will have another battalion supply them. So unless your C.O. has a really good story, I think the men will have to come from this battalion."

Grady shook his head in frustration, and walked away.

Dawson sipped the cool beer as he tried to remember if he had seen any of the "tinker toy" crushers in-country. That was the name the Seabees had given to an entire family of small construction equipment that had been designed for the

Civil Engineer Corps. In addition to rock crushers there were small road graders, bulldozers, and other earth moving equipment that could be airlifted by helicopter into combat areas inaccessible by road. He couldn't remember seeing any, and made a mental note to check when he got back to Da Nang.

As he traveled around checking jobs, Dawson didn't have the constant fear gnawing at him. Lati occupied much of his spare thinking time. He had much more to remember about her now and they were such delightful recollections.

Dawson made his usual trips down the Qua Viet and up to Cam Lo sand and gravel site. Some work was progressing on schedule, but other jobs were slowed by material being late, or the wrong material being shipped. A new ammunition storage area was being constructed, with 100-foot by 200-foot areas leveled and bounded on three sides by six-foot high earth berms. Until the storage area was finished, the ammunition was being stored in a large open area, with plenty of space between piles.

The nights in Dong Ha were much easier for Dawson even though the tempo of shelling the past few weeks had increased considerably. After work, he spent more time reading the Bible than he did reading pocket books. He was amazed at how interesting it was when he read it with an open mind. Dawson found the more he read, the more sense it made. One part helped clear up something he had read earlier.

Not quite asleep, when the first shell hit, he rolled off his cot and dropped into the mortar trench under the hooch. He did it without the panic that had gripped him in the past, and when the "all clear" sounded, he got back in bed and could sleep. How good it is to be able to control fear rather than have it control me, he thought.

When Dawson got back to Da Nang, the Commodore's yeoman said, "Lieutenant Dawson, the Commodore said he wanted to see you as soon as you got back. He's alone now so you can go right in."

Dawson walked into the office and stood in front of the Commodore's desk. "You wanted to see me, Commodore?"

"Aah, yes, Bill. Relax, have a seat. You're not going to be keelhauled. Although I think the Admiral would like to have that done, as much for who you married as for going against command policy. He's not happy at the thought of losing his best interpreter. I've been instructed to give you a letter of reprimand. Here's your copy."

Dawson quickly scanned the brief letter. "I sure can't deny the facts stated here, Commodore. Don't think I need be concerned with promotion after this, but retiring as a lieutenant won't be so bad. It will be just a little earlier than I had planned."

"I don't think you need to worry about getting passed over for promotion. I have it from a very reliable source that the copy sent to the Bureau of Naval Personnel got lost. One copy is in your service record and if it gets lost before you arrive at your next command, there'll be no record. Bill, this is something that had to be done. It'll get around, and will show we mean business about this policy."

"Yes sir, I understand. I realized the potential problem when I decided to get married. Commodore, I really appreciate the consideration you have given me."

"Keep up your good work, Bill, that will be thanks enough."

As he drove through Da Nang, Dawson thought of stopping at his apartment two blocks away. But he knew Lati would be at work, so there wasn't much point. Then he thought of stopping to see Lati at work. He had missed her very much in the past four days. As he passed near the headquarters building, the "White Elephant," he decided against stopping; it might call more attention to his unauthorized marriage.

He checked several sources trying to find out if one of the "tinker-toy" crushers was in-country. One of the equipment operator chiefs Dawson knew, told him there was one in the Da Nang-East supply yard. He called the supply yard and got the information confirmed. The man on the other end of the telephone said it had arrived last week, and was scheduled to be shipped to Chu Lai when the Seabees were ready for it.

Dawson got the weight and dimensions of all the rock-crusher components, gave them to one of the Air Force load masters, and asked him to determine if each component would fit in a C-130. A couple of hours later the Sergeant called back and assured him it could be carried in C-130s.

Shortly before quitting time Dawson checked in with Lieutenant Paul Knight, the Command Duty Officer, and told him where he would be staying that night.

Paul asked, "Do you want me to put your address in the front of the log book? Then all the Duty Officers will know where to find you."

"Well, better not, Paul. It's a sensitive subject, and I want to call as little attention to it as possible. I'll tell each Duty Officer individually."

When Dawson unlocked the door and stepped into the apartment, Lati gave a surprised, excited squeal and rushed into his arms. Her greeting was prolonged and intense, as if they had been apart for a month.

"I have missed you too much," she said in between kisses."

"You couldn't have missed me more than I did you. The days and nights up in Dong Ha were very long."

Dinner was late that night. But the two lovers didn't mind. Hunger took a back seat to other needs. Their bodies called out to each other for fulfillment, and each was satisfied. Dusk had long dissolved into night when Dawson nudged Lati.

"My stomach is complaining to me. Can you fix something? A sandwich and something to drink would be fine for me."

Lati got out of bed quickly. "I am sorry. It is not the proper way to treat my husband on his return. I planned to make you a very special dinner on your first night home. It will be late now, but I can still prepare it."

"No, my love, leave that for tomorrow. Now, something quick and easy will suit me; and what ever you do don't feel sorry. You in my arms are much more satisfying than food."

As Lati prepared sandwiches, fruit and tea, he sat at the table admiring her quick graceful movements. Being small, she appeared frail, and Dawson mused at how deceptive appearances can be. He knew well the energy contained in her petite body.

"I have the papers needed to apply for your visa. I called and made an appointment for us at the Consulate for tomorrow at ten o'clock. Will you have trouble getting off work?"

"No. Admiral Scott said he appreciated my continuing working. I never take time off like some do, so for something important, they will not mind. He said to let him know if there was anything he could do. But he said for me not to tell you of his congratulations and offer to help."

"That's nice of him. I understand his dilemma. He must enforce military policy to discourage men from marrying Vietnamese women, yet at the same time he appreciates you and is glad for your happiness. I have an idea he doesn't really disapprove of our marriage, except officially, publicly."

The next day, the Vice Consul appeared aloof and condescending as he accepted the application for a visa. He verified that they had all of the necessary papers, but wouldn't say how long it would take to process them. He said the application would have to be processed through the Embassy in Saigon, and that they were cooperating with the military command to discourage servicemen marrying Vietnamese. He told Dawson to check back with him in a couple of weeks.

At the Sunday morning briefing Dawson led off. He reported on the progress of his other major projects, leaving Khe Sanh till last.

"The Khe Sanh runway is growing into one big headache for us. I believe it should be completely re-done. The Chief in charge up there, who is an excellent earth man, says we'll not be able to keep it operational by only patching sections now and then, as we've been doing since the rains started-and I agree. I think the only way to make that runway last through this rainy season is to take up the AM-2 planks, pull out the mud, and put in a good rock base."

The commodore waved his cigar impatiently. "Hold it Bill! You're beating a dead horse. We wanted to put in a good base when we built that runway, but there's no rock available, and only one way to get it up there-by air. You know that will never happen."

"The rock situation has changed, Commodore. Rock has been located only three miles from the base."

"You've seen it? You know it's good rock, and accessible?"

"No, sir. But Chief Long has seen it, and he knows a lot more about rock than I do. He's run a quarry before."

"All right! So you've found rock. Let's assume you can get at it; what good will it be without a crusher?"

"There's one tactical rock crusher over in Da Nang-East, destined for a project down south. I've checked, and it'll fit into C-130s."

"Hold it! You're talking about my rock crusher," Lieutenant Fallon, Project Liaison Officer for Chu Lai, said. "I mean it's for one of my projects-a hot road job near Chu Lai. I'll be ready for it in the next week or so."

"Easy Ed," the Commodore said. "You haven't lost your crusher yet. Bill, what you say may be true, but it seems to me there are many 'ifs' in your plans."

"That's true, Commodore. What I need is the green light to start working out some of the problems and clear up those 'ifs.' I'm sure that runway won't hold up as the rains get heavier. If it gets closed down during really heavy rains, I doubt we'll be able to make it operational again very soon-with nothing but more mud to put back under the matting. If that happens, 4,000 Marines will be in a bad way."

"OK, Bill. You've made your point. Evidently you have a plan. Give us a quick overview."

Dawson went over his plans to get the rock into Khe Sanh. After a pause he said, "Then we close down the runway for two weeks while we muck out the mud and put in a base that will provide adequate drainage."

Commodore Rhodes shook his head. "The Marines will never let us close down that runway for two weeks. Choppers couldn't keep them supplied, and there's no way they could get enough supplies stockpiled to last two weeks."

"I believe there is a way to supply them for a short time." Dawson replied. "I've never seen it done, but I know the Airedales have the capability, using LAPES, the Low Altitude Parachute Extraction System. On one side of the camp where the terrain is level, the Marines have cleared a field-of-fire about a hundred yards wide, and plenty long enough to use as a drop zone."

"Bill, you've sold me on the concept," Commodore Rhodes interrupted. "Go ahead and get it started. I'll let the Marine top command know what's coming. Maybe that will soften them up a little when it comes time to close down the runway. Also, I can help alleviate the crusher problem. One of those small crushers is held in reserve back in the States. I'll get it sent on out here now."

Dawson changed his usual schedule, and caught the first plane to Khe Sanh early Monday morning. Before leaving, he contacted Long on the radio and told him to make arrangements for them to get out to the area containing rock.

Long was waiting with a Marine patrol when Dawson arrived. He said the Marines didn't anticipate trouble. If the V.C. became aware of them, they would think it was one of the regular Marine patrols, and hide out.

The first two miles was easy. They followed an old dirt road the jungle had reclaimed. One pass with a dozer would take out the small trees and undergrowth, and the dump trucks would be able to pass easily. The old road bed ended abruptly, and for no reason that Dawson could see. There was no evidence of a house or anything else serviced by the road.

For the next mile, they walked, pushing their way through virgin jungle or following a faint trail. As they moved along in silence, Dawson's thoughts drifted to Lati, remembering Sunday evening when they had walked hand in hand along the river. They too had walked in silence. Finally the patrol emerged from the thick jungle canopy, and started up a gentle rise covered mostly with ferns and low shrubs. One hundred yards up the slope they located the rock outcropping. The unusual looking gray ridge surrounded by green jungle on all sides, looked artificial. It was definitely out of place-some geological quirk, Dawson thought.

The Marines fanned out and set up defensive positions while Dawson and Long examined the quarry site. The west face of the rock cliff rose twenty feet above the area where the equipment would have to work.

"Well, there's plenty of rock; ten times more than we'll ever need, and it looks like good rock," Dawson said.

"Yes sir, it's decomposed granite, just what we need for a good sub-base. It's easy to get at, since there's no overburden to remove. All we have to do is blast and haul it out."

"Chief, it looks like you can make a road into here all right, except I'm worried about one section of jungle that's so thick. Isn't it going to be difficult to get rid of those larger trees?"

"No sweat, Lieutenant. A small charge at the base of each of the largest ones will knock them down. Then the bulldozers can finish the job. With the two dozers available, the road can be done in two days. It won't be no freeway, but those six-by's will be able to move in and out of here fine."

"OK, Chief. You're the pro. Have you calculated how much rock we need?"

"Should have about 10,000 yards to do the job right."

"That's a lot of rock, Chief. Once you start the operation I think you should hit it as hard and fast as you can. Maybe Charley won't realize what you're doing soon enough to concentrate his troops on the operation and close it down. How long will it take to haul the rock?"

Long got out a notebook and started figuring. "There's three front-end loaders; with the dumps I can get from the Marines, I'll have ten trucks. They'll each haul twelve yards, and I figure they can make a round trip in a half-hour. Considering the daylight we have now, we can haul about fourteen hours a day. So, barring major trouble, we should be able to stockpile enough rock in three days. Of course that doesn't include the drilling and blasting, which can be done ahead."

"Sounds good to me, but I think you're being optimistic. That seems like a lot of rock to get out of here in three days. Even if it takes four or five days, the Marines should be able to cover you that long and keep the V.C. off your necks."

Back in Khe Sanh, Dawson asked, "How did the work on the touch-down part of the runway turn out?"

"We got it completed on schedule and got the runway back in operation when we said we would. But I'm not happy with it. It was raining pretty steady for the two days we had it tore up, so the material we put back under the matting wasn't much drier than what we took out. It firmed that section up some, but it's soaking up more moisture as it rains."

"Do you think it'll last until we have the rock ready to rework the whole runway?"

"Hard to say, Lieutenant. Depends on how much rain we have, and how much traffic comes in. The small planes don't bother it much. Those C-130s cause the problem. Every time they land, they work the matting like a big pump pushing out the soft soil and leaving a void. That permits more water to collect and soften the ground deeper."

"Heavy rain can hurt your quarry operation, or at least the hauling part. It looked good out there today; not very spongy after the past days of sunshine. You'll have to schedule the work with the weather and the Marines. Do you need more men up here now?"

"Two powder monkeys to do the drilling and blasting, and I need two drills and a large air compressor."

"I'll try to get them up here this afternoon, or no later than the first plane out of Dong Ha in the morning. The Commodore is going through the Admiral to get the Marines cranked up for this operation. Have you talked with the Marines about giving your men protection between here and the rock?"

"No problem there, Lieutenant. Talked with the Gunny this morning. They're all set to put a company out there, or however many men it takes to secure the area."

"One more question, Chief. Once you get the crusher in operation, how long will it take to crush the rock needed?"

"Well, I've never used one of those little crusher, but I was told it'll put out 50 ton per hour. Once we get in operation, should take about two weeks to crush enough rock, even allowing for maintenance and minor repairs. If there's any major breakdown, or if Charley makes a direct hit with a mortar, that will increase the time required."

In Dong Ha, when Dawson told Grady the Khe Sanh runway job was to get top priority, he blew up. Dawson had to threaten to call the Commodore before Grady would agree to sending the men and equipment to Khe Sanh.

Dawson cut his inspection trip short, spending Monday afternoon and Monday night in Dong Ha checking only the really hot jobs and returning to Da Nang Tuesday afternoon.

After dinner Tuesday evening Dawson came up to the table where the Commodore and Operations Officer were lingering over coffee. "I need to talk with both of you, either now or in the morning, early."

"Have a seat, Bill. Now's as good a time as later," the Commodore said.

"It's about the runway job at Khe Sanh. I've seen the rock. I'm sure we can get it out. If the weather holds, most of what we need will be stockpiled early next week. What concerns me is getting the rock crusher up there. I'd like to send the one in the Da Nang-East yard up there now."

Lieutenant Commander Sanchez said, "Hold it, Bill. You know that crusher's scheduled to go down south soon. We've ordered one from the States for your job. It should be here in the next week or so."

"Yes, sir. I know that. But here's what I'm worried about: The repair job we did on the touch-down area of the runway won't last long because we had to put wet material back under the matting. I want to get the rock crusher up to Khe Sanh before more heavy rain forces us to close the runway. If that happens, how will we get the crusher up there? They can't air drop it like they will other supplies, once we close the runway for repairs. I think we'll be in a real bind if we don't get one up there now. When the other crusher arrives, it can go down South."

"Do you really believe the runway is that critical?" the Commodore asked.

"Yes, sir. Chief Long and I both believe it's critical."

"Then do it, Bill. I have faith in your judgment. Ed, you have the unpleasant job of appeasing Lieutenant Fallon over the temporary loss of his crusher," Commodore Rhodes said.

"Thank you, Commodore," Dawson responded. "I'll get the crusher on its way tomorrow afternoon. I'll need to give it top priority so it can bump anything but ammunition. If I run into a bottleneck, I may need some push from you."

"I'll be here if you need me, Bill."

The next morning, after having an early breakfast with Lati, Dawson went directly to the Da Nang-east supply yard to check out the crusher. He made arrangements with one of the battalions to haul the rock crusher to the freight terminal. He had to get Lieutenant Commander Ramore on the phone, to tell the officer in charge of the supply yard to release the crusher.

The rest of the morning he spent trying to convince an Air Force major and his boss that the huge piles of metal being deposited in their loading area really did have top priority; that the rock crusher and its various components were needed badly enough to bump plane loads of food, and a plane load of Marines scheduled as replacement troops at Khe Sanh. Dawson failed. The Commodore couldn't convince the Air Force Colonel over the telephone. Admiral Scott had to issue the order.

Dawson waited around until he got firm assurance his "pile of scrap iron" would get transported as soon as possible. The Major said two C-130s would deliver what they could carry later in the afternoon, and the remainder would be flown up the next day.

After lunch, Dawson contacted Chief Long on the radio, "Chief, the crusher is being flown in this afternoon. Two loads. The remainder will be there tomorrow. How's the road coming? Over."

"Fine. Should be finished today. We've done some blasting and will start hauling tomorrow. Sure didn't expect the crusher this quick. I'll need some good crusher men to set it up and operate it. I have names for you, if you can contact the Battalion. Over."

"Let me have them, Chief."

"The key man is Barrington, CD1, then Carter CM1, Fazzio, CD2, and Collins, CD2. If it's impossible to get some of those men, have Harrington select the replacements. Over."

"They'll be up there tomorrow, Chief. Any other problems? Over."

"No, sir. It's like having a Sunday picnic under a wasps' nest. But the Marines are doing a good job of taking care of the wasps. We've had no casualties so far."

When Dawson called the MCB-21 Operations Officer, and told him to send four more men to Khe Sanh, Grady did a lot of griping and complaining. Dawson told him, "Commander, I've had food, medical supplies and fighting troops bumped to get the crusher up there. The crusher's no good without men to operate it. They should be up there today if possible; and, at the latest, tomorrow. Can we resolve this, or do I need to get the Commodore to talk with your C.O.? Over."

"They'll be on the first available plane. But keep in mind, I don't have a magic machine that manufactures men! Over, and out!"

During a lull in telephone traffic, Dawson called the Vice Consul and asked about Lati's visa. The man acted like it was a strain to even give out the time of day. Finally, he confirmed that the forms had been sent on to Saigon for processing.

That night, when Dawson told Lati he had called the Consulate she shook her head, smiling. "Americans are too impatient. Everything must be done now. That is the reason you do not understand the Vietnamese. We are content to wait for events to work through time, while the American tries to push the events through time. That is what causes much of the friction between Americans and Vietnamese."

Dawson started to tell her that's why the Vietnamese had been fighting for over twenty years without resolving anything, but he held what he was thinking and said: "The reason I'm impatient is because I'm worried about getting you out of Vietnam by the time my tour of duty ends and I go back to the States. If you don't have clearance to enter the United States by the time I'm scheduled to leave, the only way I can delay my departure is to extend for another tour of duty here. I don't want to do that, but I will if your visa isn't approved in time."

Lati shook her head. "I would not like adding additional risk to your life. But we should not worry about troubles that will not be. I am sure it will all work out. What God wills, must be."

Dawson drew her close to him kissing her lightly on the neck. "I love your simplistic faith. I'm going to have to learn to trust God like you do. Like you say, let's not worry about problems that haven't arrived."

Sunday morning after breakfast Dawson asked, "How would you like to go to church this morning?"

"I would love to. I really miss going to church, but how...? Where...?"

Dawson interrupted. "I remember Reverend Holtz said he holds services for the children every Sunday morning. Let's go there. I'm sure the command won't mind my attending church instead of working. I'll go in this afternoon to take care of any urgent business."

"Attending church with all of the children will be nice. It has been so long since I have gone to a regular church service."

Reverend Holtz was happy to have them attend service. "We don't get many visitors here," he said. "The children will get a special blessing from your presence."

Chapter 16

Tuesday morning was cool and wet. Dawson's mind was filled with the problems in Dong Ha and Khe Sanh as he got job orders and blueprints together to make his trip north. He left his office loaded down with a flack-jacket and poncho draped over one arm, his .45 strapped on, and helmet in one hand. In his other hand was a small canvas bag loaded half with clothes and toilet articles and half filled with plans, work-orders.

Lieutenant Commander Sanchez called out, "Bill, I need to see you before you leave."

"Yes sir. I was on my way to the airfield. We got a new problem, or just an old one with a new wrinkle?"

"The latter I think. I got a call from an Air Force colonel who acted like we were about to lose the war. He says the runway at Khe Sanh isn't safe to land on. His pilots have been complaining for quite a while, but he thought it was just routine bitching. He flew up there yesterday, and says he wouldn't want to land a Piper Cub on that runway. He tried to get it shut down, but the Marines refuse to even consider it. Guess you better get up there pronto. If you don't think you can get a ride this morning, I'll arrange for a chopper to take you."

"I should be able to get a hop from the Air Terminal. I called earlier, and they said all flights were still scheduled even though there's a low overcast. I was going to Dong Ha, and then Khe Sanh later in the week, but I'll reverse my itinerary. I've been hearing scuttlebutt that some of the pilots are complaining about the matting developing a bow-wave ahead of them when they land. Most of the pilots I know are Marines, and they don't sweat the little problems. Anyway, I'll check it out, Commander."

The Air Force Sergeant at the passenger terminal said there was no room for passengers on the first flight going to Khe Sanh. The flight was carrying ammunition only. Dawson went out of the terminal and spotted the C-130 being loaded a hundred yards away. Running through the rain, he sloshed through large puddles to get to the plane, and then stood out of the rain under one of the wings.

Dawson intercepted the pilot, a Marine captain he knew by sight, as he started up the tail ramp. "I hear you guys are crying about our runway up at Khe Sanh."

"Not me, Lieutenant. Only when my bird won't fly; do I cry. But I'll tell you, Lieutenant, if that was my runway, I wouldn't lay claim to it. It's getting to be a mess. If the waves in it get any higher, I'm going to put in for sea pay."

"I heard you 'fly boys' were complaining about a bow wave. I want to see how bad that little ripple is, but they say there isn't room for me on the plane."

"You come on up in this bird. I'll make room-if you don't mind sitting on the deck."

The load master, checking off the last pallet of ammunition objected: "But, Captain, we've got you grossed out now. You're topped out to gross payload."

"Don't sweat it, Serge. This is my bird, and if it won't handle a couple hundred pounds overweight, then it shouldn't be on the flight line."

There were no seats, so Dawson sat on the deck with his back against the wall of the cockpit. As they roared down the runway he looked up at the ammunition piled high. Sure hope we don't have trouble on this flight. If we crash with this load, there won't be any pieces left to bury. He shook his head, telling himself to think more constructive thoughts.

The flight to Khe Sanh was bumpy. All Dawson could see through the distant porthole window were gray clouds rushing by.

The Flight Engineer came out of the cockpit and leaned over yelling in Dawson's ear. "The pilot wants you to have a bird's eye view of the landing. We're about one minute from touchdown. You can stand right behind the pilot. Hang on tight to the bar over his head when he hits reverse thrust to slow this bird down."

The plane was in a steep descent. Dawson wished he hadn't been invited to this front-row view. As the windshield wipers swished back and forth rapidly, he could see only rain splattering against the windshield and gray clouds rushing at them. He logged it in his mind to recall this moment whenever he had problems, and be glad he was an engineer, not a pilot. He wanted to ask the pilot something to get reassurance that everything was fine, but on second thought, decided it best not to distract him.

The flight engineer's "minute" seemed like an hour. When the pilot said, "I know the runway's down there someplace; we should see it anytime now," Dawson shuddered, remembering the mountains surrounding Khe Sanh. He gave an audible sigh of relief when Khe Sanh suddenly appeared just ahead.

But his relief was short lived. When the heavily loaded plane dropped onto the aluminum planked runway and the pilot gave the propellers full reverse pitch, the plane squatted and groaned. A bulge in the AM-2 planks started when they touched down, and grew alarmingly. Before they had gone more than a hundred yards, the bow wave, preceding them by a few feet, raised up almost as high as the cockpit.

The pilot pointed and grinned up at Dawson. "See what I mean? Some ripple, huh?"

Dawson didn't reply. His eyes were seeing it, but his mind refused to believe it. He tried not to think about the tremendous stress on the aluminum planks. The manufacturer of this new runway matting had said it would stand considerable stress, but Dawson knew it wasn't designed for what it was being subjected to now. If one plank breaks loose, it's all over, he thought.

The matting dropped back down as the plane came to a stop near the end of the runway. Dawson shook his head. He would've never believed what he had just been through without seeing it himself.

As they taxied to the off-loading area, Dawson asked, "How long has the matting been rising up like that?"

The pilot shrugged, and looked at his copilot. "The last two or three days, huh, Jake?"

"Yeah, sounds about right. Before, it was a lot smaller bow wave; like only two or three feet," the young copilot said.

"If they listen to me they won't let another plane land on this runway until it's repaired. I don't know why there hasn't been a serious accident already. That has to be the most hazardous situation I've ever seen," Dawson said, shaking his head.

"I sure didn't know it was that bad," the pilot said. "My dad told me what good builders the Seabees were during the Big War, so I figured you fellows put this runway together so it wouldn't come apart no matter what."

"Well, we are good," Dawson said, smiling. "But not that good! The only one holding that matting together is God, and I'm afraid He may turn it back over to us mortals anytime now."

Dawson went straight to Colonel Richardson's office. After five minutes, he realized it was a waste of time. The Colonel wouldn't consider closing down the runway. Dawson tried to get the camp commander to go out and watch the next plane land.

"It would make no difference," Richardson said. "Just be wasting my time. All I know is they've been making it in OK so far; and I need supplies and ammunition or I won't be able to hold on to this camp."

At the communications hooch, it took a half-hour to get Lieutenant Commander Sanchez on the radio. Dawson described the condition of the runway in detail. When he said the matting grew into a bow wave over six feet high, he knew Sanchez discounted his figure as an exaggeration because, Dawson wouldn't believe it if someone told him that story. After pleading and then insisting, Dawson got Sanchez to agree to present the problem to the Commodore immediately, and call him back within an hour.

Dawson felt helpless; deep inside he knew what the answer would be when it came, but there was nothing more he could do. For a moment he considered getting the Chief and his men to start tearing up the runway, but he knew they wouldn't get much done before the Marines stopped them. He would be court-martialed and the runway would remain the same-a time-bomb.

Borrowing a jeep, Dawson drove to the rock crusher to find Chief Long. He saw the mountain of rock near the rock crusher, and the smaller hill of crushed rock at the other end. Even with the rain falling, a cloud of dust billowed out of the crusher as it spit out a continuous stream of crushed rock. Thank God the crusher is here and working, he thought.

Chief Long gave a perfunctory salute as he came up to Dawson. His face showed fatigue and stress brought on by the long working days, and nights with little sleep.

"How's it going Chief?"

"Well we're making rock, Lieutenant. But we've had our share of problems. This 'tinker toy' crusher sure doesn't compare with the big ones."

"Is it going to be up to crushing all of the rock we need for the runway?"

"It may grunt and groan a bit, but it'll do it if I have to hold it together with bailing wire."

"Chief, have you seen what happens to the runway now, when those C-130s land?"

"In the past few days, only from up here. I've done everything I can to get them to close down the runway, but no one listens. My measuring the bow wave won't help. But from here I can tell the wave is almost even with the cockpit. When it comes apart and they lose a plane, then the runway will be closed."

"I'm exerting as much pressure as I can to get it closed now. If we get it shut down today, can you get it back in operation in two weeks-even considering the rock not yet crushed?"

"Guess we can, Lieutenant, if you get me more men to operate the equipment for the runway repairs. We got plenty of bodies, but I'll need more equipment operators. You can tell the Brass for me that I said it'll be a lot easier and faster to repair if we close it, than if one of those big birds buries itself in the runway."

Dawson was drinking a cup of coffee in the communications bunker when the Red Beach radio operator came on the air. Commander Sanchez said there was no way the Commodore could get the Marines to close the runway, because of the tactical situation. Dawson knew the Commander had his orders, and it was useless to pressure him further.

Dawson went to the hooch where some of the Seabees slept, and where they had a makeshift office. One young Seabee sat at a packing-crate-desk typing material orders.

"I need a movie camera. Do you know anyone that has one?" Dawson asked the Constructionman.

"A movie camera? Well, sir, the only one I know of is the one Garrett has."

"Where can I find him? It's urgent."

"He took hot coffee over to the crusher crew. Should be back in a few minutes. He said he was coming right back."

Dawson helped himself to a cup of coffee, and then paced around the hooch for the next five minutes. The rain pattering on the tin roof drummed into Dawson's mind that he was running out of time. He visualized one of the C-130s loaded with ammunition crashing into a mass of flying AM-2 runway planks-and then the huge explosion.

When a young boy of eighteen, with a friendly tired face came in, the Seabee at the typewriter said, "Hey, Garrett, the Lieutenant wants to talk to you about your camera."

Dawson went over to the entrance where Garrett was taking off his rain gear. "I understand you have a movie camera."

"Yes, Sir. Want to see it?"

"I want to use it. Actually, I want you to take pictures of the runway for me."

Garret, frowned. "Only got one roll of film. It's half used up."

"I'll get a roll at the PX. You can take yours out and then reload it later."

"Sorry, Lieutenant, but you won't have any luck. I've been trying to get more film. They don't have any now."

"Then we'll use what you have left. I have to get film of the runway."

"Well, sir with all due respect, I don't like that idea. I got some good pictures on the roll, and sure don't want to lose them. What do you want pictures of that messed up runway for anyway?"

"Garrett, this is extremely important. I need pictures of the runway as a C-130 is landing, to show to the Commodore and generals so they'll let us close the runway and re-do it. I need pictures to show the Brass how dangerous it is. It may save many lives"

"Well, sir, I'd like to help, but I'm worried about you getting me for having porno pictures. Yeah, see, on my last trip over to Lang Vie delivering supplies, I saw two Montagnard girls washing clothes and taking a bath in a stream. I stopped and took some good pictures. They didn't mind. One of them had a real good set of boobs and..."

Dawson interrupted: "Don't sweat the porno bit. I personally guarantee you won't get into trouble over the pictures you have. I'll see that you get the film back; at least the part with the girls on it, plus a new roll the next time I come up."

"OK, Lieutenant. But I sure do want the film back. There ain't much to do to take our mind off the V.C. We were planning to have a little skin-flick."

"You get your camera. I'll find out when the next C-130 is expected in."

"I can help you there," Garrett said. "I checked with the cargo people, and they said one is due in from Da Nang in half an hour."

"Get your camera and we'll drive over to the runway in a few minutes. You take the movies. I'll use my 35mm and get as many still shots as possible."

When they got into position ahead of the touchdown area, they heard the whine of the four motors of the C-130 approaching through the low overcast. Less than a quarter of a mile away, it broke through the clouds and lined up for landing.

"Garrett, I want you to start taking pictures just before the plane makes contact with the runway, and then follow it with your camera until it comes to a stop. I don't care about any part of the plane except the nose. So keep focused on the nose of the plane and the runway matting swelling up right ahead of it."

Dawson managed to get six shots with his 35mm camera before the C-130 stopped at the far end of the runway.

Garrett, shook his head when he turned off his camera. "Never saw it so close before. I sure wouldn't want to land in one of those planes. Don't see how that matting is holding together."

Dawson arrived back in Da Nang shortly after noon. When he got back to Red Beach, he got the photo lab to develop his film immediately. In the headquarters building he met the Commodore leaving his office.

"Thought you were in Khe Sanh, Bill."

"I was, Commodore, but the runway situation is really bad. Film is being developed that you must see now, sir."

"I'm on my way to a meeting. Can it wait?"

"No, sir. You need to see it now. The photo lab said they would have it ready in half an hour."

"Since I called the meeting, I guess I should be able to delay it for half an hour, if it's really that important. Bring it to my office when it's ready."

Dawson made arrangements for a 16mm and 35mm projector to be set up in the Commodore's office, and told Sanchez what he was doing, before walking over to the photo lab. After picking up the film, Dawson stopped by Sanchez's office and told him he was ready to start.

When the two naked girls appeared on the screen, the Commodore gave a low whistle, and said: "Well, maybe this will be worth delaying my meeting. I didn't know any Montagnard women looked that good, or possibly that reflects on how long I've been away from home."

"Sorry, Commodore, this belongs to one of our Seabees. It was the only film and camera I could locate up there. He had it half used when we took the pictures of the runway. I'll run it 'fast forward' if I can find the right knob."

"That's OK, Bill. I don't mind a bit of distraction. It's been quite a while since I've seen anything that could take my mind off this war."

When the runway and large C-130 filled the screen, it made a sharp contrast with the peaceful scene of two girls washing clothes and bathing. Very quickly the wave of runway matting built up until it was almost as high as the nose of the plane.

Commander Sanchez shook his head. "If I didn't know you better, Bill, I would think this is trick photography."

"I'm seeing it but I don't really believe it can happen," Commodore Rhodes said. "I thought you were exaggerating the problem, Bill, but if anything you understated it." Calling to his Yeoman, he said: "Sampson, get Admiral Scott on the telephone. Ed, I want you to take my place at the meeting with the Third Engineers. You know what my position is concerning responsibility for roads and bridges. They'll listen to you as well as they would me. It's imperative we get Khe Sanh closed down immediately."

Commodore Rhodes spent several minutes convincing Admiral Scott that the problem was urgent enough for him to view the film immediately. Finally, the Admiral agreed and said General Harrington would be in his office when they got there.

"Bill, get the photo lab to chop off the first part of that film," Commodore Rhodes said. "If we show it over there, I doubt our young Seabee would get his prize back. Meet me at my jeep. I want you there to back up the film. The Marines have a hairy situation at Khe Sanh. The general was adamant on keeping the runway open, but that film should change his mind."

When Rhodes and Dawson arrived at Admiral Scott's office there was little conversation before Dawson showed the film and slides. General Harrington acted stiff and irritated at having to rehash the Khe Sanh runway problem again.

After viewing the film, Admiral Scott said: "I see why you wanted an emergency meeting. I've never seen anything like that before. Is it as bad as it looks, Rocky?"

"Worse. According to engineering estimates, the matting should have separated long before it took that much stress," Rhodes said.

"I have to admit it looks bad. But if it's hung together this long, surely it'll hold until we get some clear weather, and can get more ammunition stockpiled up there. We can't close down Khe Sanh's only means of supply," General Harrington said.

"General, I don't see how we can leave it operational a minute longer." The Commodore was emphatic. "Think what will happen if that matting separates. The men on the plane will die, and who can tell how many men on the ground. Do you think you could explain such a loss of life after seeing this film? I want to make myself clear on this. I recommend, in the strongest possible terms, that we close the runway immediately. I'll not bear the responsibility if you continue using it."

"Commodore, do you realize we have over 4,000 men up there, and intelligence has given us an estimate of over 20,000 Viet Cong in the hills around them? Such a move may be what they're waiting for to launch a full-scale attack. I don't want another Dien Bien Phu." Harrington paced in indecision. "It would be irresponsible to continue as it is, I agree. Are you sure there's no way to fix it quick and get it right back in service?"

"I brought Lieutenant Dawson along to give you details. He's been working on the problem since it surfaced. Bill, give them the facts and figures."

"General, there's no quick fix possible now. That's what we've been doing since the rains started. There's no dry dirt left to stuff under the matting. We did that before, but it only lasted for a few landings before the runway was right back where it is now.

"All the rock we need is stockpiled near the runway, half of it already crushed. We can start immediately, and the remainder of the rock will be crushed before we need it."

"And what do my men do for ammunition and food supplies for two weeks? Harrington asked. "Choppers can't keep up with the demand."

Dawson continued: "The field of fire cleared on the northwest side of the camp is large enough to use LAPES, which can supply everything but ammunition. Helicopters will have to do that job. After two weeks you'll have a runway with a good base, that has proper drainage and should last through this rainy season and the next one."

Harrington went to the window, his hands gripped tensely behind his back. His mind searched for a way out of this dilemma. But he knew there was only one solution.

"All right, we'll shut it down. Can I use your phone Admiral? Hello, flight line? This is General Harrington. Put your officer in charge on the line. Captain, this is General Harrington. We have an emergency situation with the runway in Khe Sanh. No more planes are to land there. I said no more. If there's one on its way there, tell him to return. Helicopters are OK. Be sure Phu Bai and Dong Ha get the word on my order too."

Commodore Rhodes stood to leave. "General, I understand your concern, but I think this is the only course of action open to us."

Harrington looked grim. "God help us, Gentlemen, if Charley launches an all-out attack on Khe Sanh while the runway is down and the weather too bad to get close air support."

Back at Red Beach, Dawson got Chief Long on the radio. "Chief, I want you to start complete overhaul on the runway now. No more planes will land there until it's repaired. If the Marines give you trouble, tell them to contact General Harrington. It's closed by his order. Chief, you contact your Battalion and tell them who you need to get the job done. Tell them I'll have a chopper there in the morning to fly the men to Khe Sanh. We have two weeks to get it done. If it goes one day over, we'll be up to our ass in generals and admirals."

Dawson arranged for a Marine chopper to take him to Dong Ha the next morning and then on to Khe Sanh. At Dong Ha he appeased Grady, and five minutes later took off with eight of his men.

From the chopper, Dawson surveyed the activity on the runway, and scanned the hills surrounding the small plateau. It's like a small island surrounded by a raging sea, he thought. I wonder if the V.C. will pounce on Dong Ha in force now? Once they see we've taken away their only supply line, will they make the big push the Brass have been worried about?

As they swooped in low, Dawson saw the runway was alive with Seabees and Grunts dismantling the matting and hauling it out of the way so the earth moving equipment would have room to operate. After dropping the Seabees off, and getting assurance from Chief Long that everything was on schedule, Dawson got the chopper pilot to take him to Lang Vei.

From the air it looked like the new camp was rapidly taking shape. Ensign Johnson gave Dawson a quick tour of the camp. "The defensive bunkers have been completed, and are in operation. We're working on the buildings now, which are mostly underground. The rain slowed us down some, but we're making steady progress. We're keeping up with material delivery by Special Forces."

After tramping over the red, muddy hilltop, Dawson was surprised at the progress. The Seabees were obviously putting forth extra effort to compensate for adverse conditions. Johnson has excellent leadership ability for such a young officer, he thought. I must remember to mention that in my report, when this job is finished.

"We've closed down the runway at Khe Sanh," Dawson said. "So any material you get from here on will have to be air dropped, or delivered by chopper. I suggest you order about double what you'll need; since there may be fifty percent loss when it's dropped."

When Dawson got back to the helicopter, the pilot said, "Just got word over the radio, a C-130 is on its way to make the first low-altitude cargo-drop. It's due at Khe Sanh in twenty minutes. I've never seen an actual cargo drop. So unless you're in a big hurry, Lieutenant, I'm going to set down at Khe Sanh and get a bird's eye view of the drop."

"Fine with me, Captain. I'd like to see how it works too. I'm curious to see how much survives."

Five minutes later the chopper set down on the Khe Sanh parking apron. Dawson and the pilot walked rapidly the quarter mile to the western defensive perimeter and got in the fighting trench with the Marines. They looked out over one hundred yards of relatively flat ground completely cleared. The bald area ran parallel with the trench for a half mile.

The big silver plane appeared suddenly breaking through the low cloud cover about a mile south of the men in the trench. The pilot dropped the plane down so he was just clearing the tree tops. Just as the plane cleared the trees the first drogue parachute popped out, and the first pallet of goods almost hit the trees. When the plane cleared the trees, it dove sharply and then flared-out thirty feet above the ground.

The first pallet falling from over 100 feet, broke apart on initial impact, and sacks of flour raised a white cloud as they exploded when they hit. Pallet after pallet popped out of the rear of the plane. After the first one, the others had only thirty feet to fall, and the impact diminished. Some of them bounced once or twice before the pallets and packing crates broke apart, scattering their cargo. A few of the pallets tumbled down the muddy field, and came to rest intact.

The air was filled with the roar of the plane's four engines, the thundering sound vibrated the ground when they were given full power at the end of the clearing. Then the plane pulled into a steep climb to miss the trees and mountain.

Cans of food, and coffee and boxes of C-rations dotted the field. Off to the right patches of green covered the reddish-brown earth, where boxes of fatigues and boots had broken open.

Dawson walked out to the impact area as the work crews fanned out across the field like cotton pickers. He was surprised at the amount of items usable from the pallets that broke open. The pallets and crates were built to absorb much of the shock on impact, providing some protection for the goods. Dawson pulled one jar of dill pickles out of the mud and placed it beside muddy boxes of crackers.

The pilot dropped Dawson off at Dong Ha instead of going back to Da Nang. When he got to MCB-21 headquarters, he found the C.O. and Ops. Officer together. He explained the seriousness of the situation at Khe Sanh. "I doubt a more critical situation exists in the I Corps. It has priority over any other job we have going. If Chief Long says he needs something, he should get it now. We can worry about the paperwork later."

In the past few weeks Charley had increased his harassment shelling. The low cloud cover made him less open to air strikes, and his artillery location was more difficult to spot for return fire, because fewer reconnaissance flights were possible. Incoming rounds stopped work several times a day, and sleep was interrupted on the average of three times each night. The loss of sleep, nagging fear, and mud were debilitating. Efficiency dropped, work slowed and morale sagged.

In spite of the Viet Cong and the weather, the Bees were completing most of their projects on schedule, at times, by stretching the twelve-hour workday to fourteen and sixteen hours. Youth kept their bodies going from dawn to dark and beyond, into the midnight watches in muddy trenches. The young men matured ten years in one. They arrived young, carefree, hardly more than boys, but their faces grew more somber day by day as each one, in his own way, braced against the fear of battle. They accepted responsibilities few civilians are ever required to shoulder.

The stress and long hours dug deeper lines in the faces of the older men. They had to call on hidden inner reserves to keep up the pace, to set the example for younger men. They imparted their knowledge and skills in time condensed capsules. Their bodies thinned and hardened, but at the end of each long day their steps slowed, and their shoulders weren't quite as square as their profession demanded.

Dawson's face clearly told he belonged to the "older" group, as he sat wet and hungry in the chopper beating its way toward Da Nang. The night before in Dong Ha he was in and out of the mortar trench five times. When he arose at 0500 he was already tired. In the afternoon he waited at the Dong Ha air terminal for an hour, for the C-130 he thought would take him to Da Nang.

The plane had finished off-loading its cargo, and the load master was getting ready to load passengers for the return trip. But when the airfield started receiving incoming rounds, the pilot revved-up his idling engines, and had the big plane rolling down the runway before the crew captain could get the ramp up and doors closed. They were airborne before the fourth shell hit. That was standard procedure now the V.C. had stepped up their shelling.

After the "all clear" sounded, Dawson was looking for a ride back to the MCB-21 camp to spend another night, when the sergeant in charge of the air terminal, quietly told him that a helicopter was on its way in with wounded, and would be going to Da Nang immediately after off-loading.

As the chopper settled on the parking apron near the Da Nang Terminal, Dawson knew it would be another hour before he could get to the regiment, and that much closer to seeing Lati. When he thought of her and how soon they would be together, a warm excitement flowed through him pushing aside the cold and hunger and thoughts of war.

Lati greeted him with an enthusiastic hug and kisses. She was ready for bed, wearing the pink lace nightgown Dawson had bought her. Still holding herself tight against him, her head pressed against his chest, Lati asked, "Can I fix you something to eat?"

"No, I got a snack at the mess. I'm tired and dirty. What I need is a shower and then early to bed for a good night's sleep."

As she walked toward the bed, Lati glanced over her shoulder with a look both shy and coquettish. "To bed early, for sleep only?"

"Well, I'm not really sleepy yet, so we can talk for a while," he teased.

After making love, with Lati cradled in his arm, Dawson said, "See, I told you we would have time to talk." She gave him a soft pinch as he continued: "Tomorrow I'm going to call the Vice Consul again. I know you say, 'patience,' but my orders are due in any time now, and I want to insure you will accompany me back to the States."

He felt the slight lift in her shoulders as she answered drowsily, "You know best, my husband, but I am not concerned."

When Dawson called the Consulate soon after getting to work, the secretary took his name and then after a short pause, told him the Vice Consul couldn't speak with him now. Dawson had the feeling he would get the same answer if he called back later. So after taking care of material problems for Dong Ha and Khe Sanh, he stopped by the Consulate shortly before noon.

"I'm Lieutenant Dawson, and would like to speak with the Vice Consul."

The Vietnamese secretary said, "I don't think he can see you now."

"You tell him I'm here and want to see him. It will take only a few minutes."

When she came back into the reception room, the secretary said, "As I told you, Lieutenant, he can't see you at this time."

"Is there anyone with him now?" Dawson asked.

"No, but he's very... Wait! You can't go in there!"

The little bald headed man looked up startled from the pile of papers on his desk, as Dawson stomped into his office.

"I understand how busy you are, but this will take only a minute or so, and I'm sure you can spare that much time." Dawson tried to keep the anger he felt from reflecting in his voice.

With a resigned air of condescension, the Vice Consul said, "I don't appreciate you barging into my office in this manner. But since you have already disturbed me, tell me what you want."

"I want to know what you have heard on my wife's visa."

"I haven't heard a thing.

"Have you inquired of the office in Saigon to find out what the delay is?"

"No, Lieutenant, I've not called Saigon about your problem. And I don't intend to bother them. They'll act on your request when they get to it."

Anger and frustration boiled up inside Dawson. He wanted to pick up the indifferent little man and shake him until he understood the urgency. But he realized nothing would be accomplished, and that he would end up in real trouble. "If I can't get the information through you, Mr. Vice Consul, I'll go through other channels."

When Dawson tried to see the Consul in the next office he was told the Consul was out of town and wouldn't be back for three days. The secretary also advised that the Consul could be seen only by appointment, and further, that he didn't concern himself with such matters as visas, which was handled by the Vice Consul. Dawson drove angrily to Red Beach for lunch, thinking unpleasant thoughts about diplomats.

Lunch balled up in his stomach. It lay there like a lead weight as he worked in his office trying to juggle material from priority projects to more urgent ones, and stretch the manpower available to satisfy escalating demands. For a time he forgot his own personal problem. Crucial projects demanded all of his thinking and planning capabilities. Shortly before time to quit, one of the yeomen came in.

"This is your lucky day, Lieutenant Dawson. Your orders are here." He dropped a copy on the desk.

Dawson pushed aside the plans he had been studying, and scanned the single page.

Lieutenant Smith, who had relieved Ed Fallon as Project Liaison Officer for Chu Lai, asked, "Where are you going, Bill?"

"San Diego, my first choice; sure can't beat that. I think this is the first time in my Navy career I've gotten my first choice of duty. I leave in three weeks."

"Man, that's terrific! You're definitely a short-timer."

"Yeah, it's good in one sense, but also makes for a problem. My wife doesn't have her visa yet." He picked up the phone and asked for Admiral Scott's office.

When Lati came on the phone, he said: "Hi, this is Bill. Don't fix dinner tonight. I have some things to do and will stay here after work."

"Oh? I have a special meal planned for tonight. I can fix it when you get there." Disappointment was evident in her voice.

"No, I'll eat at the mess. I won't he very late. See you later." Dawson didn't exactly lie to Lati. He didn't have work to do, he wanted time to think, to talk with some of the officers, and have a couple of beers.

Dawson had a beer at the bar while waiting for dinner to be served. When anyone got their orders, it was a big event, and the "grapevine" spread it through the officer ranks rapidly. All of the officers congratulated him and wanted to know where he was going and when he would leave.

The food was good, but Dawson only picked at it and tried to keep up his end of polite conversation with the others at the table. As he sat half tuned-out to the light banter flowing across the table, Dawson realized all of his old buddies were gone. There wasn't anyone whom he could talk to, or that he wanted to discuss his problem with. After another beer and losing a fast game of cribbage, he left for Da Nang. Didn't solve any of my problems there, he thought. Best I get home before dark. Don't really like driving this road after dark. Sure don't want Charley to solve my problems permanently.

When he entered the apartment, Lati gave a squeal of delight. "I am happy you did not stay late. I could hear trouble in your voice when you called me. I want to share your trouble, if it is something you can share with me."

"It concerns you. When I talked with the Vice Consul this morning he had no information on your visa, and he doesn't really care. The Consul was gone, so I couldn't see him. Then this afternoon my orders came in. I leave Vietnam in three weeks."

"Oh, that is good! Only three more weeks. Where will you go?"

"You mean, where will we go? My orders are to San Diego, the perfect spot for us. All I have to worry about now is getting you there, and I can't do anything through military channels since I violated policy when we got married. There's not time for me to go through my congressman. So there's really nothing I can do. You said the Admiral told you he would help. Do you think he meant it?"

"Oh yes, I am sure he did, but he said his help would have to be through the back door. What did he mean?"

Bill laughed and gave Lati a quick pat. "What he meant, my love, is that since he's supposed to enforce regulations here, he can't help someone who has disobeyed an order, or at least other people can't know he has helped. So whatever he does will have to be done discreetly."

"Now I understand. I had thought to ask you what that meant before, but we never have much time together, and I forgot. What should I ask the Admiral to do?"

"Explain that the request for your visa was sent to Saigon over two weeks ago, and we haven't been able to get a report on its status. Tell him I must leave in three weeks, and want you to be able to go with me."

Lati got up from Dawson's lap, but he held on to her hand. "I will talk with the Admiral tomorrow," she said. "Can I get you some food? "Would you like a beer?"

"No."

"What do you want?"

Dawson made an exaggerated frown, feigning deep thought. Then with a mischievous twinkle in his eyes said, "If you come back into my arms I think you'll be able to figure out what I want."

Lati giggled as she sat on his lap and encircled his neck with her arms. And for the rest of the evening the war and visa problems were forgotten.

From the relative safety of Da Nang, Dawson felt responsible as he listened to intelligence reports of increased fighting at Khe Sanh. He felt guilty because he had forced the issue, closing the runway, but he knew he'd done the right thing-there was no alternative. If he hadn't got the runway closed so the Bees could work on it, the runway would've closed itself soon. Then the four thousand men at Khe Sanh would've been in a much worse situation. Even though he told himself he had done what was necessary, at times he felt as if he alone had endangered all of those men.

When clouds enveloped the mountains and air support was impossible, the Viet Cong increased their shelling and mortar attacks. At night they regularly probed sectors of the Marine's defensive positions. Marine patrols reported a continuing build-up of forces surrounding Khe Sanh. The strength of the enemy was no longer a matter of conjecture. The patrols confirmed that the Americans on the isolated plateau were surrounded by a horde of Viet Cong in the mountains around Khe Sanh. And they were the best North Vietnam had, not young boys from villages that the Viet Cong pressed into service regularly, but regiments of well trained, well equipped North Vietnamese Army.

The North Vietnamese badly needed a morale booster for their troops who had been taking a beating whenever they had been forced to stand and fight. The American military feared they would try to pull off another Dien Bien Phu. If they could wipe out four thousand of America's best, possibly the tide would turn and the United States would pull out as the French had done. Speculation by the American military was that the Viet Cong were willing to sacrifice as many men as necessary to take Khe Sanh.

With the anti-war sentiment being demonstrated in the United States, it was quite possible such a loss would cause the politicians to take complete charge of the war and withdraw American support to the South Vietnamese. Ho Chi Minh and his generals were well aware of the actions of a noisy American minority. When Dawson read of the protests and statements by prominent Americans supporting the North Vietnamese, he wondered if they considered the effect it had on men in places like Khe Sanh. Did they even think about how many Americans were being killed because of their actions.

The first stop on Dawson's next trip was Khe Sanh. Although it was overcast, the rain had stopped and the clouds were far above the mountains. From the helicopter it was evident that good progress was being made on the runway. The mud had been mucked out, crushed rock was being placed and then compacted with dozers-since conventional compactor rollers weren't available.

Chief Long said the job was progressing better than expected. Considering all of the incoming rounds they were receiving day and night, the runway work was staying on schedule.

"Charley put my crusher out of business for a while yesterday. They got a direct hit with a mortar round. But we were only down for a couple of hours while we did a little cutting and welding."

"Do you have all the help you need?" Dawson asked,

"Sure do, Lieutenant. Could use more and bigger equipment, but as far as manpower, it's no sweat. I have some of the best equipment operators in the battalion, and when I need muscle, the Grunts are ready and willing."

Dawson ate lunch at Khe Sanh, and while waiting for a chopper to take him to Dong Ha, two C-130s arrived with cargo. Dawson got in the trench near the drop area. The first plane had large timbers and other construction material for Lang Vei. When the first bundle of 12" square by 20-foot-long timbers hit the ground they broke apart and tumbled down the cleared area like giant tooth picks. The second plane dropped food and other supplies, with the same results as Dawson had seen before-about a fifty percent survival rate.

As the second plane made its low-level pass, with drogue chutes pulling out one pallet of goods after another, mortars started impacting in and near the drop area. The Marine's 105mm battery answered, and the incoming stopped abruptly.

Visibility was too good, and the Marines had spotted the source of the mortar fire when the first one left the tube.

Two choppers came in around 1400, loaded with ammunition. They were rapidly unloaded and then loaded with nine wounded and three bodies to be transported to the hospital in Dong ha. They had no room for Dawson. He dove into muddy mortar trenches three more times that afternoon while waiting for a ride. It was 1700 before he got a seat on a chopper heading for Dong Ha.

When he got to the Battalion headquarters it was after 1800. Dawson had just got to the Officers' mess and had his plate filled with cold leftovers when an artillery round hit on the other side of camp. All of the officers who were having a beer after dinner were in the mortar trench, ten feet from the mess, before the alert siren sounded. Dawson managed to drop into the trench without losing much of the food on his plate. As more shells came in, he ate the cold spaghetti and meat balls while squatting in one end of the trench.

Three times that night Charley lobbed in a pair of shells. He was becoming more and more proficient at harassment fire to keep everyone from getting a good night's sleep. As Dawson huddled in one of the trenches under his hooch, he thought of the men up at Khe Sanh. Their situation was so much worse, it made the danger at Dong Ha seen insignificant.

The MCB-21 Operations Officer had been replaced by Lieutenant Commander Rick Nelson. Dawson found it a welcome change from the "can't-do" attitude of the previous Ops Officer. Nelson had been on-board for little over a week, and was absorbing the myriad of details rapidly. This trip Dawson spent much of his time in Dong Ha, going over the many projects in progress and those coming up.

The days in Dong Ha flew by for Dawson as he checked on one project after another from Qua Viet to Camp Carroll. But the evenings, after work, and the nights seemed to move at half-time as he thought of Lati and worried about being able to get her out of Vietnam by the time he would have to leave. In the back of his mind, a nagging voice told him it was possible she wouldn't get her visa before he departed. From Dong Ha all he could do was worry.

Arriving in Da Nang at the end of the week, Dawson could hardly wait until he got to the apartment to find out if Lati had any new information on her visa. She had a delicious smelling Chinese dinner waiting when Dawson arrived.

After a quick kiss, his first question was, "Did you find out anything about your visa?"

"Not very much. There seems to be a problem..."

Dawson interrupted, "Didn't the Admiral help? Didn't he try to find out something for you?"

Lati sighed tolerantly. "You are so impatient. Please let me explain. The Admiral did help. He had his aide inquire for me in Saigon. All he learned was that the request for my visa has been received, and is being processed. He couldn't find out how soon it would be approved. The man at the Embassy in Saigon said they have so many requests to process, there is a backlog now, and he couldn't say for sure when they would get to mine. But he did say for the Lieutenant to call back early next week. By that time he might be able to tell how long it'll take."

Dawson paced back and forth across the living room. "Early next week! Don't they realize I'll have less than two weeks to go by then? They act as though we applied for an extra cigarette ration, or made some other insignificant request. No one seems to care. I'm the only one really worrying about getting you out of here with me. That seems to be all I can do, worry. Well, I'll wait till Monday, but if we don't have definite information by then, I'll take action. What I'll do I don't know, but I will do something."

Lati became nervous and lightly bit on her lower lip, when Dawson became angry. She looked down avoiding his eyes, and then said, "I was sure you would get back today, and I have prepared a nice dinner. Can we eat now before it gets cold? I have made something special. I think you will like it."

Dawson gave her a hug. "Of course, we can eat whenever you want. I'm sorry to take my frustration out on you. I feel time closing in on us and I don't know what to do."

He didn't talk about the problem during dinner. He tried not to even think about it, but was only partially successful. After dinner he sat sipping a cup of tea and reading the latest copy of Stars and Stripes. An article on the front page did little to soothe his worries. In fact it added new fuel to his worry-fire. The article reported on a faction in Congress that was putting pressure on the President to pull out of Vietnam. Dawson didn't think that could happen very soon, but it gave him more cause for concern.

If we start pulling out our forces, the South Vietnamese government will fall like a house built with playing cards, he thought as he stared off into space. If I can't get Lati out with me, and that should happen, there wouldn't be one chance in a million of getting her out then."

He looked at Lati and asked, "Do you realize what can happen if I'm sent back to the States and you have to stay here?"

She gave a small helpless shrug. "I think my visa would be approved soon and then I would be able to come to you in California. It would not take long I think."

"But what worries me is, when I leave here I'll not be able to return. If there's a problem concerning your visa, I'll not be able to do much from seven thousand miles away. Even if I took leave, I don't believe they would grant me permission to return to Vietnam. Can't you see why I'm filled with such dread when I see no action being taken on your exit visa?"

Lati came around the table and put her arms around him. "I know it is a big worry for you. And I want very much to go to California with you, but there is nothing more we can do now except pray. It is in the hands of God you know."

Sunday morning after the briefing, the Commodore said, "I would like to see you for a few minutes, Bill."

When everyone else had gone Commodore Rhodes said: "Sit down. I want to talk with you about the problem you're having getting a visa for your wife. You realize that Admiral Scott can't really lean on anyone to expedite processing, not if he's to enforce rules concerning servicemen marrying Vietnamese. I'm in the same boat. Officially, there's nothing I can do. But I have a good friend in Saigon, you may know him, Captain Vorhees."

"Yes, sir; I met him once in Washington. I really don't know him other than that."

"Well, he's not in a command position there, he's on the Staff, so he could make some inquiries without causing a big flap. If you want, I'll call him and ask him to check on the visa."

"Commodore, I'll appreciate that more than I can tell you. With me leaving so soon, I'm very concerned. I've even considered trying to extend, but at this late date I doubt my request would be approved."

"You're right there, Bill. Your relief is already on his way. Besides, the job you have takes you into some mighty hairy places. I was asked by the Bureau to extend for a few months, otherwise I doubt that I would have. Anyway, don't worry, things will work out fine."

Monday evening when Dawson got to the apartment, even though Lati greeted him with enthusiasm, he knew something was wrong. He held her close as he asked, "Did you hear anything from Saigon?"

"The lieutenant talked with the man at the Embassy, who said he had found our application, but didn't think it would be processed for two or three weeks. I am sorry, Bill. I dreaded telling you, I knew how unhappy this news would make you."

"Well, it doesn't surprise me. This is what I was afraid of, and why I wanted to have someone check on it. Didn't the lieutenant try to get the fellow at the Embassy to expedite it?"

Lati gave her endearing, helpless little shrug. "He asked if the processing could be speeded up. But the man at the Embassy said so many people are trying to get to the United States now, that the system is really clogged. He didn't know any way my request could be pushed ahead of others. Many influential Vietnamese are waiting and have tried to push their requests through fast. Now the Embassy won't respond to pressure, unless it comes from high up."

They ate dinner in silence. Dawson didn't really taste the food. His mind was going in circles trying to figure out another angle, some action he could take. He really couldn't come up with anything. After dinner, before they went to bed, he said: "A friend of the Commodore's is going to check on your visa also, but from what you've said, I doubt he can do much good. I guess we can only hope for the best, and pray."

The next morning, as he was getting ready to leave, Dawson said, "Honey, I'm really sorry I must leave you at a time like this. I'd like to stay here in Da Nang and pound on desks, and make someone do something. But duty comes first. Besides, from what the man at the Embassy said, I don't know what I can do that will have much effect. So I'll do what I have to, and will see you in a few days."

Chapter 17

As the chopper beat its way to Khe Sanh, a light rain fell. Most of the time they were flying in clouds with zero visibility. Dawson was the only passenger, and he had to do some fast talking to get the Marines to make room for him. After he got aboard, he wasn't at all sure he should have argued so hard to get a seat. Ammunition of various types was piled high around him, and a pallet of ammunition was slung under the chopper. As it swung around in the air currents, it made the chopper lurch and yaw. The pilot told Dawson every chopper going to Dong Ha carried as much ammunition as possible. Even then they couldn't keep up with the demand.

Approaching, even through the rain, the white rock made a welcome contrast with the red earth. As much rain as they had received in the past few days, he was surprised to see such progress.

Chief Long looked tired and haggard, as did the other Seabees working in the area. Even the perfunctory salute he gave, when Lieutenant Dawson approached, told of his exhaustion.

"From the air the runway's looking good. We've got a little over a week to meet our deadline. Going to make it, Chief?"

"Sure thing, Lieutenant. The men are getting a little tired of working in the rain all the time. But it's not cold, so they're holding up OK."

"How is the morale?"

"Well, sir, considering where we are and circumstances, I would say the men's morale is very good. Now they can really begin to see the results of their efforts, it has added a boost to their drive and enthusiasm. Did you hear about the attack last night?"

"No, I left Red Beach this morning before the briefing. What happened?"

"Charley tried to breach the northwest perimeter near our crusher and equipment storage. Actually they did overrun the Marines' position. But reserves rushed over to that sector wiped out the V.C. who had made it through. They were sappers, headed straight for our crusher area. Between the shelling, all through the night and the attack, none of us got much sleep. Guess that's why we look so pooped today."

"I know it's rough being up all night in a mortar trench, and then having to put in a long, hard day's work. I wish I could relieve the pressure on you, but I don't know how. Could you use more help from the Marines?"

"Not right now. There's all the Grunts I want, standing by whenever I need them. Now, most of the work is with the equipment and crushing and putting the rock in place. In the next day or so we'll start laying runway matting; then I'll need a lot of bodies."

"Anything I can do for you while I'm here? Is the Colonel giving you a hard time?"

"No. He's been very good to us. Visits the job several times a day, and gives the men a real boost with his praise."

"I'll report to the Commodore that we can expect the runway to be finished on schedule. Right?"

"Unless Charley gives us a rougher time than he has so far, I'm sure we'll finish on time. I really wouldn't want you to tell anyone else, but I think we'll be ready for the first plane one or two days ahead of our two-week schedule. Let's keep that between you and me. It will be a good surprise if it works out that way."

"Right, Chief. I'll hold to our regular completion date in my report. Now I need to get to Lang Vei. Do you know if any convoys are going over there today?"

"No sir. The Marines said this morning, based on reports from their night patrols, they wouldn't want to go over there in less than company strength. Charley is swarming all over the area."

"Thanks, Chief, I'll see if I can talk the chopper pilot into making a quick stop. See you next week."

Dawson located the Marine pilot having a cup of coffee. "Captain, I need to get to Lang Vei, and Charley has the area sewed up so I can't go by road. What's the chance of getting you to take me? I'll need to be on the ground only a few minutes."

"No sweat, Lieutenant. I've never been there, and would like to see the place. They don't have anything for me to take to Dong Ha, so I'm ready whenever you are."

The new Lang Vei camp, perched on top of the hill, looked quite formidable from the air. The concrete bunkers were situated so that they could provide covering fire for the adjacent ones. All of the fighting trenches, the double coils of concertina wire with claymore mines in between, made Dawson think he would hate to try to take the camp with a regiment.

Ensign Johnson showed Dawson around with much pride. The camp was about ninety-percent complete. It was fully occupied now, and the other camp had been abandoned. The two men paused near the entrance to the underground headquarters bunker.

"Good thing you warned me to order extra material, otherwise I wouldn't have had enough to complete the job. I'll have this completed sometime next week.

I'm returning to the Battalion at the end of this week, but will leave a few men to wind up the little problems. The command headquarters, the sleeping quarters, the mess hall and the ammo storage all leak. It's a problem when the roofs are underground; water can come in any one of six sides. We're correcting the above ground drainage to drain the water away from the bunkers and eliminate the problem."

"Phil, you've done a super job up here. One of the things I've really appreciated is you didn't cry about not being able to get the job done because you didn't have all of the equipment and material needed, or because the weather didn't cooperate, or because of constant enemy attacks. You've done a good job of improvising. You're a fine Seabee; and that's as good a compliment as you can get out of me. Hope you stick around, the Navy needs more officers like you."

"Thanks, Bill. This has been a real challenge for me. Except for being shot at and mortared or shelled day and night, I've enjoyed this job. I'm seriously considering staying in the Civil Engineer Corps, making it a career. But I have another two years to decide that."

"I'll see you down in Dong Ha next week, Phil. I have only two weeks left in-country. My relief is due in any time now. So next week should be my last trip up here."

Dawson was about fifty feet from the chopper when an incoming mortar hit fifty yards the other side of it. The pilot had never killed his engine, and from the cockpit he waved urgently as he started revving up the engine. Dawson sprinted the last few yards. The crewman helped him climb up as the chopper was lifting off. From the air Dawson saw two more mortars hit much closer to the helicopter pad.

During the three days Dawson spent in Dong Ha, he avoided dwelling on the visa problem by keeping extra busy during the day. But it was harder at night when he read until he got sleepy. He planned to leave Dong Ha Thursday evening, but when he was ready to go, he couldn't locate a plane or chopper leaving, so he had to spend another night in Dong Ha. He lay awake that night thinking about how much nicer it would be in Da Nang, in relative safety, and curled up with Lati in his arms.

In the morning he located a Special Forces chopper going to Da Nang early. The pilot, an Army major, whom Dawson knew from flying in and out of Lang Vei, dropped him off at Red Beach. Had the chopper gone on to its destination, the Special Forces headquarters in Da Nang-East, it would've taken Dawson another hour and a half, at least, to get back to Red Beach.

Commander Sanchez called to Dawson as he walked by his office, "Bill, the Commodore wants to see you. I think he's in his office now."

"Thanks, Commander. I'll go see him right away."

As he knocked on the unpainted 2 x 4 entrance, Dawson thought: No one can complain about our boss going in for frills like some of the top brass. His office isn't painted, and it doesn't even have a door.

"Come in, the door's open," Commodore Rhodes called out. "Oh, hello, Bill; my attempt at humor for the day. Have a seat. I want to give you news on your wife's visa. Captain Vorhees said he checked with the Embassy, and was told that your wife's visa was being processed, but it would be at least three weeks before it could be issued."

"Well, at least they're consistent. That's the same thing Admiral Scott's aide found out."

"When I talked with Vorhees, I told him how soon you're leaving Vietnam, and asked him if he could expedite processing. He said his friend on the Embassy staff told him the exit visa issue was so sensitive that the only way your wife's visa could be moved to the top of the pile was by going to the Ambassador himself. And it would take someone with a lot of clout to get the Ambassador to violate his own orders. So he concluded there isn't a thing that can be done. I'm sorry, Bill. But it should be only a week or so before she can join you in the States. It will give you time to get things squared away with a place to live and such."

Dawson watched as the Commodore filled and tamped tobacco into his pipe. "Commodore, I appreciate your efforts, and next time you talk with Captain Vorhees thank him for me. Leaving a week or so ahead of Lati is no big deal. If I could be sure she'll get her visa and follow me in a couple of weeks, I wouldn't be worried. But I have a gut feeling something will go wrong, and they'll not grant her a visa. If that happens and I'm in the States, what can I do then?"

"I understand your concern, Bill, but the likelihood of that happening is slim. I'm sure she'll be in the States with you soon. Now, how about a quick rundown on Khe Sanh."

"Yes sir, that's a lot bigger problem than my personal ones."

"Bill, pressure is really building up around that camp. The generals are very concerned. They're surprised Charley hasn't already made a major push to try and take Khe Sanh. From what I gather it's one of the worst tactical situations we've faced in this war. So how does it look? Any problems that will delay completion?"

"No sir. When I was there on Tuesday it looked good. We'll complete on-schedule."

"Any chance of completing earlier, Bill?"

"Well, there's always that possibility. If the weather clears up, or if Charley quits harassing them so they could get more work done, it's possible they could finish a day or so ahead of schedule. But I sure wouldn't want to project that as probable."

"If you find that you can complete ahead of schedule, be sure and let me know first thing."

"Will do. While we're on the subject of Khe Sanh, Commodore, I wanted to talk with you in private before I left. I really think Chief Long should get special recognition for the job he's doing. Ensign Johnson should too. He's done an excellent job at Lang Vei under really trying conditions. I know it isn't my job to make such recommendations, but I want you to know my feelings in case commendations come down from the Battalion. I'm going to mention it to the C.O. when I'm up there next week."

"Thanks for the input, Bill. I appreciate knowing your views. I've already had a good report on Johnson from the Special Forces brass. They think we've done a superb job on the new Lang Vei base. From their description and yours, I would like to get up to see that place. But I doubt I'll ever have time. Make your recommendations to the Battalion C.O. He should know how you feel."

Lati took Dawson's report on the status of her visa with her usual calm. She said, "I am not concerned. It will all end for the best."

He smiled and gave her an extra hug. "How could anyone stay pessimistic around you? I know I've been thrashing around like a calf being branded. And it's done no good. But I had to try everything I could. The frustrating part is, there really wasn't anything I could, or can do. Now I've come to that realization, maybe I can stop being such a bear and try to make our last few days here more pleasant."

"Yes, we will have little time together before you leave."

Dawson's relief arrived Saturday morning. Lieutenant John Cramer wasn't a mustang, and Dawson didn't know him. But when they met at lunch in the officers' mess, Dawson knew they would get along fine. He was sure that he would be leaving his job in capable hands. Cramer didn't get any time to get settled. He started with Dawson right after lunch.

Dawson made arrangements for Cramer to get his arrival intelligence briefing on Monday morning. As they drove from one location to another, Dawson gave him an overview of what his duties would be. He introduced him to key personnel in both Regimental supply yards. In addition to having a degree in mechanical engineering, Cramer had good practical know-how, from his part time work in the construction industry while in college.

Cramer was twenty-eight, but had the maturity of a man several years older. He had sandy, curly hair, and his blue eyes reflected his interest in everything around him. They also told you he had a sense of humor. Dawson was impressed with his ability to grasp and retain names and all the other details being thrown at him very fast.

After Cramer's intelligence briefing, Dawson took him around to the different air terminals and helicopter pads ending up at the Da Nang Marine terminal.

"This is where I usually catch a hop up north, either to Phu Bai, Dong Ha or Khe Sanh," Dawson said. "Tomorrow, we'll go directly to Khe Sanh. Remember, I told you that was our hottest project; only choppers get in there now."

"Yes, I remember Khe Sanh. It was a topic of discussion at the briefing this morning. They really took a pounding last night. The Viet Cong probed their perimeter defense three times. The lieutenant giving the briefing said the C.O. up there thought the V.C. were going to launch a full scale attack. That other place, Lang Vei, had action almost all night. Sounds like I'm inheriting some hot territory."

"You're right there. The one thing I can guarantee you about this job is that you'll not get bored."

Tuesday morning the sun came up bright over the South China Sea. The sky was cloudless. Dawson and Cramer were at the Marine helicopter pad at 0630, and managed to squeeze into the first helicopter going to Khe Sanh.

Cramer was much impressed with the beauty of the terrain rushing by under them. Dawson had forgotten the beauty of the country, light green rice paddies making a striking contrast with the rich red soil and the emerald hue of the sea, and then as they flew over the mountains, the dark green carpet of jungle. For Dawson the beauty had been lost in the carnage. But Cramer, with the innocence of a new arrival, kept pointing and exclaiming.

Dawson thought, If I listen to him, maybe I can recapture the beauty in my mind. Then, when I'm far from here, possibly I can remember the beauty instead of the horror of battle, the terror of waiting for the next shell, the strange looking pile of things that turned out to be bodies, and the sickening stench of human blood.

For a moment, as they approached Khe Sanh from the east, Dawson could see it all through Cramer's eyes. The long narrow falls reflected in the sun like shimmering silver tinsel. The sheer cliff at the beginning of the runway made a rugged contrast with the smooth, shining aluminum planks that began near the top of the cliff. It would be a beautiful sight if I didn't know what was down there, Dawson thought. The acts of man seem to blot out the beauty of God's creation.

About half of the runway was in-place. Dawson breathed a sigh of relief, now he was sure it would be finished ahead of schedule. And he hoped Charley had missed his best opportunity for taking Khe Sanh.

They were half way across the parking apron headed for the crusher site, when some of the rose color was blown off Cramer's glasses. A mortar exploded between them and the helicopter, so close they felt the concussion-but fortunately, none of the shrapnel. They were in one of the worst possible places during a mortar attack-far from any mortar trench.

"Let's go," Dawson said, as he broke into a run.

The second round hit before the men got to the mortar trench near the crusher, and before the helicopter got off. Fortunately, Charley missed the helicopter again. They didn't have a chance with the third round; the helicopter was airborne before it hit. Dawson and Cramer were in the relative safety of a trench when it hit, both of them well winded.

One of the Marine spotters had picked up the mortar's position, and Marine artillery saturated the hillside. When the shelling stopped, the helicopter went in low, raking the area with its machine guns.

When Cramer got his wind back, he said, "I hope you didn't arrange this just to impress me."

"Not me! Charley must've thought you needed indoctrination. Lately, anytime a helicopter lands, the odds are about five to one it gets mortared. The V.C. are willing to risk a couple of men and a mortar tube for the chance at one of our choppers. And it looks like it's paying off for them."

Cramer looked out over the flat terrain as Dawson pointed to the skeletons of three helicopters visible where they had been pushed out of the way after being hit and burned. "Then one of my primary survival tactics will be to get away from planes as soon as they land," Cramer said. "I must be more out of shape than I realized. The run over here with the flack jacket and all the other gear, really got me winded."

"Yeah, I know. That's why I didn't say anything for three minutes after we got here. Guess the show's over, let's find Chief Long."

The Chief climbed out of a trench near the area being filled and compacted. He waved at Dawson and Cramer. As they walked by the high stacks of AM2 matting, Dawson gave Cramer a quick rundown on the matting. When Dawson told him each plank cost almost $2,000, Cramer gave out a low whistle.

"John, this is Chief Long, one of the sharpest equipment chiefs I know. Chief, meet Lieutenant Cramer, my relief. I have my orders, so this will be my last trip up here. Things are really looking good. I bet you like this weather."

"Yes, Sir. We can make good time on a day like this. If I could get them to park a helicopter over in that area all the time, so we could be sure the in-coming was going over there, then we could keep right on working and I could have this runway ready day after tomorrow. As it is, I can almost promise it by Friday."

Dawson slapped the Chief on the back. "Wow! Outstanding! That's three days ahead of schedule. Is that firm enough to make public?"

Long hesitated. "Well, it's not a sure thing. If the weather turns sour, or if Charley keeps us in the trenches a lot more, it won't be ready by Friday. So I'd like to put off telling the world for another day."

"OK Chief-it's your show. I'll give you a call tomorrow. You'll know by then, for sure. Be in the communications center at 1600; I'll call you. Then I'll let the Commodore know. It's good politics if he can be the one to tell the Admiral and the General."

"Fine with me, Lieutenant. I won't tell the C.O. here until after I talk with you. Some men are waiting for me, so I had better get with it." Reaching out to shake Dawson's hand he said, "It's been a pleasure working with you, Lieutenant. You're not nearly as hard-nosed as I'd been told."

Dawson laughed. "Well, Chief, I'm only a hard-nose when people don't put out, and I sure couldn't put you in that category."

Chief Long turned to Cramer. "Welcome to our mountain retreat. The accommodations aren't plush, but we always provide a warm welcome." With that, he gave a snappy salute and walked toward his crew of Seabees and Marines, working shoulder to shoulder.

Dawson chuckled as the two men walked back toward the main part of the camp. "Well! I've never seen Chief Long in such a jovial mood. He must feel really good about getting this project completed. He has good cause to feel proud; it's probably the most important job he's ever done."

The C.O. was in his office when Dawson and Cramer entered. Dawson introduced the two men and told the colonel this would be his last trip to Khe Sanh. "Well, I envy you that, Lieutenant. I want to tell you that your men have really worked their tails off on the runway. Looks like it'll be ready before next Monday. Can I plan on that?"

"I wouldn't plan on it being finished early. The men are working to get it back into operation as soon as possible, and may have it completed early. But there are too many ifs to give a firm schedule change at this time."

"Fine, Lieutenant. I understand. We'll be ready for it whenever we can get it. I have a staff meeting in five minutes, so if there's nothing else, gentlemen, I need time to go over some notes."

Outside the hooch Cramer said, "I'll bet he doesn't have a sense of humor. At least he doesn't show it."

"I doubt there would be any humor left in me if I'd been here as long as he has, and had the responsibility for over four thousand men." Dawson said. "It must be very difficult being responsible for all these men and see the choppers take out bodies day after day. If I was given the choice of his job or being on the front line pulling the trigger, I believe I would choose the front line."

"Well, Bill, as far as I'm concerned, this whole place is the front line!"

In the communications center, Dawson asked if they knew of any helicopters from Dong Ha due in soon. The sergeant behind the desk said: "I don't know of any, but from voice traffic on the radio, there's a Special Forces helicopter landing at Lang Vei. I think I heard the pilot say they were going to Dong Ha next."

"Get the pilot on the radio and ask if he can drop in here for two passengers on his way to Dong Ha."

The helicopter pilot responded to the sergeant's call, "I almost got my tail rotor blown off by a mortar in Lang Vei, so I don't want to stop unless it's an emergency."

The Sergeant looked at Dawson and shrugged. "What do you want me to tell him?"

Dawson came around the desk and said, "Let me talk to him. This is Lieutenant Dawson, one of the Seabees who built your new base at Lang Vei. It isn't an emergency, but I need to get down to Dong Ha as soon as possible."

"I think I've carried you up here before. Yeah, I can give you a ride. Will be there in four, and will use landing approach Bravo."

Dawson gave the mike back to the Sergeant to close out the transmission, and then asked, "What did he mean 'approach Bravo'? Sounds like he's in a fixed wing and thinks he has more than one runway to use."

The Sergeant laughed. "He knows what he's doing. He's being extra careful. That's code telling us he will make a quick set-down at one place, and then hop over to another spot to pick you up. Charley usually sights his mortar in on the first spot and doesn't have time to get it sighted in on the location Bravo. Check in with the sergeant at the staging area. Tell him a chopper's coming in using approach Bravo, and he'll tell you where to be for a pick-up. I suggest you hustle a bit. If you aren't there when he arrives, I doubt he'll wait."

They jogged to the staging area and located the sergeant in charge. The helicopter came in sight as they explained to the sergeant. He pointed west and said to go down the taxi apron about 100 yards until they came to a white X on the matting. The helicopter flew directly over them as they ran down the edge of the taxi apron. By the time they found the X and backed off a dozen yards, the helicopter had landed two hundred yards east of them. It touched down for a few seconds, then lifted off and headed straight for Dawson and Cramer.

The helicopter was dropping down on the X when a mortar round hit near the first place it had set down, and two seconds later one exploded close to the first one. The helicopter rested on the ground barely long enough for Dawson and Cramer to scramble aboard.

As the helicopter lifted off and then followed the directions of the Marine spotter to where the mortar rounds came from, Cramer shouted in Dawson's ear, "At my Stateside briefing, they told me that most likely I wouldn't see combat. What they should've told me is that I'll get shot at, but may not get to shoot back. I see what you mean about this job not being boring."

The helicopter hovered near the area of dense jungle the Marines were shelling. Then the shelling stopped. As the wind cleared away the smoke, two figures were spotted running. The helicopter heeled to port. The port machine gun issued one long burst, and the two V.C. fell and didn't move.

When the helicopter started gaining altitude, Dawson talked to the pilot on the intercom. "My relief is with me, and I would like for him to see Lang Vei, in case we have more work there. Can you fly back over there?"

"I can give you a fly-over. But I'm not setting down again. The V.C. are riled up like a nest of hornets that's been whacked with a stick. They've shelled and mortared Lang Vei five times since breakfast."

"A fly-over's fine. At least he can get a look at it from the air."

As the pilot flew a low, slow circle around the hill-top fortress, Dawson gave Cramer a brief description of the underground bunkers, and the other major construction in its completion stage.

When they settled onto the helicopter pad at Dong Ha, Dawson told the pilot, "Thanks a lot. We really appreciate the ride. I have only this trip to check Lieutenant Cramer out on my job. Really needed to get down here as early as possible, so we can inspect the projects in progress."

"No sweat, Lieutenant. Buy me a beer if you ever see me in the States. So long, Lucky," the pilot said.

While they waited for transportation to the battalion camp, Cramer told Dawson, "When I volunteered for duty in Vietnam, I thought I would be a company commander in a battalion with a group of men under me. We would be right out in the thick of things, really doing something important. Then when I got my orders to the Regiment, it was a let-down. I thought I might as well have stayed in the States with my wife and children as be stuck in Vietnam behind a desk. But when I got here and found out what my job was to be, I thought, well, at least I would get to see plenty of country. Now, I see that I didn't need to worry about not getting in the thick of things. If today is any example, it may get thicker than I like before my tour of duty is over."

"John, as I said earlier, you sure won't get bored with this job."

For the next two-and-a-half days Dawson and Cramer inspected jobs in and around Dong Ha. By noon Thursday they had seen most of the work in progress. Two jobs right in Dong Ha remained to be inspected after lunch. At 1600 they stopped at the Battalion Communications Center, and Dawson got Chief Long on the radio.

"How does it look, Chief?"

"It's a definite go for tomorrow; we can have it operational by noon."

"That's terrific! Great job, Chief! I'll pass this on to the Commodore and the Command here right away."

Dawson got connected to the Commodore by radio. When he told him the runway would be back in service Friday morning, the Commodore was ecstatic.

"You're sure? There's no chance of a delay?" Commodore Rhodes asked.

"I'm as sure as I can be of anything in this country. Chief Long will tell the C. O. at Khe Sanh in a few minutes. I thought you would like to be the one to give the Admiral the good news."

"Right, Bill. I appreciate the call. I'll bring him up-to-date right away. And when you get back here, the drinks are on me."

After inspecting the frozen food storage project and the addition to the hospital, the two lieutenants checked in at the air terminal for transportation to Da Nang.

As they relaxed on the noisy, vibrating C-130, Cramer asked, "Do you know how many times Dong Ha went to Red Alert while we were there?"

"No, I didn't count. I just dropped into a trench each time the siren sounded."

"Well, I kept track, and it was fifteen times. I'm really surprised anyone can get much done with all of the interruptions and loss of sleep."

Dawson leaned back and closed his eyes. "Yeah, that's a real problem, and I'm continually amazed their production stays up. Some people down south, where they may get an attack once a week, if then, don't understand that factor when they compare battalion man-days with work accomplished. But I remind them of the difference in working conditions, whenever the subject comes up."

Cramer shook his head saying: "When we left Khe Sanh, I thought Dong Ha might be something like Da Nang. What a miscalculation. The situation isn't as threatening nor the atmosphere so tense as at Khe Sanh, but I wouldn't like to live there."

Dawson grunted, "The troops joke about coming from Khe Sanh to Dong Ha for rest and relaxation; and troops in Dong Ha joke about going to Da Nang for R & R. Guess there can always be a worse place than where you're at; but there've been times I didn't think so."

Arriving at Red Beach, Dawson was disappointed to learn the regiment was having a "dining-in." He had been looking forward to being with Lati as soon as he finished work. But he had to call and tell her he wouldn't be home until later.

What prompted the pomp and polish was the early arrival of Captain Bayshore. He was to set up a new regiment in Phu Bai to supervise all battalions north of Da Nang. Rumors had been going around that such a reorganization was being considered. But Dawson hadn't really concerned himself with it, since he expected to be gone before it occurred. The commodore scheduled this "dining-in" to get all of the officers together to meet the new regimental commander. Attendance was mandatory.

If Dawson hadn't been thinking about Lati, he would've enjoyed the dinner. The food was excellent. The Vietnamese girls were in their best ao dais, and in high spirits as they served the dinner. Wine was served with the meal and cigars and brandy after, and the two speeches were short and interesting.

After the speeches, the officers migrated to the bar area. Dawson took his brandy into the lounge and finished it as he kibitzed a game of cribbage. His intention was to slip out as soon as he thought he could, without being missed. He was almost to the front door when he heard the commodore call.

"Bill, come on over here and collect the drink I promised you."

Dawson walked to the end of the bar where Commodore Rhodes and Captain Bayshore were talking with some of the battalion commanders.

"You've met Captain Bayshore, haven't you?"

"Yes sir. I met him before dinner. Good to see you again, Captain Bayshore."

The Commodore ordered a drink for Dawson. "I was telling these gentlemen how happy the top command is about getting the Khe Sanh runway back in operation early. Charley waited too long, he missed his chance to have a good shot at taking that place. I think we can all breathe a sigh of relief."

Dawson made polite conversation for a while as he finished his drink. When he set it down on the bar, the commodore asked, "Ready for another one?"

"No thanks, Commodore. I would like to be excused. Some personal business needs my attention."

"You go right ahead, Bill. I'd want to do the same if I were in your shoes."

It was 2200 by the time Dawson got to the apartment. Lati was sitting at the table, reading, in her most feminine nightgown. She rushed into his arms as though he had been gone for months. After hugging and kissing him, Lati said: "I have missed you so very much, and could hardly do my work today thinking about being here with you this evening. Then you had to go to that military dinner. I know I should not complain, but I was even more lonely tonight knowing you were there, and so near."

"I'm sorry I couldn't get home earlier. I didn't want to go to the dinner, and even thought about saying I was ill, but then they may have made me go to the hospital. So I decided that wasn't a good idea. I promise we'll spend as much time together as possible until I leave. Sunday I'm sure I can get the whole day off, and we can go for a walk along the river; or better than that, we'll drive up to Monkey Mountain. Have you ever been up there?"

"No, but I would like to go."

"Have you..." Dawson hesitated and then continued, "I don't suppose you've heard anything new on your visa?"

"No. Nothing. The Admiral's aide said it would do no good to call again."

"I suppose he's right, but I'll check on it tomorrow. If I can't get anywhere, then I'll try to put it out of my mind, so I won't make our last few days miserable. I'll hope and pray it'll work out fine as everyone tells me it will."

Friday morning Dawson got the Commodore's permission to call Captain Vorhees in Saigon. From Vorhees he got the name and telephone number of his friend at the Embassy. An hour passed before he could get another line to Saigon. But he finally got through to Hal Morrison at the Embassy.

"This is Lieutenant Dawson in Da Nang. Captain Vorhees, talked with you last week about my wife's visa. I know at the time you said the processing would take two to three weeks. I'm calling to see if there's been any change in that schedule."

"Yes, I remember Vorhees asking me about your wife's visa. I checked on it and gave him the information available. I'm sure nothing's changed, Lieutenant, except it's one week further along in processing."

"Mr. Morrison, I'm leaving Vietnam in four days, and I'm very concerned about my wife getting out of here. Can you do anything to speed things up? Is there any additional fees or funds I can provide to speed up the process?"

"I'm not going to take offense at your suggestion. But please keep in mind, you're talking to an American diplomat, not a Vietnamese. If I were willing to respond to offers of money, I could have been very rich before now. Many wealthy Vietnamese have offered me large sums to expedite their visas, but they waited their turn like the rest. There really is nothing more that can be done."

"I had to make one last attempt. I didn't mean my offer as a bribe. One more question, sir: Any possibility of my wife not being granted a visa?"

"Now that, Lieutenant, you should be able to answer better than I. I don't know her background. But if she hasn't been involved in things like the black market or drugs, or hasn't had ties to the Viet Cong, I know of no reason she can't be granted a visa. I'm sure you realize that doing a background investigation is the major part of the processing. That's what is in progress now."

After putting down the telephone, Dawson sat thinking a while. Then he picked up the phone and asked for the Naval Support Activities Headquarters. The Admiral's aide answered the phone. It took him a few minutes to get Lati to the telephone. Dawson told her, "I just talked with someone at the Embassy who said they were already in the process of doing a background investigation on you. Have you heard anything about it?"

"No. No one has asked me any questions or said anything about me being investigated."

"Before you leave today, ask the officer in charge of personnel, and the Admiral, or his aide if they have been contacted about you. At least then we may be able to tell how far along they are."

Starting Friday morning, Dawson let Cramer make the decisions, with Dawson looking over his shoulder giving advice, or making corrections where necessary. When he got stuck on a critical material problem, Dawson told him who to contact to resolve the bottleneck or lack of material.

Getting Cramer brought up to date on the material status of each project was the most difficult part of the turnover process. In weeks past Dawson had juggled material to meet immediate needs. If material arrived for project A, and work couldn't start for some reason, he diverted the material to project B which was ready to go, except for the lack of material. This diverting and swapping went on all of the time. But it became a serious problem if suddenly they gave the green light for project A to proceed, and the replacement material for it hadn't yet arrived. The customer became irate when he learned his material had been used on another project. Sometimes it meant borrowing from a third project to keep things running on an even keel.

Dawson had kept rough notes on which job owed what to whom. But they weren't specific enough for someone else to follow. So he made more detailed notes for Cramer, for each project and hoped he hadn't forgotten something.

"John, I realize in the States, under normal conditions, diverting material from one construction project to another was a definite no-no. But here we must swap or borrow to meet combat requirements. You must learn how far to carry this expedient, because it's usually your decision, and if you're not careful your tail will end up in a crack."

Lati had an elaborate dinner prepared when Dawson got home. When he whistled at the candles, flowers, and wine on the table, she said: "Well, I thought I had better feed you well, to compete with the fancy dinner you had last night. I want you to remember my dinner at least as well as the one last night."

"With two fancy dinners in a row, I may get spoiled and want to eat like this all the time. But you can be sure it's not only your cooking I'll remember."

"Then maybe it is the pretty clothes I need to worry about. I remember you were quite impressed with the way the girls looked last night. Will you remember me in this?"

She twirled around, the tails of the organdy top half of her ao dai flared, showing more of her soft beige satin pants.

Dawson paused in deliberate thought. "I'm not sure if you can take my mind off those girls or not. Spin around one more time so I can decide."

She tossed her head and said, "Well, if you are not sure, I may as well get busy in the kitchen."

As she turned to go, Dawson reached out and caught her arm, drawing her to him. "Now, why do you worry about how well I like your cooking or what I think of you all dressed up? Though I like your cooking and think you're a very beautiful woman, that isn't why I'll remember you, why I love you. It's because of your gentle nature, your concern for others, the grace you display when you move and speak. It's simply because you are you. Don't you realize I would love you if you couldn't cook and if you weren't beautiful? Those qualities I appreciate, but they're simply added bonuses."

She snuggled close to him. "You are very kind with your compliments. I was not really serious, well, not very." She pulled away and then stopped, looking over her shoulder and asking, "But do you like the way I look tonight?"

He laughed, and said: "Yes. I think you look stupendous. So good, in fact, unless you get dinner on the table soon, I may not be able to get my mind on food."

As they ate, she told him she had found out someone from Saigon had called asking questions about her. The personnel officer said he gave an excellent report on her, and the investigator seemed satisfied.

The rest of Vietnam, at least the men in mortar trenches, those out on patrol, or waiting in places like Gio Linh for the next incoming round or the next full-scale assault on their perimeter, lamented the slow passing of time. But for Dawson and Lati the next three days zoomed by like three minutes.

Saturday he made sure Lati would he able to cash the money orders, he was leaving with her, at the American military post office in Da Nang. After the Sunday briefing Dawson hurried home to Lati, and for the rest of the day he didn't let her out of his sight.

Monday he helped Cramer clear up loose ends, and then called the Embassy in Saigon: "Mr. Morrison, when we talked last week you gave me an approximate time when my wife's visa would be ready; can you give me anything more definite now?"

"Your wife's file arrived at my desk this morning, Lieutenant. Everything looks in order. The background investigation gives her a clean slate, so there should be no problem-it's a matter of processing now."

"I wouldn't press you on this, Mr. Morrison, but I'm leaving Vietnam tomorrow morning. Is it possible for you to give me a date when her visa will be ready?"

"Well, I don't know. Another week should do it. Hold on a minute, I'll talk with my office manager."

After what seemed a very long minute to Dawson, Morrison returned to the telephone. "We'll finish with it here on Friday and send it to the Da Nang Consulate on the courier plane Saturday. Your wife can pick it up one week from today."

"That's the best news I've heard since I got my orders back to the States. I really do appreciate your efforts, Mr. Morrison. I can leave here now with a much less troubled mind."

When Lati arrived at the apartment Dawson grabbed her in his arms lifting her off the floor and whirled around the room shouting, "It's approved! It's approved!"

After he set her down, Lati asked, "What do you...? You mean my visa has been approved?"

"Yes. I called the Embassy. You can pick up your visa one week from today. I also talked with the Vice Consul. He said there would be no other delays. I checked on flights, and the first reservation I could get for you is on Wednesday."

"Oh, that makes me so happy I could cry. Now you can quit worrying. I told you everything would work out fine."

"Yes, I know you did. Well, this is one 'I-told-you-so' I don't mind."

Tuesday morning Lati wanted to accompany Dawson to the airfield, but he said, "No, Lati, I don't like prolonged good-byes. It's better if we say our good-byes here."

After a quick breakfast and many goodbye kisses, Dawson rushed to the Da Nang airport and boarded the State-side bound Continental flight. The packed plane took off into a sun breaking over the calm South China Sea. It was a beautiful sight, providing an exhilarating feeling for the planeload of military men. Dawson felt a tug at his heart at leaving Lati. But his spirits brightened with the thought that they would soon be together again.

With a deep feeling of gratitude Dawson thought: Lord, thank You for bringing me safely through this time and place where so many men have died. I thank You for Lati, who has brought me comfort and understanding. And thank You for the inner peace You have given me.

Glossary

105mm   105 millimeter artillery piece.

III MAF   Third Marine Amphibious Force.

Ao dai   Type of dress worn by Vietnamese women.

ARVN   Army of the Republic of Vietnam.

ASAP   As soon as possible.

Berm   A mound or bank of earth used to contain or protect.

CP   Command post.

CDO   Command Duty Officer.

Claymore mine   A defensive weapon set above ground. When detonated, shoots 700 steel balls in a wide arc.

Concertina   Coils of razor wire used around the camp perimeters.

Cumshaw   Something acquired or accomplished through bargaining, or as a favor.

DMZ   Demilitarized Zone. A narrow strip dividing North and South Vietnam, which was supposed to be a neutral zone.

Grunt   1) A Marine foot soldier. 2) Lineman's helper.

H and I   Harassment and Interdiction Fire.

Hooch   Tin roofed building of tropical wood construction, used for barracks or offices.

Hot-stick   A wood or fiberglass pole of high insulation used to work on high voltage lines.

KIA   Killed in action.

LCM	Landing Craft Medium. A shallow draft boat that can be beached for loading and off-loading men and supplies.
LDO	Limited Duty Officer.
LST	Landing Ship Tank. A seagoing craft that can carry vehicles and tanks, and off-load directly onto the beach.
MAC V	Military Assistance Command, Vietnam, (senior U. S. military command in Vietnam).
MCB	Mobile Construction Battalion.
Mike Boat	See LCM.
Mustang	An officer who came up through the enlisted ranks; a colloquial term for an LDO.
NAVFOR V	Naval Forces, Vietnam, (senior U. S. Naval command in Vietnam).
NCR	Naval Construction Regiment.
Piaster	Monetary unit in Vietnam.
R & R	Rest and relaxation.
RVN	Republic of Vietnam.
SIMPCOM	Project designation for Simplified Communications.
UDT	Underwater Demolition Team.
Weaps	Slang for "weapons carrier;" a 3/4 ton, 4-wheel drive vehicle.

About the Author

Don Windle

Don Windle is a retired Naval officer who writes, hikes, and fishes in the mountains of Northern California. After surviving three wars, he is happy to live with his wife, Bessie, in the tranquility of a rural area. His tour of duty in Vietnam with the Navy Seabees inspired his writing the novel, WHERE BEES SWARM.

More Clocktower Books you'll enjoy

You can find more exciting Clocktower Books at clocktowerbooks.com. Most of these titles can also be ordered at Barnes & Noble (barnesandnoble.com) and Amazon (amazon.com), as well as your local bookstore. If you are a fan of Science Fiction, Fantasy, and Horror, check out our free Web-only magazine *Deep Outside SFFH* at outside.clocktowerbooks.com.

We Never Said Goodbye (and other stories) by Dan Murr. This is a first-rate collection of nonfiction by highly esteemed columnist Dan Murr. With a master's precision and bold insight, Mr. Murr paints for us the horrifying last night of the Edmund Wilson, a ship doomed on the Great Lakes during a monster storm. ISBN: 0-7433-0352-0.

Lion of Scythia by Max Overton. The Greek empire is on the move. When Nikometros, a Greek soldier and nephew of Alexander the Great, engages the Scythian horsemen, he is captured, not only by their army but also by the beautiful high priestess. Soon, Nikometros is a part of the tribe, bound by honor and love to help his one-time foes as they struggle to keep their lands from invaders. ISBN: 0-7433-0096-3.

Maya by Nirmala Moorthy. Maya is a courageous and strong woman who could step from the pages of fiction for the enthralled reader. Three sisters grow up in a fascinating but repressive household in modern India. All three women face the multiple faces of Fate as American-Indian novelist Nirmala Moorthy weaves a tale of anger, struggle, loss, anguish, and bittersweet triumph. Told as only an insider can tell it, with delicate and perfect detail that will delight the imagination and engage the senses. A tale that has delighted readers as it reaches across cultures and boundaries. ISBN: 0-7433-0067-X.

Printed in the United States
20460LVS00004B/115-156

9 780743 300209